VALLEY OF SAINT ANNE

DAVE GIOIA

ISBN 979-8-99293-272-0 (softcover)
ISBN 979-8-99293-273-7 (ebook)
Library of Congress Control Number: 2025912998

This book is a work of fiction. Names, characters, places, and incidents are the product of the author's imagination or are used fictitiously. Any resemblance to actual locales, events, or persons, living or dead, is purely coincidental.

Printed in the United States of America.

DEDICATION

To Diana and Joe

CONTENTS

CHAPTER 1

Morning Jog

Kate jogs past Newport Beach Pier and watches the sky brighten and the clouds change color as the sun rises above the houses lining the boardwalk, facing the Pacific. It would be much more convenient to jog around her block in Costa Mesa, but there's something about being by the ocean that makes the extra effort well worth it.

Her time alone in the early morning, before having to face the routine and responsibilities of the day, is important. It gives her a chance to think through whatever she needs to and helps her stay in shape, which has become even more important in the last few years as the pounds have become easier to put on and harder to take off. Her fortieth birthday is approaching and while she tells herself age doesn't matter, she can see its effects in the mirror each morning and doesn't want to give in to it.

She notices the men who glance at her as they jog past. She can tell they like what they see: pretty face, bright blue eyes, nice figure, long honey-color hair, pulled through the back of her blue sailing cap and streaming behind her like a mustang's tail. She's been approached from time to time, when doing her warmup or cool down stretches, and asked out on dates, but she's always politely declined, as she has the occasional offers from customers at work. Ever since she and Ed divorced, she's been content being alone.

She didn't think there'd be any problem with jogging, but checked with her doctor, who assured her there was little to worry about. She just needed to be careful, which she has been ever since she first learned she has hemophilia. She rarely even thinks about it anymore.

It was a concern when she got pregnant, though. She knew the odds of her passing the gene along are fifty-fifty. If she did and the baby was a boy, he'd have the disease; if a girl, she'd be a carrier. She worried about it during her pregnancy and was relieved when the test showed Deirdre doesn't have the gene.

She glances at her watch. Ed's been on her mind more than usual lately. His relationship with Rita has always been rocky and based on the little he's shared with her and what she hears from Dee Dee, things seem to be worse than ever. Despite everything, she thinks fondly of Ed. He coaxed her back to life after the experience with Bobby, which seems like a dream now, a nightmare, something that happened to a different Kate.

She met Ed at CSU Long Beach. He was majoring in Criminal Justice and she in Psychology. He wanted to be a cop and join a local force, and she had only a vague idea of what she wanted to do. She thought learning more about what makes people tick couldn't hurt, no matter what she ended up doing, and she was right. It comes in handy as a manager in retail.

It was several years after Bobby's death and she still felt like she was living in the dark, at the bottom of a deep hole, removed and isolated from people, and being in another relationship was the farthest thing from her mind. She and Ed were taking the same American Lit course one semester, and she soon became aware of his amorous glances.

One day after class he asked her to have a cup of coffee. Her initial reaction was to decline his offer, but his smile was so sweet and his expression so hopeful as he searched her eyes and waited for her answer that she agreed. They walked to a nearby coffee shop and sat at a table outside. They chitchatted about this and that: she enjoys reading current bestsellers, romance novels are a guilty pleasure; he enjoys going with his buddies to the desert to ride ATVs, and to Lake Havasu to party. They talked about family, hers having arrived in Southern California from Ireland by way of Halifax, and his from Germany by way of Mexico City.

"Look out right!" she hears from behind her and narrowly misses being knocked to the asphalt by a couple on rented bikes. Tourists! They're the one drawback to jogging here.

She was won over by Ed's patience and persistence. She knew he sensed her reluctance to become involved with him much beyond having a friendly cup of coffee together now and then. When the course was over, they wished each other well. Ed gave her his number, which she took without giving him hers, and they didn't see each other again for several years, until the day she went through that intersection on Beach Boulevard.

She noticed the motorcycle cop on the side of the road as she did. The light was yellow, and she thought she'd made it through in time, but looked in her rearview mirror and saw the cop swing onto his motorcycle and he was quickly behind her with blue lights flashing. It was Ed. He let her off with a warning and they began seeing each other.

He was right about his three older sisters. He'd told her they were critical of every girl he ever brought home. When Kate finally met them, they stared at her coolly and she knew they'd be talking trash about her as soon as she left. She asked him afterward if it was because she's white and he assured her that his sisters didn't discriminate based on skin color. He'd had Latina and white girlfriends and even one Asian — there did seem to be a lot of them — and his sisters found them all equally unworthy.

His parents liked her, though, which was all that mattered. She was neutral to the idea of getting married and content just living together as a couple, but agreed to when she became pregnant. Dee Dee was born and life as a family began. Ed seemed a model husband and father. Then the phone call came.

She was in the kitchen in their home in Costa Mesa. Ed was at work and Dee Dee, then seven, was at school. Kate had picked up a birthday cake and candles to celebrate Ed's birthday after dinner. The home phone rang, and she noticed before answering it that the caller ID was blocked. The man didn't introduce himself. He said that his daughter was a high school senior, and that Ed had been seeing her for some time. She asked how he'd gotten the number and realized as soon as she did that it was an idiotic question, prompted by panic. The man sounded embarrassed and a bit apologetic but determined. He said his daughter was a very bright, talented young woman, that she had a great future ahead of her and that he didn't want it spoiled by something like this. He'd appreciate it if she'd have a talk with her husband and ask him to do the right thing and leave his daughter alone. She said she would, and he thanked her. She placed the phone on the table, sat with her hands folded in front of her and stared blankly out the window. It was the first time in her life she'd been betrayed, and the feeling was like having a venomous worm squirming inside her, poisoning her as it fed on her mind and body. Was it the first time Ed had been unfaithful? How many other women had there been?

In retrospect, she shouldn't have confronted Ed at the dinner table. It was an indication of how distraught she was. Right moment? There's never a right moment to confront your husband about his infidelity, or so she thought. She told Ed about the call as delicately as possible, as much not to anger him as to keep the conversation over Dee Dee's head, and when she asked if he understood, he looked at her like he was ready to pick up his knife and plunge it into her heart. He pushed back his chair, stood and began pacing back and forth like an enraged animal in a cage. He finally stopped and looked at her and then at the birthday cake. He picked it up and threw it against the wall above her head, screaming at her to mind her own fucking business, and left, slamming the door behind him. Dee Dee was terrified and when Kate told her a few weeks later that she intended to divorce her dad, Dee Dee was sad but seemed relieved.

Rita arrived with Ed to pick up Dee Dee for one of his weekends and Kate's first impression of her was "fiery." She and Rita are about the same height, but that's where the similarity ends as far as appearances go. Rita's a Latina with dark brown, almost black eyes and creamy light brown skin, and that day she wore her long black hair up in a sexy topknot, fastened with a red elastic with charms on it. She wore a red halter-top and skintight black jeans and red open toe heels, and her manicured fingernails and toenails were painted the same color red as her lipstick. Rita struck her as a woman who could go toe to toe with any man, and she knew by the way Rita looked at her that she was considered an adversary. She was only a little surprised to hear Rita's lawyer. At the time, she thought maybe this fiery woman is just what Ed needs.

She's never witnessed the two of them having one of their famous fights, but when Dee Dee first shared with her that they'd had one and described it to her, she could easily picture the scene. She'd like to think their fighting isn't her problem, but it is because Dee Dee's subjected to it. She feels sorry for Ed but concerned about how his stormy relationship with Rita is affecting Dee Dee. She doesn't think she has grounds to deny Ed visitation rights. For now, it's just a continuing concern and Dee Dee seems to be dealing with it well. She's a resilient kid. Kate glances at her watch. Time to head back and get ready for work.

* * *

Dee Dee sits at her desk and opens her diary to the first page. She decides to read her first entry, written on her birthday last year and which she hasn't read since, so she will in honor of her birthday. She knew whom she was going to write to, having recently read Anne Frank's *Diary of a Young Girl* for school. She found it thoroughly engrossing, profoundly sad and touchingly hopeful.

Friday, December 31, 2010

Dear Anneliese,

I really enjoyed reading your diary and it's so sad what happened to you. Knowing you the way I do, though, I'm sure you kept your spirits up and were very brave to the end.

I hope you don't mind me writing to you. I don't think you will. I thought about writing to Kitty, but Kitty was your friend, so I thought I'd write to you. Let me tell you a little about myself.

My name is Deirdre Beyer and today's my twelfth birthday. Deirdre was my mom's grandmother's name, but my mom says everyone called her Dee Dee and that's what everyone calls me. You wonder why they even bothered to name us Deirdre? Go figure!

My mom and I live in Costa Mesa, California. So does my dad but he doesn't live with us. My parents divorced when I was seven. It's no big deal. It seems everybody gets divorced these days.

I asked my mom for a diary and a fountain pen like the one you used and got them for my birthday! The pen came in a red leather case, just like yours did! The pen is messy but I'm getting used to it. You may be wondering why I don't just use my computer to keep my diary. It would be a lot easier. Now that I think of it, you wouldn't be wondering about that. I don't think you knew about computers. It's a funny thing. Writing the way you did makes me feel like you're right here with me.

My life is nothing like yours was. You suffered so much. I have it pretty good. My mom's really nice. So is my dad. I see him on weekends. His wife's name is Rita. She's okay, but she drinks and they fight a lot. It's awful! I know you know what I mean.

I want to visit the Secret Annex someday. I want to be where you were and feel what it must have been like for you. Maybe I'll know better being there.

Well, that's all for now. I'll write again soon.

Yours, Dee Dee

P.S. I like the name Anneliese. It's very pretty. Anne is nice too, but I like Anneliese better. Saying it is like singing. I hope you don't mind me calling you that. By the way, my middle initial is also M. I know yours is for Marie. Mine is for MacKenna. That's my mom's maiden name ("maiden" sounds so old fashioned).

I can tell you that having your birthday on New Year's Eve sucks! I never have a party on my birthday. My friends' parents are always too busy with their own parties! I guess I shouldn't complain. You didn't have much of a party on your birthday, either.

She flips through the pages to the first blank page and stares down at it, tapping her pen lightly against her lips and twisting one of her braids as she considers what to write. She glances at her last entry, written last week on the day before school break, and "Kids can be so stupid!" catches her eye. What happened that day is still fresh in her mind, and she feels the raw emotions she felt then well up in her and decides to read it.

Wednesday, May 18, 2011

Dear Anneliese,

You know how some of the kids at school and especially Carlos and Juan and Ramon like to tease me about my braids and call me "Heidi." I usually don't let it bother me, but this time it did. it did today. Rosa and I were minding our own business at lunch, and they came over with some of their friends and sat at our table. Carlos had his usual dopey grin on his face. He looked around at his friends and said, "She thinks she's Mexican American! How stupid is that?" Everyone laughed except Rosa and me. It made me really mad.

My dad's family is from Mexico City. They lived there a long time before they came here, so doesn't that make me Mexican American too? I think so. Do you have to look a certain way to be Mexican American? I don't think so. Look at you. You were Jewish but you were born in Germany and grew up there speaking German. Okay, my Spanish isn't so good but I'm learning and it's getting better. But didn't that make you German? I think so. The funny thing is, I look more German than you do! My dad's family came from Germany when they moved to Mexico. Kids can be so stupid!

Yours, Dee Dee

She hears her mom arrive home and call from the kitchen, "Ready to go, honey?"

Yeah!" Dee Dee says.

"Bag packed?" Kate asks from the bedroom doorway.

"Uh-huh!"

"I'll take a shower and we'll have breakfast."

"Okay," Dee Dee says. She puts her pen to the top of the blank page and begins writing.

Friday, May 20, 2011

Dear Anneliese,

I don't have much time to write this morning. I'm staying with my dad and Rita this weekend. We're going to Universal Studios in L.A. tomorrow. It's a theme park. I've never been there, and it should be fun, but I already know it won't be. I don't know what will happen to spoil things, but something will. Just wait and see! I remember reading about all the times something stupid happened to spoil fun things for you. I'll write soon.

Yours, Dee Dee

* * *

Kate punches in her code at the employee entrance to Bloomingdale's at South Coast Plaza and joins the other managers for a brief morning meeting in Bridal. There's nothing much to report about Mens, her department. She stands afterwards, just before store open with her staff, listening to the Assistant Store Manager share news about today's promotions and in-store events and looks around at the familiar faces. She sees the new hire, Matt Tildon, standing by the escalators with Sharam, the top producer in Men's Suits, the Armani specialist and always impeccably dressed, and Roberto, another associate in Men's Suits. Matt's been hired part-time, and she remembers what he shared with her about himself in the interview. He's a student at CSU Long Beach, which is her alma mater, studying Fine Arts photography. He hasn't worked in men's clothing before, but said he was eager to learn and that he'd give it his all. She liked his positive attitude.

It's Matt's first day. He's young, in his early twenties, maybe six feet and handsome with short dark hair and brown eyes. He's wearing a suit, which is company policy for associates in Men's Suits. It's the same one he wore for the interview, and he looks as uncomfortable in it now as he did then. It's probably the only suit he owns. Still, he looks good in it. Something about him looked familiar when she first met him, and she still has the feeling she's seen him before but still can't remember where.

She visits Men's Suits mid-morning as a covering manager to see how things are going and finds Sharam, Roberto and Matt, standing in front of the cash-wrap counter chatting, which, strictly speaking, they shouldn't be doing, but it's a slow day so far with few customers in the store and none in Men's Suits, so she lets it go. She arrives in front of them, phone in hand and hugging her clipboard to her chest. "How's it going?" she asks Sharam.

He raises his eyebrows slightly and looks around the empty department.

"Things will pick up," she says encouragingly.

"Let's hope so." Sharam says.

She looks at Matt. "Welcome to Bloomingdale's," she says brightly. "I'm sure you'll enjoy working here."

Matt smiles. "I'm sure I will."

"How are these guys treating you?" she asks, nodding at Sharam and Roberto.

"These guys are great," Matt says. "I've got a lot to learn."

Sharam places a hand over his heart and bows slightly. "What I know, he'll know," he says solemnly to Kate.

Kate smiles. She always enjoys Sharam's well-mannered style, which seems so "old world." It's refreshing. "I'm sure he will. Let me know if anything comes up." She looks at Matt. "Glad to have you here."

"Glad to be here," he says with a smile.

She feels his eyes on her back as she walks away and there's that feeling again that she's seen him before but still can't remember where.

* * *

Matt leans against the pool table next to his and Amber's, sips his beer and watches her line up a shot. It's as if he took a photograph of her the moment he first saw her and has been standing over a developing tray in a dark room ever since, watching the image slowly emerge and become better defined as new details appear. He remembers vividly that day they first met at the beach volleyball courts by Huntington Beach Pier.

It was late afternoon on a gorgeous summer day, with the sun a yellow-orange ball about an hour or so above the horizon, "magic time," when the quality of the light gives the world a warm intense glow and a super real cinematic look. He and his friends had been surfing and decided to top off the afternoon with a few games. His friend Dibs's girlfriend Janey showed up with a friend Matt had never seen before. They sat on the wall by the boardwalk watching them play. The friend was beautiful and obviously into pink. Her shoulder-length blonde hair was kept off her face by a pink barrette. Her lipstick and nail polish were pink. She wore a pink bikini top, white shorts and Day-Glo pink flip-flops. She posed on the wall like a calendar pinup from the Forties. Posing seemed to come naturally to her, like she was born to model. What he found intriguing about her was the way she looked at people, observing them from behind the bright colors.

They finished the game and he and Dibs walked over to them and Janey introduced her friend as Amber. He noticed her muscle tone and asked if she's into sports. She looked up at him and shielded her eyes.

"I row, open water," she said.

"Ah. Surf?"

"Never got into it."

"Amber knows Becca," Janey said.

Matt nodded and looked back at Amber. "Business Admin?"

"Finance."

"Let's have a beer," Dibs said.

They walked from the beach across Pacific Coast Highway and sat at an outside table, sipping their beers and watching the sun sink slowly toward the horizon. He glanced discreetly at Amber's face, admiring the way the deepening light from the setting sun seemed to make her skin glow. "So, what's your plan?" he asked her.

"Be a broker and make tons of money."

"Cool."

"Might skip the MBA. Not sure it'll buy me anything."

"Things have kind of changed in the industry since the meltdown, haven't they?" Dibs asked.

Amber looked at him coolly, "Nothing has changed. Nothing ever will. Money runs the show, which is why the Feds bailed out the banks. Profits and bonuses are better than ever. All the regulation in the world won't stop people from making money. If there's money to be made, they'll find a way to make it."

"Yeah," Janey said, "at our expense."

It was subtle, but he saw the displeasure in Amber's expression. Whatever it was she was about to say to Janey, she kept it to herself, and he knew it wasn't out of deference to him. Amber looked at him.

"What's your major?" she asked.

"Photography." He remembers the way she raised her eyebrows slightly, just enough to let him know she was unimpressed.

"What's *your* plan?"

"Make a career of it." He could see her trying to reconcile "photography" and "career" in her mind and doing a quick calculation of what the merger of the two might yield. It didn't seem she thought it could amount to much.

"What type of photography?"

"All sorts."

"Can you make a living at it?"

"Depends on what you mean by 'living.' Anyway, if I'm going to spend most of my life working, I'd rather do something I love doing."

"I guess," she said dismissively.

"You're up, shutter bug," he hears her say. He picks up his cue, slowly chalks it and gazes absently at the table. It was a few weeks after they first met that he saw her again. He and Dibs and another friend were having a party. He knew Janey was cool toward Amber, but she asked him if he wanted her to invite her and he said sure, it would be nice to see her again. Amber arrived once again wearing a profusion of pink. He watched the affect her presence had on the crowd in the living room as she entered. Every head turned her way and the men, especially, continued to glance at her throughout the evening. They mingled and chatted with his friends, and he watched her as she studied the framed photographs on the walls.

"These yours?" she finally asked.

"Yeah."

She eyed an abstract photo. "What's that?"

"A detail of the *Catalina*. It's an old steamer that used to ferry tourists to and from Catalina Island. It ran aground on a sandbar in Ensenada harbor and was rusting away for years. They finally cut it up for scrap."

"I was a kid the last time I visited Mexico," she said. "I wouldn't go there now if you paid me."

"I go to Ensenada now and then," he said. "There's a campground overlooking the ocean. It's a beautiful spot and cheap."

She glanced at him. "I'm not into camping. We've spent millions of years trying to make life easier and more comfortable. Seems like going backward to me."

"Sharpens your appreciation for all the creature comforts. Anyway, I enjoy it. Let's get some fresh air."

They stepped out onto the patio, made their way through the crowd and sat in the dark. "So," he asked, "you think you'll be pretty good at the money game, huh?"

She looked up at the evening sky. "Yeah. I think I've got what it takes."

"How so?"

"Any broker can make a sale when an investor calls and says, "Buy me this or that," but getting people to put their money at risk, hoping for a great return but with no guarantee? That's an art."

"The power of persuasion?"

She looked at him and narrowed her eyes slightly. "Yeah, I'm really good at getting people to do what I want."

He sipped his beer and let her words sink in. He knew this was an important detail, the most important so far. "Yeah?"

"Yeah." She leaned a little closer and looked from his eyes to his lips. "If you were my boyfriend, you'd do whatever I want."

"Huh. And what if I didn't want to?"

She stroked his arm lightly. "I'd make you."

"How?" He studied her blue eyes as she came closer and even in the darkness saw they looked paler now, an icier blue, and she brought her lips to his and he felt her hand on his thigh and then move to his crotch and then a squeeze. A lot more detail had filled in and he was curious to see how the rest of the picture would develop.

* * *

Kate hears the familiar sounds of Dee Dee arriving home from her weekend with Ed and Rita. She closes the romance novel, puts it on the coffee table, stands and walks to the front door and opens it to see Dee Dee's glum and Ed's nervous expressions. "Have a good time, honey?" she asks Dee Dee. "Uh-huh," she hears Dee Dee say as she walks quickly past without looking up. Kate turns and watches Dee Dee cross the living room, head down and shoulders hunched, carrying her overnight bag. Kate looks back with concern at Ed. "How'd it go?"

He fidgets with his keys. "I think she had a good time. It's hard to tell with her these days. Seems like she has a lot on her mind, and she doesn't talk much. I don't have to tell you."

"Well, it's not surprising given the situation."

He narrows his eyes. "Meaning?"

"Just that she's a twelve-year-old kid dealing with divorced parents."

"She's got plenty of company," he says. "She can handle it."

Kate wants to ask how things are with him and Rita but thinks better of it. She's learned from experience that letting Ed take the lead in sharing information about his marriage is a less confrontational way to find out what's going on. Anyway, she'll get a good account of how the weekend went from Dee Dee. "Take care," Kate says.

"Yeah. See you."

She lingers in the doorway and watches Ed walk to his car. Rita has changed him, wearied and aged him. Kate can see the sadness and worry in his face and the defeat in his shoulders and can't help feeling sorry for him. She watches him drive away, closes the door and walks to Dee Dee's bedroom where she finds her unpacking her overnight bag. Kate leans against the doorway and crosses her arms. "So, how was it?"

Dee Dee shrugs. "Okay. It was really crowded, and the lines were way too long. Rita complained about it all day."

"It can be frustrating. I don't like waiting in long lines, either."

"Yeah, but I bet you don't complain about it."

"Well, everyone's different. That's just who she is."

Dee Dee rolls her eyes. "Tell me about it."

"All set for school tomorrow?"

"Yeah."

"Want to come read with me?"

"I'm gonna write in my diary."

"Okay, honey. Put your dirty clothes in the hamper."

"I will," Dee Dee says. She sits at her desk and opens her diary and flips the pages to the next blank page. She doesn't reread anything. She wants to get straight to setting her thoughts down, She unscrews the cap of her pen, smoothes the blank page with her palm and begins writing:

Sunday, May 22, 2011

Dear Anneliese,

Well, I told you something would happen to spoil things and I was right! The lines were really long to get on the rides, and we spent most of the day standing around waiting. I didn't mind so much. I expected it. All the theme parks are like that. Rita never stopped complaining! Honestly, I don't know why she even came with us. She should have stayed home. My dad tried his best not to let her get on his nerves, but he finally got mad, and they started to argue. They even argued in the car on the drive home. All they seem to do together is argue! Really, I don't know why they stay together.

I know that a lot of arguing went on in the Secret Annex (you called it "bickering" but it's the same thing) and that you thought it was odd how easily grown-ups argue about stupid things, and that you thought it was something children did and outgrew. Well, I can tell you that nothing has changed!

I understand why people in the Secret Annex argued so much. You were all stuck together in that small space for so long, but my dad and Rita aren't stuck in their house. They can go wherever they want. Still, they argue all the time. I think if they'd been in the Secret Annex they would have killed each other! You wrote, "You only really get to know a person after a fight. Only then can you judge their real character." You're probably right, but it seems to me that after so many fights, my dad and Rita should have learned that they're not right for each other. Even I can see that! Why do they stay together? It doesn't make any sense to me.

I wish my mom would meet someone. She doesn't seem to mind not having a husband or a boyfriend, but I think she's lonely. It's nice to have someone to do things with instead of always doing things by yourself. I asked her if she wanted to get married again and she said, "If it happens, it happens. We'll see." She doesn't seem to care one way or another. Maybe she's still getting over Dad. I'm not really sure, but I guess I understand the way she feels. After all, I'm happy doing things by myself. I spend a lot of time alone. Of course, I have friends, but I don't have a boyfriend, and it doesn't bother me. I'm sure I'll have a boyfriend someday, probably in high school. That's a long way off.

Yours, Dee Dee

P.S.: About my mom getting married again or having a boyfriend, I have to say I like the way things are now with just the two of us living here. We get along really well. Sure, she gets on me sometimes, like when I put off doing my homework until the last minute or don't clean my room, but she never really gets mad and we never argue. My mom's great! I know you and your mom didn't get along so well and you felt she was always taking other people's sides when they complained about you or picked on you. It must have felt awful! I know you're happy for me.

CHAPTER 2

The Brennans

The terra cotta tiles on the roofs of the estate homes in Amber's parents' gated community in Newport Coast glow in the late afternoon light. Matt pulls up to the guard shack and the uniformed security guard picks up his clipboard, leans out and eyes his license plate, his Jeep and the surfboard sticking out the back. "How can I help you?" the guard asks with a polite smile.

"Matt Tildon. I'm here to see the Brennans." He watches the guard scan the guest list and glance at him, a little suspiciously he thinks, and open the gate.

"Need directions?" the guard asks.

"All set."

"Enjoy your stay."

He parks in front of the Brennan's house and takes the roses he bought for Amber's mom from the passenger's seat, gets out and looks back at the Jeep by at the curb. It's the only car to be seen and he knows the garages of the houses in this cul-de-sac are filled with expensive luxury automobiles. He has the feeling his Jeep is affecting property values. Amber answers the door.

"Hi," she says cheerily.

"Hi," he says, not as cheerily.

They enter the house and Matt sees Amber's parents, gazing down at him from a large studio portrait hanging on the wall in the white marble tiled vestibule. He recognizes it as the work of a photographer in Laguna Beach whose stock in trade is portraiture of the well-heeled local gentry.

He takes in the interior of the house as he follows her. To the left is a study with mahogany walls and bookcases and a large desk, and to the right a sweeping staircase. They pass an entertainment room and a spacious well-equipped kitchen with enough hanging copper, stainless steel and cast-iron pots and pans to put most restaurants to shame. The dining room is appointed with a large crystal chandelier and a long sideboard and table surrounded by a dozen high back chairs. To the right is an enormous living room with matching gold, silver and crystal chandeliers suspended from a vaulted ceiling. Persian rugs cover the floor and there are two long couches facing each other and winged back chairs grouped together at either end of the room, all upholstered in dark brown leather. Oil portraits of the family in ornate gilt gold frames hang above a large fireplace. Through the floor-to-ceiling windows he sees a panoramic view of Pacific.

He's been in some expensive homes before but nothing like this. He estimates that most of his family's house could fit in the living room and imagines what it must have been like growing up here. Its size would have affected anyone. He can see Amber in his mind's eye as a little girl looking right at home in it. He understands better now why she is the way she is, although it's still unclear how he fits in the picture.

She's shared a bit about her family with him. Her father's name is Court and he's a hedge fund manager. Her mother's name is Alicia and she volunteers her time doing fund raising work for organizations in the community, most notably the local children's hospital. This is a special occasion because Amber's older sister Cryssie is home from Wellesley College on a visit.

He follows her outside to the large stone-paved patio and sees her parents and Cryssie seated around a table under a pergola. He's struck by the contrast between the sweeping view of the Pacific and the way Cryssie's sitting, feet up on the chair, arms hugging her legs, chin resting on her knees. Her parents smile as they approach, but Cryssie keeps her head and eyes down and picks nervously at the skin on her knee. Matt gives the flowers to Amber's mom and she thanks him and tells him he didn't have to do that and sends Amber to the kitchen to get a vase to put them in. Court says he hopes Matt likes steak. Matt says he does and glances at the barbecue, easily longer than his Jeep. Amber returns with the flowers in a vase and two beers and puts one in front of him. She sits across from him next to Cryssie, which he finds curious.

He sips his beer and studies the faces around the table. He sees that Amber has Court's icy blue eyes and square jaw and Cryssie her mother's brown eyes and oval face. Unlike Amber, Cryssie isn't wearing any makeup. Her hair is dark brown and cut short and she's cute in an edgy sort of way, although his impression is that she probably doesn't see herself as cute and wouldn't consider being told she is a compliment. She's slender and lacks Amber's muscle tone, and while Amber wears little diamond studs in her earlobes and doesn't have any tattoos, Cryssie has three silver studs in the crescent of her right ear and her upper arms are covered with tattoos of purplish, red-tinged feathers. She and Amber both sit in silence as he and Court make small talk. Cryssie doesn't so much sit as perch on her seat, not looking at her father, but listening carefully to him with her head tilted slightly and her ear turned toward him. Court tells Matt that he hears from Amber he's a photographer and says he likes Helmut Newton's work.

"What about Maplethorpe?" Cryssie asks without looking up.

"Not into that stuff," Court says without looking at her.

Cryssie frowns. "What? Flowers?"

Matt hasn't been with the Brennans ten minutes and can see they're far from a happy family. Court and Cryssie are like two ticks in an ashtray circling each other. Alicia seems long-suffering and resigned to the discord between the two of them. He has the feeling there are wounds in the family that have never healed, festering wounds that might erupt at any moment. Alicia asks if he's a native Southern Californian. He says he is but that his folks moved here from Utah and notices the slight rise of Alicia's and Court's eyebrows and knows what the next question will be.

"Are you Mormons?" Alicia asks.

He notices Cryssie glance at her mother, and then at him, and then look down at her knee and begin picking nervously at it again. He smiles at Alicia. "My folks are Kentucky Baptists. My dad got a good job offer in

Salt Lake. They're open-minded people. They let me and my sister make up our own minds about religion. I'm with Freud."

Cryssie looks up at him. "What do you mean?"

"It's time we moved beyond it."

She narrows her eyes. "Ever been in therapy?" she asks and looks back down at her knee.

He sees Amber and her parents shift nervously in their seats.

"What's your dad's line of work?" Court asks before Matt can answer Cryssie's question.

"General contractor."

"How's business?"

"He's had a pretty hard time of it the last few years. My mom's a nurse. They do all right."

"How old's your sister?" Cryssie asks.

"Nineteen."

"What's her name?"

"Jenn."

"What's she like?"

Matt sees the others becoming increasingly uncomfortable, Amber most of all and she looks at her sister, frowns and crosses her arms.

Cryssie glances at her. "What?"

Matt smiles. "Jenn's a great kid, talented musician, straight A student, going to Stanford in the fall." He sees Cryssie's impressed and keenly interested now.

"What instrument?"

"Violin and piano. She's been playing the violin since she was three."

"What's she going to be?"

"A doctor."

"Is she gay?"

Amber jabs her sister in the arm with an elbow. "Cryssie!"

Cryssie scowls at her. "In case you haven't noticed a lot of intelligent talented women are."

Matt laughs. "It's a good question. I've always just assumed she's straight. She has lots of gay and straight friends, but she's never really had a boyfriend or girlfriend. She went to her senior prom with her friend Jeff, who's gay. So, I guess the answer is I don't really know."

"She's your sister," Cryssie says. "Why don't you ask her?"

He grins. "Why don't you?"

"Maybe I will."

Cryssie strikes him as the type of person who means what she says, and he has the feeling she will. He sees this last exchange proved too much for Amber and her parents and watches Court walk to the barbeque to busy himself with the steaks and Alicia and Amber to the kitchen to collect things for the table. "How do you like Wellesley?" he asks Cryssie.

She shrugs. "It's okay."

"I hear Boston's a fun town."

"Yeah, it's okay. It's too damn cold. I went skiing once in New Hampshire. I fell down all day and froze my ass off. That was it for me. P-town's nice. It's a fun place to hang out."

"What's it like?"

"A lot of the locals are descended from old Portuguese fishing families. You'd think there'd be no way they'd tolerate gays, but they've accepted them into the community. More places should be like that."

"You?"

"Bi. What're you doing with Amber?"

"Whaddya mean?"

"Why are you wasting your time with her? You two are on different planets. She's my little sister and I love her, but I know her. She likes to toy with men. I don't think she even likes them." Cryssie looks around at the house and the patio. "Anyway, this is what she's used to, and she won't settle for less. I don't know what most photographers make but I'm pretty sure it's not enough to support this lifestyle. That's why you're here, to rub your nose in it." She looks at him. "I'm sure I'm not telling you anything you don't already know."

"No, you're not. I guess I got sucked in."

"Yeah, she's good at that."

He shrugs. "I was curious to see what else there might be."

"I'll save you the time and trouble," she says. "More of the same."

* * *

Matt escorts his customer from rack to rack, showing him the different suits available in his size and glances now and then at Cryssie, who's standing across the aisle in Men's Accessories with a Medium Brown Bag in her hand, checking out the items in the display case while she waits for him to be free. Her unexpected appearance is a pleasant surprise.

"When's the sale begin?" the customer asks.

"Wednesday."

"Thanks. See you then."

Matt hands him a card and sees Cryssie wait until the customer's gone to walk over. "Hey! Whadja buy?" he asks.

She rolls her eyes. "A pair of torn jeans. These prices are insane."

"Amber here?"

"Upstairs, spending a bundle on girlie stuff. Working tomorrow?"

"No, I'm off."

"Doing anything later?"

"No, why?"

"Let's hook up. What time are you off?"

"Six."

"I'll pick you up."

He finds her waiting in a light blue BMW 650i Coupe, he guesses her mother's car, by the employee entrance. He gets in and sees she's wearing her new expensive, black "distressed" jeans, a black hoodie and black flip-flops and also, unlike yesterday, make up, not a lot, just lip gloss and a little eye shadow. He smiles. "Lookin' good."

"Date face. You should feel honored and privileged."

"Where're we headed?"

"Malibu. First, we're stopping at Santa Monica Pier for chili dogs and fries and a ride on the Ferris wheel."

"Cool."

"Our parents used to take us there when we were kids. It was a bright spot in an otherwise shitty childhood. I like to visit it from time to time. It keeps me connected to pleasant memories."

"What's in Malibu?"

"Our beach house. We rent it out during the season."

The house is dark and smells musty as they enter and turn on lights and open the blinds. They put beer in the fridge and each take one outside to the deck and settle in chairs, Cryssie sitting, he notices, as she did the evening before, with her feet up on the edge of the chair and hugging her legs. It's a moonless night and at first, they can barely differentiate the strip of sandy beach from the ocean, but slowly their eyes adjust to the darkness. They listen to the steady low rumble and hissing of the surf and watch wave after wave break on the shore. Out of the corners of his eyes he sees her reach into the pocket of her hoodie and remove something. A pillbox? She twists off the cap and takes out a small pill and holds it up.

"Hug drug," she says. "I'm into hugs. Want one?"

He holds out his hand and she places a pill in his palm. He puts it in his mouth and sees her do the same. She holds out her bottle to him and they clink.

"Here's to hugs," she says.

"To hugs." He sips his beer and sees her do the same.

"Has she met your family?" Cryssie asks.

He shakes his head.

"Have you offered to take her to meet them?"

"No."

"Has she asked?"

"No."

"She's not going to. She's not interested."

"Probably not."

"Do they even know about her?"

"I've mentioned her."

"I want to."

"What?"

"Meet them."

He grins. "I think the person you really want to meet is my sister."

She looks at him and raises her eyebrows. "And your point is?"

"What was Amber like as a kid?"

"Like most second children. She watched the shit I went through. She learned to fly beneath the radar. Who can blame her? And they spoiled her rotten, which didn't help. I think they did it out of guilt for treating me the way they did. They treated her like a little princess."

"What's she doing at Long Beach? Your folks could send her to any school."

"She wanted to be a big fish in a small pond. So, had enough punishment?"

"Yeah. I guess I've just been avoiding ending it."

"Don't worry about hurting her feelings. You won't."

He sips his beer and stares out at the darkness. "Does she know we're here?"

"What difference does it make?"

"Did she ask you to talk to me?"

"Afraid you're being dumped? Pride hurt?"

"It's funny. I'm not and it isn't.... I wish I weren't wired this way."

"You can't fight human nature. Believe me, I know."

They sit silently, staring out at the ocean and feeling increasingly expansive and connected without speaking as the drug takes effect. She stands and faces the ocean with her arms outstretched. "I need a hug."

He stands and faces her and wraps his arms around her and feels her arms wrap around him. He closes his eyes and concentrates on the feel of her body. She seems so small in his arms, so delicate, like a bird. He can feel her heart beating against his chest. Is he just imagining it or are their hearts beating in time together? He opens his eyes and sees her studying his face and then look into his eyes and he looks into hers and they stay that way what seems to him a very long time. Finally, she brings her lips to his and they kiss for what seems an equally long time. She finally draws her head back and smiles.

"Let's fuck," she says.

They undress in the bedroom in the dark, climb onto the bed and lie silently in each other's arms. Holding her feels different than holding Amber, the few times she's allowed him to. There's less of her there and he imagines this is what it would feel like holding a shadow in a dream.

He kisses her lips, her cheek, her ear, her neck, her shoulder. He can just make out her breasts in the dark. "They're not much," he hears her whisper, "but they're sensitive." He kisses her nipple and feels her shudder. He sucks it gently and it quickly hardens in his mouth. "Do that all night and I'll be the happiest girl in the world," he hears her whisper.

The sky is just beginning to lighten when they finally lie resting in each other's arms. The rest of her body, he discovered, is as sensitive as her breasts. He also discovered more piercings. That was a pleasant sensation. "Let's watch the sunrise," she says. "I'll make coffee."

They sit on the deck, Cryssie with her hoodie up, and Matt can just see her nose and chin poking out. She takes a pack of cigarettes out of her pocket and a cigarette out of the pack and one for him and hands it to him. She lights them both and they sit quietly for a while, smoking and sipping coffee and watching the occasional jogger and beachcomber pass by, and the gulls and small shorebirds dart in and out of the breaking waves, pecking in the sand in search of the first meal of the day.

"When did you know you were bi?" he asks.

She flicks the ash off her cigarette. "I've been attracted to both sexes as long as I can remember. I had my first same-sex experience when I was thirteen. My friend Barbara lived nearby. She was a tall, sweet shy kid with wavy blonde hair and bright blue eyes and a big smile. We'd sit on my bed with the door closed and talk about sex to feel each other out the subject, you know? We were clueless and wanted to explore. I made the first move. I asked her if she wanted to feel what it would be like to have her breasts touched. I'll never forget the look on her face. She was nervous and embarrassed, but curious and she nodded. At first, I touched her through her tee shirt. She liked it. I loved it. I loved making her nipples hard. Then I got her to lift up her shirt and let me feel them through her bra. It was white cotton and decorated with a cute little bow, very girlie. I finally got her to pull up her bra. Her breasts were beautiful, big for her age. The fact that my mother was downstairs and could have appeared at any time made things thrilling, but I knew she wouldn't bother us. She didn't want to know what was going on. That's who she is. I kept telling Barbara to relax and not worry, but she was always afraid the door would suddenly open. Pleasure fueled by fear. It was a turn on." Cryssie takes a long draw on her cigarette and blows the smoke out in a stream. "She was okay with touching. She could close her eyes and imagine I was a boy, I guess, but she didn't want to kiss. As much as I wanted to kiss her, she wouldn't let me. The last time we were together she told me some boy in her class had asked her out and that was the end of that. We were more acquaintances than friends after that. When we'd run into each other, I could tell I made her uncomfortable. I was her dirty little secret."

"I dunno. Seems pretty normal to me."

"The difference being that most kids stop there. One or two same-sex experiences and you're over it. As soon as girls experience boys, they're done with girls. Same with boys, right? Not me. I got into boys and liked it, but I still liked girls." She scratches her knee through the expensive tear in her jeans and looks at him and frowns. "When am I gonna meet your family? I'm not here forever."

CHAPTER 3

Matt's Family

Cryssie watches people dressed in black wander out of the employee entrance on the side of the big white box of a store. She has the mental image of a white whale giving birth to penguins. She likes Matt. He's a nice guy, relaxed and easy-going. He doesn't say much, so it was interesting listening to him on the Ferris wheel ride describe the way he's gotten to know Amber, like he's been watching a photograph develop in the dark room. He has that artist's view of life, quietly observing and considering and sizing things up. He said he knew he and Amber weren't right for each other from the start, that he allowed himself to be led along, but she thinks that's only partly true and that he just plain miscalculated. Other men have with her sister, so far all of them.

She can tell by his polite and gentle manner that he's been raised by loving parents and that his family is close. She's longed for a family like that. Her family has served as the benchmark of dysfunction against which she's measured the families of friends she's met through the years. She's found them all to be only slightly less dysfunctional than her own. Maybe it's just Orange County, or the part of it where she grew up, the money part. She's eager to meet his family and curious to see how they are together and what it feels like being with them. Most of all she's looking forward to meeting his sister.

Matt finally appears and she takes the box of See's Assorted Chocolates she bought for his mom, her favorites he said, and gets out, locks the car, gets into his Jeep and they head toward his parents' house in Costa Mesa. They turn onto a tree-lined street in a neighborhood of modest ranch style single-family homes with just enough space between them for a walkway. "Carl and Dot, right?" she asks and sees him nod. She eyes the houses, so close together. What must it have been like growing up here? It's like having your neighbors in the next room.

They pull up to the curb and park in front of a beige stucco house with brown wood trim around the windows. "Home sweet home," she hears him say. Her first impression of the house is that it could probably fit in her parent's living room. The green window boxes filled with peonies and cyclamen catch her eye and she notices that the bushes are neatly trimmed and the grass in the small front yard is mowed and carefully edged. It's nice, very homey. Matt gets the beer from the back of the Jeep, and they walk up the path to the front door and enter the house.

"Hey, Mom!" Matt calls.

Cryssie sees Dot standing in the kitchen with her back to them and studies her as she turns. She's pleasantly plump with short, light brown hair and bright brown eyes and a round smiling face.

"Hi, honey," Dot calls and comes to meet them, wiping her hands on a dishtowel. She drapes it over her shoulder and hugs Matt.

"This is Cryssie," he says.

Dot gives her a hug. "So nice to meet you!" She steps back and sees the present Cryssie's holding out to her with both hands. "You didn't have to do that!"

"Matt said they're your favorite."

"They are! How thoughtful and sweet of you, dear!"

Cryssie likes Dot a lot, likes everything about her, her welcoming manner and the way she wraps an arm around hers and leads her to the kitchen. She's just arrived and already feels at home in a way she never has in her parents' house.

Matt puts the beer in the fridge and takes out two. "Jenn here?"

"She'll be right back," Dot says. "She went to get wine." She looks apologetically at Cryssie. "Carl and I don't drink."

"I probably shouldn't either," Cryssie says and takes the beer from Matt and looks around the kitchen, which seems about the size of her parents' pantry and strikes her as all the kitchen any family should reasonably need. "Your home is lovely."

"Thank you, dear."

Cryssie smiles as Dot takes her arm again and leads her to the backyard where she sees Carl, his back turned to them, standing over a smoking grill with a pair of tongs in his hand. She smiles again as she feels Dot give her arm that gentle squeeze. It feels like they're already best friends.

"I hope you like barbequed chicken," Dot says.

Cryssie grins. "Love it." Dot gives her arm another gentle squeeze and leans closer.

"Spicy?"

"The spicier the better," Cryssie says, her grin widening into a smile. She's smiled so infrequently in her life and can't remember the last time she did and can feel her facial muscles performing beyond their usual limits. It's a nice feeling.

"Carl, honey, meet Cryssie."

Cryssie watches Carl turn. He's big and burly. His short-cropped curly hair is strawberry blonde and his eyes light blue and his cheeks ruddy. He looks like a builder, a man who makes things with his hands and takes pride in his work, the type of man you can rely on, unlike her father, who's also big and burly but builds nothing you can see and whose sole purpose in life seems to be to take everything from you without your ever noticing. She sees Carl smile and put out a hand that seems twice the size of hers and she takes it and watches hers disappear into it.

"Nice to meet you," Carl says, smiling and nodding toward Matt. "What's this guy doing with someone as pretty as you?"

Cryssie feels herself blush and Dot give her arm another gentle squeeze. When was the last time she blushed, and at such a predictably polite compliment? She can't remember that, either.

"Matt says you live in Newport Coast," Carl says. "I worked on those houses."

"Well, you did a great job. My parents love to show off their home."

"Not much of that type of construction going on these days. I don't think there will be again anytime soon."

Cryssie hears Dot sigh and give her arm a now familiar-feeling gentle and comforting squeeze.

"It's hard for everyone these days," Dot says, "but we have a lot to be thankful for. Two wonderful children, a nice home, good health."

Cryssie's conscience stirs. In fact, things aren't hard for everyone. They are for most people, but her parents don't want for anything and she's knows Matt's parents know that. As far as material things go, she and Amber are fortunate to be their parents' children and have enjoyed a life of luxury, but when it comes to parental love, they're poverty stricken.

"Hey!" Cryssie hears and turns to see a smiling young Asian woman a little taller than herself, with long glistening black hair, walking toward them with a glass of white wine in her hand. She must be Jenn and she's wearing a white tee shirt cut off above her navel revealing a flat and firm tummy, and low waist shorts that show off the graceful curve of her hips and her long shapely legs. Jenn's face reminds Cryssie of the white porcelain statuette of an Asian woman in a flowing robe posed elegantly holding a lotus flower that's been sitting on a table in the upstairs hall in her parents' house for as long as she can remember. She's always admired it and wondered what it would be like to be a woman that beautiful. Looking at Jenn is like looking at that statuette come to life.

"Come meet Cryssie, honey!" Dot says, waving Jenn over.

Cryssie watches Jenn walk toward her and stop in front of her and glances down at her hand as she holds it out to her. Her long slender fingers are ring free and her fingernails are perfectly formed and unpolished and she takes Jenn's hand in hers as she would that statuette's, carefully, cautiously and gratefully.

"Nice to meet you," Jenn says.

Cryssie looks up and studies Jenn's face, her almond skin, dark brown eyes framed by wing-like black eyebrows, long black eyelashes, short slender nose and full pink lips. It's a face whose natural beauty would only be marred by makeup. She realizes she's still holding Jenn's hand and lets it go. "Same here."

Jenn's noticed Cryssie's glances from the moment they sat at the dinner table, Cryssie directly across from her beside Matt. She could see Cryssie was trying her best to keep her eyes on Matt or her parents when they were speaking but couldn't manage it. Now, with the meal over, Jenn's sitting back, relaxed, with an arm draped over the back of her chair and her legs crossed, talking with Cryssie about college and she's struck by her adoring expression and the fact that she's no longer even trying to hide the fact that she can't take her eyes off her. She doesn't know quite what to make of it since she knows Cryssie and Matt spent the night together in Malibu. "I thought about applying to Wellesley," Jenn says. "If I weren't on the pre-med track, I probably would have. What's your major?"

"Economics," Cryssie says.

"What got you interested in it?"

Cryssie fidgets with her fork. "The mess the world's in, the unequal distribution of wealth and resources, the exploitation of the poor and weak, the fact that in the same country, the same community, a few people can have everything while most people have relatively nothing. I'm all for capitalism, but things seem out of whack. I'd like to understand why better, you know? I dunno, maybe try to do something about it?"

Jenn smiles. "I admire you for wanting to try."

Cryssie gazes at Jenn's eyes and savors the compliment. She wants to leap across the table and throw her arms around her and cover her with passionate kisses but continues fidgeting with her fork. "Thanks."

Carl sits back and crosses his arms. "That's the way the world is. I don't think it's going to change anytime soon."

Dot sighs. "Well, let's be thankful for what we have." She looks at Cryssie and smiles and raises her eyebrows. "Ready for coffee and dessert?"

"I'll help," Cryssie says, pushing back her chair.

Dot puts a hand on her arm. "You stay right there."

Cryssie watches her and Jenn stand, pick up plates and walk toward the kitchen. How she wishes she could stay right here — *forever.*

Matt and Cryssie drive in silence back toward South Coast Plaza, Cryssie staring straight ahead with her hands folded in her lap. She can't stop thinking about how she might have turned out differently as a person had she been raised by Dot and Carl, perhaps not as wary and prickly and cynical. Most of all, she can't stop thinking about Jenn and picturing her face. She made a conscious effort to record every detail, including that tantalizing tiny mole on the right side of her upper lip. They exchanged contact information and told each other they'd keep in touch. Was Jenn just being polite? She hopes not. She looks at Matt's profile. The fact that Jenn was adopted drew her attention to the fact that he doesn't resemble either of his parents. She's been meaning to ask him ever since they left. "You adopted?"

"Yeah."

"I thought so. You don't look like your folks. Does she know anything about her biological parents?"

"Yeah. They live in Xinzhou, China, not far from Beijing. At least they did when she was born."

"Has she ever met them?"

"No."

"Does she want to?"

"She thought a long time about that. My folks were willing to pay for the trip, if she wanted to go, but she decided it was better not to. She figured there must have been a good reason her parents gave her up for adoption and she wasn't sure they'd want to see her again."

"Did she ever try to contact them?"

He shakes his head. "She moved on."

"How about you?"

"I don't know anything about my biological parents."

"Do you want to? Aren't you curious?"

"No."

"Any chance your folks would adopt me?"

He glances at her and smiles. "What time's your flight?"

"Seven."

"Out of John Wayne?"

"Yeah."

"I'll take you."

"Amber's taking me. Meet me there if you want."

* * *

Matt waits on a bench outside Cryssie's departure terminal at John Wayne Airport, thinking about everything that's happened between them in the last week, and especially about the visit with his family. They like her and she likes them and it's clear that she really likes Jenn. It's unclear how Jenn feels about her. He couldn't read anything more than that she enjoyed meeting Cryssie, but maybe he was missing something. It's also unclear how Cryssie feels about him and where he figures in the equation. It's an interesting situation.

He catches himself. It's typical of him to be wondering about how everyone else feels instead of trying to figure out how he feels. He likes Cryssie and enjoys being with her and would like their relationship to continue, but she's about to get on a plane and travel three thousand miles away. It's not necessarily an obstacle. He's okay with a long-distance relationship, but it is a consideration. The big question mark is Cryssie's feelings for Jenn.

He sees Amber's car pull up and she and Cryssie exchange a few words. Cryssie gets out and takes her suitcase from the back seat. Amber, he sees, is keeping her eyes straight ahead, avoiding eye contact with him. Cryssie closes the door, Amber pulls away and she walks up to him. He stands and sees her eyes are reddish and her face puffy. "You okay?" he asks, giving her a hug and peck on the lips.

"Didn't get any sleep. I need coffee."

"Be right back," he says.

She sits on the bench and takes the pack of cigarettes and lighter out of the pocket of her hoodie. She takes a cigarette out of the pack and lights it, inhaling deeply. It's one thing to be bi, but it's another to have strong feelings for a brother and sister. It seems inevitable that she's going to hurt one of them and possibly both. Why is she the way she is? She's been asking herself that question for as long as she can remember and is no closer to an answer now than she was after a year of meeting with the shrink her parents sent her to, when they told her they didn't think her interest in her female friends was "normal," whatever that is. They could have been understanding and supportive but made her feel like a freak instead.

What a nightmare the shrink was with her endless questioning. Was she abused as a child? Did she view her mother as a sexual object? Was she envious of her father's penis? Was she subconsciously trying to replace him? Was her id out of control? What a load of bullshit and a total waste of her parents' money. It serves them right. She has this much to thank her shrink for, though. She did help her gain a better understanding of her bisexuality.

Her shrink's simple explanation was that people are born with a biological switch and that sometime around puberty the switch gets turned on by attraction to the opposite sex, in which case they're heterosexual, or the same sex, in which case they're homosexual. With some people, both sexes turn it on, in which case they're bisexual and with others neither sex turns it on, in which case they're asexual. She was careful to stress that one's sexual orientation is neither "good" nor "bad" just biology, although given the fact that most people are heterosexual, being perceived as being "different" can and usually does make life more difficult.

Still awake at 3:00 am in her bedroom, lying on the bed, staring blankly at the TV screen with the sound off, she decided to go sit outside on the patio and smoke a joint. Maybe it would relax her.

She thought about Charlie the chameleon in her grade school science room. Everything about him fascinated her, the way he looked, the way he moved, the way he rotated his eyes, his incredibly long tongue, but most of all his ability to change color. At a time when she was beginning to become aware of the fact that she was different, she identified with him. Charlie was living proof that you didn't have to be one way or another. When she got her first tattoo, it was a chameleon, clinging to a stick on the small of her back.

Still, she grapples with the question of whether she's the way she is because of nature or nurture. To others it might seem a distinction without a difference, but the answer is important to her. If it's nature, then her attraction to both sexes is instinctual. If it's nurture, then it's a matter of choice. She's always believed it's nature, but she's always had her doubts, and they came calling when it seemed the night would never end. Why would she choose to be attracted to both sexes? It doesn't make any sense, unless....

There's no question in her mind that changing color was part of Charlie's nature. He did it to survive, to make himself invisible to predators and prey alike. The nagging suspicion she's had for some time is that she does it for the same reason, not consciously, but subconsciously. She had the feeling her shrink also suspected as much and who could blame her, given her relationship with her parents? Wouldn't she want to seek acceptance and affection and love from whomever seemed willing to give it and, at the same time, wouldn't she want to protect herself from being disappointed and hurt? The conclusion makes sense, as it does every time she argues this side of the question. The problem is that it always feels wrong. Neither Matt nor Jenn showed any sign of being attracted to her. She was attracted to them. She's the pursuer. She's not so much a chameleon changing color to suit the situation as she is a leopard that can't change its spots. She doesn't want to hurt anyone but can't help the way she feels, and her feelings for Jenn are stronger than her feelings for Matt.

Matt comes walking up to her. "Here ya go," he says, holding out a cup to her.

She takes it and cups it in her hands. She feels exhausted and cold and the heat against her palms feels good and comforting. "Thanks."

He sits beside her. "So, what's up?"

She draws on her cigarette, blows out a stream of smoke, glances at him and looks down at her shoes and shrugs. "I dunno. You tell me."

"I dunno."

She looks up at him. "We don't know much, do we? Listen, all that stuff I said about being concerned about the unequal distribution of wealth? It's bullshit, hypocritical. I could have severed my ties to my parents long ago and struck out on my own, done anything to support myself, but I didn't. They pay my tuition and my rent and give me a big fat allowance each month. I'm a spoiled brat, plain and simple, just like Amber. You don't need more of that shit."

He can see in her eyes now that she wants their relationship to remain a friendship and knows the reason why and grins. "You're head over heels for her."

She searches his eyes and looks at his grin. "It's that obvious?"

"Yeah."

"You okay with it?"

"Sure."

"That's a relief," she says and looks back down at her shoes. "I've never felt this way about anyone before. I can't explain it. I've never been afraid of making a fool of myself before either, but I am now."

"Sounds like love."

She looks up at him and stabs her cigarette out in the ashtray. "That's what I'm afraid of." They stand and hug and she rolls her suitcase toward the entrance and turns back. "Good luck with Amber! You're gonna need it!"

He waves and watches the doors slide closed behind her. Well, it was short but sweet. He's glad he met her and has the feeling she's going to be in his life for a long time to come. He has her to thank for getting him off his ass about ending things with Amber, although he's still not looking forward to it. Ending relationships is always a pain.

* * *

The strobe lights pop as they flash, filling the studio with bursts of white light and the battery packs sigh as they discharge. "Good. Just a few more." Matt watches Amber through the lens as she changes poses, nude on a white cube in front of a light gray muslin backdrop. "Good." He circles her, the strobes popping and flashing and the battery packs sighing.

The idea of producing a series of large format black and white nudes for his senior project occurred to him the first day he met Amber, when she was posing on the wall. He knew it would be good and sees now that it'll be better than good. It'll be *damn* good. She's a natural. When he first suggested it to her, she was reluctant to pose nude, but he explained that her face wouldn't appear and she felt better about it and agreed. She said she knows all about being a headless body, which struck him as curious.

The strobes pop and flash and the battery packs sigh. "Good." Of course, he put it off until the end of the semester and was reluctant to call to ask if she was still willing to pose. He fully expected her to blow him off and was pleasantly surprised when she said she would. It was the first time they talked since Cryssie's visit, and no mention was made of what happened between them. He doesn't know if she knows what did, or does and doesn't care, but suspects he's about to find out.

Amber imagines herself being held captive in a closet, lying on her side with her knees tucked against her chest, her feet tied together at the ankles, her hands tied behind her back and a gag in her mouth. She imagines the feel of the rope around her wrists and ankles and strains against them. "Great," she hears Matt say, and she knows her posing this way is turning him on. By his own admission she fascinates him. He can't figure out what makes her tick and here's the answer, staring him in the face and he just can't see it. How easily men are pleased and how easy it is to use that pleasure to manipulate them. That's what makes the game fun. This one's over, though. Posing for him is closure.

"Great," she hears him say and lies on her back, still imagining herself bound. "Arch your back a little more," she hears him say. "Like that. Good." Cryssie was close when she asked if she thought their parents were prescient when they named them Crystal and Amber, Cryssie being emotionally fragile and she feeling numb and stuck. It's fanciful thinking. The truth of the matter is their parents made them the way they are.

Cryssie was even closer when she said that Matt's just the latest man she's punishing for not measuring up to their father. For someone who says she hates shrinks so much, her sister sure acts like one sometimes. Cryssie should concentrate on trying to be less emotionally needy. It's a sign of weakness and unbecoming. Poor unloved Cryssie. She thinks she has problems? She doesn't know the half of it. Anyway, if her sister hates their father so much, then why does she continue to let him support her? She's a hypocrite. As for herself, she has no qualms about taking his money. He might be a monster but he's a successful and wealthy one, and she admires that. "All set," she hears Matt say and opens her eyes and looks up at him.

"Let me take some portraits and I'll treat you to a beer."

* * *

Matt studies Amber's face as she checks out people at the tables around theirs. She's such a physically beautiful person, but such a cold human being. It's a shame. What type of man would make her happy? Probably one like her dad. The waitress arrives with their glasses of beer and places them on the table. Matt glances up at her, "Thanks." He looks at Amber, picks up his glass and holds it out to her. "Cheers."

She stares at him and picks up hers and clinks his. "Yeah, cheers."

"Thanks for helping me out." He says.

"No problem."

"You're a natural. With your looks and talent, you could model professionally."

"I have bigger and better things in mind."

He places the glass on the table and leans back and crosses his arms. "So, let's talk."

"About?"

"Us."

"There is no 'us.' There never was."

"Then why were you interested in me in the first place?"

"I wasn't. You were interested in me. I let you tag along."

He cocks his head and smiles. "Come on. This 'ice goddess' persona of yours has to be a pose. No one's that cold."

She fixes her eyes on his. "You're a smart guy, but you have a lot to learn." She raises her eyebrows. "Anyway, look who's talking about poses? Where's your crown, Prince Charming? Malibu?"

"Fair enough." He sits forward and holds out his hand and smiles. "Friends?"

She looks at his hand, stands, slinging her bag over her shoulder, looks down at him and raises an eyebrow. "You're all the same."

He sips his beer and watches her go. She tried to sound so blasé but the bitterness in her voice was unmistakable. Someone must have gotten to her and whoever did got her good.

CHAPTER 4

Ed and Rita

Ed stands in the bedroom in front of the full-length mirror, tying his tie. He glances at Rita, who's standing with her back to him at the sink in the bathroom, putting the finishing touches on her makeup. He isn't looking forward to this evening. He doesn't enjoy going out with her anymore. She's unpredictable in social situations and he's afraid she'll do or say something outrageous that will embarrass him in front of his co-workers and superiors. She told him to relax and stop worrying, that she'd behave, which she always says, but the fact of the matter is she's an alcoholic and drunks, like all addicts, can't be trusted.

He eyes her tight-fitting red dress, one of her favorites and the one she was wearing the first time they met. He loved the way she looked in it then and couldn't take his eyes off her that evening. Now he thinks she looks like a hooker. The irony isn't lost on him. Her sexiness was the main reason he was attracted to her. He's always been partial to the wild, loose, hard-partying type. Kate was the only exception. But Rita has lost her appeal for him. He sees her step back and examine herself in the mirror above the sink, turning her head this way and that. She picks up her vodka tonic from the counter and takes a sip, then turns to face him with raised eyebrows.

"How do I look?" she asks.

"Nice," he says and sees her frown.

"'Nice'? Waddya mean 'nice'? You look at me in this dress and you say 'hot' or 'sexy'! Not 'nice.' Are you a man? You used to be." She shakes her head, clucks, turns back to the mirror and touches up the lipstick at the corners of her mouth with her pinky.

"We're going to a department dinner dance, not an adult entertainment awards ceremony," he says.

"Very funny," she says, smoothes her eyebrow with a fingertip and takes another sip of her drink.

He glances at her. You'd never guess she's an attorney and a good one. When he and Kate divorced, Rita's brother Ricky, a fellow officer, mentioned he had a sister, attractive and a lawyer, and also recently divorced, and asked if he'd like to meet her. When Ed arrived at her apartment to pick her up for their first date and she opened the door, he had a hard time putting together in his mind the person he saw standing in the doorway and the fact that her day job was representing undocumented immigrants. She made the sexy portrayals of women lawyers on TV seem tame, and when they ended up back at her apartment, she proved a tigress in bed. It was one of the wildest nights of sex he'd ever experienced, and when they were lying together afterward, she asked him if the reason he and his wife divorced was because he cheated on her. He said it was, and she said that if she ever caught him cheating on her, he'd be sorry he was ever born. He believed her.

His fidelity doesn't seem to be a big issue with her these days. They rarely have sex anymore, and when they do, it's usually initiated by her to appease him after pissing him off during one of her drunken tirades. What he wants to do is divorce her, but he can't afford to. Given what he's already paying in alimony and child support to Kate and what Rita would exact from him, he'd be living out of his car. He's trapped. Rita comes out of the bathroom, sipping her drink.

"Why is she even here this weekend?" she asks testily. "You knew we had this function. You should've rescheduled."

"It's my weekend and she'll be fine alone for the evening."

Rita opens the jewelry box on the dresser, fishes around in it and selects a gold necklace with a thick woven chain and large pendant that drapes to her cleavage. She looks him up and down as she fastens it around her neck. "You need new clothes. You look like a cop in a suit."

"I am a cop in a suit."

"Precisely."

Dee Dee's eager to see how Rita's prepared herself for the evening. She'll be wearing lots of makeup, as usual, and probably the red dress, her favorite, and big jewelry. She's probably also tipsy by now. Dee Dee hears them on the staircase and glances up from the TV at her dad, standing in the doorway, and sees Rita behind him and the drink in her hand. Dee Dee hates being right about Rita and knows she's an embarrassment to her dad.

"We'll be back around eleven or eleven-thirty, honey," Ed says, walking over to Dee Dee. "If anything comes up call. Okay?"

"Yeah," Dee Dee says, and her dad gives her a kiss on the top of her head. She sees Rita set her drink down on the coffee table and strike a pose for her.

"How do I look?" Rita asks.

Dee Dee looks her up and down. She's reminded of every "evil woman" character she's seen on TV and in the movies, the ones that always end up beaten and bloody or dead. "Nice."

Rita rolls her eyes. "You and your father! Two peas in a pod!"

* * *

Rita sips her drink and eyes the three couples seated around the table with her and Ed and Ricky and his wife Estella. She recognizes them from past functions, and they introduced themselves when they all sat down, but their names escape her now. Dick and Jane, Jack and Jill — What difference does it make? They're chatting about work and kids and school and recent trips they've taken on vacation, none of which interests her. It's the typical small talk of pampered middle-class people who complain about how hard it is to get by, while enjoying a standard of living most people in the world envy and can only dream about.

They know she's an immigration attorney and how heated she can become about the plight of undocumented immigrants trying to gain legal status, so they're careful to steer clear of the subject, which leaves her with nothing to say or do but drink and listen to mindless chitchat and then to the Chief, who's taken the podium and is commending various members of the department, Ed among them for his investigative work in vice and narcotics that helped indict the Gomez brothers for drug trafficking.

Ah, the Gomez brothers, two Guatemalans who were kids when they came to the U.S. illegally with their parents. What's the real crime? Crushing poverty in their home country. Faced with conditions like that here, we'd all flee to Canada.

Her own parents immigrated illegally from Ciudad Obregón in Mexico. They came to Santa Ana because they had family living here legally. She and her brother were born here, but when she was three, her parents were deported, and they left her and Ricky to be raised by their aunt. One or two twists of fate and her brother's story could have been the Gomez's. To hell with borders.

She worked hard to get her parents Green Cards and eventually citizenship, but they're among the very fortunate few. These people around the table could care less about undocumented immigrants. For the most part, California turns a blind eye to the problem and, anyway, Ed and Ricky and the rest of the force have better things to do. But they're part of a system that cares a great deal about the "problem," largely for political reasons. Undocumented immigrants are a convenient "other" to use to strike fear in the citizenry. She's sleeping with the enemy.

She looks around for the waiter. "I asked how you're doing," she hears Ed say in a lowered voice next to her ear. "Fine," she says. "I need another drink."

"You've had enough."

She glares at him. "I'll tell you when I've had enough." She stands and walks unsteadily toward the ladies room as the Chief thanks everyone for coming. The ladies room is empty when she enters and she hears the applause in the ballroom as the door closes behind her.

Sitting in the stall, peeing, she hears the ladies room door open and chatting women entering and filling up the place. She wipes herself, flushes the toilet and stands, steadying herself with one hand on the toilet paper dispenser and pulling up her panty with the other, and when she's arranged herself as best she can she opens the stall door and finds a woman standing there, waiting her turn and looking at her with concern.

"You all right?" the woman asks.

"Fine," Rita says. The woman steps aside to let her pass and Rita takes a couple of steps and stumbles, and another woman catches her outstretched arm and holds her up as she steadies herself. "Thanks," Rita says and looks back down at the level floor tiles. "They should fix that before they have a lawsuit on their hands," she says and can hear how slurred her speech is now.

She stands at the sink, washing her hands and keeping her head down. She can feel the women's eyes on her back and can well imagine what they're estimation of her is and what they're thinking: Her poor husband. She's too drunk and angry with herself to feel humiliated.

The music is loud and the dance floor crowded as she makes her way to the table with a fresh vodka tonic in hand. She notices people glancing at her but concentrates on keeping her eyes on the back of her chair watching her step. Ricky and Estella and Ed are the only ones at the table, and they look up at her with concern as she arrives. Ed pulls her chair back and she sits.

"Howya doin'?" he asks.

"I wish people would stop asking me that."

"We're just concerned about you, Sis," Ricky says.

"Everybody is apparently."

Estella glances at her phone and looks at Ricky. "We should probably get going. It's getting late."

Ricky nods, still looking at his sister with concern.

Rita takes a long sip of her drink. "Finish up and let's go," she hears Ed say. "No," she says, "let's dance. That's why we came, right?" She sees Ed and Ricky and Estella exchange worried glances.

Ed puts his arm on the back of her chair and leans close. "I don't think that's a good idea."

She pushes him away and glares at him. "Stop pissing me off! Either dance with me or I'll find someone who will!"

He glances at Ricky and Estella, then at the people on the dance floor. He looks at Rita and slowly shakes his head. "Rita —"

She pushes her chair back and stands. Ed tries to grab her but she's just out of his reach and as she turns toward the dance floor, she looses her balance and falls, knocking over chairs. The clatter can be heard above the music and people near her on the dance floor stop, turn and stand looking down at her, sprawled on the floor. "Is she okay?" Rita hears a woman ask and another ask, "Is she hurt?" and Ed say, "She's fine, she just tripped," making excuses for her as he always does in these situations.

She knows she's out of control and that her behavior is sloppy and shameful, but also that nothing's going to change, so why bother feeling ashamed? Ed helps her up and almost has to carry her to the car and manages to get her in. She stares out the windshield at the blur of taillights as she rides home. He hasn't said a word since they left the hotel, and she knows he's pissed and rightly so. She is an embarrassment.

She used to be so strong. She learned from her parents' experience what happens to the weak and vulnerable, the powerless and unprotected, and swore to herself she'd never allow anyone or anything to have control over her, but she met her match in alcohol. She used to be able to drink as much as she liked and keep it together. In college she partied as hard as anyone and woke up the next morning clear-headed. She was so strong then, but things began to change with Dan.

They were both just starting out in their careers, he as a criminal defense attorney, and they began dating and getting to know each other. They both said family was important and that they wanted to have kids, two, maybe three. They married and for the next few years concentrated on work. Like most young professionals, they allowed it to consume them and saw very little of each other. He seemed fine with it, but she felt a growing dissatisfaction with their situation and began bringing up the subject of family. She noticed that each time she did, his response was always the same. It wasn't the right time, they weren't earning enough money and couldn't afford the loss of her income, he couldn't devote the time necessary to be a good father and didn't want to burden her with the responsibility of raising a kid alone. It was always one excuse or another and it created friction between them that naturally led to arguments about petty things, and they drank to dull the unpleasantness of situation.

They both liked to drink, but their monthly liquor bill soon doubled. She remembers the awful feeling of gradually losing control over her life and being unable to do anything about it. All she had to do was stop drinking, but she couldn't, and when she became resigned to that fact, "couldn't" became "wouldn't." She somehow managed to pull herself together each morning and go to work and do a good job, but Dan lacked her resiliency, and his practice suffered. The last she heard he was still a drunk and just scraping by.

When they divorced, she promised herself she'd get sober but she didn't, and every time she tells herself she should, or Ed tells her to join AA or check herself into a rehab clinic, she uses Dan's excuse not to. It's not the right time. It's never the right time.

* * *

Dee Dee hears her dad and Rita arrive home, and Rita's complaining voice over the sound of the TV and the popcorn she's munching. She can tell by her dad's expression that he didn't have a good time and knows why when she sees Rita behind him, unsteady on her feet with that dazed look on her face she gets when she's had way too much to drink.

"Hi, honey," Ed says. "Everything okay?"

"Yeah." Dee Dee says and glances at Rita. When Rita's like this it usually means there's going to be a fight. Dee Dee watches her dad walk upstairs, removing his suit coat, and Rita walk toward the kitchen. She hears the familiar sounds of ice cubes tinkling in a glass and the slam of the refrigerator door, and then a cabinet door open and slam shut. She sees Rita return with a drink in her hand and walk slowly and carefully up the stairs, holding onto the banister to steady herself. She hears the slam of her dad and Rita's bedroom door, and it isn't long before she hears the muffled sounds of their voices, low at first but getting louder.

Rita leans against the bathroom doorway with her drink in her hand and stares at Ed as he stands in his underwear in front of the closet, arranging his suit on the hanger. "I know your precious daughter hates me."

He glances at her. "Shut up."

"Darling Kate would never act this way, would she?"

"I said shut up!"

"Why don't you get down on your knees and beg her to forgive you? Maybe she'll take you back. You can be one big happy family again!"

He closes the closet door and points at her. "Stop shouting. I mean it. Dee Dee can hear you."

Rita tilts her head, cocks her hip and puts a hand on it. "Oh, the little princess can hear me! What the fuck do I care? She's gotta grow up sometime!"

He takes a step toward her. "I'm warning you for the last time."

"Who the fuck do you think you are, telling me to shut up?" She throws the glass at his head, but he ducks, and it shatters against the wall behind him.

He moves toward her. "That's it!"

"Yeah? What are you gonna do about it?" she asks defiantly.

He intends to slap her, but his anger gets the better of him and the punch sends her falling backward into the bathroom, where her head bounces off the tile floor and she lies sprawled and moaning.

Dee Dee hears the loud thud and picks up her phone and calls her mom. "Hi, honey," she hears her mom say, sounding surprised, "what's up?" "Can you come get me?" Dee Dee says. "I don't want to stay here."

"What happened?"

"Rita's drunk. They're having a fight. This one's really bad."

"Get your things together. I'll be right there."

Ed kneels beside Rita, pressing a cold washcloth to her bruised and swollen left eye and cheek. She's disoriented but begins coming around and looks up at him angrily.

"You son of a bitch!" she screams, "you fucking son of a bitch!" She swings at him wildly. "I'll kill you!"

He pins her arms against the floor. "Calm down. I told you to shut up and you wouldn't listen. You were asking for it."

She can't argue with him. She was asking for it, begging for it the way a soldier mortally wounded in combat begs to be put out of his misery. She wants to cry but won't give him the satisfaction. "Let me up," she says calmly. He cautiously lets go of her arms and helps her to her feet. She stands at the sink, looking at her bruised and swollen face in the mirror as she runs cold water on the washcloth. "I'm sorry," she hears him say, "I didn't mean to hit you that hard." She shrugs, wringing and folding the washcloth, then presses it against her eye and cheek. She stares at his reflection in the mirror. She doesn't know whom to feel sorrier for, herself or him.

"I'm going to check on Dee Dee," he says and is alarmed to find her sitting on the couch in the living room with her overnight bag beside her. "What's up?"

"Mom's coming to get me."

He feels his anger rising again. "Why did you call Mom?"

"You guys were fighting. I don't want to stay here."

"We were just having a disagreement, Dee Dee." He can see that she thinks his explanation is ridiculous and she has that determined look in her eyes he knows so well, just like Kate's. "I'll call her."

"I'm going," Dee Dee says firmly.

He opens the front door and Kate peers around him and sees Dee Dee getting up from the couch with her bag. She looks at Ed. "What happened?"

"Everything's fine. She didn't need to call you."

Kate narrows her eyes. "She's coming with me," she says and sees Rita come down the stairs in her robe. She stops midway, crosses her arms and stares down at her icily. Judging from the size of the bruise on Rita's face, she's pretty sure Ed hit her. She holds out a hand to Dee Dee. "C'mon, honey."

Ed pats Dee Dee's back as she passes. "Sorry, honey." He watches them walk to Kate's car, get in and drive away. He wonders if Dee Dee will ever want to come back to the house again or if Kate will get a court order preventing her from coming. He closes the door, turns and looks at Rita, still standing on the staircase staring down at him. He can't force her to get sober, but her drinking is poisoning every aspect of his life. If she continues this way, she'll destroy him, whether or not that's her intention. He watches her turn and walk up the stairs, then hears her footsteps as she walks down the hall to the bedroom. He sighs and follows her.

They lie in bed in silence, staring at the TV. "When was the last time we made love?" she finally asks.

He was anticipating this question and just waiting to see how long it would take her to ask it. "Sex is the last thing on my mind."

"We used to fuck like rabbits. What happened?"

"Things changed."

"What?"

"You're drinking."

"I was a drunk when you met me. It didn't bother you then."

"Not a falling down one."

She sighs, moves closer to him, wraps her arms around his and snuggles against him. "Let me make it better, baby," she says.

He looks at her. The hurt expression, the doe eyes, the pleading "little girl" voice — It's all a pathetic act and as angry as he is at her, at the moment he pities her.

She pouts and turns her bruised and swollen eye and cheek toward him. "Didn't I take a punch like a big girl? I know I deserved it."

"I'm sorry."

"I know you are, baby." She slides her hand beneath the covers and strokes his chest. "Kiss it and make it better."

He leans toward her and kisses her cheek.

"Hmm…," she purrs, closing her eyes. "That's nice. Kiss my eye, baby. It needs it too."

He kisses her eye and feels her hand sliding downward.

"Fuck me, baby," she says softly, "I know you want to."

He didn't and knows he shouldn't, but does now, as he always does when they play this tired game of pretending to make up.

* * *

Kate sips her tea and scans the headlines on her iPad. Protest in the Arab world continues to dominate the news. There seems to be turmoil everywhere and she certainly feels it in her life lately. She looked in on Dee Dee when she returned from her morning jog and found her still sleeping. Good. Let her sleep.

She spent the entire jog thinking things over. She feels sorry for Ed, but as infuriating as Rita's behavior might be, that's no excuse for hitting her. She doesn't want to prevent Dee Dee from seeing her dad, but things between Ed and Rita are clearly out of control and she doesn't think their place is a good environment for her. She'll see what Dee Dee has to say.

Kate showers and dresses and puts bowls and spoons and glasses on the kitchen table for breakfast. Dee Dee comes shuffling and yawning into the kitchen, rubbing one tired eye with the back of her hand. "Mornin,'" Kate says cheerily. "Sleep well?" Dee Dee nods and sits and Kate fills the bowls with cereal and milk, the glasses with orange juice and sits across the table from her. "You okay, honey?"

Dee Dee nods and picks up her spoon, looking down blankly at her bowl.

Kate watches her put a spoonful of cereal in her mouth and chew slowly. Dee Dee obviously has a lot on her mind. What kid wouldn't after last night's experience? And she probably has questions. Kate's always told her they could talk about anything, that she could ask her about anything, and she'd give her an honest answer. It was easier when Dee Dee was younger, but as she's gotten older and her questions have become less those of a child and more those of a young adult, pointed and probing, it's been hard to resist the temptation to sugar coat her answers. All the more reason not to. Dee Dee looks up at her.

"Did Dad ever hit you?"

"No, honey."

"What would you have done if he did?"

"Divorce him."

"But you did. If he didn't hit you, why did you?"

Kate feels her stomach muscles tighten. They haven't had this conversation. When she and Ed divorced, she told Dee Dee it was because they "had their differences." It seemed the appropriate explanation at the time. It doesn't now. "He was unfaithful."

"Meaning?"

"He was seeing another woman."

"Who?"

Kate can't bring herself to tell her twelve-year-old daughter that her dad was seeing an eighteen-year-old high school student. It's just too unseemly. Not now. Maybe someday when she's older, if she's still curious and asks. "A younger woman."

"Was it because he thought you were old?"

Good question and one Kate asked herself at the time. "I don't know, honey."

"How did you find out?"

"Someone told me."

"That must've hurt."

"It did. I couldn't be with him after that."

Dee Dee glances at the wall. "Is that why Dad got angry and threw the birthday cake?"

Kate nods. "There's only room for two people in a marriage. I'm not talking about kids, of course. There's plenty of room for kids, but a husband and wife have to be able to trust each other, and part of that is trusting that they're not seeing other people. Know what I mean?"

Dee Dee's watched "Big Love" on TV with her mom, about the Mormon husband and his three wives, and her mom explained that polygamy is a practice the Mormons long ago denounced, but that it's still practiced by some people here in the US and in some other cultures. Having more than one wife is different than her dad seeing another women without telling her mom. She gets that. "Yeah. I feel sorry for Dad, though. He sure isn't happy with Rita."

"No, he isn't. How do you feel about staying at Dad's?"

"I dunno. That was scary. I have to think about it."

"Yeah. Well, today's kind of a bonus day. I was planning to go to the Getty Center. I've wanted to see it ever since it opened. Wanna go?"

"What's it like?"

"Lots of art, paintings and sculpture and stuff. I've checked it out online. The place looks beautiful."

"Where is it?"

"L.A., on a hilltop just off the 405."

Dee Dee shrugs. "Sure."

CHAPTER 5

A Trip to the Getty Center

Whenever Kate's on the 405, where Bobby was killed, she feels lingering bitterness. She knows it's crazy to feel that way about a freeway, but she does. At least it's Sunday and traffic has been flowing, and they've made good time. "See the white buildings up on the hill?" she asks Dee Dee, "That's it. The view must be spectacular from there."

Dee Dee peers out the windshield at the white buildings off in the distance. They look like a modern version of a castle and the closer they get the more impressive they seem.

They board the tram for the winding trip up the hill and stand looking out the window in the front of the first car. As the elevation increases and Los Angeles comes into view in the distance, Dee Dee has the feeling she's rising up to another world. The tram rounds the final turn and the sand-colored stone-faced buildings come into view. The sunlight reflected off them is so intense that they seem to glow. It looks to her like the setting of a fairy tale, a place where charming princes and enchanted princesses and knights in armor on horses battling fire-breathing dragons would feel right at home.

Dee Dee waits in the visitor center as her mom rents audio tours, standing with her head back, gazing up at the glass ceiling high overhead. She feels tiny in the big open space.

Kate walks over and studies the museum map. "Wow! There's a lot to see! Let's start with the paintings. If we don't see everything we can always come back."

They enter the first gallery and are surrounded by Italian religious artwork from the 13th and 14th centuries. They move from painting to painting, stopping to listen to the commentary in their headsets. Kate is mindful of the fact that religion hasn't played much of a role in her life. Her parents are Methodists and brought her to church every Sunday, but religion never interested her much and it was around the time she turned sixteen that her trips with them to church on Sunday became less frequent and she finally stopped going altogether. She and Ed weren't churchgoers, either, and what Dee Dee knows about Christianity she's learned from conversations they've had about the meaning of major religious holidays and TV specials at Christmastime.

They stand in front of Tommaso del Mazzo's *Annunciation,* with the archangel Gabriel kneeling in front of the Virgin, and the dove of the Holy Spirit descending over her head, and God and the angels looking down from above. Kate notices Dee Dee remove her headset and look up at her quizzically and Kate removes hers.

"Was she really?" Dee Dee asks.

"What?"

"A virgin?"

Kate laughs and an elderly couple standing near them does too. She glances at the man, who looks at her sympathetically.

"Good luck with that one," he says, smiling and shaking his head.

She looks down at Dee Dee. "I don't think so. Not literally. I think the story is that way because it helps people understand that Jesus was the Son of God."

"But Joseph was her husband. Wasn't he good enough?"

The elderly couple walks off, laughing and shaking their heads again.

Kate and Dee Dee move on through the galleries and the epochs in the development of European painting. Dee Dee marvels at the realism of the still lifes by the Dutch and Flemish painters and, toward the end of the exhibition, she's struck by the little girl in Fernand Khnopff's painting *Jeanne Kéfer.* The girl is hauntingly beautiful and looks small and vulnerable, standing alone on a porch in front of a big door. Dee Dee thinks she knows how she feels, and now more than ever.

She's fascinated by the paintings of voluptuous rosy-hued nudes. The women seem so at ease and unselfconscious about their bodies, like it's perfectly normal for adults to lounge around with no clothes on. The most fascinating one is Théodore Géricault's *Three Lovers.* Two women and a man are on a bed. The woman lying on the left has big breasts and a big round tummy and she's gazing at the other woman and the man, who are embracing. The woman embracing the man is wearing a white dress, but only just, and has her back turned and you can just make out the man's face over her shoulder. His expression and especially his eyes look more like an animal's than a person's. Dee Dee stares transfixed at the painting as she listens to the commentary and hears that the "nudity and relaxed pose" of the woman on the left "evoke the classical tradition of representing repose after lovemaking" and that "encoiled in her lover's arms and with her legs provocatively exposed, the woman in white is an active participant in the amorous act, rather than a passive object." She's not sure what all that means or what to make of the feelings this painting has aroused in her, or where to begin with the questions it's brought to mind. She removes her headset and looks up at her mom quizzically again.

Kate glances down at her, removes her headset and grins. "Pretty racy, huh?"

"Three people?"

Of course, Dee Dee's thinking about their conversation at breakfast about her dad's infidelity. If they're going to talk about how humans are, at bottom, animals, with animal desires that need to be satisfied, there's probably no better time to do it than now, standing in front of this painting. "It's not about love. It's about lust."

"What's that?"

"Sexual desire. It's an urge, like being hungry. When you're hungry you eat, right?"

Dee Dee stares at the painting. She has an inkling of what her mom's talking about. She's felt something stirring between her legs lately. It's a new feeling, just a tingling, but it feels nice and she's curious about it. "Is that what Dad was doing?"

Kate's reluctant to answer and feels relieved when Dee Dee doesn't press her for one and is happy to move on.

They step outside the gallery onto the terrace, walk to the wall and stand admiring the panoramic view. They can see all the way to the San Gabriel Mountains in the east, Long Beach in the south, Santa Monica in the west and the shimmering Pacific beyond. Below them is a beautiful garden arranged around a large circular pool with rows of sculpted white and red azaleas in the middle of it, forming a curving and interlocking design. It looks to Kate like a symbol of some kind. Is it and does it have a meaning? Gazing at it, she imagines her understanding of it is like Dee Dee's of sexual desire at this point in her life. She can only wonder about it and beyond that, there's only guessing.

They walk down the stairs to the garden entrance and follow one of the zigzagging tree-lined paths leading through it to the pool, stopping to admire the trees and plants and flowers. Kate's familiar with some of them, the plane trees, lavender, sage and verbena, and identifies them for Dee Dee, but most are exotics she's never seen before. It's like walking through a wonderland.

They arrive at the end of the path and stand admiring the azaleas in the pool. Kate lifts her gaze to the opposite side of the pool and sees the people there, standing and strolling on the path through the garden. She notices a man on one knee, photographing flowers, and even though his arm obscures his face, she recognizes him. It's Matt from work. Her instinct is to walk over and say hi, but she hesitates. She's a manager and he's an employee and they should keep a respectful distance. It seems silly. "C'mon, honey. Let's check out the other side."

Kate studies Matt as they approach. He's walking slowly toward them along the path with his camera at the ready, inspecting the flowers. "Hi," she says brightly. He glances up at her and smiles, then looks at Dee Dee and back at her.

"Hey," he says.

"What a coincidence."

"Yeah, a nice one."

"This is my daughter Dee Dee."

"Matt. Nice to meet you," he says and grins. "Like your braids. Very cool."

"Thanks," Dee Dee says, smiling up at him.

Kate's struck again by the feeling that she's seen Matt before, but she's given up trying to think where. He probably just reminds her of someone, although she can't put her finger on whom, either. "First time here?" she asks.

"No, I've been here a few times. I love this place. I came to check out the new portrait exhibition. Great photographs. How about you?"

"First time," Kate says and looks around at the garden. "It's so beautiful."

He holds up his camera. "Let me take a picture of you and Dee Dee."

"Sure. That would be nice."

He walks them over to a spot with the pool, stream, waterfall and topiary in the background. Kate and Dee Dee stand close together and smile at the camera, Kate with an arm around Dee Dee's shoulders and Dee Dee with an arm around her mom's waist. "Got it," he says. They walk over and stand on either side of him and look down at the picture. He sees Dee Dee make a face and glances at Kate and sees that she's not too happy with the way she looks, either. He grins at the prospect of having some fun with them.

"I always look awful in photographs," Kate says.

"You guy's headed back to the tram?" he asks.

"Yeah."

"Mind if I walk with you?"

"No, not at all."

"I'll show you where the water in the pool comes from. It's pretty cool. We can check it out on the way. There's a path crisscrossing the stream leading up to it."

They gather around the window in the back of the last car and watch the museum and the peek-a-boo views of Los Angeles recede in the distance. Matt holds the screen on the back of his camera so they can all see the photos. "Check these out," he says and steps slowly through them. There's one of Kate and Dee Dee close together on the bridge over the stream, smiling and looking down at the water rushing toward the pond. There's one taken from a low angle of Dee Dee, gazing up at water from the stream's source, dripping into a cutaway cistern. Her innocent and rapt expression resembles that of the Virgins and saints gazing heavenward in the religious paintings.

"You look beautiful in that one, honey," Kate says.

There's one of Kate and Dee Dee facing each other. They're gazing at each other's eyes and Kate has a hand on Dee Dee's cheek and is smiling tenderly at her. Matt's particularly pleased with this one, which seems to him to have captured perfectly in their expressions and poses the love between a mother and daughter. His mother loves him, but she's never looked at him the way Kate's looking at Dee Dee in the photo.

"That's a great one of you, Mom," Dee Dee says.

The last one is of the two of them, smiling and walking hand in hand toward the camera.

Kate's amazed and looks at Matt. "They're lovely. I didn't even notice you photographing us."

"I love shooting candids. That's when you see people as they really are, when they don't know they're being photographed."

Hearing this reminds Dee Dee of the comment her mom made about John Edwards, the Presidential candidate who seemed to be the model husband and father, but who was discovered to be having an affair with his videographer and to have had a child with her. "Character is who you are when no one is watching," her mom said. She got it, but was uncomfortable with the idea that people could somehow see what she does in private.

Matt takes a pen and piece of paper from his shirt pocket and hands them to Kate. "Give me your email address and I'll send them to you."

"Sure." She's about to write down her personal address but catches herself and writes down her work address instead.

* * *

Kate and Dee Dee talk about the Getty all the way home; how much they enjoyed the visit; how beautiful the place is and how spectacular the view is; their favorite paintings; what a coincidence it was running into Matt and what a nice guy and talented photographer he is, on and on.

They're still talking about it as Kate folds and puts away clean clothes in Dee Dee's dresser and Dee Dee sits at her computer, gazing at the outfit she's designed using the fashion design program she got last Christmas. She clicks on the outfit to reveal the nude model, then on the model to make the outfit reappear, back and forth. She's more interested in the nude model than the outfit. The model is rendered realistically and looks like an attractive young woman in her late teens with a slim figure and pert breasts and a pronounced mound between her legs, and Dee Dee's feeling that tingling sensation between her legs that she has been lately. She hears her mom close the drawer and clicks on the nude model to make the outfit reappear.

"I still can't figure out how Matt did that," Kate says, shaking her head and walking over to Dee Dee, "photograph us without our noticing. It's amazing." She stands by Dee Dee's side and looks at the outfit on the model. It's as good as anything hanging in Young East Sider at the store. "I like that. You have a great eye for design."

"Think so?"

"Yeah, I do. Come on, honey, it's time for your bath."

Dee Dee closes the bathroom door, turns on the water, adjusts the temperature and lets the bathtub fill. She takes off her bathrobe and hangs it up on the door and examines her body in the mirror above the sink, turning this way and that. Her body doesn't look anything like those of the women in the paintings. Neither does her mom's. Will she have big breasts and curvy hips, or will she look more like her mom? Probably like her mom. She turns sideways and looks at what there is of her breasts and her flat stomach and slightly curved back and small buttocks. There's not much to her yet.

She tests the water with her toe, settles into the tub, picks up the bar of soap and rubs her body with it, beginning at her feet and working her way up. She puts the soap on the side of the tub and settles back with her chin just above the water and closes her eyes, conjuring up the painting of the two women and the man on the bed.

She knows about sex, about vaginas and penises, about how babies are made and how they develop and are born. She's seen porn at Rosa's. The people in porn are professional actors. Having sex is their job and they get paid to do it. The three people in the painting are different. The painting is like a candid photograph and the three people look like they're really enjoying themselves and don't care who sees them.

She moves her fingertips slowly in circles around her nipples, feeling her body tingling all over, but especially between her legs. The sensation there is stronger and different. She moves one of her hands to between her legs and strokes herself. She's washed herself in the bath hundreds of times but never touched herself like this. She's been thinking about doing it and wondering what it would feel like and seeing the painting made her finally want to and it feels good, as she knew it would. It would probably feel even better if someone else was touching her.

She sits at her desk in her bathrobe, tapping her pen lightly against her lips as she reads her last entry, then unscrews the cap and smoothes the blank page with her palm and begins writing:

Sunday, June 5, 2011

Dear Anneliese,

So much has happened since I last wrote to you! I was supposed to stay at my dad's this weekend. He and Rita went to a party Saturday evening and came home early. As usual, Rita was drinking before they left and when they got back, I could tell she was drunk. They had a big fight in the bedroom and even though they had the door closed, I could hear them from the living room. It sounded awful! I got really frightened and called my mom to come pick me up. When we were leaving, Rita came downstairs and she had a big bruise on her cheek and around her eye and her face was swollen. My mom said maybe she fell and hurt herself but we both knew my dad hit her!

I think of you and the others living together for so long in the Secret Annex. Sure, you had arguments, but no one ever hit anyone! Maybe they did and you just didn't write about it, but I don't think so. I feel so sorry for my dad. It must be awful living with someone you hate so much. I can't imagine it. Anyway, I don't want to stay at my dad's anymore. It's just too scary. I haven't told my mom yet, but I'm going to. Maybe my dad and I can just do something together during the day on the weekends. We'll see.

My mom and I went to the Getty Center in Los Angeles today. What a great place! It's high up on a hill and you can see for miles from there. I thought about you so much! I really wish you could have been there to see the paintings. You would have loved it! I know how much you liked Greek and Roman mythology. There were lots of paintings about it. I checked out the website when we got home and copied down some of the names of the gods and goddesses. You probably know them all. I only knew a few of them, like Bacchus, Cupid, Mercury, Mars, Venus, Diana and Pan. But I'd never heard of the others. I'll read about them. There's a lot to learn and it'll be fun.

There were lots of pictures of naked women! They don't look the way we do today. They're big! Not fat. Big and beautiful! I asked my mom why women don't look like that now and she said skinny is healthier. I guess it is, but I look at fashion models and they're way too skinny! Some of them look like freaks and even die because they don't eat enough!

We met a man named Matt in the garden who works with my mom. He's a really good photographer. He took photos of my mom and me when we weren't looking and they look great! He's nice. I like him.

I did something when I took a bath this evening that I've never done before. I touched myself. I don't mean like washing myself. I played with myself, with my boobs and between my legs. My boobs are tiny, but it still felt good and especially between my legs. I got so excited! I know you did the same thing and now I know how it felt! All warm and tingly! And then I thought about what it would feel like if someone else touched me the same way.

I bet it would feel even better! I wonder when it will happen and who it will be. We'll see.

Yours, Dee Dee

P.S.: Did you and Peter touch each other like that? I know you held hands and put your arms around each other. I guess not. You would have written about it. Only a couple of weeks of school left! Can't wait to visit the Grand Canyon!

CHAPTER 6

Rita in Court

Rita sits at the respondent's table in the Immigration Courtroom in the Roybal Federal Building in downtown Los Angeles with her clients, Aracelle Medina-Castillo and Leticia Rios-Medina, Aracelle's seven-year-old daughter, both from Tijuana and undocumented immigrants. With them is Aracelle's sister Belicia, a U.S. citizen who lives with her American-born husband Juan in Santa Ana and with whom Aracelle and Leticia are now living. Rita and her clients are waiting, as is the Department of Homeland Security Trial Attorney seated at the prosecution table next to theirs, for the Immigration Judge, the Honorable Monica Nuñez, to return from a brief recess she called to review the facts and the arguments before delivering her decision to grant or deny asylum for Aracelle and Leticia. Rita knows the Judge well. She's thorough and fair and treats respondents in her courtroom with dignity, which can't be said about all Immigration Judges.

It's been a long and difficult process, and it would have been so much easier if only her clients had entered the country with the proper documents, but Aracelle didn't want to risk visiting the U.S. Consulate in Tijuana or seeking asylum at the border and for good reason. She feared for her life. She still does. How brave this diminutive, soft-spoken woman is, sitting calmly beside her with her hands folded in her lap. Would she have had the courage to do what Aracelle did? As tough as she thinks she is, she isn't sure.

Aracelle's husband Rodolfo Rios-Alvarez is head of *Motosierra Roja*, the Red Chainsaw cartel that operates with impunity in Tijuana and whose drug trafficking operations are extensive throughout Central and South America and the U.S. There are outstanding warrants in the U.S. and Mexico for Rodolfo's arrest on charges of drug trafficking and accessory to murder. *Narcocorridos* about his exploits, his creative methods of disposing of rivals and his womanizing fill the airwaves in Tijuana. His bad temper is legendary and Aracelle bore the brunt of it at home. He abused her horribly, often beating her until the features of her face were almost unrecognizable. When Rita saw the photos Aracelle's mother had taken of her in the hospital after the last beating she felt nauseous. Ed's punch was a love tap in comparison.

According to Aracelle, Rodolfo is also a jealous man, and he kept her under constant surveillance, which is why she didn't dare approach the Consulate, the border or even government officials in Tijuana, most of whom are on the cartel's payroll. Her brother Fidencio, also a member of the cartel, arranged for her and Leticia to travel to the U.S. concealed in the trailer of an 18-wheeler owned and operated by a friend's cousin, who's authorized to carry freight back and forth across the border. Fidencio, Aracelle and Leticia met the driver in the dead of night, which they were able to do unobserved because Fidencio had hired freelancers to kill the man Rodolfo had keeping an eye on his wife. It was a brave thing for Fidencio to do because, as Aracelle told Rita, if Rodolfo ever finds out, he will certainly have Fidencio killed, and it will likely be a particularly gruesome death, since Rodolfo will consider his actions to be not just a betrayal of the family but of him. He's fond of having people dismembered by chainsaw and encased in concrete and thrown out of airplanes over the ocean, and she tries not to think of her brother meeting such an end.

It was Belicia who called on behalf of Aracelle and her daughter. Rita met with them and took notes as Aracelle told her story in Spanish. Rita then informed them in Spanish about the procedure for seeking asylum and advised them about how she would proceed and what would likely happen. As with all her clients, she wanted Aracelle and Leticia to be well-informed about the process and legal proceedings, which can overwhelm people in their situation, who are always fearful and feel powerless.

Rita would file an affirmative Asylum Application with Immigration and Customs Enforcement. She would also file a FOIA request with DHS to see what information, if any, they had about Aracelle and could use against her in court. They would be fingerprinted by USCIS and copies of their biometrics and biographical information would be sent to the FBI. They would be interviewed by an Asylum Officer and, hopefully, that would be the end of it, but likely not, because they'd entered the country as they did and DHS would push for detention. If the Asylum Officer didn't grant asylum, their case would be referred to Immigration Court and they would receive a Notice to Appear at a Master Calendar hearing. They might be granted asylum at the hearing, but if not, DHS would request that Aracelle be detained and she could post bond. Leticia would remain in Belicia's care. The next step would be a Merits Hearing in Immigration Court. They might be granted asylum at the hearing, but if not, they could appeal. Rita urged Aracelle to be completely forthcoming about the fact that she's the wife of a drug trafficker and murderer, especially given the agencies involved, DHS and the FBI. Aracelle agreed and Rita began the Executive Office for Immigration Review paperwork process and building her case.

As she told Aracelle at their first meeting, the Immigration Courts have been much more favorably disposed in recent years to grant asylum to women suffering physically abusive treatment by their husbands. As evidence of the abuse, Rita had the photographs and Aracelle's medical records from the hospital in Tijuana. She had affidavits from her doctor, her mother and her father stating that they often saw Aracelle bruised and bloodied and that Aracelle told them it was the result of having been beaten by her husband at home. Finally, she had Leticia's eyewitness testimony to some of the beatings. Add to this Aracelle's own testimony and it seemed like she had a pretty strong case. All DHS had, she thought, was the fact that Aracelle and Leticia had entered the country without proper documents.

Shortly after submitting their information to DHS and the FBI, Rita received a call from an Agent Dougherty, who shared with her that the FBI considered the Rios Pena Cartel a terrorist organization, since it routinely assassinated local civic officials in Tijuana, and Aracelle, by virtue of her relationship with Rodolfo, a member and accomplice. They viewed Aracelle's abuse claim as a "family matter" to be resolved between her and her husband and the Bureau would press vigorously for her and her daughter's deportation. However, if Aracelle were to cooperate with the Bureau and provide information about her husband, her brother and the cartel, the Bureau would be more supportive of their applications for asylum. Rita discussed the conversation with Aracelle, who was clearly terrified as she listened, and asked her whether she wanted to cooperate with the FBI, explaining that it would increase their chances of gaining, asylum but that the decision was entirely up to her. "No," Aracelle said firmly, "absolutely not." She not only feared for her life and her daughter's, but she also feared for the lives of her parents. "Rodí will certainly find out," she said, "and he will kill us all."

The interview with the Asylum Officer didn't go well and neither did the Master Calendar Hearing, which was presided over by a judge Rita knew from past experience would likely be unsympathetic. In both cases and especially at the Master Calendar Hearing, during which the DHS Trial Attorney basically argued on behalf of the FBI, she sensed the Bureau working behind the scenes, influencing the proceedings. At the conclusion of the Master Calendar Hearing, Aracelle was detained by DHS and then freed on bail. Now here they are, waiting for Judge Nuñez to return with her decision. Rita feels Aracelle's hand on her forearm and looks at her.

"I want you to know you've been a very good advocate," Aracelle says. "Whatever the decision, we appreciate what you've done for us."

Rita nods. "Thank you."

"If there's ever anything I can do for you, please let me know."

Aracelle's offer strikes Rita as odd. What could she possibly do for her? Share her favorite tamales recipe? She sees the door to the judge's chamber open and watches Judge Nuñez enter the courtroom and fixes her eyes on hers. "All rise," she hears the deputy say. She stands with the others and studies the judge's face as she walks to her chair and sits at the desk. "Be seated," she hears the deputy say. She sits and tries to read the decision in the judge's expression, but her face is a mask of judicial impartiality as she puts on her reading glasses, positions papers in front of her, picks up a pen and writes on one piece of paper and then another. She puts down the pen, removes her glasses and looks at Aracelle and Leticia.

"It's the decision of the court to grant the respondents' request for asylum," the judge says.

Rita's pleased but feels exhausted, the way she always does each time she's able to successfully defend her clients. She stares blankly at Judge Nuñez, who continues looking at Aracelle and Leticia as the court interpreter repeats the ruling in Spanish. Rita feels Aracelle grip her arm and hears her whisper, "Many thank, many thanks."

The judge looks at the prosecutor. "Does DHS wish to reserve appeal?"

"We do, your Honor."

The judge nods and picks up the two order forms she's just signed, looks at Rita and holds them out to her. "Counselor."

Rita stands, walks to the bench and takes the documents. Judge Nuñez is looking at her with slightly raised eyebrows and just the hint of a smile. "Thank you, your Honor," Rita says and turns and sees Aracelle, Leticia and Belicia huddled together at the respondent's table, their arms around each other, tears streaming down their cheeks. She knows she should feel elated, overjoyed, but as she walks to her seat, her stomach feels queasy and her only thought is that she's long overdue for a drink and can't get to her car fast enough. It's well stocked with nips.

She's almost to her car in the dimly lit underground parking garage, rolling her brief case behind her and anticipating the first of the nips she'll soon be downing, when her phone rings. She fishes it out of her suit coat pocket, glances at the screen and sees the caller's ID is blocked. "Hello?" she asks. "You're dead, bitch," she hears a man say coolly in Spanish. It stuns her and she feels the blood draining from her face and unsteady on her feet. Before she can say anything, she hears the call terminated. She has a pretty good idea who it was.

She sits in her car, finishing the second nip and feeling a little calmer, but still shaken. Should she have a third? She could use it but probably shouldn't. She has a long drive home in rush hour traffic. She sits back in the seat, folds her hands in her lap and closes her eyes. Why didn't she see this coming? Aracelle did. That's why she said what she did. She'll call her. Maybe her brother knows something and can help her. As if things weren't bad enough, there's the other unexpected development she's been trying not to think about. She should have foreseen that one too and has no one to blame but herself for letting it happen. She was drunk and wasn't thinking straight. It all seems too much, and she tries to put the key in the ignition but can't because of the way her hand is shaking. She finally gives up and pounds the steering wheel with her fist. "Shit!"

* * *

Rita sits at the kitchen table, working on her third vodka tonic, the drive home in rush hour traffic on the 405 now a blurry memory of blurry taillights. She hears Ed arrive home and looks up as he enters the kitchen. She watches him walk to the fridge, open it and take out a beer.

"How'd it go?" he asks.

"We won," she says flatly.

"Hey, congratulations!" He sits across from her and opens the can and studies her face as he sips. She's always like this when she wins cases, pleased she won, but exhausted and subdued, worn out from the effort, but he notices something different about her attitude and expression and especially in her eyes. She looks haunted. "You okay?"

"Rios called," she says.

"Yeah? What'd he have to say?"

"'You're dead, bitch.'"

He shrugs. "I wouldn't worry about it. Probably just wanted to rattle your cage."

She stares at him dumbfounded. He's probably right but — Jesus! Would he even care if they killed her or would he feel relieved? Well, now's as good a time as any to share the other news with him. "I'm pregnant," she says and keeps her eyes on his as he sets his beer on the table and slowly sits back in his chair. She can't read how he feels about it any better than she could the judge's decision and waits for some reaction for what seems a long time, not knowing what to expect. She's relieved to see his features soften and surprised to see a smile appear. He's actually looking at her tenderly, although after everything she's put him through, she doesn't know why he would or should. Of course, it's the baby he's happy about and the prospect of redeeming himself as a father with a new kid.

She feels her eyes filling with tears and they're not tears of joy, but of despair at being pregnant and a hopeless drunk. The tears begin streaming down her cheeks and she watches him push back his chair, stand and walk around the table to her. She feels him put his arms around her and hold her tightly and rest his chin on the top of her head. "You have to stop drinking," she hears him say softly. As if she could. Why should she? She's not even sure she wants the baby.

CHAPTER 7

Steve and Cyn

It's a perfect day for sailing off Newport Beach, with a stiff onshore breeze. The race has shaped up pretty much the way most of them do, with one exception. Steve's usually the one in the lead with Chris trying to catch him, but his crew took a few moments too long resetting the sails as he steered *Raptor,* his J-35, around the last marker buoy and up into the wind, and it cost him the lead. Now he's about a boat-length-and-a-half behind Chris, and his only chance of winning is to overtake him at the next marker buoy and make a run for the finish, wing and wing with his spinnaker flying. *Raptor* and Chris's *Spare Change* are virtually identical, but Steve knows his is the faster boat because of the edge he has over Chris at the helm. Steve's crew is crouched to create as little wind resistance as possible. They're doing what they can to assist him, but at this point they all know it's up to him and what he can do with *Raptor* heading into the wind.

He grips the helm just tightly enough to control the boat but loosely enough to feel and anticipate its behavior. He has *Raptor* heeled over as far as she'll go, riding the edge of the wind, and the boat feels like a giant knife, slicing through the water. He watches Chris steer a course toward the next marker buoy that will take *Spare Change* around it as close as possible, preventing Steve from overtaking him on the leeward side. It's a long shot, but if he can overtake Chris at the marker buoy on the windward side, there's a chance he can steal *Spare Change's* wind while his crew resets the sails and unfurls the spinnaker. Even if it's only for a few moments, it could give him just the advantage he needs to win this race. No risk, no reward. He has to go for it. That's how he's gotten where he is.

At twenty-nine, he's come far. The Sisters of Charity at the parochial school in New Rochelle his parents sent him to nurtured his early interest in mathematics and it blossomed into love, and his ability to grasp higher principles was prodigious. He majored in Mathematics at MIT and received his graduate degree from the Sloan School, which he attended on full scholarship (his parents couldn't have afforded the tuition). His thesis about new applications of advanced analytics in developing investment strategies came to the attention of Ira Weiss, the founder and CEO of PACBOND in Newport Beach, one of the world's leading bond trading companies. All the major players were courting him, and he was surprised that PACBOND, a company in such a risk averse business, would be interested in him, but Ira flew Steve out from Boston, and he had lunch with Ira and Connell MacAllister, head of the London office and Ira's second in command. Ira and Connell were fascinated as they listened to his ideas. Steve remembers Ira smiling and asking, "Mind if I keep these?" as he picked up the cocktail napkins covered with Steve's scribbled formulas and put them in his jacket pocket. They made him an offer so attractive he could barely disguise his astonishment, and he's proven to be worth every penny. His ideas generate huge profits for the company, for which he's handsomely compensated, and *Raptor* is part of the reward for his labor and the lifestyle he enjoys as a result.

Accepting the position at PACBOND was itself a bit of a risk. His friends at Sloan ribbed him about wasting his time in an unexciting and unglamorous industry. "Where's the money?" they asked. He'd have a better chance of getting rich selling life insurance, the said, but his decision paid off and now he's set, with a gorgeous wife he can afford to indulge, a beautiful home with an ocean view in Corona Del Mar, expensive cars, a yacht, membership at a prestigious country club in Newport Beach and vacations at luxurious resorts.

Growing up the son of an Italian American family in the North Bronx, Steve Aquilina longed for a better life, but he never imagined he'd achieve anything like this. Everything he dreamed of having just ten years ago he now has and more. What he doesn't have yet is this race and he wants it badly.

Steve's managed to bring *Raptor's* bow abreast of *Spare Change's* stern with less than two boat-lengths to go to the marker buoy. He edges *Raptor* up closer to the wind. Through the helm he feels the boat shudder slightly, then lurch forward, gaining speed. His crew has the spinnaker and spinnaker pole and reaching strut ready to go and are poised, waiting for his command. Both boats are at the marker buoy as Steve brings *Raptor's* bow abreast of *Spare Change* on the windward side. "Helm's a-lee!" he yells and puts *Raptor* hard to port. His crew springs into action and works quickly to let out the mainsail and raise the spinnaker. He positions *Raptor* directly between *Spare Change* and the wind, and as his spinnaker fills and billows out, Chris's sags noticeably. Confident now of the race's outcome Steve savors the moment and gives Chris a tug on the bill of his cap as he overtakes him. No risk, no reward.

* * *

Steve drives along Pacific Coast Highway in Newport Beach headed home. He notes the now familiar effects of the recession that are visible even in this affluent community. There are more than a few "For Lease" and "For Sale" signs on the vacant commercial real estate along PCH and a surprising number of realtors' open house signs in his neighborhood in Corona Del Mar. He knows there are many homeowners in town who haven't made mortgage payments in over a year and are just waiting for the banks to foreclose. This little corner of the world, though, a community that includes Corona Del Mar, Newport Beach and Newport Coast, still has the unmistakable look and feel of money. It's evident in the multi-million-dollar homes, the yachts, the expensive imported cars and jewelry on the wives and girlfriends at dinner parties. He's even come to associate the smell of the eucalyptus-scented air with money.

He takes a prepaid cell phone out of the center console and calls Tommy Tran to see if Thien will be at the club later. Tommy says in that heavily accented clipped way of his that she will, and also that new girl

Kialee Chris liked so much last time. Good, Steve says, they might see him later.

He turns onto his street and sees Armando's white pickup truck parked by the curb in front of his house. Cyn's kept Armando busy with remodels and renovations ever since they bought the house. What now? he wonders.

He grabs a beer in the kitchen and finds them upstairs in the master bedroom, standing in front of her walk-in closet. They turn as he enters, and he nods toward Armando and looks at Cyn. "Hey," he says, "what's up?"

"I'm glad you're home," she says. "We're discussing this closet area."

"What about it?"

"Honey, I need more space. I've got nowhere to put things anymore!"

He looks at Armando and grins. "Some problem, huh?"

Armando smiles and shrugs.

"What are we looking at?" Steve asks him.

"Well…," Armando says.

"What difference does it make?" Cyn says. "It'll cost what it costs."

"Right," Steve says. He sips his beer and reminds himself that it's all part of the deal.

Of the several secretarial candidates HR sent him to be interviewed when he first arrived at PACBOND, Cyn was by far the most attractive and struck him as the easiest going and most fun to be with. If they were going to work together every day, why not make it enjoyable? The icing on the cake was that she's a redhead and has green eyes. He'd never been involved with a redhead and had always fantasized about what it would be like.

As time went by, they got to know each other. They were both in their mid-twenties, single and unattached. He's from the Bronx and she's from a small town in Indiana. She worked as a waitress when she first arrived in Southern California, then in retail sales and finally decided to get her associate's degree online in administrative office management. He was learning to sail and thinking about buying a boat. She'd only been on a boat once, on a cruise to Ensenada with her ex-boyfriend, and was seasick the entire time. They both said they were ambitious and wanted to succeed and were willing to work hard to do it. They both wanted to get married someday, although her parents' marriage was a disaster and he'd always wondered if he could be satisfied having sex with only one woman, which didn't surprise her.

He looked forward to seeing her at work each day. She was always dressed nicely and always wore 4-inch heels and had quite a collection of them. Just looking at her in them was a turn on, but watching her walk in them was sheer delight. He was attracted to her and knew she was to him, but they managed to keep their relationship strictly professional for many months, until the company Christmas party.

It was a Friday night affair at the country club in Newport Beach he'd joined shortly after arriving from Boston. Ira was a member, as were all the top executives at the company. It was the first time Steve saw Cyn outside of work. She wore her hair down, a short emerald green skirt and off-white, sleeveless, silk halter blouse and matching emerald green high heel sandals. She looked stunning. They chitchatted a bit over a drink, but spent the rest of the evening mingling separately, and whenever he glanced at her, he found her glancing at him.

As the party wound down and he was saying his good-byes, he looked for Cyn but couldn't see her and figured she was in the ladies room. He was walking to his car when he heard her call, "Hey, boss! Wait up!" He turned to see her running toward him as best she could in her heels. He glanced at the entrance to the club to see if any of his colleagues were standing there and saw only the uniformed attendant at the valet parking stand. Cyn said she'd had a little too much to drink and asked if he'd mind giving her a ride home, saying she could pick up her car in the morning. She said she was really embarrassed, and he said, hey, these things happen, no problem, and off they went.

As they drove up PCH toward her apartment in Costa Mesa, he did what he always does when faced with uncertainty, analyzed the situation and calculated the risk. Was she really drunk or was this just a ploy to lure him back to her apartment? He'd soon find out. If her plan was to have sex, what were the possible consequences? He hadn't read the employee handbook but was pretty sure that while romantic relationships between employees of equal status were permitted, they weren't between managers and employees. The question was whether he could trust her to be discreet. He'd love to find out what she was like in bed, but was it worth the risk?

He pulled up to the curb outside her apartment building and she opened her eyes, looked at him, placed a hand on his forearm and thanked him for the ride. She said she'd invite him in but didn't think that was such a good idea because of work, that she didn't want to jeopardize his job. Hearing this, her stock with him soared. He grinned at her and said what they did in their private life was their business, and she said, yeah, she guessed he was right and they leaned toward each other and kissed.

He quickly learned the answer to his first question. She was far from drunk and had him on the bed and out of his clothes in no time. He watched her undress pose for him in her green silk lingerie. When she slowly removed them, she revealed a tantalizing, neatly trimmed triangle of red pubic hair. She was every bit as earthy in bed as he'd anticipated and the revelation came when they lay in each other's arms after making love, both exhausted and glistening with sweat. She smelled like no other woman he'd ever been with, and her scent affected him as no other woman's had. He nestled his nose in her armpit and felt he could be perfectly happy to remain that way forever, nuzzling and smelling her and enjoying the feel of her stubble against the tip of his nose.

They ended up spending the weekend together and he was delighted to discover she's as enjoyable a companion out of bed as in. As wonderful as the sex was, it was talking with her that really hooked him. It was a joy. She was impressed with his academic credentials and confident about what she knew and curious and interested in learning more about what she didn't. Had he met his partner? He pondered the question as he drove back to his place late Sunday evening and realized when he arrived home that he'd been smiling ever since he left her.

When he arrived in his office Monday morning, he found a small bouquet of tulips in a glass vase waiting for him on his desk. He read the card: "Thanks for a great time!" They began seeing each other regularly on weekends and she stayed at his apartment in Newport Beach. They were very careful about their behavior toward each other at work and allowed themselves only one bit of fun, using his top desk drawer as a drop box for notes to each other. A typical one waiting for him in the morning might read, "Guess what I'm wearing for underwear? Nothing!" It made seeing her throughout the day thrilling. It all seemed like harmless fun to him, and they carried on this way for months.

Then one morning, shortly after he arrived in his office, Cyn appeared in the doorway and asked if she could talk with him in private about something. Her expression and tone of voice made him think he was about to hear she was pregnant, although she'd told him she used birth control. He said sure and she closed the door and walked to the front of his desk. He asked what she wanted to talk about and she grinned and said, "The fact that I'm really horny right now." He grinned and said there wasn't much he could do about that at the moment. She walked around his desk. perched on it, gave him a sexy look and asked, "Are you sure?" She said she'd bet he could think of something and parted her legs. He hesitated and she pouted. "Just this once?" she pleaded. She wouldn't ask again, she assured him. She'd be good. He reluctantly slid his hand up her leg and discovered that today was a "Nothing!" day and that she was very wet. She closed her eyes and he stroked her, and it didn't take her long to climax. She opened her eyes and smiled and said, "Thanks. Back to work." With that, she stood and left the office, leaving the door open. He had the feeling the encounter had a purpose beyond satisfying her horniness, but he couldn't think of what it might be. He called Cyn that evening and asked her what the hell that had been about and she said, sounding genuinely apologetic, "I'm sorry. I slipped up. I promise it won't happen again."

The call from Marion, the stony ex-Marine HR manager, came a couple of days later. During their only previous meeting when Steve first arrived at PACBOND, Marion struck him as viewing employees with suspicion and her primary mission being to defend the company against them. Steve settled into the chair across the desk from her and tried to disguise his nervousness. She said that Ira had asked her to have a chat with him and Steve's skin went cold. Not good. She said it had come to her attention that he and his secretary were seeing each other outside of work and asked if he were aware of the fact that romantic relationships between managers and employees were prohibited by company policy. He felt his nervousness verge on panic. He wondered if Marion knew about what had happened that day in his office. Was the place wired with hidden surveillance cameras? Could they legally do that? She reminded him that sexual harassment was grounds for immediate termination. She told him not to be naïve and said that he knew as well as she that if his secretary lodged a sexual harassment complaint against him, he'd be hard pressed to disprove it, and that if she took the company to court, she'd win. The takeaway was that Ira considered him a valuable asset, but that he was putting his job and the company at risk, that Ira didn't want or need the bad press that would result from a lawsuit. Steve left Marion's office feeling like he had a target on his back, that he'd tripped a wire and was now on the corporate radar screen.

He knew he should be furious with himself for having put his position at the company at risk, but he wasn't. His decision to sleep with Cyn that night and then to continue seeing her had been calculated and it was the right one. He'd never been happier in his life. There had to be a solution to this predicament. He just couldn't see it yet. He called Cyn that evening and filled her in about his meeting with the Marion. Cyn said it was time they talked and why didn't they have dinner at his place Friday. She'd make steak tartar for him, one of his favorite dishes.

They were on their best behavior at work the rest of the week. Cyn visited his office only when necessary and they said as little as possible to each other. No notes, no teasing or joking, just business. The situation felt intolerable to him. He imagined it was what life must have felt like living in the Soviet Union or one of its satellite states, always with the suspicion that someone was watching and listening, recording your every word and movement.

Cyn waited until they'd finished eating and he'd had a few glasses of champagne before telling him she had something she wanted him to watch. She picked up the remote and pointed it at the TV screen. It popped on and there he was, sitting at his desk in his office. Judging from the angle, he figured the video recorder was on a shelf in the bookcase across from his desk. Why he hadn't noticed it was beyond him. It must be a small one and it's probably black, making it hard to see. Maybe she put tape over the recording light, so it wouldn't be visible? He watched as she entered the frame and stood between him and the recorder and realized it was that day she asked to talk with him in private. Her back was to the recorder all the time, but he was clearly visible and when she perched on the desk, it was obvious from his expression and what could be seen of his arm that he was touching her between her legs. He could barely contain his anger at her for having trapped him, and at himself for having allowed it to happen. He asked her what she planned to do with the recording, and she raised her eyebrows.

"Get you," she said.

He asked her what the hell that meant and she brushed his cheek with her fingertips.

"Relax, baby," she said, "there's nothing to worry about."

It didn't help. She asked why he thought most relationships failed and he said, "I dunno. You tell me." She said because people are foolish and dishonest with each other and themselves, and that her parents are a perfect example. She was sure they thought they loved each other and told themselves money didn't matter, so long as they had enough to get by, and that they'd never let having kids spoil the romance in their marriage. Money *did* matter, though, and having kids changed everything. Her dad had an affair when her mom was pregnant with their last child, and her mom made his life a living hell after that. She felt sorry for her parents, but she wasn't going to be like them. She took his hand in hers and searched his eyes with a worried expression.

"Do you really and truly love me?" she asked.

He was about to tell her he did, but she didn't let him speak.

"Listen," she said, "I know you do, and I know you'd be miserable if I were out of your life. I'd be too. Most people never find the person they're searching for. They end up settling. I've found my person, and I know you've found yours. You need a partner who's as sharp as you are, and you have to admit I got you good. So, let's get married. The deal's really simple. You want to fool around? Fine. I'm not worried about other women. You'll never find another me."

He chuckled and shook his head. "You're too much."

"I know," she said, grinning, "so are you. We're made for each other."

She gave notice at work, moved in with him and busied herself house-hunting. She found their home in Corona Del Mar and they moved in and began life together. She got her realtor's license and started a business, specializing in executive relocation. Ira recommended her to his business network and now her business is successful, and her services are in high demand.

They took a weekend trip to Las Vegas, were married and had the time of their lives. In a city filled with beautiful women, none were more beautiful or as attractive to him as Cyn, and when they climbed into bed each night, he devoured her and fell asleep with his nose nestled in her armpit, breathing in her scent, perfectly content.

CHAPTER 8

Little Saigon

Cyn sends Steve off for an evening of "playing cards with Chris." She places her glass of wine on the desk in the study, sits and taps a key to wake up the screen. The property she's researching for another of Ira's referrals appears. Their relationship with Ira and Adele changed dramatically after she left the company, and especially when they married. Shortly after they returned from Las Vegas, a wedding present arrived from the Weisses, together with an enormous bouquet of flowers. The card on the flowers read, "Our warmest wishes. Mazel Tov! — Ira and Adele," and the one on the large gift box, "Keep it filled with love!" The gift was a silver Japanese bowl, which she saw online cost close to nine thousand dollars. She and Steve are now on the invite list to the two parties the Weisses host each year at their estate home in Coto de Caza, one on the Fourth of July and the other on New Year's Eve. The Fourth of July party will be their first and it isn't far off. She has to begin thinking about what to wear, definitely something new and summery.

Steve parks on a side street off Beach Boulevard in Little Saigon in Westminster, well down the block from the entrance to Tommy Tran's "gentlemen's club", as Tommy likes to call it. Westminster is home to the largest population of Vietnamese outside of Vietnam. The families are all from what used to be South Vietnam and left the country in the Seventies, after the Americans departed and the Communists took over. Some feared for their lives, others were simply unwilling to live under the new regime. They'd been Westernized and embraced capitalism, which they practice ruthlessly in their own manner.

Tommy came to the States with his parents and sister. His restaurant is around the corner in the front of the building on Beach Boulevard. This is the back of the house operation. It's styled after the better clubs in Saigon, as the city is still called by the Vietnamese here. No one calls it Ho Chi Minh City. Once inside the club, customers are in a red, black and chrome mirrored cocoon of self-indulgence. Steve has no illusions about the place. It's a combination gambling den and whorehouse with high-class pretentions, a fun place to hang out now and then. For an annual membership fee of fifty thousand dollars, payable in cash, he gets the run of the place.

Steve swipes his card through the reader, enters and is greeted by Tommy's wife Hue. He always enjoys seeing Hue. She's cheerful, gracious and polite and manages Tommy's business skillfully, maintaining a tight ship with a light hand. As always, her hair is decorated with a lily, her namesake flower. She sings a welcome in Vietnamese, bowing and waving him into the large room. He sees the club is crowded this evening. Despite the recession, there's still plenty of money in Orange County. He follows her to the table where Chris and two other club members he knows are seated, playing Texas hold 'em. Hue pulls back a chair for him. He sits and she places a hand on his shoulder.

"Scotch?" she asks.

"Thanks." The men at the table study their cards. "Gentlemen," Steve says and sees them nod without looking up. The man to his right is a successful plastic and reconstructive surgeon whose practice is in Newport Beach and Adele Weiss is one of his clients. "How's business?"

The man smiles. "I'm going to retire early on your boss's wife," he says, keeping his eyes on his cards.

Hue returns with a glass of Steve's favorite scotch and a box of cigars. "Thanks," he says. He takes a cigar, lights it and joins the game. A couple of drinks and most of the cigar later, he decides he's had enough. "Not my night," he says. "I'm out while I still have a roof over my head." He finds Hue waiting for him at the bottom of the stairs. She smiles and bows slightly as he approaches. He stops by her side and she leans close to his ear. "Tack Room," she says, and he can hear her smile in her voice. She knows it's his favorite.

He taps lightly on the door and after a moment Thien opens it and smiles up at him. He takes a moment to admire her. She looks heavenly, as she always does. Her shoulder-length black hair glistens, her eyelids are blue and her lips bright red, making her small heart shaped mouth stand out against the pale, almost translucent skin of her face. She's wearing a red silk robe decorated with embroidered dragons and matching red heels. She takes his hand and leads him into the room.

It's appointed with a private bath, a king size canopy bed draped with red silk fabric flowing to the floor, an entertainment center with a large flat screen TV, a wet bar, a long burgundy upholstered couch and a round black lacquer coffee table decorated with an arrangement of lilies in a white porcelain vase, and next to it a round mirrored plate. The walls are covered in dark red leather and accented with weathered boards running floor to ceiling. They're decorated with crops and whips and harnesses, and one wall has two large black wrought iron rings bolted to it an arm's-length apart. The room seems to leave little to the imagination, which forces him to use his and is why it's his favorite. He makes himself comfortable on the sofa as Thien pours him a glass of scotch at the wet bar. She hands him his drink, settles next to him on the couch and runs her fingers lightly through the hair at the back of his head.

"You want get high?" she asks, grinning and holding up her hand, forming an O with her thumb and index finger. She closes one eye and peers playfully at him at him through the O.

"Sure." He watches her stand, walk to the entertainment center and return with a long-handled silver pipe and lighter and a small red leather box. He was introduced to opium at Tommy's and enjoys its high. It's not always available, so this is a treat. She kneels on the floor in front of him, places the items on the coffee table and opens the box.

"You smoke," she says, "I make you feel real good."

He watches her remove a piece of folded foil from the box and carefully unfold it, revealing a small black ball of opium. She places it in the small bowl of the pipe and offers the pipe stem-first to him with a nod of her head. She picks up the lighter and holds it at the ready. He puts the stem between his lips and leans forward. She flicks the lighter and holds the flame over the little black ball. He watches the flame dip as he draws the smoke into his lungs, listening to the opium crackle and hiss. Almost immediately he has the sensation that his skull is dissolving and his brain expanding. He studies Thien's face. She's smiling and looking up at him expectantly.

"Good?" she asks.

"Hmm," he says and takes another long draw. She appears to be sinking, and he realizes it's because his eyes keep drifting up toward the ceiling. He tries hard to focus, and the room suddenly comes alive. One moment a formula he's been working on appears engraved in gold on the red leather wall in front of him, the next he's with a princess in the palace stables and dragons are racing in circles around her.

"I make you feel real good now," she says.

He watches as she stands, unties her robe and lets it fall to the floor around her feet, revealing white silk lingerie. She hands him the lighter and he takes another long draw, filling his lungs with smoke, and watches as the little ball begins to glow. She undoes her bra and drops it to the floor, then slowly pulls down and steps out of her panty. He stares at her shaved mound and the tiny red heart tattooed above it. She takes the pipe and lighter from him, takes a long draw and hands them back, then kneels in front of him, keeping her eyes on his as she unbuttons and unzips his jeans. He lifts himself off the couch and she pulls down his pants and underpants to his knees, then rests her hands lightly on his thighs, leans forward and wraps her lips softly around the head of his cock. He feels as if the center of his being is now inside her mouth and that his heartbeat and breathing are being controlled by the gentle pulsation of her lips and the strokes of her tongue. He watches as her lips move farther down his shaft until her nose is nuzzled against his groin. He wants to come but she plays him like an instrument, skillfully bringing him back from the edge and up to it again and again.

He's shuddering now. How long have they been doing this? It seems forever and he feels ready to explode. She draws back her head, lets his cock free and smiles at him. This is why she's his favorite. She knows just how to please him. She stands, turns around and bends over, looking back at him and swaying her ass as she places her hands on her ass and spreads her cheeks. He gazes at her anus, cutely puckered like a mouth waiting to be kissed, perfectly round and rosy-hued. He's always amazed at how small her opening is, yet how easily he can enter her. She has many heavenly attributes and it's the one he admires and enjoys most. She reaches back, takes his cock and slowly guides it in, settling down on it until it's all the way in.

"Ooo," she coos, "so big!"

She seems to weigh nothing and looks to him like a sprite on a rocking horse. He closes his eyes and imagines her to be a tiny princess and himself her magnificent steed, and that she's riding him naked through the kingdom, flaunting her privilege as royalty before the peasantry. Well, he'll show "Her Royal Tininess" who's riding whom here. He reaches up and gathers her hair in his hands, close to the base of her skull, and pulls hard, bending her head back. She bobs on his lap and shouts, "Aiyee!" at each forceful thrust. He feels himself verging on coming and begins thrusting against her so hard that if he weren't holding her by her hair, she'd be thrown off and the feeling as he empties himself in her is sublime.

She rides him until he's still, then lifts herself off him, puts on her robe and walks off to the bathroom. She returns with a basin of warm lemon scented water, a washcloth and hand towel. He watches her kneel and carefully bathe him and pat him dry. Cyn's right. As much fun as Thien is, his interest in her is limited to what goes on in this room, and when he leaves, he does so happily and she's probably just as happy to see him go.

He hands her five twenties at the door and gives her a kiss on the forehead. "Buy yourself something nice," he says.

She smiles up at him. "You my favorite guy."

It's past one when Steve arrives home, bleary-eyed and still buzzing from the scotch and opium. The house is dark. He lets himself in without turning on the lights, rearms the alarm and heads up the stairs. From the bedroom doorway he can make out Cyn's body under the covers, turned toward the window with her back to him. He undresses, climbs into bed and snuggles against her.

"Have fun?" she asks. "Hmm," she hears him say and feels his hand on her hip. She remembers how it felt living in her parents' house after her mother learned of her dad's infidelity. No place felt safe. Her mother should have left him or forgiven him. Either would have been better than the life of always simmering resentment toward each other they've been living all these years. It's much better this way. Steve can share his body with whomever he pleases. It isn't important. What's important is being the only woman in his heart and mind. She rolls over and brings her face close to his, sniffing his neck and shoulder and smelling the lingering scent of perfume. She pulls back the covers, pushes him onto his back and smells her way down his chest and stomach to his lemon-scented cock, which she finds ready and waiting for her. Good, she thinks, taking it in her hand and straddling him, now for the main event.

CHAPTER 9

Dee Dee's Portrait

Sharam studies the photographs in Matt's portfolio, slowly turning the pages. Matt was surprised to learn from him that he's an architect and also a photographer, and that when he and his wife arrived from Iran, they took jobs in retail because it was the quickest and easiest way to begin earning a living. Sharam brought in his portfolio, filled mostly with photographs of buildings he'd designed, but also some impressive portraiture and scenes of people and places in Tehran. The guy's good and Matt's eager to hear Sharam's opinion of his work.

"These are very good," Sharam says, "especially the candids." He arrives at the black and white nude series and raises his eyebrows. "Interesting...."

"I wanted to treat the human body purely as abstract form."

"Yes, I can see that. The composition is nicely structured. You'd make a good architect. These are very erotic, verging on pornographic."

"It's a fine line between the two."

"You walked it nicely. Well, whoever's body it is, she's very beautiful."

"My ex-girlfriend Amber," Matt says and smiles. "We broke up the day I shot those."

Sharam looks at him. "How ironic." He spots Steve and Cyn approaching. Thank God for PACBOND, one of the few remaining companies where suits are still required at work. "Steve! Cyn!" Sharam says. "So nice to see you!"

"Hey, buddy," Steve says, "got your message." He glances down at the portfolio on the counter and sees the black and white nudes. "Whose portfolio?"

"Mine," Matt says.

"Mind if I take a look?"

"Not at all."

Cyn puts her Blooingdale's Big Brown Bag filled with purchases from Women's upstairs on a chair, walks to Steve's side and looks down at the photographs as he slowly turns the pages.

"I'll put your suits in a dressing room," Sharam says. "Whenever you're ready."

"Thanks," Steve says, "Be right there. Who's the model?" he asks Matt.

"My ex-girlfriend."

"Professional?"

"No. She's a finance major. Following in her dad's footsteps. He's a hedge fund manager in Newport Beach. Makes a ton of money."

Steve glances up at him. "What's her name?"

"Amber."

"Last name?"

"Brennan."

"Huh," he says and looks back down at the photographs. "Her dad's on our Board."

Cyn knows her man. He's already plotting to get Amber into bed and not just because she has a beautiful body. Sex is the driving force, of course, just as it is behind his trips to Westminster, but this is different. He must see some advantage in bedding the daughter of a Board member. It seems risky, but then, risk excites him. It's what she loves about him most. She studies the nudes as Steve slowly turns the pages. Amber has a beautiful body, all right, but the guy's clearly a talented photographer. Not everyone could capture it like this. She tried her hand at photography once and learned from experience that it isn't as easy as it looks.

Her best friend in high school Kathy's dad was a professional photographer and did weddings and portraits. He had all sorts of photography books, and her two favorites were a book of Diane Arbus's photographs and one of Ansel Adams's. On the face of it, the photographs couldn't have been more different, Arbus's of freakish-looking people whom she made look ordinary, and Adams's of the natural world, which he made look monumental. Still, she recognized in both the same objective eye and ability to let the subject speak for itself.

Her parents gave her a digital camera for Christmas, and she took it with her everywhere. She photographed people in town when they were unaware, hoping to capture something interesting in unguarded moments, but she knew everyone and the photographs just looked like snapshots of neighbors. She photographed the fields and trees and streams in the gently rolling countryside, but everything looked flat and uninteresting. She read the owner's manual and figured out how to take a picture of the "Speed Checked by Radar" sign beside the road on the outskirts of town, with streaked cars coming and going in the background, suggesting they're traveling over the limit. The sign is an open joke in the community. Everyone knows the police never set up a speed trap there or anywhere else and most people do speed past the sign. She was hoping to capture that in the photograph, to make a statement, but it just looked like a sign by the side of the road with streaked cars behind it. It was around that time she decided she needed a change of scenery and began thinking about moving to California.

"I'll try on the suits," Steve says.

"Be right there," Cyn says and turns the page. "What's your studio rate?" she asks Matt without looking up.

He's sure that discussing a potential photography job with her on the sales floor is against company policy, but she asked. He should probably quote her a thousand dollars, not including prints, as Dieter does his customers, but what if she thinks it's too much? He doesn't want to offend Sharam's customer's wife.

Cyn glances at him and sees he's uncomfortable discussing business and reluctant to quote her a price. He's probably afraid she'll think he's overcharging her. He's cute and young and inexperienced. She's enjoying this. It's a turn on. "Would two thousand cover it?"

"Yeah. More than."

She smiles and raises her eyebrows just enough to indicate she might be interested in getting more for her money.

"You know, prints, supplies," he says.

She holds out her hand. "Give me your card."

He grabs a note pad, writes down his contact information, tears off the sheet and hands it to her.

She glances at it, folds it, tucks it in her shoulder bag and picks it up. "Thanks," she says and walks toward the dressing rooms, looking back over her shoulder. "I'll give you a call and we'll schedule a time."

Matt watches her go and admires her butt and the way her calves look in those heels. He closes and zips up his portfolio and notices Kate walking toward him, phone in hand and hugging her clipboard to her chest.

"How's the sale going?" she asks.

"Pretty well."

"That your portfolio?"

"Yeah. I brought it in to show Sharam. He wanted to see my work."

"It shouldn't be here on the sales floor."

"I know. That occurred to me. Sorry."

"Mind if I look at it during lunch?"

He hands it to her. "Not at all."

"Thanks for sending me the pictures from the Getty. They're really beautiful."

"Glad you like them."

"See you later," she says and turns and walks away.

He watches her go. He's always considered Kate attractive, and just as he admired Cyn's body, he now admires Kate's. He has to admit that even though she's in business dress and isn't wearing heels, she has a great body and especially so for a middle-aged woman.

Kate sits at her desk in the office, going slowly through Matt's portfolio. His work is very good, and she particularly likes the portraits. She takes a bite of her sandwich, turns the page and sees two black and white photos of a nude in what strike her as very provocative poses. The photos take her by surprise and even though she's alone, she glances around the office. How silly. She studies the model's body. Whoever she is, she's beautiful. Is it his girlfriend? Could be. He's a good-looking guy. Makes sense he'd have a beautiful girlfriend.

She turns the page and sees two more photos in the series. One of them shows the model's body from mid-thigh to below the neck. The picture is taken from above and her back is arched and her torso slightly twisted. She seems to be struggling. Her legs looked squeezed together and something about her torso, the way her breasts are straining up toward the camera, suggests that her hands are bound behind her back. The photo strikes her as being right on the line between erotica and pornography. She's not a prude and she's seen her fair share of porn, but she much prefers erotica. It's subtler, more suggestive.

She wonders what it must be like to pose nude. Could she do it? She doesn't think so. She'd be too self-conscious about her body, even though it's still in pretty good shape. She hears the keypad on the office door beeping and knows it's Sharianna, her curvy, buxom black colleague. When Sharianna taps the keys to enter the code, there's a swing to the rhythm, as there is to everything she does.

"Hey girl, watcha doin'?" Sharianna asks, dropping her keys and phone on her desk and sashaying over to Kate. She stands beside her with a hand on a cocked hip and looks down at the black and white nudes. "My, my, what have we here? Whose portfolio?"

"Matt's."

"The new guy in Men's Suits?" Sharianna asks with surprise. "Now, that is one fine lookin' man. I'd like to get me some of that. She his girlfriend?"

"Don't know," Kate says and slowly turns the page. "Could be."

Sharianna sashays over to her chair and plops down. "You seein' anyone?"

"Uh-uh."

"When's the last time you had a date?"

"Can't remember."

"Girl, you need to get yourself in circulation or you're gonna end up an old maid."

"Can't," Kate says and slowly turns the page. "I've been married and have a kid."

"Okay, spinster!"

"Same thing."

"A-L-O-N-E! Get it? Don't you ever feel like goin' out and havin' fun?"

Kate shrugs. "Anyway, I haven't met anyone."

"Ain't gonna happen sittin' at home. You want me to hook you up, girl, you just let me know."

"Thanks. You're a peach." Kate closes and zips the portfolio. Maybe she'll have Matt do a portrait of Dee Dee. She's been meaning to have one done taken to hang over the fireplace.

CHAPTER 10

Ira and Adele

Ira unlocks the door to the flat in Mayfair, turns on the lights and rolls his suitcase across the threshold. It's been a month since he was here last and the place smells musty. He turns on the air conditioner, pours himself two fingers of cognac, settles into an armchair in the living room and puts his feet up on the ottoman. These trips to Tel Aviv to visit his mother are physically and emotionally exhausting. Her health is failing and she's frail now. She feels like a bird when he embraces her. He's tried for years to convince her to come live with him and Adele, but she won't budge. She's stubborn and strong willed, just as his father was. It's a good thing too, otherwise he wouldn't be sitting here now, relaxing with a drink in his hand and gazing at this luxuriously appointed living room and expensive artwork on the walls. He wouldn't have been born or, if he had, would have been killed, as the members of his family were, who remained in Germany until it was too late to leave.

He takes a cigar from the humidor on the coffee table and snips off the end. He lights the cigar and settles back in the chair. It puzzled him when he was younger why they didn't see the writing on the wall and leave when there was still time. He's read volumes about the Holocaust, but his father's explanation, shared with him on the occasion of his Bar Mitzvah, remains the best. "They were frogs in a kettle," his father said, "comfortable swimming in familiar waters. They felt the water getting warm, then warmer and didn't realize until it was too late that it was boiling. Why didn't they leave? Germany was their home. The Jews were an important part of society and had contributed greatly to German culture. It's not so easy to just pack up and leave all that behind. And remember," his father said, "the world turned its back on the Jews. Even America didn't want to take us in. We were betrayed and it played right into Hitler's hands. It was all the proof he needed that the Jews were a global problem the world wanted to be rid of, and he was only too happy to oblige."

As beautiful a city as Munich is, whenever Ira's there, he feels surrounded by ghosts. It was his family's home for many generations. His mother's family settled there in 1880, fleeing the pogroms in Russia. An ancestor on his father's side helped establish Chewra Talmud Tora, the first Jewish association in Munich, in 1808. Fortunately, his father had the foresight and courage to leave when it was still possible to do so, but only just.

In 1937 the Nazi-German government's "Aryanization" policy was in high gear, putting financial pressure on Jewish-owned businesses and causing them either to fail or sell out to the government. As the pressure on his father's pharmaceutical distribution business increased, his father decided that as difficult and dangerous as it would be, the time had come to flee the country and resettle his family elsewhere. At the urging of his distributor in Spain, a good man and friend, his father decided on Seville, an ironic choice. While the Spanish state under General Franco was sympathetic to the Axis Powers and provided them material support, Spain was officially non-belligerent and allowed Jews to take refuge there, four hundred years after expelling them. Ira was born in Seville in 1950 and wasn't even a year old when his father again relocated the family, this time to Tel Aviv, the capitol of the new Jewish state.

Ira's never forgotten what his mother said when he asked her why they named him Ira. "So you will be always vigilant," she said, "always on your guard. To survive, you must be." How right she was. He decided early on that the less people know about you and the more you know about them, the better. The image of a boiling frog is never far from his mind.

He sips his cognac, picks up the pre-paid cell phone from the coffee table and punches in a number. "Hello?" he hears Sami say and smiles, always amused by the sound of his Lebanese Cockney accent. "Mister Black," Ira says.

"Mister Black! Arrived safe and sound then, have we?"

"Just confirming."

"My sincere apologies, Mister Black. Lara can't make it, family business of some sort. Expect Olga."

"Olga?" he asks with concern.

"Nice girl."

"Experienced?"

"She's new. She'll do well enough I think."

Ira sighs. Women experienced in this sort of thing are rare. He's only known two, Leslie and Lara. Lara is good, but there'll never be another Leslie. "Fine," he says, resigned. He ends the call and puts the phone on the coffee table. Leslie introduced him to it, and he's never experienced anything like her since.

London was a wild place then. The Swinging Sixties had begun to liberate the English from their post-war psychological and emotional torpor, and by the end of the Seventies the era of dangerous self-indulgence, of cocaine and eight balls and designer drugs was dawning in London as it was in New York and Paris. He was, what, thirty? He met Leslie when he and a friend decided to cap off an evening of partying by visiting a high-class bordello. Leslie was the daughter of a peer, who amused herself by working as a prostitute there. He chatted with her in the lounge area over drinks. They hit it off and she led him to a room. They began with heated foreplay on the couch and made their way to the bed. "I'm into breath play," she said.

He smiles as he remembers his reaction. He was nonplussed. He'd never heard of such a thing and his mind raced to imagine what it was all about. He knew he looked a fool as he watched her open the nightstand drawer and remove a large, clear plastic bag and hand it to him. "There's nothing like coming when you're on the verge of blacking out," she said. "Hold the bag tightly around my neck, love, and squeeze. I'll tap your arm if I need air." Hovering above her, his hands around her neck, looking down at her face through the foggy plastic bag as she gasped for breath, her eyes wide and glazed and her mouth open so wide he could see down her throat — Well, it transported him to a place he'd never been before, and when she came she thrust herself against him so hard he was afraid she would injure herself. He tried it himself with her doing the squeezing and enjoyed the sensation, but it was nothing compared to the way he felt when he did it to her.

Poor Leslie. Drugs did her in. How he wishes she were still alive and here with him now. Sami had a hard time finding a girl who was willing to try breath play. He finally found Lara and she proved worth the wait and the expense, and she's only gotten better over time. He likes to think his tutelage is responsible for that.

The intercom buzzes and he gets up and pushes the button. "Yes?" he asks. "I am Olga," he hears a young woman with a distinctly Slavic accent say. He buzzes her in and waits for her at the door. Russian probably. The trade is filled with them these days. Young women desperate for money have become one of Russia's leading exports. He hears a light tap on the door and opens it. "Please," he says and waves her inside. He studies her as she stands in the middle of the living room; beige sweater with the sleeves pushed up; skin-tight black jeans and black boots. She's tall, on the thin side, with short toffee-color hair, dark brown eyes and Slavic features. Her complexion is pasty and the skin beneath her lower eyelids is purplish. She's attractive but could use a bit of makeup. She's obviously nervous, clutching the strap of her large, black, leather shoulder bag with both hands and waiting for instruction. He waves her toward the couch and she sits, perched nervously on the edge of the seat cushion with her back straight. "Please, make yourself comfortable," he says. "A drink?"

She nods "*Da,* thank you," she says and takes the bag from her shoulder and sets it on the floor.

"Vodka?"

She nods again.

He walks to the sideboard, fills two small glasses, returns and hands one to her and sits down next to her. He smiles and holds up his glass. "*Ypa.*"

She forces a smile. "*Ypa.*" she says and takes a sip.

"Where are you from?"

"Moscow."

"How long have you been here?"

"Mmm...." She searches for the words in English and how to put them together. "Six month," she says, unable to pronounce the "s" at the end of 'months.' "Not so long."

"You've done this before?" he asks and sees she has no idea what he's asking her about and mimes placing a bag over his head. "Breath play?" She looks perplexed and he realizes Sami didn't even bother to explain the job to her. He smiles reassuringly and pats her knee. "It's all right, my dear. You'll do fine. I'll show you what to do."

How unsatisfying the evening is so far, sitting here struggling to make himself understood. Lara has such a keen wit, and he misses the conversational foreplay while enjoying drinks on the couch. He puts his hands around his neck. "To stop," he says, holding up a hand, "tap my arm," and taps his arm. "Understand?" She watches his movements like an attentive schoolgirl and mimics them, putting her hands around her neck and indicating "stop" with her hand and tapping her arm. He smiles and nods. "*Da,* good." Sami should be paying him to teach this woman. He'll have to have a word with him. This type of thing can't happen again. It's tedious.

He leads her to the bedroom and begins to undress. He watches her in the valet mirror as she quickly removes her clothes, climbs onto the bed and sits waiting for him with her legs to one side, leaning on an arm. He hangs his clothes on the valet, climbs onto the bed and sits in front of her. He can see the apprehension in her eyes and smiles and holds her hand. He puts his hand gently on the back of her neck and draws her to him, hoping to feel her body relax a bit as they kiss, but it remains rigid. The poor girl is scared to death. He feels her place an arm around his waist and a hand on his back. Good, that's better. Go easy. He brushes her nipples with his fingertips and feels them harden. Good. Her body is beginning to respond. He pulls her arm from around his waist and guides her hand to his penis and strokes her forearm to encourage her. She squeezes him gently and begins stroking him and in moments he's erect. Good. He leans her back slowly onto the bed, opens the nightstand drawer and removes the plastic bag. She stares wide-eyed at it, and it occurs to him that she probably didn't understand that it was going to be placed over her head, not his, that is, if she understood anything he said to her. His suspicion is confirmed when he moves the bag toward her head and she grabs his wrists and stops him. "Relax," he says. "You want the money?" She nods and reluctantly lets go of his wrists. "Good, let's continue." He lifts her head off the pillow and places the bag over it, gathering up the opening in his hands as he spreads her legs with his knees and positions himself between them. He squeezes her neck tighter as he enters her and gazes down at her face as he begins slowly pumping. She looks terrified and is already gasping for air.

How different the experience is with someone so inexperienced. It's nothing like with Lara and even less so than it was with Leslie. The excitement he felt with Leslie was exquisite as he gazed down at her, her lips parted slightly, her nostrils flared, her eyes looking increasingly unfocused and glassy, deliberately bringing herself to the verge of unconsciousness and then gently tapping his forearm, signaling him to open the bag a bit to let her breathe and then begin the process again, over and over until he felt her wanting to come and they would together, forcefully and gloriously. How he misses her. There will never be another like her.

He feels Olga struggling beneath him. No amount of imagining will make her expression look anything other than what it is: utterly terrified. The situation is a disaster. Best to get it over with quickly and be done with it. He closes his eyes and gathers up the opening of the bag, tightens his grip on her neck and quickens the pace and force of his thrusting, pinning her arms to the bed with his elbows. He feels her legs kicking and her torso wriggling and opens his eyes to see her head moving rapidly from side to side and the concavity in the bag where her mouth is sucking against it.

He closes his eyes. Just a few more thrusts and he'll come. He feels hot liquid squirting against the inside of his thighs and hears a rude noise. The smell of feces and urine fills his nose and mouth. It can't be, can it? He empties himself in her, loosens his grip on her neck and lowers himself on top of her. As the pounding of his heart subsides, he's aware of her stillness and lifts up his head and looks at her face. Her eyes are wide open, her pupils dilated, and her open mouth is frozen in a gasp. He removes the bag from her head and puts two fingers on her carotid artery and two on her wrist and his ear to her chest. Nothing. He gets up and looks down at her body and the mess she's made on the bed between her legs, some of which is on his thighs.

He heads to the bathroom and showers. The stench is worse when he reenters the bedroom, and he holds his breath crossing it. He stops in the doorway and takes a last look at her body and turns and shuts the door behind him.

He picks up her bag in the living room, sits on the couch and begins examining its contents: Cosmetics pouch; ring of keys; wallet; Russian passport, Olga Arsov-Baranski, age 22; tampons; birth control pills; condoms; chewing gum; glass pipe; straight razor; cigarettes; lighter; small brown teddy bear with a red heart on the collar around its neck; aspirin; prescription medication. He reads the label: Digoxin. He opens the wallet: Eighty-one pounds, three pence in paper and coin; Russian driver's license; National Health Service card; fortunes from fortune cookies, all, unfortunately, wrong; plastic folder of pictures. He looks through the pictures: Olga with her parents, judging from the resemblance, all smiling; Olga with her boyfriend, presumably, both smiling; Olga when a little girl, bundled up in a parka and crouched down in the snow with her arm around a Husky that's sitting beside her with a paw on her chest, Olga smiling at the camera and the dog with its eyes fixed on hers. He puts the wallet back in the bag, picks up the phone and calls Uri. "Hello?" he hears Uri ask. "Uri, Ira. I have a cleaning job for you."

"Where?"

"The flat in Mayfair. It's a mess. I'll be gone within the hour."

"No problem."

* * *

The meetings with Connell and the London staff went well. They've stayed on top of unfolding events in the Middle East and North Africa and have been taking steps to protect PACBOND's investments there by devising strategies that will enable the company to profit from various outcomes on a country-by-country basis. It was good having Steve there. His ideas and suggestions are always fresh and inventive.

As Ira and Connell always do when he's in London, they enjoyed themselves in the evenings at their favorite private club. Their friendship goes back to when they were young bucks, working together in the City of London, and Connell continues to be his only confidante other than Adele. What he confides to Connell he wouldn't to Adele and vice versa. They're the counterweights in the gyroscope that keeps him upright and sailing on a steady course through life. It was all he could do to keep his mind focused on business or pleasure, though. He couldn't get the image of Olga's lifeless body, lying in the mess on the bed out of his mind. It would have been nice to unburden himself. Connell might have been shocked, but he would have understood and not judged him. As much as he wanted to, as much as it would have eased his feelings of guilt and remorse, he didn't. It's better to keep the door to that room in the house of many rooms that is his life shut and locked.

He remembers his reaction to that analogy when he first read it in the New Testament. He was taught that Jesus was a prophet who was an impertinent upstart, a brash irritant in society, a real rabble-rouser. Jesus was wise, though, and Ira was taken with his parables and metaphors and analogies, like the house of many rooms, which describes his life perfectly. How he would like to have Jesus here now, sitting across the desk from him at home in his study, to discuss things that most people can't fathom, that can only be discussed with someone as wise and compassionate and forgiving as he was.

He works his way through what seems an endless number of emails and can't get Olga's image out of his mind. He's killed people before, but always deliberately. They were enemies of Israel, terrorists plotting death and destruction. They deserved to die and when he killed them, he didn't give their deaths a second thought. Olga's death feels different, like the murder of an innocent and made worse because of the circumstances, which are unquestioningly sordid. The experience has shaken him. It will take some time and doing but he will get her image out of his mind. He must.

Thank God for Uri, who called the next day to say he'd taken care of everything, having replaced the mattress and bedding and left the place spotless. Ira has no doubt. There's no one better at clean up than Uri and that's the least of his talents. There'll be no trouble with Sami. He received his payment, which is all Sami's concerned about. Sami won't question Olga's disappearance. Girls come and go all the time in his business.

Ira looks at the photograph of his parents on the desk next to his computer screen. The picture was taken on a day trip to Mikhmoret near Tel Aviv. They're in their forties, standing on the white sandy beach in bathing suits, an arm around each other's shoulders, smiling at the camera. Lavi and Matanya, the "lion" and the "gift of God." Well, the lion is long dead, and God's gift is failing. Nothing lasts, including, hopefully, the image of Olga in his mind. He needs to plan his next trip to see his mother. At the rate she's losing weight, she won't last much longer.

He looks at the photograph next to the one of his parents. It was taken on Copacabana beach in Rio de Janeiro on a vacation he and Adele took some twenty-five years ago, long before she began "enhancing God's handiwork," as she describes her trips to her cosmetic surgeon. They're also in bathing suits with an arm around each other's shoulders and smiling at the camera. A stranger took the photograph, a handsome young man who was lying with his beautiful companion on a blanket next to theirs. It occurs to him that he doesn't know who took the photograph of his parents and has never asked. Probably also a stranger. He'll ask his mother when he sees her. She'll know. She may be failing physically but mentally she's still razor sharp.

Looking at Adele's smiling face and fit body in the picture, it occurs to him that they haven't been intimate in a long time. Why is that? It's not that he no longer finds her desirable. Her body has changed, of course, and her skin is not as smooth as it once was, but her touch has lost none of its tenderness and the feel of it none of its thrill. Anyway, his desire for her has never been based merely on physical appearance, but on who she is as a person, her intelligence, wit and, yes, sensuality. She's a very good partner in bed. Does she no longer desire him? Has she lost her appetite for sex? Is it no longer important to her? He finds it telling that he doesn't know. He needs to pay more attention to her.

He hears her approaching in the hall and sees her enter the study carrying a cup and saucer. She places them on the desk next to him and puts a hand on his shoulder. "Thank you, my dear," he says. "Just what I need." He picks up the cup and blows on the coffee and takes a sip.

Adele gazes at the photograph of his parents. "I wish your mother would come. I know she won't, but I think of her so ill and so far away…." She shakes her head and sighs.

He puts an arm around her waist and gives her a squeeze. "And how are you?"

"Fine," she says and lightly strokes the back of his neck.

"Good, then give me a kiss."

She leans down and gives him a peck on the lips.

"A proper one."

She raises her eyebrows and smiles. She hasn't heard this signal in some time and welcomes it. She's been wondering if they'd ever make love again, or if he'd lost interest in her in that way, despite all her efforts to make herself look younger. Maybe it has just been because he's so busy at work and traveling so much. She brushes his cheek lightly with the backs of her fingertips and brings her lips to his. She feels his hand slide slowly down to her butt and massage it. She was hoping to feel this signal, which means they will certainly be making love later. She's only too happy to oblige him. He needs it, the poor dear, worrying so about his mother and his company. It will take his mind off things.

Ira comes padding out of the bathroom nude and looks at Adele. She's in her nightgown, propped up against pillows, reading and doesn't look up. He smiles and climbs into bed and settles in under the covers next to her on his back with his arms behind his head, displaying his chest to good effect. It's a far cry from when they first met. As shy as she was then, she couldn't take her eyes off him and was so embarrassed by the fact that her face would turn red, and she'd giggle. He loved that about her. Time was when the nightgown would have been off by now. Those were wonderful times, but times have changed and not necessarily for the worse. With age comes a deeper appreciation of intimacy, and this is how they play the game now, with subtlety and nuance. He switches off his light and looks at her. "Interesting?"

"Hmm...."

"Very?"

This is the final signal she was waiting to hear and looks down at him and smiles coquettishly. She places the book on the nightstand, turns off her light and lies in the dark on her side facing him, waiting for his summons.

"Come here, little fox," he says.

She snuggles her body against his, rests her hand on his stomach and nuzzles his shoulder. "I was afraid you'd lost interest, my love," she says softly.

"I've neglected you. I'm sorry for that."

She kisses his shoulder and rests her head against it. "I was thinking recently of the first time."

"It was fantastic."

"That's what you said then. I was so afraid, and you were so patient and gentle. I was already in love with you, but after that even more." She brushes his stomach with her fingertips. "I wish I could have given you children."

"We tried. Anyway, I'm not sure I'd want to bring children into this world."

"It's a better one than our parents knew."

He's not so sure. He turns on his side to face her. "If we'd had children, they might have come between us. They often do between couples. We might not be lying here in the dark now, about to make love." He strokes her cheek and kisses her, and she sighs.

"It was God's will."

He's not so sure about that, either. He puts his arm around her waist and massages the small of her back, gently pulling her body closer. He feels her hand sliding along his abdomen and arrive at his penis and close gently around it, as only her hand does, tentatively at first, as if touching a delicate object, like the shy young woman she was when they first met and, where certain aspects of intimacy are concerned, still is and will always be. He gathers up her nightgown, pulls it over her head, tosses it aside and lowers himself on top of her and kisses her. She places her hands on his buttocks and caresses them, guiding him into her and drawing him close.

He hears his phone on the nightstand ring and ignores it. Not now. He pushes deeper inside her and hears the call go to voice mail. Her hands are at the back of his neck now. She's hanging on him and meeting his thrusts with perfect timing. She's as good a lover as ever, even better, like a prima ballerina who's learned how to wring maximum effect out of the slightest movement of her body. He feels her legs wrap around him and knows by the sound of her breathing and moaning that she's approaching orgasm and a long overdue one. They'll have one together to remember. He feels her pressing her legs against his sides, signaling him to thrust deeper and faster. Her mouth is by his ear, and she cries with pleasure at every thrust, softly at first, but louder as she nears climax and then steadily. They come together and he holds her tightly as she catches her breath and calms, then slowly rolls over on his back and takes her hand in his. She giggles and he waits for her to say what she always does when they've exhausted themselves making love and she's finally recovered.

"Phew! You're a bull!"

He remembers the call, picks up the phone, listens to the message and places the phone on the nightstand. He takes her hand again and gives it a squeeze. "She's gone," he says.

"Oh, my God!"

He feels her squeeze back and snuggle against him and press her forehead against his shoulder. The question of who took the photograph of his parents will forever go unanswered now, as so many questions will. The one question that haunts him he knows the answer to. The reason Olga is dead isn't because she didn't understand or try to stop him. It's because he prevented her from stopping him to satisfy himself. Making love with Adele did take his mind off Olga, but now the image of her lying in the mess on the bed is back in his mind. "May she rest in peace," he hears Adele whisper. Yes, both of them. The question is will he?

CHAPTER 11

The Weisses' Party

It's a warm July evening with the brown hills in the distance bathed in golden light and the sky filled with wispy clouds as Steve and Cyn head toward the Weisses' home in Coto de Caza. Steve's gotten to know Ira fairly well since he's been at PACBOND, but he suspects there's a lot more about the man that he doesn't know.

Ira's shrewd and calculating and very secretive. What he's learned about his background is that he grew up in Tel Aviv, worked in intelligence, studied at the London School of Economics, established himself as a broker at a bond company in the City of London and rose quickly through the ranks. He's heard stories about Ira's early years in London. Apparently, he was quite the partier and ran in a social circle that included the sons and daughters of peers and Saudi royals. According to Connell, Ira bedded an impressive number of women; American debutantes visiting London on their tours of the UK and Continental Europe; runway models; aspiring actresses. Ira and Adele were sweethearts in Tel Aviv and married just before relocating to the States.

By all appearances, Ira is a model of probity and decorum, but there's something about him. His occasional trips, for instance. He'll be gone for a week and even his secretary has no idea of his whereabouts. He makes his own travel arrangements for his personal trips. The rumor is that his destination is Bangkok, which raises all sorts of questions in

Steve's mind. Nothing would surprise him. Everyone has a secret life of one sort or another. Some are just more interesting than others.

Cyn stares at the white paddock fence bordering the tree-lined street and watches it pass by in a blur. It reminds her of a racetrack and how appropriate that it would. It is a race, after all, and winning is the price of admission to this exclusive gated community. Not just winning but winning big, and if you want to live here among the elite, you do whatever it takes.

The downstairs of the Weisses' home is crowded with people and Cyn can see through the living room windows that the backyard is just as crowded. It's still early in the evening and Ira and Adele are stationed in the living room, close enough to the front door to greet arriving guests. Ira's impeccably dressed, as usual, wearing a navy blazer and open collar, dark blue, hound's tooth check dress shirt and light grey gabardine dress trousers and cordovan loafers, all undoubtedly Brooks Brothers, which she knows is his favorite place to shop for clothes. Adele looks very nice in her ivory, chiffon A-line dress with a ruffled collar. It's a classic look. The last time she saw Adele was at the company Christmas party when she lured Steve back to her place. He's mentioned that Adele's had more work done and the new evidence of her surgeon's handiwork are clearly visible. Her features are beginning to look alien and aquatic. Well, if it makes her feel better about herself, good for her. She can afford it and what's the harm?

Ira notices them and waves them over. Cyn gives Adele a hug and hands her the box of chocolate truffles she's brought for her, telling her not to share. Adele tells her she didn't have to do that and how sweet and thoughtful of her and thanks her profusely. Ira comments that she's the only person who thought to bring Adele a gift and that it's very much appreciated. His saying this strikes Cyn as somehow significant, like he's letting her know that she enjoys a special status in their lives, although she could just be imagining it. He has a way of making even the most off-hand remark seem significant.

Ira introduces them to the couple he and Adele have been chatting with, Court and Alicia Brennan. So, the plot thickens. Cyn studies them closely. Court's a tall man with a broad chest, ruddy complexion and big smile showing lots of teeth. Alicia's short and reserved. Her smile, what there is of one, looks forced and frozen and her sparkling jewelry strikes Cyn as a distraction to keep people from looking at her eyes and noticing that their peering at you warily, as if from behind a mask. It occurs to her that Amber might be here too. Things could get very interesting indeed.

"Hear you sail," Court says to Steve.

"J-35. I race."

"Used to race. I have a Swan 62 now. Don't get her out as much as I'd like."

Cyn can tell by the slight rise of Steve's eyebrows that this Swan whatever-it-is is an expensive boat. She's learned a bit about sailboats since she's been with Steve and wouldn't be surprised if Court's boat cost him a million and probably a lot more.

Court looks around at the crowd. "My daughter Amber loves to race. She's here somewhere. I'll introduce you. She's a good hand."

"I can always use crew," Steve says.

Cyn knows Steve's entire being is now focused on meeting Amber and she admires the way he's managing to disguise his eagerness and excitement. She feels a hand on her arm and sees it's Ira's.

"Excuse us," he says to Steve and Court. "We'll leave you two salts to talk shop." He leans close to Cyn's ear. "May I see you for a moment?"

"Sure, Ira." What's this about? She knows all about his Machiavellian personality. He's smiling benignly as he leads her toward his study, but she feels like a fly caught in a web.

"After you," he says and waves her into the room. He closes the door and escorts her to the couch. "Please, make yourself comfortable." She sits and he sits beside her and pats her knee. "I think it's time you and I got to know each other better. Steve's an extraordinary person. You know how highly I regard him. I consider him an invaluable asset to the company. Because he is and because you're his wife, I want us to have a closer relationship, to be able to talk about things freely, in strict confidence, for the benefit of, well, all parties concerned."

Cyn's still wondering what the hell this is all about and looks at him uncertainly. "Okay."

"Cognac?"

"Sure."

He pours a finger of brandy from the decanter into each of two snifters, hands her one and watches as she takes a sip. "You know, I'm very proud of what I've accomplished here, of what I've built, and I'm very protective of it. I don't want to see it compromised in any way."

"Of course."

"I was in intelligence, many years ago in Israel. I was good at the craft. It's all about understanding people. Getting them to tell you what you need to know is easy. Getting them to do it without their realizing it, that takes real skill."

"I'm not sure I understand, Ira."

"Of course. Forgive me. Are you and Steve happy together?"

She finds the question a bit presumptuous. "Yeah."

"Normal relations?"

"I guess, whatever that means."

"He sees other women?"

She finds this question irksome and wants to tell him it's none of his damn business but thinks better of it. She realizes what this is all about. She's being tested. She remembers those white fences that reminded her of a racetrack and thinking that it is a race, after all. She's about to run one and it's a steeplechase. Each of Ira's questions is a hurdle and she's just arrived at the first one. If she balks and pulls up, she fails, but if she jumps and even if she stumbles and falls, she passes. She has the feeling he already knows the answer to this and every other question he'll ask. She nods and watches him sip his brandy, not taking his eyes off hers, and when he lowers his snifter the benign smile is gone.

"Well, we all have our vices," he says. "The important thing is how we manage them. You allow it?"

She nods.

"Encourage it?"

"No."

"Do you see other men?"

"Are you coming on to me?"

He smiles and pats her knee. "Of course not. I'm just trying to understand the type of relationship you have."

"Open. Anyway, I'm not looking, and the opportunity hasn't arisen."

"Ah, opportunity. How would Steve feel about it if you did? Would you tell him?"

"Good question. I think he'd be hurt and, no, I probably wouldn't."

"So, your marriage isn't really so open."

"I guess not."

"You feel that giving him his freedom is what you have to do to keep him."

"Yeah, I guess so."

"I'm sure you know about Westminster."

She feels a jolt and searches his eyes. He does know everything.

He reaches into his coat and takes out his phone. "You have your phone?" He watches her take it out of her bag and holds his up so she can see the screen. "Put this number in it. If you or Steve ever need my assistance, call this number." He watches her enter it. "Good. I'm sorry if I alarmed you. Not everyone could have had this conversation with me and been so candid and honest. You're a remarkable woman and I have nothing but the utmost respect for you."

"What's the point, Ira? Is there something you want me to do?"

He smiles and pats her knee. "No. Just look after Steve." He nods toward the door. "Shall we?"

She sees Steve through the crowd of people in the backyard, standing by the fence with a beautiful young blonde in a tight-fitting black cocktail dress. It has to be Amber. She knew he'd find her eventually. Whatever they might be talking about, she knows the black and white photos are vivid in his mind and that he's imagining what it would be like to have that body of hers all to himself in bed. Steve notices her approaching.

"Hey, honey. This is Amber."

Amber has a great body, all right, and obviously enjoys showing it off. She's wearing just enough dress to be decent. She has her father's blue eyes and features and seems removed and watchful like her mother, and her expression tells you she's favoring you with her presence. "Nice to meet you," Cyn says and sees Amber force a polite smile.

"She's going to crew," Steve says happily.

"How nice," Cyn says, trying to sound happy for him. They have to talk. They're living under a microscope and Amber's dangerous.

* * *

Steve gazes at Amber as she looks around at the people in the club lounge. She knows how to crew, all right, better than most of his buddies, and she's a hell of a lot nicer to look at. It was just the two of them and he worked her hard. He couldn't take his eyes off her then and he can't now. In a way she's a lot like Cyn. He can see she's always thinking, planning three and four moves ahead. He knows Cyn's right, that Amber's dangerous, but the prospect of putting this trophy on the wall is worth the risk. The waiter puts their drinks on the table, a pale ale for him and a dry gin martini with a twist of lemon for her. Steve holds up his glass. "Here's to winning."

Amber holds up hers. "To winning."

"You did great."

"Thanks. It was fun. I haven't sailed in a while."

"You'd never know it."

"Your wife's attractive. I hear her business is doing well, thanks to Ira."

"It is." He heard the hint of condescension in her voice at the end and noted the slight rise of her eyebrows to match.

"I hear she keeps you on a pretty long leash," she says.

He tilts his head and narrows his eyes slightly. "What else do you hear?"

"I know pretty much everything there is to know about you."

Huh. This woman's more like Cyn than he thought, just as calculating, only colder. He sips his beer and watches her sip her martini.

"My father knows everything that goes on at PACBOND. He keeps me posted. So, your wife's okay with you chasing after me?"

"Your dad tell you that?"

"He didn't have to. I could tell by the way she looked at me at the party. She doesn't like the idea, but she's not going to do anything about it. I get the feeling she puts up with a lot with you. I'd think twice about getting involved with me if I were you."

"Why's that?"

"I can ruin you."

He feels a rush of adrenaline and sips his beer. He didn't think he'd ever meet someone as masterful at the game as Cyn. Amber has him right where she wants him, right where he wants to be. "What turns you on?" he asks.

"A man who's willing to risk everything for the privilege of being in my presence."

He studies her eyes. He's not sure what to say and the only thought in his mind is getting her into bed, although it's clear now that it's going to require more effort than usual.

"I amuse myself with men like you. I love seeing the expressions on their faces when they realize the trap's been sprung on them."

"Pretty cold."

She raises her eyebrows and gazes at him coolly. "The only reason you're interested in me is because you think I'm a piece of ass and want to get me into bed. Am I right?"

"Not exactly."

She slowly lowers her eyebrows. "Right. You also foolishly think that being involved with me can somehow work to your advantage at the company, that my influence with my father might prove useful to you."

He's impressed. She's pretty much put her finger on it.

"I have to say I'm losing interest in you, Steve. The game seems over before it's begun." She looks around at the people in the lounge and then fixes her eyes on his. "I guess I'm not surprised. My father knows everyone at this club and so does Ira, and you decide to bring me here, as if everyone can't see what's on your mind? It's written all over your face."

He forces himself to keep his eyes on hers. He knows he's only imagining people glancing over their shoulders at the two of them, and also that he's being skillfully manipulated. It's incredible how well she knows how to turn him on. He drains the rest of his beer and puts the glass on the table. "Let's go."

* * *

Steve leaves Amber's apartment, gets in his car and begins the drive home. She continued her skillful manipulation of him all evening. The woman's unbelievable. He wanted to do everything imaginable to her, but she let things go only so far, and as far as attending to his needs was concerned, forget it. He's still stiff as a rod. She's a cock tease and he figures her plan is to satisfy a little more of his appetite each time they meet, rewarding him with treats as she would a dog. He's convinced now she's even more masterful at the game than Cyn. When he was leaving and kissed Amber at the apartment door, she told him she expected an expensive present next time. He'll have to think about what to get a heartless spoiled brat who already has everything.

Cyn hears Steve arrive home and pauses the movie, eager to hear the details of his evening with Amber. She listens to him toss his keys on the counter in the kitchen and get a beer from the fridge. She can tell by the noise he's making that things didn't go as he'd hoped. He sits beside her and gives her a peck on the lips. She smells Amber. She watches him slouch back and sip his beer and stare at the paused scene on the screen.

"What are you watching?" he asks.

"*XXY,* an Argentinean flick. It's good."

"What's it about?"

"A teenage girl who was born with a penis. She's living as a girl and has to decide if she wants to be a girl or a boy. She could develop either way."

"Huh. Which do you think she'll choose?"

"Probably stay female."

"What would you do if you were her?"

"Dunno. I can only imagine what it would be like, how it would feel."

He looks at her and grins. "Ever wish you had a penis?"

She glances at the bulge in his jeans. "I have one. What's it been doing?"

He shrugs and looks back at the screen.

Just as she suspected. "Not much, huh?"

He shakes his head.

"Wow! And you spent the entire evening with her? She's good. You know it isn't going to end well."

He nods.

There's nothing more to say, not now. She glances at the bulge in his jeans again. He needs relief. It's all part of the deal.

* * *

Matt and Dieter lean against the display case with their arms crossed, gazing up at the surfboards hanging from the ceiling, an appropriate bit of interior decorating on Dieter's part for a business named Surf City Photography and a constant reminder of where he'd rather be. "Been out lately?" Dieter asks.

Matt shakes his head. "With school and work, no time. I'm thinking about a trip to Ensenada soon. I'll surf Trestles on the way."

"Surfed it Sunday."

"Yeah?"

"Uppers. Good sets."

"Cool."

Dieter notices an attractive redhead arrive at the door. "This her?"

"Yeah." Cyn looks even more beautiful to Matt than he remembers her being. She's wearing her hair up in a twist and a green halter-top that almost matches the color of her eyes, white linen shorts and straw wedge sandals. He notices she isn't carrying a garment bag. Maybe she has an informal portrait in mind. She'll look great in color. He introduces her to Dieter and leads her to the studio.

Cyn makes a slow circuit as Matt busies himself with the camera on the tripod. She looks up at the lights hanging from the grid and around at the light tables and props against the walls. She sees the white cube darling Amber posed on. The black beanbag chair next to it looks more comfortable. She walks to the gray muslin backdrop and runs her palm lightly across its surface. "The scene of the crime, huh?"

He glances at her and smiles. "I guess you could call it that. So, what do you have in mind?"

She walks slowly toward him. "Black and white nudes. I thought that was clear." He looks surprised and concerned.

"I didn't get that," he says.

She stops in front of him and raises her eyebrows. "Is there a problem?"

"No, I guess not."

She nods toward the door. "Does it lock?"

"Yeah."

"Lock it."

He walks to the door, locks it and begins moving the white cube in front of the backdrop.

"Let's use the beanbag."

He pushes the cube back against the wall and places the beanbag in front of the backdrop.

She fingers the hairpins at the back of her head. "What do you think? Hair up or down?"

"Let's do both. We'll start with it up and then let it down."

She smiles and nods. "Good."

He stands by the camera and watches her step out of her sandals, remove her clothes and place them neatly on a chair. She turns to face him, and his eyes are drawn first to her nipples, which are almost the same color as her hair, then to the neatly trimmed triangle of public hair, a slightly lighter shade of red.

She's watches him as he admires her body and glances at his crotch and sees it's having the predictable and desired affect on him. He looks up at her and smiles.

"You have a beautiful body."

"Thanks. Let's see what you can do with it." She walks to the beanbag and settles on it. "The photographs of Amber are good, very erotic. I want mine to be more...." She narrows her eyes and purses her lips. I dunno...."

"Edgy?"

"Hmm...."

"Sexy?"

"Hmm...spontaneous...interactive."

"I'm not sure I know what that means."

"Neither am I. Let's find out."

He removes the camera from the tripod and plugs in the cord to the power packs. "Do you want me to shoot just your body or your face too?"

"You're the artist. I told you what I want. Tell me what to do."

"Okay, kneel, facing the backdrop with your arms together in back, like your bound, looking over your shoulder at the camera."

She isn't surprised but is a little disappointed that he's headed in the direction of repeating what he did with Amber. He must assume she wants the same thing, which isn't at all what she wants. She's not sure yet what she does want, not entirely, but it's not that. "How's this?"

"Good." He begins shooting and moving around her. "Now turn sideways to the camera and reach back and hold your ankles."

"Like this?"

"Arch your back more and push your chest up, like you're a pin up. Good. Head back, more. Really stretch your neck."

"Like this?"

"Yeah. Kneel toward the camera and put your hands on your thighs. I want your arms straight and your shoulders hunched, and I want you to squeeze your breasts between your arms. You're still a pin up."

"How's this?"

"Good. Tilt your head a little and look at the camera out of the corners of your eyes. You're a naughty girl. What happens to naughty girls?"

She pouts at the camera. "They get punished."

"Right. Punish yourself."

She holds her nipples between her thumbs and forefingers and squeezes them.

"Fan out your other fingers. Good. Pull hard."

"Until it hurts?"

"Yeah." He studies her face through the lens and sees her grimace. Her expression looks genuinely pained. She's either in pain or a good actress. "Okay, I'm going to shoot while you let down your hair. These pictures are for your husband, right?"

"Yeah."

"Imagine getting him off just by letting your hair down."

She thrills at this idea. He's definitely on the right track now. Is it possible? Could she actually do it? She reaches up and fingers the pins at the back of her head, arching her back and straining her torso upward and twisting it slowly. She removes the pins and holds her hair in her hands and eyes the bulge in Matt's jeans as she slowly lets it down around her shoulders. Maybe she can.

"Good. Kneel facing the backdrop and put your head down and your arms out in front of you. I just want to see your ass. Up a little higher. Good. Now, put your hands on your cheeks with your fingers fanned out."

"Like I'm going to spread them?"

"Yeah, but not yet. Good. Okay, now spread your cheeks and put your fingertips around your rim."

"Like this?"

"Spread 'em a little more. I want them to radiate out around it. Good." He sees her squirm.

Is he into that? She's not sure but either way she lingers, wanting him to get a good look at her. When he has, she slowly rolls over on her back and looks up at him with raised eyebrows, waiting for instruction.

He looks at her flush cheeks and neck and hovers over her. "Put an arm behind your head with the elbow out and the other between your legs. Arch your back."

"Like this?"

He watches her stroke herself between her legs. "Yeah." He frames her face. "Look up at the camera. Good, just keep going."

"Should I come?"

"If you like."

"Do you want me to?"

"Yeah." He watches her close her eyes and turn her head to the side. "Imagine your husband's standing over you. You're getting yourself off for him." He sees her look up at him out of the corners of her eyes and remove her arm from behind her head. He feels her hand on the bulge in his jeans and her squeeze.

"Like this?"

"Yeah." He feels a tug at his zipper and watches her as she unzips his jeans and feels her hand pulling down the waistband of his boxers.

"I want your cock in the pictures."

He straddles her and squats over her as she pulls him down to her and watches her press his cock against her cheek and give it a kiss on the tip and a lick along the shaft, then open her mouth and wrap her lips around it, gazing up at his eyes as she sucks. He can tell by the way she's moving her body and her moaning that she's coming and feels himself coming too, and when he has and tries to withdraw, he feels her hand pushing hard, against his butt, holding him against her. She's intent on draining the last drop out of him and is looking up at him dreamily. He's unsteady on his feet and finally she lets go of him. He steps back and takes his eye away from the viewfinder and looks down at her. She looks like a cat that's just enjoyed lapping up a bowl of cream.

"Hmm...," Cyn purrs. "Good job."

He arranges himself and zips up and buttons his jeans. He watches her stand and walk toward the chair to get dressed and admires the back of her body. She's every bit as beautiful as Amber and a hell of a lot more fun. "I'll load the photos on the computer and we can review them."

She sits beside him and studies each photo as he steps slowly through them. They're all good, *really* good, and when he arrives at the last photo and she sees his cock in her mouth and her dreamy look — Well, that one's really hot. Looking at the photos and especially this one has made her horny and she squirms and is sure he notices. She wants him to. "I like them all, but this last one's my favorite. That'll do the trick, all right."

"Can I ask you something?"

She looks at him. "Sure."

"Your husband's cool with this?"

"Yeah."

He shakes his head. "I don't get it."

"No, you don't. You're a nice guy, sweet, but naïve. Let's go."

"Where?"

"To get a room."

"I don't get involved with married women."

"Don't be ridiculous. I paid for more, a lot more. Remember? Let's go."

* * *

She props her pillow against the headboard, reaches into her bag by the side of the bed and takes out a pack of cigarettes and lighter. She offers him one and he shakes his head. She takes one out, lights it and places the pack and lighter on the nightstand, then settles back against the pillow, crosses her arms and looks at the dreadful artwork on the walls as she inhales and slowly blows out a stream of smoke. She smiles, picturing his expression when they'd rested and she was ready for more. He was entering her vaginally again and she said, "Not there this time." It was priceless. She'll never forget it or the way his body stiffened. She could tell it was his first time, and it took some guidance, but she got him where she wanted him and once she did, he relaxed and enjoyed it. He really is a sweet guy, very polite and gentle and thoughtful, maybe a little too much so with women. She's not that much older than he. She could be his big sister and feels that way toward him at the moment. "Why haven't you done that before?"

"I dunno. No one's been into that."

She flicks the ash into the ashtray and looks at him. "How would you know? I bet you've never asked. Not something good girls do, right?"

He glances at her and looks back at the awful artwork. She's right. He's polite to a fault with women. It's his upbringing and it's hard to be otherwise. "I guess so."

"You'd be surprised what good girls are into. You could stand to be more assertive. Women like that in a man." She draws on her cigarette and slowly exhales the smoke. "I still can't picture you and Amber together. I met her."

He's surprised and looks at her. "Really? Where?"

"At a party. What's she like sexually?"

Her bluntness reminds him of Cryssie and he smiles, although the question makes him uncomfortable. Amber preyed perfectly on his lack of assertiveness, giving him only so much, knowing he wouldn't dare ask for more. "Cold."

"Yeah. My husband's seeing her."

He's even more surprised to hear this. "Seriously?"

"All because of your photographs. Funny, huh? He's not having any better luck than you did, if that's any consolation. Seeing anyone?"

"Not really. I hooked up with her sister. She was visiting from Boston. She and Amber are like night and day. We had a great time, but she's more interested in my sister."

Now Cyn's the one who's surprised and looks at him with raised eyebrows. "What is it with you and women? For a nice good-looking guy, you sure strike out a lot."

He chuckles. "Guess I just haven't met the right person yet."

"I guess." She stubs out her cigarette in the ashtray, lies on her side facing him, puts a hand on his chest and strokes it lightly with her fingertips. "When you do, make sure you tell her," she says and gazes at him. He's the first person other than Steve she's been with since she and Steve met. Matt's sweet, a nice indulgence and a quick learner and there's so much more she can teach him. She's looking forward to continuing his education. She allows Steve his fun, so doesn't she deserve to have a bit of her own? She grins. "In the meantime, more."

* * *

Cyn stops at the Post Office to pick up the mail on her way home from running errands and is hoping the album has arrived. Matt said he put it in the mail yesterday, so it should have. She's delighted to find a key to one of the package boxes in the mailbox. She takes out the mail and goes through it, glancing at each piece before tossing it in the trash. She's about to toss a small, square, white cardboard envelope addressed to her with no return address but, hesitates and looks at the back and then the front again. Something about it tells her she'd better check its contents first and she tears it open. She removes a clear CD case, looks at the CD inside and reads what's written on it in black marker:

We all have our vices.
Is this one wise?

She feels a jolt and the blood draining from her face. She glances around and reads the message again and clenches her teeth. She knows what's on the CD and who sent it. As helpful as Ira's been to her, she's filled now with the sense that he could as easily destroy her and Steve as help them if it suited his purpose. The old Midwestern expression "as independent as a hog on ice" comes to mind. There might be some debate about its origin, but there's no doubt in her mind about its meaning. She grew up understanding that it comes from a hog escaping from its pen in winter and ending up on the ice on the pond and breaking through because of its weight and cutting its throat on the ice trying to get out. It couldn't describe her and Steve's situation more perfectly.

CHAPTER 12

A Trip to the Grand Canyon

Dee Dee sits astride her mule on the South Rim of the Grand Canyon and gazes at the layers of yellowish- and reddish- and dark-brown rock forming the walls of the South Rim on either side of her. She looks down at the canyon floor far below and sees Bright Angel Trail snaking its way across it toward the dark horizontal break in the land where she knows the Colorado River is flowing. She lifts her gaze up to the walls of the North Rim in the distance. Their colors are the same as the South Rim's but appear more pastel in the haze. She knew the Grand Canyon was big but was unprepared for just how big. It's immense, almost beyond comprehension. As good as the photographs online are they don't do it justice and looking at it she doubts any can.

She and Rosa wait behind Kathy, their young, blonde blue-eyed guide, with Rosa's parents and her two older brothers and two other couples in their party behind them. Dee Dee eyes Kathy's campaign hat and long braided ponytail and sees her point toward a spot on the rock face to the right and turn in her saddle and look back at them.

"See that black speck on the ledge?" Kathy asks.

Dee Dee tries to sight along Kathy's arm but isn't sure she sees what Kathy's pointing at.

"Just to the right of that dark indentation in the rock."

Now she sees it, a baldheaded black bird perched on the ledge.

"California Condor," Kathy says, "the largest North American land bird with a wingspan of almost 10 feet, the largest of any North American bird. They were on the brink of extinction because of poaching, lead poisoning and habitat destruction, but they're making a comeback now with our help. All 22 remaining wild condors were captured in 1987 and bred at the San Diego Zoo. They were reintroduced into the wild beginning in 1991. At last count, there were 210 living in the wild. I'm pretty sure that's 87. He's been hanging around lately. If we're lucky he'll take flight."

Studying the bird in relation to its surroundings, it does seem large, even at this distance. As if on cue, the condor hops and drops from the rock ledge and spreads its enormous wings and slowly spirals upward on the column of warm air rising from the canyon floor. Dee Dee glances at Kathy, who's watching the condor. This place is so big and Kathy's not all that much bigger than she is, yet she's right at home here and seems to know everything about the place, including which of only 210 condors in the wild they're watching. Dee Dee adds "park naturalist" to "writer" and "fashion designer" on her list of things she's like to be.

"Okay, let's head down," Kathy says and gives her mule a gentle prod with her heels.

The moment seems perfect to Dee Dee as they begin the long, slow zigzagging descent to the canyon floor. This trip by mule to Phantom Ranch where they'll sleep in stone and wood cabins is the highlight of the visit and she's really been looking forward to it. She eyes the condor circling overhead through the lenses of the wraparound sunglasses her mom bought her and reflects on the visit so far.

They've camped in one of the sites on the East Rim and spent the days hiking the trails and the evenings sitting around the campfire, eating dinner, roasting marshmallows and talking. Rosa's dad is a really good storyteller, especially ghost stories. He seems to have an endless repertoire and as much as she enjoys listening to him she wishes he weren't so good. It makes it hard to get up and leave the fire and walk off in the dark to the latrine. Rosa's parents have been sleeping in their RV and she and Rosa in one tent and her brothers in another.

She's gotten to know Petey and Pauly pretty well. Petey's fourteen and Pauly's sixteen. They're both nice. Pauly's quiet and loves to read while Petey likes to tease and joke. He's taken to sneaking up behind her and pulling her braids, although not hard. She doesn't mind. It's all good fun. Yesterday afternoon she and Rosa and Petey played a game of tag while Rosa's parents were getting dinner ready. Pauly didn't want to play, calling it a "kid's game" and stayed at the picnic table reading his book. The three of them played in the woods near the campsite close enough so that they could hear the call when dinner was ready. Petey being a boy and older and faster was a good sport and made it easy for her and Rosa to tag him. He easily ran them down whenever he was "it" and she soon realized that he always chose to tag her, at first on the arm or shoulder or back but then he'd grab her butt or tag her accidentally on purpose on the chest, always laughing when he did. She knew she should probably tell him to stop but didn't.

They follow Kathy down the switchback trail to the canyon floor and stop at Indian Garden for lunch, then continue on across the Suspension Bridge over the Colorado River where they watch a rafting expedition coming down the river and wave at the people as they disappear under the bridge. Dee Dee puts "rafting down the Colorado" on her must-do list.

It's late afternoon when they arrive at Phantom Ranch and the temperature is still close to a hundred, but the air is dry and the sun feels nice and warm against Dee Dee's skin. She and Rosa check out their cabin. It's equipped with a bunk bed that sleeps two, just like the others.

They enjoy a steak dinner outside prepared by the staff and afterward Dee Dee and Rosa and Petey and Pauly take an evening walk along Bright Angel Creek while Rosa's parents sit and chat with the two other couples in their group. The air has cooled since the sun moved beyond the North Rim and the reflection of the almost full moon above the South Rim makes the rushing water in the creek look like quicksilver. Dee Dee notices Rosa and Petey talking and putting some distance between her and Pauly. "Pretty," she hears Pauly say and sees him gazing down thoughtfully at the shimmering water. "Yeah," she says. "You read a lot. I love to read too. What're you're reading?"

"*A Canticle for Liebowitz.*"

The title sounds baffling to her and she looks up at him quizzically. "What's a 'canticle'?"

"A chant, like Gregorian chant, a prayer that's sung."

"Is Liebowitz a person?"

"Yeah, a Jewish electrical engineer who worked for the U.S. military and survives a nuclear war. He converts to Catholicism and founds a monastic order dedicated to preserving scientific knowledge until the world's ready for it again. It's set here in the Southwest. It's good. You should read it."

"Do you think there'll ever be one?"

"No, but when the book was published in 1960 people were afraid there was going to be one between us and the Soviets."

She looks around at the Grand Canyon and tries to imagine what the place would look like after a nuclear war. It's already a big hole. They'd probably just destroy cities where most people live. She tries to imagine a world with few people left living in it. It's a scary thought. "What do you think it would it be like, being killed by a nuclear bomb?"

"You'd be vaporized," he says and snaps his fingers. "Poof!"

She tries to imagine being vaporized and that's even scarier. She remembers the religious paintings at the Getty Center and looks up at Pauly. "Do you believe in heaven and angels, all that stuff?"

He looks down at her. "You mean life after death?"

"Yeah, I guess."

He looks off in the distance. "No. I think people made it up to make the idea of death easier to take. It's hard to deal with the fact that when you die that's it, it's over." He looks down at her again and smiles. "If I were you I'd concentrate on enjoying life now."

She looks down at the shimmering water. She feels the same way Pauly does. It's hard to imagine that when you die there's nothing more but she suspects it's the truth. The religious paintings by the Italian artists in the first galleries at the Getty come to mind. They make the supernatural seem so real. Maybe that's why the artists painted them, to help people believe. Did the artists believe? She remembers from the audio commentary that they were paid by the Church to paint the pictures, so maybe, but maybe not.

It's interesting that as she and her mom moved through the galleries the subjects changed from religious themes to portraits of noble and wealthy people who also paid the artists to paint them. Then landscapes and seascapes and it wasn't mentioned if anyone paid to have those painted. Then still lifes of flowers in vases and glasses on tables and whatnot, then paintings of ordinary people doing ordinary things who seemed to be unaware they were being painted, as she and her mom were unaware Matt was photographing them. She thinks of the paintings of Mary and Jesus and the saints and of Jeanne Kéfer and the man and two women in *Three Lovers*. Did people just stop believing as time went on? Is that why she doesn't?

She looks up at the moon and sees it looking down at her the way God and the angels look down from above in the religious paintings. Maybe it's watching over her. Maybe there is something beyond all this. Maybe it's just being here in this big place that makes her feel so small and alone.

* * *

Dee Dee and Rosa sit facing each other on the lower bunk with a flashlight on the blanket between them, its beam aimed toward the wall. It's late and they have to be up early to leave camp. They've been chatting and Dee Dee can tell there's something Rosa has been dying to tell her, but is still keeping a secret. She's tired and is about to climb up to her bunk when Rosa leans toward her.

"Know what?" Rosa asks mysteriously.

"What?"

"Petey likes you."

Dee Dee can tell by Rosa's suggestive expression and the importance she gave this statement that she means more than as his sister's friend and she's not sure how she feels about it. "He does?"

Rosa nods and leans a little closer. "Do you like him?"

Dee Dee's not sure what to say and shrugs. "Yeah, I guess so. He's your brother."

"He wants to come visit."

Hearing this makes her uneasy. "Now? Why?"

Rosa widens her eyes. "You know. He likes you."

Dee Dee thinks she knows what Rosa's talking about, but is still uncertain whether Petey wants to come visit the two of them or be alone with her. She thinks the latter and isn't sure how she feels about that, either. "I don't know. I don't think he should. It's late."

"He won't stay long," Rosa assures her.

Dee Dee feels backed into a corner now. Rosa's her best friend and she's here as her family's guest, and as much as she thinks Petey's coming is a bad idea she's reluctant to protest. She looks at Rosa, not knowing what to say or do.

Rosa grins, reaches down and switches off the flashlight. "Be right back."

With the flashlight off the only light in the cabin is from the moon, now high overhead, and Dee Dee can barely make out Rosa in the darkness. She feels the bed sway as Rosa hops off and watches her silhouette as she tiptoes quickly to the cabin door, slowly opens it, steps outside and slowly closes it behind her.

Dee Dee and her mom have had a few conversations about sex, mostly about how her body will change and what will happen as it does. She's not thinking about those conversations now. She's thinking about the one they had when they watched a news report on TV about three local college boys who convinced a girl they met in a bar to come back to their dorm room and spiked her drink with a drug called "Roofies," and now they've been charged with rape and face long prison sentences if convicted. "Roofies" struck her as a funny-sounding name for a drug, but there's nothing funny about what the boys are accused of doing to the girl, recording themselves taking turns having sex with her when she was unconscious and inserting things into her vagina. Her mom said the best way to avoid being in a situation like that is not to allow it to happen in the first place, to be extremely cautious about strangers you meet and going places with them. Not much was said about the girl in the news report, other than that she's in the hospital and undergoing treatment. The girl's mom probably gave her the same advice. This situation feels different, though. She knows Petey. He's Rosa's brother. It's funny. She hopes Rosa will be here with them and, at the same time, that she won't be. It's a confusing situation, but also an exciting one.

She waits, her eyes now adjusted to the darkness, listening for the sound of Rosa's and Petey's approaching footsteps, but all she hears is the profound silence of the Grand Canyon. The game of tag comes to mind. This really is a situation of her own making. She was well aware of the way Petey's tags were becoming increasingly personal, and saw his expression change when he realized he could touch her anywhere he wanted and she wasn't going to stop him. Why didn't she? The thought did cross her mind to. She'd never been touched that way and wanted to be, that's why.

Finally, she hears the sound of approaching footsteps and can tell they're Petey's and that Rosa isn't with him. She watches the door slowly open and Petey enter and close it as quietly as possible behind him, then tiptoe to the bed. She feels the bed sway as he sits on it beside her.

"Hey," he whispers.

She can just make out his eyes and grin in the darkness. "Where's Rosa?"

"In our cabin. I'll send her back."

"When?"

"After."

"What?"

"You know."

She feels like a fool. It's a situation of her own making, all right, and now that she's in it, she has no idea what to do and sits quietly, waiting to see what happens next. He moves closer to her, and she feels his hand on the small of her back and starts.

"You okay?" he asks.

"Yeah," she says, thinking her voice sounds strange, thin and squeaky.

"Ever made out?"

"No."

"It's fun. You'll like it."

His voice sounds different now, not teasing or boasting or bratty, but confident and encouraging. She searches for something to say, but can't think of anything. She's relieved to feel him gently pull her toward him and goes willingly. She hears his breathing and feels his lips against hers, warm, pressing softly, and then a bit harder. Jeanne Kéfer and the woman in *Three Lovers* come to mind. She knows how that little girl feels, so small compared to the door behind her and looking so vulnerable. She has an inkling how the woman embracing the man in *Three Lovers* feels. Of the two feelings, the woman's is far more desirable and she'd like to experience it.

She can tell by the way Petey's holding her closely, but not too tightly, and stroking the small of her back that he's done this before, and she follows his lead. She doesn't want to make more of a fool of herself than she already has. She feels the tip of his tongue between her lips, brushing against her teeth. She knows what French kissing is and has always wondered if it would feel gross having someone's tongue in her mouth. She parts her teeth enough to let his tongue in and it doesn't feel gross at all. She puts her tongue in his mouth and feels his tongue twirling slowly around hers. It feels nice.

She feels his hand moving slowly from the small of her back around her waist to her stomach and then up toward her breasts. She remembers touching herself in the bath and wondering what it would feel like if someone else were touching her. This is what she wanted, after all, and why she didn't stop him from touching her when they were playing tag. Her body thrills when he places his hand on her pajama top and fondles her breast, and the thrill increases when he takes her nipple between his thumb and forefinger and gently squeezes and rolls it. He moves his hand inside her pajama top and she feels the same warm tingling between her legs she did in the bath, but it's different now, more intense.

With her arms around his neck and her face pressed against his shoulder, she imagines she looks just like the woman in the white dress in *Three Lovers*. Her body is a twig compared to the woman's, but she imagines she does and even more so when she feels his other hand on the inside of her thigh at the top of her leg. She knows where it's headed and shudders when she feels him touch her between her legs. She feels his hand take hers and place it on the lump in his boxers. She's surprised by how hard it is and feels him begin moving her hand back and forth, showing her what to do.

"Don't worry," he whispers, "you won't break it."

She hears the amusement in his voice and feels her cheeks and neck flush. It's a good thing it's dark or he'd see how embarrassed she is. She's never touched a boy anywhere, let alone there, so how would she know? She wraps her hand around it and gives it a squeeze and is surprised by how warm it feels.

"Hmm," he whispers, "that feels good."

She moves her hand slowly back and forth and feels his hand sliding inside the waistband of her pajama bottom to between her legs. So, here it is, the moment she's been wondering about and she was right. As good as touching herself feels, being touched by someone else feels even better. She closes her eyes and imagines what his fingers look like, stroking her there, and spreads her legs wider. With one hand stroking him and the other around his neck, hanging onto him, she really does feel like the woman in *Three Lovers,* given over completely to sensual pleasure, to the enjoyment of sex.

The sensation between her legs is a new one and she feels her body on the verge of doing something it's not quite able to do yet. She feels like she's melting but stiffens when she feels his fingertips probing her opening, wanting to enter her. The girl who was raped by the boys comes to mind and the thought frightens her. She wants him to stop but what if he doesn't? "Don't," she whispers and is relieved to feel his fingertips withdraw and his hand begin stroking her again. She relaxes a bit and concentrates on enjoying the feeling, but stiffens again when he pulls down the waistband of his boxers and places her hand on his penis and she pulls her hand away.

It shouldn't make a difference, stroking him through his shorts or actually holding him in her hand, but for some reason it does and she feels like Jeanne Kéfer again, small and vulnerable. "Don't stop," she hears him whisper, "you do it really good." Does she? Does he really think so? He probably said that just to get what he wants, but she wants to believe him and it gives her the confidence to take him in her hand again and slowly stroke his penis and it feels even warmer now.

She hears his breathing quicken and feels his body stiffen and thinks she knows what's about to happen. "Don't stop," she hears him whisper urgently and feels his body begin jerking and then wetness on her hand and the air is filled with a musty animal smell. She watches him lie back on the bed, wipes her hand on his boxers and sits looking down at him in the dark, waiting to see what happens next.

"That was great," he whispers, sitting up and pulling up his boxers.

She watches him stand, tiptoe to the door, open it and leave, leaving the door ajar. She sits there, listening to his footsteps grow fainter. She climbs up to her bed and gets under the covers and lies there, staring at the ceiling. She hears Rosa returning and the door close. She listens to her tiptoeing quickly across the floor and feels the bunk sway as she climbs on bed below.

"So? How was it?" Rosa whispers.

Dee Dee knows Rosa's dying to hear the details, but she isn't going to tell her anything. What happened between her and Petey was just too personal too intimate, and anyway, she hasn't even begun to sort out how she feels or what she thinks about what happened. "G'night," she whispers, turns on her side and curls up, pulling the covers under her chin and smelling Petey's lingering scent on her hand as she does.

It's just before sunrise as they prepare to mount the mules and begin the long trip back to the South Rim. Dee Dee listens to the small talk around her, yawning and trying to keep her eyes open. She lay awake a long time thinking about things and didn't get much sleep. She glances again at Petey, who's standing with his back to her, talking with Pauly. He hasn't said a word to her and is avoiding making eye contact with her. She's trying to understand why he's acting this way after doing what they did last night. Does he think less of her now? Why would he? Her mom's always said that sex is a good thing, a natural part of life. Well, what happened last night felt good, most of it, anyway, the last part was kind of yucky, and natural and she doesn't feel at all ashamed of herself.

* * *

Back across the Colorado River, Dee Dee and Rosa clean up the campsite after dinner while Rosa's mom and dad pack up the RV, getting ready to leave in the morning. Petey and Pauly are in their tent, getting their things together. Petey still hasn't said a word to Dee Dee and has avoided making eye contact with her. She isn't just puzzled by Petey's behavior now, she's angry about it, although she's been doing a good job of not letting it show. She ties up the plastic bag filled with paper plates, cups, napkins and plastic utensils and carries it to the trash bin. She sees Petey crawl out of his tent with a flashlight in his hand and walk toward her. He stops in front of her and she stares at him, waiting to hear what he has to say. She's heard the term "sheepish expression" before and now she knows what it looks like.

"Wanna go for a walk?" he asks.

"Sure."

They walk along a path they've taken before that leads through the woods to the edge of the East Rim, Petey lighting the way. They're a good distance from the campsite and surrounded by woods when he switches off the flashlight and stops. She takes a few more steps and stops and turns to face him. "Why are you stopping?" she asks and he walks up to her and puts his arms around her waist. "No," she says, pushing him away and stepping back.

"Why not? We did it last night."

"Because of the way you've treated me all day. You haven't said a word to me. You haven't even looked at me. Why?" She glares at him and waits for his answer. There's just enough light to see that he looks guilty now.

He shrugs. "I dunno…you know."

"No, I don't know," she says angrily. "That's why I'm asking."

"I dunno," he, sounding helpless.

"That's not good enough," she says and walks quickly past him toward the campsite. "Hey," she hears him call, "I'm sorry, okay?"

Sunday, July 3, 2011

Dear Anneliese,

What a great trip! I can't believe how big the Grand Canyon really is! You really can't tell from the photographs. You have to see it to believe it!

It was really nice of Rosa's parents to invite me to go with them. Her dad had to make reservations a year in advance and it cost my Mom around $500 to send me! Can you believe it? I am so thankful to her, and I've been thinking about what I can do for her in return. I haven't come up with anything yet, but I will.

We stayed in a campsite on the East Rim and hiked all over the place. Rosa and I slept in a tent and so did her brothers. Her parents slept in the RV they rented for the trip. We ate our meals around the campfire. Rosa's dad is a good cook. He's also a good storyteller. He told ghost stories when we sat around the fire in the evenings. The stories were really spooky and made me think twice about getting up to go pee.

The best part of the trip was at the end when we went to Phantom Ranch across the Colorado River. We rode there on mules. My mule's name is Daisy and when I got off her at Phantom Ranch, I felt like I was still riding her! I've gone fishing with my dad off the coast a few times and felt the same way when we got back on land, like I was still on the boat!

At the beginning of the trip to Phantom Ranch we saw a California condor. They're very rare. Our guide Kathy told us that there are only a couple hundred of them living in the wild. Kathy knows everything about the place. I really like her and learned a lot from her. Anyway, the condor was perched on a cliff and while we were looking at it, it took off and flew! How great is that! We were really lucky to see it fly. Those birds are big! You wouldn't believe how wide their wings are! They make the ravens that were always trying to steal food at the campsite seem tiny, which they're not.

When we were riding across the Colorado River we saw people in rafts going down the river. It looked like a lot of fun and I'm definitely going to do that someday. It's on my list.

We stayed in cabins at Phantom Ranch. They're pretty old and made of stone with wood roofs. Rosa and I had our own, her brothers had theirs and her parents theirs. The cabins have bunk beds. I slept on top and Rosa on the bottom. I was the guest and let her have it. I didn't mind. As it turned out, I didn't get much sleep anyway. More about that in a minute.

I know I've mentioned Rosa's brothers before, but I haven't told you anything about them because I didn't really know them very well before this trip. Pauly is 16 and Petey is 14. Their names are actually Paul and Peter, but that's what everyone calls them.

Pauly's kind of quiet and loves reading as much as I do. He told me about a book he's reading, "A Canticle for Liebowitz." I copied down the title because I knew I wouldn't remember how to spell it correctly! "Liebowitz"? Forget it! I wouldn't have figured that out in a million years, although I'm sure you wouldn't have had any problem spelling it.

Anyway, he said it was about these monks who take care of scientific knowledge after a nuclear war. It made me wonder what life would be like if there really was a nuclear war. I don't think there'd be anything left. I sure hope it never happens. I just realized you have no idea what I'm talking about.

Did you believe in life after death? I wonder. You never mentioned anything about it. I asked Pauly if he did, and he said he didn't. He thinks people just made it up because they're afraid of death. I think he's right. I'm not sure I'd even want to live forever. What if I got bored? Where would I be then? I think we keep people alive in our memories, the way you're alive in mine. You'll always be alive because people will always be thinking of you. Anyway, Pauly said I should concentrate on enjoying life now. I think that's pretty good advice.

So, now let me tell you the most important news about the trip. You remember I was wondering who the first person to touch me would be? It was Petey! I never would have guessed him. As I said, I hardly knew him before the trip. It happened in the cabin the night before we were going to leave Phantom Ranch. Rosa and I stayed up late talking on her bed and she said that Petey told her he liked me and was going to come visit. I thought she meant with her there, but she went to go get him and he came alone. I should have known. We took a walk that afternoon along Bright Angel Creek and Rosa and Petey went ahead of me and Pauly and the two of them were talking about something. I asked Rosa the next day if they were planning the whole thing then and she admitted they were.

Anyway, I sat on the bed in the dark, waiting. He came in and sat next me and asked me if I'd ever made out, you know, kissing and petting, and I said I hadn't, which you know is true. And then he put his arm around me and kissed me and I kissed him back. He even put his tongue in my mouth and I put mine in his! Did you and Peter do that? If you did, you never mentioned it. At first he touched my boobs through my pajama top and it felt great. Then he put his hand inside my top and played with my boobs and squeezed my nipples and that felt even better! I knew he wanted to touch me between my legs and I'll be honest with you, I wanted him to and let him and that felt unbelievable! He tried to put his finger inside me, but I stopped him. I knew it would hurt and, anyway, I didn't want him to.

It's a funny thing. At first, I touched his penis through his boxer shorts and I was okay with doing that, but then he pulled down his shorts and put my hand on it and the idea of actually touching it threw me. I don't know why, but it did. Anyway, I stroked it until he came all over my hand! YUCK!!! I wiped my hand on his boxers. I hope his mom doesn't notice it when she does the wash.

Anyway, being touched by someone else felt as good as I imagined it would, even better! He left and Rosa came back and I could tell she wanted to hear all about it, but I didn't say anything and not because I felt embarrassed or ashamed. It just didn't seem right telling her about it. I know you understand.

So far, so good, but get this. The next day Petey wouldn't say a word to me or even look at me. I was surprised and couldn't figure out why he was treating me that way, especially since we'd done what we did. All day he treated me that way and it wasn't until after dinner back at the campsite that he asked me to go for a walk with him. I said sure and off we went. The only reason

I went with him was to see what he had to say for himself. We were about halfway to the East Rim when he stopped and turned off the flashlight and put his arms around me. He wanted to make out again! Can you believe it? I wouldn't let him. I asked him why he'd been treating me the way he was all day and guess what he said? "I don't know!" What kind of an answer is that? I think I know, though. It took me a while to figure it out. I think he felt less of me because I let him touch me and felt he could whenever he wanted. I hope he learned a lesson.

Well, I've got to catch up on my sleep. I can't keep my eyes open. I'll write soon.

Yours, Dee Dee

P.S.: This shows you how tired I am. I forgot to mention my period! There's no blood yet, just clear discharge. I told my mom and she's going to buy pads. It's funny. I've thought so much about it and wondered what it would be like. I've heard so many stories about girls and their periods that I didn't know what to expect. Well, here it is and all I can say is it's no big deal, so far, anyway. It's like being touched for the first time. When it finally happens all the wondering and worrying is over. It does feel kind of strange, though, knowing that I could actually have a baby now. It's hard to believe, but girls my age used to. Who knows? Maybe they still do somewhere!

P.P.S: One last thing. I'm pretty sure you masturbated. Everyone does. Well, I guess some people don't, but most do and especially kids, all the time. Did you orgasm? I've read about it online and some women say they were able to at 3 and others not until they were 10 and others not until they were 20 and some say they never have and aren't able to. I know I can. I just haven't gotten there yet, but I felt myself get really close with Petey, probably because it was someone else touching me. I know I will soon. I really hope you did. It would be so sad if you didn't.

CHAPTER 13

Jenn Visits Cryssie

Jenn finishes the chapter, bookmarks her place, closes the book, leans back and looks out the window at the vast checkerboard expanse of cultivated land far below and the Rockies slowly receding in the distance. In two and a half hours she'll be in Boston, a place she's never been. Her only trips east have been to Louisville to visit her grandparents when they were still alive and Washington, D.C., with her high school Model UN group. Having been born and raised in Southern California, where everything, with the exception of Mission San Juan Capistrano, seems new, she likes the feeling of oldness in the East, of an America that was already established when California was just being settled. She imagines Massachusetts will look a lot like Norman Rockwell's paintings.

When Cryssie invited her to come visit, Jenn thought why not? Her summer job teaching kids to play the violin and piano in the outreach program at the community center is volunteer work and, anyway, she'd wanted to do some traveling before beginning her studies at Stanford in the fall. She feels she's gotten to know Cryssie well in the course of their email correspondence. She's a fascinating and complex person with a lot on her mind, which she shares freely without self-editing. Her brand of blunt honesty was jarring at first, but Jenn's used to it now and has come to appreciate it.

Cryssie's conflicted about her family's wealth and has a contentious relationship with her parents, and especially her father. The problem seems to be a clash of values, but there's probably more to it than that. Her sister Amber apparently has no problem with her parents or their wealth. Amber admires her father and is following in his footsteps into finance. It's interesting and curious how two people can be raised by the same parents yet develop so differently. She and her brother are different people, but they're more alike than different, both close to their parents and embracing their parents' values.

Jenn's looking forward to seeing what life is like in Jamaica Plain, the part of Boston where Cryssie lives. It seems like an interesting place. In the 1600s and 1700s it was a farming town, an early transportation hub and home to what the town history describes as "a small but choice circle of elegant, graceful and cultivated people used to wealth and accomplished in the arts of life." It's been undergoing a process of gentrification in the last decade and is home to a large LGBT community. Given that fact and the photos of Cryssie's friends on her Facebook page, all of whom look gay and seem like quite a cast of characters, she wouldn't be surprised to learn that Cryssie's also into women, which would be fine by her.

Jenn's own sexuality has always been a bit puzzling to her. She enjoys being affectionate with her close male and female friends, hugging and holding hands and cuddling, but isn't really interested in having sex. When she feels the desire, she pleasures herself. She knows she's a textbook asexual but resists self-identifying as one. She prefers to think of herself as "sexually independent."

* * *

Cryssie waits in Baggage Claim, her eyes fixed on the top of the escalator. It still hasn't sunk in that this is really happening, that Jenn is actually going to appear at any moment. It seems like a dream and as thrilled as she is, she's also apprehensive. It took her a long time to work up the courage to ask Jenn to come visit. Of course, there was the ever-present fear of being rejected, but she was surprised by how nervous she felt when Jenn said she'd like to come. She waits and watches, standing on tiptoes each time she sees a pair of shoes appear at the top of the escalator. Clunky-looking black Doc Martens ankle boots — Definitely not Jenn.

Did Matt tell Jenn about Malibu or that she has strong feelings for her or that she's bi? Probably not, but that doesn't make her any less nervous or apprehensive. She's determined to try to keep her feelings in check and behave. She doesn't want to make a fool of herself and jeopardize their friendship. Whether or not she'll be able to is another matter. She's full of good intentions but knows it'll be a struggle.

She thrills at the sight of black ballet flats and tight black jeans and glances at the ankles. It's Jenn! Cryssie watches her glide gracefully down the escalator, standing with that erect posture of hers, looking like a goddess descending from the heavens. It's the first time she's seen Jenn with her long hair pulled back in a ponytail and likes the way it shows off that beautiful face of hers.

She makes her way to the front of the crowd and sees Jenn looking around, searching for her. She wants to run to her and leap into her arms but manages to restrain herself. Still, she can't help bobbing up and down on the balls of her feet like a kid in anticipation of hugging her and feeling her hug back. She waves and catches Jenn's eye and Jenn smiles, waves, steps off the escalator and walks up to her. "I can't believe you're really here!" Cryssie cries gleefully and closes her eyes as they hug, savoring the feeling of Jenn's body pressed against hers.

* * *

The restaurant on Centre Street is trendy and crowded and Jenn takes in the scene as they follow the hostess to their table. Most of the customers are young and middle-aged women, casually dressed in tee shirts and shorts and jeans. The haircuts are short and there isn't much makeup being worn. She sees some of the woman sporting tattoos and that the preferred jewelry of those wearing any is a stud or two or three in the side of one ear, although she also notices wedding bands on the ring fingers of same-sex couples here and there. The people strike her as the modern-day equivalent of that small but choice group of early residents and Cryssie seems to know quite a few of them and stops to say hi and introduce Jenn as they make their way to their table. They settle in and Jenn looks at Cryssie with raised eyebrows. "Wow! You sure are popular!"

Cryssie shrugs. "I throw a lot of parties," she says and grins. "I still can't believe you're really here."

"It's great to be here. I've been looking forward to it."

They order glasses of wine and Cryssie sips hers and gazes at Jenn as she peruses her menu.

"The pulled pork looks good," Jenn muses.

"It is," Cryssie says, "try it. How's Matt?"

"You probably know better than I," Jenn says without looking up. "I haven't seen or spoken with him lately. Is he still seeing your sister?"

"I'd be surprised if he is."

"I think I will try the pulled pork," Jenn says and puts down her menu. "It's odd that he never brought her home to meet us. He always brings his friends home."

"It's just as well," Cryssie says.

"I understand she's really beautiful."

"She is." Cryssie takes her phone from her bag and scrolls through the photos to the picture of Amber posed on the wall by the volleyball courts by Huntington Beach Pier and hands the phone to Jenn.

"Wow! She's beautiful, all right. Still, if she really treats men the way you say she does, I can't imagine what they were doing together. I know my brother well."

Cryssie shrugs. "She's a siren. She loves luring sailors onto rocks."

"She must be pretty good at it," Jenn says and hands back the phone. "Matt's no fool."

Cryssie looks at the photo and smiles. "I'm glad they met," she says and gazes adoringly at Jenn. "If they hadn't, I wouldn't have met you."

Jenn can see in Cryssie's eyes and hear in her voice that what she suspected is true, that her feelings run deeper than friendship and probably much deeper. She shouldn't be surprised and feels foolish that she is. She's felt it from the moment Cryssie arrived and sensed it in her emails by the way she seemed purposefully to steer clear of the subject of feelings. Cryssie was probably afraid that if she shared hers, she wouldn't have come. Would she have? She doesn't know. What she does know is that there aren't three thousand miles between them now, that she's sitting across the table from Cryssie and they'll be spending a week together.

Jenn tries to hold her gaze but can't and feels herself blush and glances nervously at the women at the tables around them.

Cryssie grins. "You're cute when you blush."

"Please stop. You're embarrassing me."

Cryssie looks at her impishly. "Okay, for now"

* * *

Jenn looks around at the spacious well-appointed living room. "Wow! Nice digs!"

"*Mi casa es tu casa,*" Cryssie says and nods toward the hallway. "Your boudoir's on the left. Glass of wine?"

"Sure. Be right back," Jenn says and rolls her suitcase toward the bedroom.

They sit across from each other in the living room with glasses of wine in hand, Cryssie in a chair with her feet on the coffee table and Jenn on the couch with her legs tucked under her.

"What's it like being adopted?" Cryssie asks.

Jenn laughs. "That's like asking a fish what it's like being a fish."

"Yeah. I guess. Any feelings for your biological parents?"

"Not really. If I went back to Xinzhou, I could spend the rest of my life there and never fit in. I don't know anything about being Chinese. I'm sure my biological parents would seem as strange to me as I would to them."

Cryssie stares down into her wine glass. "I've got the opposite problem. I know my parents and our family's history all too well. I asked Matt if he thought your parents would adopt me. I wasn't kidding."

Jenn looks around again at the living room. "They seem to provide for you pretty well."

"It eases their conscience. I hate it."

"Then why do you let them?"

Cryssie searches Jenn's eyes. "I dunno. Maybe I'm a spoiled brat."

"You don't strike me as being a spoiled brat."

"Maybe I feel it's the least they can do to make up for the way they've treated me."

"How's that?"

"Like they wish I'd never been born, that I'd just go away, disappear, vanish."

"Why?" Jenn asks and watches Cryssie struggle with the question.

"That's what I'd like to know. I've been asking myself that question for as long as I can remember."

"Have you ever asked them?"

"I wouldn't give them the satisfaction. Anyway, if I did, they wouldn't give me a straight answer. Enough wallowing in self-pity," Cryssie says and sips her wine.

Jenn got a sense from Cryssie's emails of how deeply affected she is by her relationship with her parents, but now she sees firsthand how confusing and painful it is for her. "So, who's coming to the party tomorrow?" she asks brightly to change the subject.

"Bea and Mia, Wellesley friends. Mark and André. They live here in town. Mark's a fashion designer and André teaches at B.U."

"What subject?"

"Spanish Lit. Sarah and Di own a pastry shop on Centre Street. Mary Sheehan and Pru Prescott."

"Who're they?"

"Mary's the Secretary of State and Pru's her chief of staff. They're neighbors."

Jenn raises her eyebrows. "Of Massachusetts?"

"Yeah. Pru's people are rich as Croesus. If you want to be her new best friend, ask her about her family's history. She loves to talk about it."

"I will. They all sound interesting. Should be fun."

Cryssie gazes at Jenn, which is all it seems she's been able to do since the moment she arrived. It's still early for Jenn but late for her and she feels exhausted from having been in such a high emotional state all day. She wants nothing more than to take Jenn's hand and lead her to bed and hold her in her arms while she falls asleep. She yawns and covers her mouth.

Jenn smiles sympathetically. "Go to bed. I'll read awhile."

"Yeah. I think I will."

Cryssie lies in bed in the dark, staring at the ceiling. As tired as she is now, she can't fall asleep. She's savoring the feel of Jenn's good night hug and can't get the image of her sitting on the couch reading her book out of her mind. Having her so near is thrilling and maddening and she knows she won't fall asleep until she relieves herself of all this pent-up sexual energy. How would Jenn's long slender fingers feel fingering her body the way she does the strings of her violin? It's crazy to be jealous of a violin but she is.

* * *

Jenn stands beside Cryssie in the kitchen, waiting for people to arrive and listening to Bea tell them about her and Mia's upcoming trip to France and Spain. Jenn sips her wine and studies the two young women. They're both dressed in tees and jeans and sneakers, and they both wear their hair cut short and no makeup, like Cryssie. Bea is boyishly good-looking with dark brown hair and Mia cute with sandy hair, and they have personalities to match. Of the two, Bea does most of the talking and Mia stands beside her with her arms around her waist and her chin resting on her shoulder, gazing at her sweetly with doe eyes.

Mary and Pru arrive and join them in the kitchen. Mary looks to be in her mid-forties and maybe fifteen years older than Pru and strikes Jenn as looking very Irish, like the Kennedys. Her blonde-streaked light brown hair looks expensively coiffed and ready for the cameras. She's dressed conservatively in a crisp white dress shirt, navy slacks and navy equestrian slip-ons. Pru's also dressed conservatively in a pink dress shirt, navy pleated skirt and navy flats. Her brown hair is close cropped, which makes her round face seem even rounder. She's quick to laugh and when she isn't speaking, she smiles pleasantly. Pru strikes Jenn as the perfect partner for a politician. Mary offers her assessment of what's happening in the Middle East and North Africa, that it's really the beginning of the end of the European colonial period since the despotic regimes were put in place by the European powers and propped up for decades to continue to serve their interests. There's no telling how things will turn out, Mary says, but you can bet that State is scrambling to try to stay on top of unfolding events. Listening to Mary, it's clear to Jenn that she aspires to higher office.

Sarah and Di arrive with a box of pastries. Sara looks like one of her own confections, short and round with milky skin, blue eyes and long strawberry blond hair. Di is tall and thin with short spiky black hair. Sara's glasses are gold wire rim and Di's are thick black horn-rimmed. Sara's wearing a white tee and blue bib shorts with white ankle socks and blue sneakers. Di's wearing a black tee dress that falls shapelessly to her knees and thick sole black work boots. Like Bea and Mia, the two young women strike Jenn as complementing each other perfectly.

Mark and André are the last to arrive and based on appearances strike Jenn as a curious couple. Mark is tall and thin with a wreath of black hair, a long face, sharp bird-like features and piercing dark brown eyes. His outfit is all black and body hugging, and she assumes his own creation. André is shorter than Mark and his expression and brown eyes seem melancholy. Maybe it's because he teaches literature day in and day out. His complexion is dark, Mediterranean, and his wavy brown hair is shoulder-length. He looks every bit the academic in his tan plaid sport coat, green and brown check shirt, khaki slacks and burgundy loafers. She's curious what brought these two together from the worlds of fashion and academia, beyond physical attraction. She watches Mark and André saying their hellos to their friends until they finally arrive in front of her, Mark fixing his eyes on hers the way she imagines a hawk fixes its on a field mouse's.

"This is Jenn," Cryssie says.

"Delighted," Mark says and takes Jenn's hand. He looks down and studies her long slender fingers. "I hear you're a violinist. I'm sure you're very good."

"I play pretty well," Jenn says.

"Don't be modest," he says matter-of-factly and studies her face. "Do you model?"

She laughs and shakes her head. "No."

"You should. You're gorgeous."

She feels herself blush. "Thanks."

"My husband André."

André takes Jenn's hand and bows slightly. "A pleasure. He's right. You should model. Your beauty is fresh, unique." He looks at Mark. "Like Kaj's."

"That's what I was thinking," Mark says, still studying Jenn's face and now with narrowed eyes.

"Who's she?" Jenn asks.

"He," Mark says, "a Dane we met in Patagonia. We're connoisseurs of beauty."

"Ah, well, I'm flattered," Jenn says nervously. She glances around and notices that everyone in the kitchen is following her exchange with Mark and feels uncomfortable being the center of attention and completely unprepared to deal with a personality as intense as his.

"Thank your parents," Mark says, again matter-of-factly.

The idea that she should be thankful to her biological parents for anything blindsides her emotionally. She thought she was long past the feelings of anger and resentment at their having abandoned her and now here they are again, overwhelming her. She looks at Cryssie and sees she knows she's in desperate need of being rescued.

"It's too crowded in here," Cryssie says, taking Jenn's hand and leading her to the living room, where they're joined by the others, carrying drinks and wine bottles and trays of hors d'œuvre and pastries from the kitchen, and soon enough several groups form and as many conversations are underway.

Cryssie sits perched on the arm of Mark's chair, the alert hostess at the ready. She surveys the scene and tunes into the various conversations. Mark and Sarah and Di are bemoaning the current state of the economy and the affect it's having on their businesses. Bea and Mia are discussing their travel plans with André and he's giving them suggestions about places to visit and restaurants to eat at in Barcelona, his hometown, and Madrid, where he studied and received his Baccalaureate before coming to the States. Jenn's telling Mary and Pru about sightseeing in Boston today and Mary laughs and says she's never taken a duck boat tour on the Charles River, and maybe as Secretary of State she owes it to the Commonwealth to do it, on her own dime, of course.

Jenn asks Pru about her family's history and Cryssie gazes at Jenn as Jenn listens attentively to Pru's story about how her ancestors came over on the Mayflower and built a shipping business importing potash from Canada, and then carrying more lucrative cargo, opium, rum and slaves, and added carbon black to the business portfolio in the mid-1800s. Her family used their wealth to back political candidates and support politicians in office who served their interests. It's funny, Pru says, as heavily involved in politics as they've always been, unlike the Cabots and Kennedys, no one in her family has ever had any interest in actually being a politician. They've always preferred to remain behind the scenes and act as kingmakers.

Cryssie's studied Jenn's face so intently from the moment they first met that she can read her well now. She saw Jenn glance at Mary as Pru began telling her story and saw her notice Mary put a hand on Pru's back and look at Pru proudly and admiringly, which she always does when Pru speaks of her family. Cryssie can see Jenn's wondering whether the reason Mary is with Pru is her family's money and political influence, as Cryssie did herself when she first met Mary and Pru and heard Pru's story. In fact, Pru's family lavishes both on Mary and does so for one reason and one reason only: the two women are deeply in love, just as she is with Jenn and wants Jenn to be with her. Gazing at Jenn, surrounded by her friends, relaxed, engaged and enjoying herself is like gazing at the piece of the puzzle that's been missing in her life. She feels a hand on hers and looks down at Mark and sees him looking up at her with those piercing eyes of his.

"Penny for your thoughts," he says.

She smiles and looks at Jenn. "I'm happy."

"I was wondering why you haven't seemed yourself this evening."

She looks down at him and frowns and nudges his shoulder playfully.

As usual, Mark and André are the last to leave. Mark's a notorious lingerer. He brought up the subject of modeling again with Jenn and is insisting that she'd be great at it and should give it a try, that he'd be happy to put her in touch with his contacts in the business and would love for her to model for his ads. Cryssie's relieved when André politely brings the conversation to an end and guide's Mark, now gloriously drunk, to the door and she and Jenn busy themselves cleaning up, Cryssie loading the dishwasher and Jenn retrieving glasses and plates from the living room.

"I like your friends," Jenn says.

"They like you."

"They're an interesting couple."

"Who?"

"Mark and André."

"Mark's a character."

"He reminds me of my friend David. They have the same eyes and the same way of looking at you. André was telling me about what life was like for his grandfather during the revolution and the Franco regime. I realized how little I know about modern Spanish history."

Cryssie watches Jenn head to the living room to collect more things for the dishwasher and the trash. This feels so nice, cleaning up together after a party and chatting about the evening. This is the way life should be, the way she wants to live, with someone she loves and respects. God, how Jenn turns her on! She's doing a good job of behaving herself, but it isn't easy.

Jenn returns, carrying empty wine bottles and puts them in the trash. "Mary invited us to the symphony," she says. "I told her we're going to the Cape. Maybe another time."

Cryssie savors the words "another time." How lovely they sound and how hopeful they make her feel.

Jenn leans against the counter and crosses her arms. "Do you have any straight friends?"

"Yeah," Cryssie says, closing the dishwasher and turning it on and looking at her. "Glass of wine? I'm having one."

"Sure."

They sit across from each other in the living room and sip their wine. Cryssie's content just gazing at Jenn, but she can see Jenn has something she wants to talk about and can pretty much guess what it is, given her question in the kitchen. She also sees Jenn's reluctant to begin the conversation. Well, they have to have it sooner or later so better sooner. "I'm bi," Cryssie says.

"I thought you might be." Jenn looks down at her wine. "I'm not really into women or men. I have women friends and men friends, but they're just friends."

"Do you enjoy sex?"

Jenn nods and shrugs. "Just not with other people I guess."

"Have you ever?"

"Once. I was curious. I figured I should find out what it was all about. It wasn't a pleasant experience."

"Guy or girl?"

Jenn smiles. Cryssie would ask. "Guy."

"Wow! One bad experience and you gave up?"

Jenn looks at Cryssie uncertainly. She was about to share something with her but caught herself and takes a moment to consider carefully. If she does, she'll give Cryssie just the opening she knows she's been hoping for and she's not sure she's ready for what will likely happen. If she doesn't, she'll keep Cryssie at a safe distance emotionally and she's not sure she wants to. Cryssie's just sitting there, waiting patiently, but clearly eager to hear what she has to say. It seems silly now, holding back like this. "Sex isn't the only way two people can express love and affection," Jenn says cautiously.

Hearing this thrills Cryssie. It's like the front door to Jenn has suddenly swung wide open. She tries her best not to let her excitement show. She doesn't want to scare Jenn off and knows that if she shows her the way she feels right now, she'll run screaming back to California. "How else?" she asks as calmly as possible.

Jenn looks down at her hands and shrugs. "Holding hands, hugging, cuddling."

Cryssie takes a deep breath. "Can we?" She sees Jenn look up at her, still uncertainly, and search her eyes for what seems a long time as she considers her answer. Finally, Jenn smiles and pats the seat cushion beside her. "Goodie!" Cryssie cries and leaps up and scampers over and snuggles against her. "This is more like it," Cryssie says and takes Jenn's hand in both of hers and looks in her eyes. "You're okay with me having feelings for you? You're not afraid of me?"

Jenn shakes her head.

"Good," Cryssie says and rests her head against Jenn's shoulder. She wants to tell Jenn she's never felt so happy but doesn't. It would only overwhelm her. She knows she must let Jenn feel her way along in their relationship. They have a week together, so she's content to let her take her sweet time doing it, for now anyway.

"What's it's like," Jenn asks, "being attracted to both sexes?"

Cryssie lifts her head and looks in Jenn's eyes. "Normal, natural." She rests her head back against Jenn's shoulder. "Let's sleep together. I'll behave. I promise."

They lie in bed in their tee shirts and underpants and cuddle in the dark. They can feel each other's warm breath against their faces. "G'night," Jenn whispers.

"G'night," Cryssie whispers, "sweet dreams." She brings her lips to Jenn's and kisses her softly and thrills at the feel of Jenn's lips pressing back against hers. She watches Jenn turn on her side with her back to her and gazes at her in the darkness. She lies awake and waits until she hears by the sound of Jenn's breathing that she's drifted off and then slowly snuggles against her. She smells Jenn's hair and the skin on her neck and shoulder, breathing in deeply as she masturbates and bites her lip to keep from making noise as she climaxes. She's thankful to be here, in bed with her love and tells herself it's okay this way, for now, anyway.

* * *

They drive along the spine of the Cape on Route 6 toward Provincetown and Jenn has the feeling they're on a journey to the end of the world. As the miles go by, the land bordering the two-lane highway continues to narrow until they reach the top of a rise in North Truro and see the highway and sand dunes ahead, with Cape Cod Bay on one side and the Atlantic on the other and Provincetown in the distance with the Pilgrim Monument rising above the town. Jenn read that the monument was built to commemorate the arrival and stay of the first European settlers in New England and the signing of the Mayflower Compact, and that it's the tallest all-granite structure in the country. From a distance this picturesque seaside town seems an unlikely place to be home to an

LGBT community. Maybe it's because it's located at land's end, far from prying eyes in Boston. She's eager to see what life is like here.

They spend the days like happy tourists, whale watching, taking long walks on the beaches and visiting the shops on Commercial Street. Their favorite is Shop Therapy, with its exterior covered with psychedelic paintings and filled with sex toys and drug paraphernalia and off the wall postcards. At day's end they enjoy seafood dinners in cozy restaurants and drinks afterward in lively bars featuring over the top female impersonators. Afterward they stroll slowly hand in hand back to their room at the inn, open a bottle of wine, draw their chairs up to the picture window and sit side by side, holding hands and gazing out at the moonlight shimmering on the bay. Tonight is their last in P-Town and they're treated to a spectacular sight as the full moon slowly descends toward the horizon in the southwest, finally touching the bay and sinking out of sight in a blaze of light.

"That's amazing," Jenn says softly. "I've never seen anything like that."

"Neither have I," Cryssie says. "Maybe it's a sign."

Jenn hears the sadness and worry in Cryssie's voice and looks at her. "What do you think it means?"

"That everything ends, no matter how beautiful."

Jenn squeezes Cryssie's hand. "You would think that."

"Why wouldn't I? You're leaving." Cryssie sighs and leans her head against Jenn's shoulder. "It sucks."

They snuggle in bed in the dark, Cryssie thinking about Jenn's departure. She feels like a prisoner on death row, facing execution in the morning. Her time is running out and there's nothing she can do to forestall the inevitable. At least they're here together now. Concentrate on now. "You masturbate, right?" Cryssie asks and isn't surprised by Jenn's silence.

"Yeah," Jenn finally says.

"What do you think about when you do?"

"I dunno…lying in a beautiful peaceful place…a meadow filled with wildflowers."

"You don't think of someone?" Cryssie sees Jenn shake her head. "Would you now, with me?"

With the moon gone Jenn can barely see Cryssie's face in the darkness, but there's just enough light from the street to see the longing in her eyes. It's a sweet romantic idea, a way for them to be intimate without physical contact, which she knows is why Cryssie suggested it, in deference to her. Masturbating was the farthest thing from her mind. Could she? She realizes the more important question is shouldn't she? Cryssie's been so good about behaving herself all week and is obviously miserable about the prospect of her leaving tomorrow and wouldn't it really be the right thing to do? After all, they'd just be masturbating together. She settles on her back and closes her eyes. "I dunno...I'm not sure I can with you here...I'll try."

Cryssie lies with her head on the pillow and watches Jenn slowly move her hands beneath the covers. "Where are you?" Cryssie asks and draws back the covers so she can watch Jenn touching herself. She can just make out Jenn's frown.

"Shhh," Jenn says, caressing her breasts through her tee shirt and arching her back slightly and squirming her hips. "On a beach...lying in the sand...listening to the waves."

Cryssie thinks of their walk to Jeremy Point in Wellfleet. With no one around they stripped and lay side by side in the sand. She couldn't take her eyes off Jenn's body. "Jeremy Point?"

"Shhh," Jenn says. Jeremy Point was nice. She didn't mind Cryssie admiring her body. In fact, she was flattered and kind of turned on by it. It was a new feeling, as so much of what she's felt on this trip has been. She's not thinking of Jeremy Point now, though, or any other place on the planet. She's in that private place in her mind she goes to when she pleasures herself, a warm sandy beach like Jeremy Point but different, where only she exists.

Cryssie caresses herself and watches Jenn slide her hand down along her stomach and inside her underpants. She sees Jenn's legs part and watches her hand as she strokes herself and her other hand caressing her breast and hears Jenn's breathing quicken and become deeper. She's never wanted anything more than to touch Jenn right now, but what will happen if she does? Will Jenn let her? Will she freak out? Will it end their relationship? At this point she feels she has nothing to lose. She's already going to lose Jenn tomorrow when she gets on that plane. She has to close the final distance between them and show Jenn how she feels. She reaches down and places her hand lightly on Jenn's and feels her body stiffen. She kisses Jenn softly on the cheek and waits and finally feels her relax a bit and when she does, wraps her fingers around Jenn's wrist and slowly guides her hand out of her underpants to between her own legs and places her hand between Jenn's.

"It feels strange," Jenn whispers.

"It's just new, different," Cryssie whispers and sees Jenn's face turn toward her and her eyes searching hers and she searches Jenn's and they both seem frozen in the darkness, neither taking her eyes off the other's and neither moving her hand. "I want to make you come," Cryssie whispers. "I want us to come together."

"I'm not sure I can, or that I can make you come."

"Don't worry about me. I will when you do." Cryssie brings her lips to Jenn's and kisses her softly, keeping her lips on hers as she slowly strokes her between her legs. She feels Jenn's hand resting motionless between her own legs. Just having her hand there is enough and the fact that she hasn't taken it away is encouraging. She concentrates on touching Jenn as lightly as possible as she strokes her, brushing the insides of her thighs with her fingertips. She feels her part her legs a bit more. Good. Go slowly. Don't rush.

Jenn closes her eyes and tries to return to that private place in her mind but can't. Her entire being is now focused on the movement of Cryssie's hand between her legs. It feels good but at the same time like an intruding foreign object. She wants to give herself over to the pleasure of it but the fact that it's someone else's hand doing the pleasing, or trying to, is preventing her. It's beyond frustrating. It's maddening.

She thinks she knows what's at the bottom of her problem with intimacy. It's always in the back of mind, where she's managed to keep it until now. Having been abandoned once she didn't want it to happen again. She couldn't do anything about it the first time and decided early on that the best way to prevent it from happening again was to never put herself in the position of trusting someone's feelings for her, no matter how deep they seemed to be. She did a good job of walling herself in emotionally and everyone's left her alone, except Cryssie, who's been relentless in her pursuit of her.

She remembers what Cryssie said about the moon, that maybe it was a sign that everything ends no matter how beautiful. Jenn heard the worry in Cryssie's voice, worry that she's the one who's going to be abandoned. Jenn takes a deep breath and tries to concentrate on the feel of Cryssie's hand against her skin. Cryssie's being so gentle and her hand does feel nice and the way she's brushing the hair on her mound as she strokes her feels nice too. Jenn can tell Cryssie wants to be more passionate in her lovemaking but is holding back, handling her carefully like she's that porcelain statuette she told her she reminds her of. Is she really that delicate, that fragile? She realizes her hand has been between Cryssie's legs all this time and she's been doing nothing to please her. She begins stroking her and feels her push harder against her hand. "Look at me," she hears Cryssie whisper and opens her eyes and sees her gazing at her.

"I want you here, baby, with me," Cryssie whispers, "not somewhere else. I want to see your eyes when you come."

Jenn gazes at her as they stroke each other. Cryssie's expression is so sweet and her eyes so filled with love. Jenn realizes that no one has ever looked at her this way. It's the look of someone who wants her so badly she'd do anything and give everything to be with her. She feels her climax approaching and when it comes, her orgasm is deeper and stronger than any she's ever experienced. She can't keep her eyes open any longer and holds Cryssie's hand tightly, breathing in deeply and blowing out slowly and watching the pinpoints of light exploding on the insides of her eyelids. There seem to be thousands of them, and they remind her of sparklers on the Fourth of July. She feels Cryssie's body snuggling against hers and her cheek pressing against her shoulder and opens her eyes and sees her looking at her gratefully.

"Thank you, baby," Cryssie whispers, "that was amazing."

"Yeah…it was…and scary."

"Scary?"

"Letting someone get that close."

Cryssie nods. "I know the feeling." She strokes Jenn's cheek with a finger. "I feel as much like an orphan as you do, baby. Maybe that's why we found each other, so we can take care of each other."

Jenn smiles at the thought. Two orphans alone in the world, taking care of each other. She has no idea where things go from here, but in the moment it doesn't matter. All that matters is being here together. "I love you," she hears Cryssie whisper. It's the first time someone other than family has said that to her. She knows what they mean when they say it, and she knows by the sound of Cryssie's voice that she means something entirely different. She feels like she's on a high wire. It's dizzying and exhilarating and she's afraid she'll fall at any moment but lying here beside Cryssie she thinks maybe she can maintain her balance. "I love you too," Jenn whispers and feels Cryssie squeeze her and press her face against her neck and then feels the warmth of her tears on her shoulder. She listens to the low rumble of the distant surf and tries not to think about tomorrow and knows Cryssie's doing the same.

* * *

They're running late from the Cape and the road leading to Jenn's departure terminal at Logan is jammed. Cryssie eyes the State Trooper in his blue uniform and black Sam Brown belt, jodhpurs, black over-the-calf boots and peaked cap. The State Police in Massachusetts remind her of jackbooted Nazis and seem to act like them too. The Trooper walks toward them along the line of parked and double-parked vehicles. His expression is stern and he's pointing at drivers and motioning them to move on. Cryssie drives to the far end of the terminal and pulls to the curb in front of two State Police cars.

Jenn looks back at the Trooper. "Maybe we should park in the lot."

"We don't have time. Anyway, the cops are busy back there."

"I don't want you to get a ticket."

"Don't worry."

They walk back toward the terminal entrance and pass another Trooper, standing beside an unattended car, writing a ticket. He glances up at Cryssie and nods toward her car. "That yah cah, Miss?"

"Yeah, I'll be right back."

"If you leave it unattended," he says, "it's gonna get ticketed and towed."

"Let's move it," Jenn says anxiously.

Cryssie glances back at the car. "I'll risk it."

The Trooper looks down at his ticket book and continues writing. "Suit yahself."

They stand on the sidewalk by the Skycap station, holding hands and gazing at each other's eyes, Cryssie trying her best not to get teary. "I wish you could stay," she says.

"I wish I could too," Jenn says. "This has been an amazing trip. You're turn next. Come visit me this fall at Stanford."

Cryssie nods. "I love you."

Jenn wraps her arms around Cryssie and kisses her and whispers in her ear, "I love you too. Thank you."

"Think of me," Cryssie says, stepping back and wiping her eyes with a finger.

"I will. Promise."

"You better get going."

Jenn grabs the handle of her roller bag and turns to go. "I'll call when I get back," she says over her shoulder.

Cryssie nods and watches Jenn walk quickly toward the automatic doors. She waves at Jenn when she glances back over her shoulder again and feels alone and lost the moment the doors close behind her and she's gone. Cryssie turns and walks toward the far end of the terminal and glances at the stern-looking Trooper, standing in the road, pointing at drivers and motioning them to move on. She sees her car is still parked in front of the two police cars, so at least she didn't get towed. She doesn't see anyone at that end of the terminal and assumes she didn't get a ticket, either. She's not far from her car when a door to the terminal adjacent to the parked police cars opens and a Trooper, this one wearing a campaign hat, walks out and over to her car, taking out his ticket book and a pen as he does. She quickens her pace. "Hey!" she shouts, breaking into a trot. The Trooper glances at her, looks back down at his ticket book and begins writing. She arrives in front of him and stands facing him with her hands on her hips and holds out an upturned hand toward the ticket book. "What are you doing?"

"Citin' yah, Miss," he says without looking up. "Yah cah's unattended and pahked illegally."

She glances back at the Trooper in the road at the far end and sees him looking over his shoulder at her. Did he call him? The son of a bitch probably did. "I was right there! You saw me! You had to give me a fucking ticket?" She sees the Trooper's jaw clench and his eyes narrow.

"Just doin' my jahb, Miss."

She watches him finish writing the ticket, rip it out of the book with a flourish, walk around to the front of her car and tuck it under the wiper blade. He walks toward the police cars parked behind hers and she walks quickly to her car and grabs the ticket. "Fucking cops," she mutters. "Pahdon?" she hears him say. She gets in and looks in the rear-view mirror and sees the Trooper sitting behind the wheel of the car directly behind hers. She should have listened to Jenn and parked in the lot. The Trooper was right. He was only doing his job. She has to stop taking out her anger with her father on every male authority figure. It would be so much easier if Jenn were here. She's so calm and levelheaded, the opposite of herself. Fuck! She rests her forehead on the steering wheel. The fall seems such an impossibly long way off. She hears a loud angry sound burst from the Trooper's car and looks in the rear-view mirror at the flashing blue lights and slowly pulls away with the Trooper right behind her. The fall — Fuck! She'll never make it.

CHAPTER 14

Consuela's Quinceañera

Dee Dee gazes at Rosa's cousin Consuela, transfixed by the sight of her seated in an ornate chair on a draped platform at the front of the hotel function room. Dressed as Consuela is in a billowing white satin gown with ruffled sleeves and wearing a silver necklace with a cross pendant and a sparkling headpiece, she looks like a beautiful young princess on a throne. Consuela's flanked on the right by fourteen Maids, representing her first fourteen years, all cousins, Rosa among them, wearing bright blue gowns, and on the left by her Honor Chamberlain, her older brother, and the Maids' fourteen Chamberlains, also all cousins, Petey and Pauly among them, wearing black suits and shirts and bright blue ties. It's an amazing sight.

Dee Dee read about Quinceañera and learned that it's based on a very old Aztec tradition, the Ceremony of Woman, which predates the arrival of the Conquistadors and that the Spanish adopted it as they did most Aztec traditions as part of their effort to Catholicize the native population, just as the Christians adopted pagan rituals and tailored them to suit their own purposes. The Thanks Action Mass in the church earlier was a solemn affair with Consuela kneeling in front of the congregation, holding her white prayer book and rosary beads and bouquet of flowers, which she laid at the feet of the statue of the Virgin of Guadelupe. The Mass was the most important part, but it's clear that everyone's been looking forward to this moment and the party that will follow.

She watches as Consuela's father, looking elegant in his black tuxedo and white ruffled shirt and black bowtie, replaces her headpiece with a tiara and presents her with a scepter. Consuela is now a princess of God and the world with power and authority and responsibility for her life. Together with the scepter she holds the Last Doll in her lap. The doll looks like a miniature version of Consuela and represents the last things she'll think about as a child, now that she's focused on the things of a young woman. The doll is festooned with ribbons, one of which Dee Dee knows Consuela will give as a keepsake to each guest.

Dee Dee watches Consuela's father lower himself to one knee before her and remove her white patent leather flats and gently guide each white-stockinged foot into a white patent leather high-heel shoe, also symbolizing her transformation from a girl to a young woman. He stands and Consuela beams up at him. The guests at the tables stand and clap and shout out congratulations and Dee Dee stands and claps along with them.

She gazes at Consuela and her Court of Honor, posing for photographs, and wonders what her fifteenth birthday will be like? Maybe she'll get together with Rosa and a few friends. Maybe they'll have pizza somewhere, go to a movie, but nothing like this. Why not?

She glances around the room and is reminded that she's the only blonde blue-eyed person present. Do you have to look like Consuela to have a Quinceañera? Is there a rule about it? Anyway, her dad's family is Mexican American so doesn't she qualify? It would be so cool! Her own high heels! She's only seen her mom wear high heels a few times and hers aren't even as high as Consuela's. So what if she only wears the dress once! It would be worth it! She has to make it happen!

The photographer takes the last portrait and Consuela walks on her father's arm to the middle of the dance floor. They pose for photographs and then begin dancing to the music of the First Waltz. Dee Dee watches them moving gracefully together, Consuela radiant and her father looking at her proudly. Dee Dee wonders if her dad knows how to waltz. Maybe he can teach her. It looks pretty easy. The DJ invites the Maids and Chamberlains to join Consuela and her father and now the dance floor is filled with swirling couples, another amazing sight.

The dance ends, the cousins return to their tables and Consuela begins circulating on her brother's arm. Dee Dee watches her admiringly, even though Consuela's walking a little unsteadily in her heels.

"She's so beautiful!" Rosa gushes, sitting beside Dee Dee.

"I'm going to have one," Dee Dee says.

"What?" Petey asks, sitting on the other side of her.

"A Quinceañera."

"Cool," he says.

"She can't," Dee Dee hears an older boy cousin across the table from her say and sees he's frowning at her.

"She's not one of us," he says.

"She is," Rosa says, "part, anyway. Her dad is."

Dee Dee notices the girl cousin sitting next to the frowning cousin make a face.

"If she's Mexican American," the girl says, "I'm Snow White."

"First they steal our land, then they steal our traditions," the frowning cousin says. "They won't stop till they've stolen everything."

"Don't be an asshole, Rafael," Pauly says. "She's a family friend and a guest. You're embarrassing us."

"*Por la raza todo, fuera de la raza nada,*" Rafael says bitterly.

"Cut the bullshit!" Pauly says.

"Come on," Rafael says to the cousins on either side of him and pushes back his chair and stands, "let's have a smoke."

Dee Dee watches them walk away and looks at Pauly. "What did he say?"

"'For the race everything, outside the race nothing.' It's bullshit. Don't pay any attention to him."

"What race?"

"Aztec. He's about as Aztec as the Emperor of Japan."

The remaining cousins laugh nervously.

"He and Teresa and Hector believe in Aztlán," Pauly says derisively.

The word sounds strange to Dee Dee, like something's missing in the middle. She already feels uncomfortable because of the unwanted attention and doesn't want to add the embarrassment of mispronouncing the word. "What's that?"

"Supposedly all the land Mexico sold to the U.S. because of the Mexican American War. You're sitting on it. They want it back."

She stares blankly at Pauly, trying to imagine the possibility of that actually happening.

He smiles. "Don't hold your breath."

The waiter places her salad in front of her as the three cousins return from their smoke and sit across the table. She tries not to make eye contact with them but can't help glancing now and then at Rafael and sees him frowning at her. She's comforted by the fact that she has Pauly to defend her.

She's finishing her dessert when the DJ begins playing another waltz and she sees couples get up and walk to the dance floor and begin dancing.

"Can you dance?" Rosa asks.

"Not like that," Dee Dee says and sees Pauly grinning at her.

"Come on," he says.

She's panic-stricken and feels her cheeks and neck flush. "No, I can't! I don't know how!" She feels Rosa nudge her shoulder. "Go on! Dance!" she hears Rosa say.

"I'll teach you," Pauly says, stepping toward Dee Dee and taking her hand.

She feels herself being gently raised to her feet and led to the dance floor. Her heart is pounding, the room is a blur and she keeps her eyes on the sleeve of Pauly's suit coat. He turns and faces her, takes her hand and places her arm around his waist, then his around hers. She stands stiffly, staring at his chest, waiting for instruction.

"It's easy," he says, "one-two-turn, one-two-turn. Ready?"

She's not at all ready and feels rooted to the floor, but she feels Pauly begin moving and taking her with him.

"Just follow me."

She steps on his foot and stops abruptly, feeling beyond embarrassed.

"It's okay," he says encouragingly.

She feels herself set in motion again and looks down at his feet and begins to see the pattern.

"Good," he says, "just like that. Don't step, glide."

After a few turns she feels confident enough to look up at him and sees him smiling down at her.

"You're a great dancer," he says.

She feels herself blush again. She can only imagine what color her cheeks and neck are now, probably beet red judging from the warmth of her skin. "I'm not," she says, looking up at him shyly. "You're just being nice."

"No, you are. I wouldn't say it if I didn't mean it."

She feels his arm around her waist, holding her gently but securely, and his hand cupping hers. She's really dancing now, anticipating his movements and she's confident enough to look up at him and not worry about stepping on his feet. As they turn, she sees everyone at their table watching them and smiling, everyone except Rafael and Teresa and Hector. Who cares about them? She looks up at Pauly. They aren't that far apart in height and if she were wearing heels like Consuela's, she'd be almost as tall as he is. They're not that far apart in age, either. He's only four years older. He loves to read as much as she does, and she really enjoys talking with him. He's handsome too. She feels warm and happy and doesn't want to stop dancing. She just wants to stay here in his arms, swirling round and round, but the music ends. Pauly smiles at her and escorts her on his arm back to their table and pulls back her chair for her. The dance with Pauly and his gentlemanly treatment of her is like a scene in one of her mom's romance novels come to life. She feels elated and lighter than air.

"You learn fast," Pauly says, pushing in her chair for her.

"You're a good teacher," she says, smiling up at him. "Can we dance again?"

"Sure."

The DJ is playing fast tempo mariachi music now and most of the cousins and younger guests are on the dance floor, hopping around arm in arm, but she and Pauly sit side by side at the table, talking. It's a little difficult having a conversation with the music so loud, but Pauly doesn't seem to notice and she's happy just being here with him, sitting beside him and the two of them close together. There's nowhere else she'd rather be.

She asks him why Rafael feels the way he does and listens as Pauly tells her about the Chicano Civil Rights Movement, *El Movimiento,* that began in the '60s with the goal of empowering Mexican Americans. It's pretty much fizzled out now, he says, but is kept alive by people like Rafael and Teresa and Hector. He's all for empowering Mexican Americans but has no time for extremists like them.

He tells her that he's really enjoying the book he's reading about the Spanish expeditions to Alta California to establish settlements. She knows a little about Gaspar de Portolá and Junipero Serra from her fourth-grade studies and a visit with her parents to the mission in San Juan Capistrano, and now she hears from Pauly that Junipero Serra named Orange County *Valle de Santa Ana* in honor of Saint Anne, the Virgin Mary's mother who was very popular in Spain at the time. The idea that she didn't know this and might never have learned the original name of the place, or the original Spanish name, anyway, if he hadn't told her fascinates and concerns her. What was it called before that, and before that? How many names has it had? How many different people have lived here? It's probably the same everyplace in the world! There's so much to learn and so much she'll never know. She feels overwhelmed and sees him smiling at her with eyebrows raised.

"Wanna dance?" he asks.

She was so engrossed listening to Pauly that she didn't notice the music change and hears the DJ's playing a slow song now. She looks at the dance floor and sees the dimmed lights and the cousins returning to the tables. "Sure!" she says and leaps to her feet and takes his arm and walks happily by his side toward the dance floor. She sees people smiling at them and nodding in their direction and commenting about them among themselves. She doesn't feel at all uncomfortable now being the center of attention. She feels great! He takes her in his arms and she wraps hers around him and presses her cheek against his chest and closes her eyes as they begin swaying to the music. It may be Consuela's Quinceañera but it's her party now!

Sunday, July 17, 2011

Dear Anneliese,

WOOHOO!!! You wouldn't believe how much fun I had at Rosa's cousin Consuela's Quinceañera!

It lasted all day. We started off in church and when I arrived and saw Consuela, I couldn't believe how beautiful and grown up she looked! I wore my black dress and pumps and my mom did my hair in my "grown up" style. She did my makeup too. I looked pretty good but nothing like Consuela! She was dressed all in white and looked like a princess!

After church we went to a hotel for the Quinceañera ceremony. It was pretty amazing. It was like watching Consuela grow up right before our eyes! Then we had dinner, and I can't wait to tell you about the dancing!

I sat with Rosa and Petey and Pauly and some of their cousins. There were four tables of them! Most of them were in Consuela's court. The girls all wore blue dresses and the boys wore black suits and shirts and blue ties to match the dresses. They all looked pretty cool.

By the way, yesterday was the first time I saw Petey since the trip to the Grand Canyon. I'm happy to say that he was very nice to me and respectful and I don't hold the way he treated me against him. Everyone deserves a second chance and I know you agree.

So, now for the best part! Pauly asked me to dance! And not just hopping around dancing but a waltz! I WAS TERRIFIED!!! I wanted to run out of the room! I followed him to the dance floor and just waited for him to show me what to do. Of course, the first thing I did was step on his foot! I don't know what the word is that describes being beyond embarrassed but that's how I felt. But he wouldn't let me go and the next thing I knew I was dancing! A waltz! It was so much fun and felt so good and I didn't want to stop, and when we did, the first thing I asked him was if we could dance again! We did, at the end of the party. It was a slow dance and we held each other and I didn't want to let go of him, ever!

You know how much I like Pauly and enjoy talking with him. I don't know how he feels about me, but I know how I feel about him. I really like being with him. He's 16 and I'm 12. Do you think he was just being nice to me? Do you think he thinks I'm just a kid, that I'm too young? Probably, I guess. I don't know. I sure don't feel too young.

Oh, yeah, I almost forgot. There was this older cousin at our table named Rafael and he wasn't at all nice to me. He got mad when I said I wanted to have a Quinceañera. He said that it's only for Mexican Americans, which, of course, I am, partly. Anyway, what difference does it make? I have Jewish friends who celebrate Christmas! I celebrate Hanukkah! What's the big deal? I'm going to ask my mom and dad if I can have one. It would be SO COOL!!! I'll keep you posted.

Yours, Dee Dee

P.S.: Pauly told me that the Spanish originally called where we live Valley of Saint Anne in honor of the Virgin Mary's mother. If he hadn't told me, I might never have known. It freaks me out when I think how much there is to know and that I'll never be able to know everything, even with the Internet.

P.P.S.: My mom's going to have Matt from work do a portrait of me. I have to think about what to wear. It would be neat if I could wear a Quinceañera dress!

* * *

"In a half mile," the female-sounding voice says, "continue straight, on Newport Boulevard." Kate's always amused by the odd way her car's navigation system pronounces things. She imagines a time when you won't be able to tell the difference between a person speaking and a computer or for that matter a person and a computer, but hearing this unnatural-sounding voice, that time seems far off.

She glances at Dee Dee, who's listening to music through her earbuds with her eyes hidden behind her wraparound sunglasses and her makeup and hair done just as they were for Rosa's cousin's Quinceañera. Dee Dee says she thinks it makes her look more grown up and she's right. She's looking more grown up all the time lately.

Kate glances over her shoulder at the garment bag on the back seat. Dee Dee chose the dress for her portrait: cobalt blue chiffon cut low on the bodice with thin shoulder straps. Watching her at the store, standing in front of the three-way mirror modeling the dress and studying herself Dee Dee seemed less a kid and more a young woman. She's at that age now where things begin changing quickly and Kate suspects her exploration of sex with boys has begun and probably did on the trip to the Grand Canyon. There was just something about her that was different when she returned, and it wasn't just the fact that she'd begun her period. Kate's not worried about her. Dee Dee has a good head on her shoulders and Kate knows she'll come to her if she has questions or needs advice.

Thinking of the dress reminds her of Dee Dee's desire to have a Quinceañera. Kate laughed when Dee Dee said she wanted to have one, but when she thought about it the idea made complete sense. After all, Dee Dee is part Mexican American and Ed's sisters had one. She'd just be carrying on his family's tradition. "In a quarter mile, destination is ahead, on the left."

Kate looks around the studio and notices the white cube against the wall. She walks over to it and looks down at it. It's the one Matt's model, whoever she was, posed on. It feels odd being here with him. Except for the Getty, her only experience with him has been at work. He's always been polite and respectful, but now she realizes how little she really knows about him. She remembers her reaction to the black and white photos, that they seemed almost pornographic. They were his doing, so he must be into that stuff. What was that photo session like? How did he feel, looking through the camera at the model as he photographed her? What was going through his mind? How did he feel? What type of man is he really? She sits on the white cube and watches Matt and Dee Dee check out the different backdrops, each a different color abstract design.

"Dressing room's over there," Matt tells Dee Dee. "Get into your dress and we'll see what works best." He walks over to Kate, stops at a distance and stands looking down at her. He can't help imagining what she'd look like posing nude on that cube. He imagines pretty good.

She looks up at him, her hands resting on the sides of the cube, feeling the sharpness of its edges against her palms. "Who was the model?"

"Friend of mine."

"Girlfriend?"

"Sort of, not really."

She looks down at the edges of the cube and pats them. "She couldn't have been very comfortable on this thing."

"Actually, that was kind of the point. I didn't want her to be comfortable. I wanted her to be aware of the hardness and deal with it."

Kate remembers her impression being that the model seemed to be struggling against constraints. "Were you punishing her?" She surprises herself, asking such a personal question, and feels herself blush. It was out before she realized what she was saying and now wishes she could take it back.

He laughs. "Good question. Maybe subconsciously." "All set," he hears Dee Dee say and turns and sees her standing by the dressing room door in her dress. He studies her and an idea comes to him. He walks to the backdrops, raises them and places a stool in front of the white wall. "Have a seat," he says and Dee Dee settles onto it.

Kate stands and walks over and positions herself off to the side where she can observe both Dee Dee and Matt as he works.

He removes the camera from the tripod and test fires the strobes. "Any hobbies, Dee Dee? Into sports?"

"I play soccer at school. I really love to read."

"Yeah? What's your favorite book so far?"

"Anne Frank's *Diary of a Young Girl.*"

"I've read it. Really something."

"What do you like to do, bedsides take photographs?"

"Surf." He smiles at her wide-eyed reaction to hearing this.

"Cool! I so want to learn to surf!"

"You'd love it. I'd be happy to teach you."

"Really?" She looks hopefully at her mom.

Kate glances nervously from Dee Dee to Matt. "I dunno. It's nice of you to offer. I don't want to impose." She hates being disingenuous. Of course, it would be great for Dee Dee to learn to surf, but she's having difficulty with the idea that teaching her means Matt would become more involved in her life beyond work and she's not sure how she feels about it. Her immediate reaction is that it's not such a good idea, which seems foolish. They're talking about Dee Dee learning to surf, for God's sake.

Matt moves around Dee Dee with his eye to the viewfinder, studying her from different angles. "All you'd need is a wet suit. We can surf tandem on my board until you get the hang of it. You can swim, right?"

Dee Dee nods and looks pleadingly at her mom.

"You're sure it's no trouble?" Kate asks.

He glances at her and smiles. "Yeah."

"Well, okay. Thanks," she says, still feeling uneasy.

Dee Dee beams at her mom and then Matt. "Awesome!"

"Okay," he explains, "I'm going to talk to you while I shoot, you know, move your head this way or that."

"Okay," she says eagerly.

"Great. Just keep looking straight at the camera, right at the lens, and don't let the strobes flashing throw you."

"I won't."

"Good." He frames her from the chest up. "Stay just like that, facing the camera and hold your head up just a little more. Good. Sit up straighter. Arch your back a bit. Good. Okay, imagine you're surfing for the first time." There's that beaming smile again. "You're standing on the beach in your wet suit, looking out at the waves rolling in. See 'em?" She nods and narrows her eyes a bit and peers at the camera. "You see that not all the waves are the same. About every seventh one is bigger. See it?" She nods. "You put your board in the water, lie down on it and begin paddling out. Great. Chin up a little. The water's cold, but your warm in your wet suit and you paddle up and over the waves until you get far enough out and turn your board around. You lie there, looking over your shoulder at the ocean, waiting for your wave." She's looking at the camera lens, but her eyes aren't focused on it now. She's looking through it and past it at the approaching waves. "Not this one, not the next one, and then you see it." Her eyes widen and she raises her eyebrows and parts her lips slightly. "Good. It's getting closer now. You can see it getting higher. You're timing it. You feel it lifting you up and moving you forward and you stand on your board and get your balance." There's a hint of uncertainty in her expression and he knows she's wondering if she can really do that. "You're riding along the face of the wave now and it feels like you're flying." He can see she likes that idea. "It's just you and the wave, all the way in." He looks up from behind the camera and sees she's still on her board, riding her wave, confident and strong. He smiles at her, and she looks up at him dreamily and smiles and he can see she's not fully returned from her imagining. "All set."

"How'd I do?" she asks.

"Great. You can change."

Kate watches her hop off the stool and walk quickly toward the dressing room and turns her gaze back to Matt, who's standing with his back to her, reattaching the camera to the tripod. She watched him the entire time he was photographing Dee Dee, watched the way he moved his body, bending and tilting to get just the right angle. He has a nice body and a nice butt and that's what she was looking at mostly and what she's gazing at now. "It was fun watching you work. You were great with her."

He turns and sees her raise her eyes to meet his. Was she looking at his butt? He's pretty sure she was. It seems totally out of character for her and for the first time he thinks of her solely as a woman and not as a manager at work. "Thanks. The trick is staying out of the way, just letting people to be themselves."

That's why those candids he took at the Getty look so good. "Yeah. I can see that. Everything okay at work?"

"I'm giving notice."

She starts and tries to maintain an expression of no more than curiosity, but it feels forced and the skin of her face tight. She's sure she looks ridiculous and that he can see right through her, the way her mom always did when she was a kid and had gotten into some mischief or other but swore she hadn't. Her mom would look at her and shake her head and say, "Honestly, I don't know why you even try." It's her eyes. They always give her away. "Really? Why?"

"Dieter has a web development business. It's really taking off. He asked me to take over managing the store. No benefits, but that's okay."

"We'll miss you." She's sure he can see through that comment too. People come and go in retail all the time these days. A month after he's gone few people will remember him and only one person will truly miss him and she's sure he knows who that person is. She feels completely differently now about his offer to teach Dee Dee to surf. She's relieved and happy that he did.

* * *

Kate and Dee Dee sit side by side at the desk in Dee Dee's bedroom, slowly going through the photos on the computer screen. Matt put both color and black and white versions of the portraits on the CD and the black and whites remind Kate of photos she's seen of elegant models and movie stars that once appeared in *Glamour* and *Vogue*. They're beautiful and unforgettable, even more so than color photos.

Looking at the progression of photos, Kate sees an interesting and subtle change occur in Dee Dee's expression. It takes on an increasingly dreamy and ethereal quality until in the last one Dee Dee seems there but not there, like a radiant spirit. It really is amazing how Matt was able to tune into Dee Dee and connect with her and she with him. That's when Kate began looking at him differently and admitted to herself that she was attracted to him and gave herself over to her desire to admire his body, and especially that nice butt of his, and welcomed the idea of letting him get closer to her.

"Wow, these are great," Dee Dee says softly.

"They are. Which is your favorite?"

Dee Dee clicks on the black and white version of the last photo to enlarge it.

Kate smiles. "Mine too. The one in color is beautiful, but this one's more interesting I think."

"Yeah, I do too," Dee Dee says and looks at her mom. "He's really nice. Do you like him?"

"Yeah. He's nice."

Dee Dee narrows her eyes slightly. "You know what I mean."

Kate glances at her and looks at the photo on the screen. "We hardly know each other."

"I think you like him."

"Yeah? What makes you think so?"

"The way you were looking at him."

Kate feels herself blush. Did Dee Dee really notice her looking at him? She probably did. She's a keen observer and doesn't miss much. What must she think of her?

Dee Dee grins. "See? You're blushing! I knew it! I think he likes you too."

So, they've arrived at a new place in their relationship as mother and daughter. Kate's always interested in hearing what Dee Dee has to say, but never more so than now and she knows what she's about to hear is important. "Why?"

"The way he looks at you and smiles. You should smile more. You have a pretty smile."

Dee Dee's right. She's had a lot on her mind lately and especially the situation with Ed. Kate glances at her and sees her looking at her expectantly.

"So?" Dee Dee asks.

"What?"

"Why don't you do something together? You know, go on a date? You'd have fun."

"He hasn't asked."

Dee Dee rolls her eyes. "He's just shy, like you."

Reserved, yes, and maybe a bit guarded, but shy? Well, maybe she's right. They are kind of the same thing. "I'm older than he is," Kate says and can see by Dee Dee's expression that she knows she's finding reasons and making excuses not to have fun. It feels like their roles have reversed and she's the kid, waiting eagerly to hear her daughter's advice and knowing it will be encouraging.

Dee Dee shrugs. "So what? He likes you."
Kate laughs and tousles her hair.
"What?"
"You," Kate says and chucks her under the chin. "You're too much."
"Well, ask him! You'd have fun!"
Kate looks at her tenderly. "I'll think about it."
Dee Dee studies the photo. "Good, just not too much or too long."

Saturday, August 27, 2011

Dear Anneliese,

Mom and I looked at the photos Matt took of me and they're all great! We both like the black and white version of the last one the best and that's the one we're going to use for my portrait. I can't believe how good I look! I know you know I'm not being conceited.

Matt's a really talented photographer. I told you that he's going to take me surfing with him soon. I CAN'T WAIT!!! I know he and my mom like each other. I talked with her about it this afternoon when we were looking at the photos. I told her she should go on a date with him, and I could tell she wanted to. He hasn't asked her, of course, because he's shy, just like her, so I told her to just ask him! Why not? She still might not, though. I'm going to talk with Matt about it and see how he feels. I know. I'm playing matchmaker! Why not? If I don't, those two might never get together and that would be a shame! I know they'd have fun together!

Yours, Dee Dee

* * *

Kate lies in bed, her legs together and arms straight by her sides, staring up at the ceiling. She hasn't done this in a long time. She can't even remember the last time she did. She's felt flustered emotionally and filled with sexual energy ever since the photo session and even more so since her conversation with Dee Dee. She's been alone for so long and has been content to be that way, or thought she was until she found herself staring at Matt's butt and felt desire stirring in her for the first time in ages. She'd almost forgotten how it feels.

She closes her eyes and moves a hand to her breast and the other to between her legs. Why not go out with Matt? It would be fun to do something together, just the two of them, have dinner, see a movie, take a long walk on the beach, in the evening, maybe find a spot and sit and watch the waves roll in, listen to the surf. That would be nice, just the two of them.

She parts her legs and arches her back a bit. They'd sit side by side in the sand, gazing out at the ocean. Maybe they'd talk, maybe they wouldn't, wouldn't want to or need to. Maybe he'd reach over and take her hand. That would be nice. She hasn't held someone's hand in a long time. Maybe he'd move closer and put his arm around her. That would be nice. Maybe he'd put his hand on her cheek and turn her face toward his and look in her eyes and bring his lips to hers. She hasn't been kissed in ages, either. Maybe he'd put a hand on her breast, just as hers is now, and caress it, just as she's doing now. When was the last time someone did that? She'd welcome it and encourage him to do more.

She squirms and digs her butt deeper into the bed. Maybe he'd lay her back on the sand and lie next to her. That would be nice. Maybe he'd move his hand from her breast to between her legs and stroke her, just as she's stroking herself now. She'd put her hand on that nice butt of his, the way she was thinking about doing when she was staring at it during the photo session. She'd move her hand to between his legs and they'd lie there, kissing and stroking each other tenderly, just the two of them, oblivious to everything around them, lost in giving each other pleasure. She'd forgotten how good it feels to bring herself to climax and then lie with her eyes closed, feeling content and happy the way she does now. As good as it was, she knows her orgasm would have been harder and stronger and lasted longer had they really been Matt's hands pleasing her.

She opens her eyes and stares at the ceiling. What is she thinking? She's old enough to be his mother.

CHAPTER 15

Shirin

Jenn smiles as she looks around at the lights strung in the trees bordering the beer garden near campus and back at Sharon and feels thankful to have made her first friend at Stanford on her first day here. They both arrived with their dads in the armada of cars and pickups and vans and liked each other the moment they met. They chatted while they spent the day moving their things into their dorm rooms, unpacking boxes and getting their rooms into some kind of shape. Jenn guessed correctly that Sharon's Iranian. She's attractive with wavy black hair, coppery skin and hazel eyes. She's from Irvine and her dad's a physician who teaches at UCI School of Medicine.

"My name's actually Shirin," Sharon says. "I got tired of people mispronouncing it and decided to just go with Sharon."

"It's a beautiful name. Does it have a meaning?"

Sharon rolls her eyes. "Take your pick: 'sweet,' 'pleasant,' 'gentle,' 'delicate.' It's a very girly Iranian name. What about yours?"

"Welsh, a derivative of Guinevere, you know, King Arthur's queen. It means 'smooth' and 'fair.' It was one of the most popular girls' names when my folks named me. I'm forever meeting Jennifers."

"Ah. It suits you. Since we're the first friends we've made, why don't you call me Shirin and I'll call you Gwen? It'll be our little thing."

Jenn's immediate reaction to the idea is that being called Gwen would feel strange, but she knows she's reacting the way she is because it's new and different. Isn't that what being at university is all about, experiencing and embracing the new and different? She smiles. "Sure. Why not? But you may have to tap me on my shoulder."

"Why didn't you go to UCI? It's a great med school."

"I considered it but decided on Stanford. I wanted to start fresh someplace, you know?"

Sharon nods. "I do. I love my family. We're very close. You probably know there's a big Iranian community in Irvine. I felt like I was living in a bubble."

"Do you have family in Iran?"

"Yeah, in Tehran."

"What's it like for them?"

"Like life everywhere. It's what they know and they deal with it. My aunt and uncle visit now and then. The first time they came they went to Disneyland. They loved it! Whenever they come they visit a different theme park. I think for them theme parks are the perfect antidote to the dreariness and oppressiveness of life in Iran under the mullahs. So far Disneyland's their favorite. I'm not into theme parks."

"Neither am I. I've been to Disneyland and Knott's Berry Farm once. That was enough."

"Yeah. I prefer national parks. I go to Joshua Tree sometimes."

"Never been there."

"Really? I love that place! It's so beautiful! I climb there."

"I knew you were into something. You're in great shape."

"I also play soccer and swim. Have you ever been to Yosemite?"

"I haven't."

"Neither have I. Would you like to go sometime? It's not that far from here."

"Sure. That would be fun."

"Maybe Columbus Day weekend."

Jenn shakes her head. "I have a friend coming to visit."

"Maybe he'd like to go."

"She...I dunno...maybe."

Jenn's uneasiness makes Sharon think this person is more than just a friend, and also that Jenn's confused about her feelings. "A friend?" Sharon asks delicately.

"Yeah, Cryssie."

"Tell me about her. What's she like?"

Where to begin? "Complex. She resents her parents' wealth but accepts their financial support. She feels unloved by her parents and I think what she wants more than anything is to be loved, but she's wary of people and keeps her distance. Outwardly she's tough, but inwardly she's emotionally needy." Jenn wishes she hadn't said that last part and winces mentally. It feels like a betrayal. "She's bisexual."

"She sounds complex, all right," Sharon says and grins and narrows her eyes slightly. "Are you two just friends? I get the feeling you're more than that?"

"More I guess."

"And you're not sure how you feel about it?"

Jenn shakes her head. "I'm asexual, at least I think I am. I visited her this summer and we were intimate. It was a wonderful experience, but scary. I felt so exposed and vulnerable. I'm adopted. I have abandonment issues."

"Ah. Do you distrust her feelings, or do they scare you?"

"Scare me. I'm still afraid of being abandoned, but I've come to realize that's not the issue. The issue is I'm afraid of disappointing her. She feels things so deeply. I'm not sure I'm enough for her, that I can satisfy her."

Sharon smiles. "Well, Gwen, you'll never know unless you try."

Jenn laughs and shakes her head. She's sure she'll never get used to being called that. "I know. That's what I'm afraid of. How about you?"

"No one at the moment. It's funny. I'm straight, but listening to you made me think of my best friend Sandy. We grew up together and we're still close friends. When we were kids, we used to walk holding hands or arm in arm and we still do when we're together. We kiss each other on the lips. We don't give it a second thought."

Jenn's phone rings. She takes it out of her bag and sees it's Cryssie. It's late there. "Hi!"

Cryssie smiles at the sound of Jenn's voice and moves her hand from her breast to between her legs. "Hi, baby. All moved in?"

"Yeah," Jenn says and glances at Sharon. "How are you? Where are you?"

"In bed. Columbus Day weekend seems a long way off. I miss you, baby."

Jenn stands and mouths, "Be right back," and Sharon nods.

"Where are you?" Cryssie asks.

"At a beer garden near campus with a friend," Jenn says, walking to the sidewalk. "We met moving in. Her room's next to mine."

"It is?"

Jenn hears the envy and worry in Cryssie's voice. "We just met, Cryssie. We're friends."

Cryssie stops stroking herself, opens her eyes and stares at the ceiling. "What's her name?"

"Sharon."

"What's she look like?"

"Attractive…in great shape."

"I just wanted to hear your voice. I think about you all the time, baby."

"I think about you too."

"You do?" That sounds encouraging and Cryssie begins slowly stroking herself again.

"Yeah," Jenn says. It's a white lie. The first time she pleasured herself after the trip she began by imagining Cryssie lying beside her and that they were her hands doing the pleasing, but she couldn't keep her image in her mind's eye and found herself returning to that beautiful peaceful place where she's alone.

"Talk to me, baby," Cryssie says.

Jenn knows why. "About?"

"Anything…what you're wearing."

"Gray hoodie over a white tee, jeans and sneakers. It gets cool here in the evenings."

"I know. Nice."

"Yeah, nice and sweaty. I haven't showered."

"Even better. If I were there, I'd lick you clean."

Jenn knows she would too. She can hear Cryssie panting and pictures her lying there in the dark with her eyes closed, the phone pressed to her ear, stroking herself. She remembers vividly how Cryssie sounded as she approached orgasm in P-Town and hears her making the same urgent cries that sound like a mixture of agony and ecstasy and they reach a crescendo and then there's silence.

"Phew!" Cryssie finally says. "Thanks, baby. I needed that. I can't wait to see you and hold you in my arms and kiss you all over."

The desire and longing in Cryssie voice makes Jenn wonder again if she has it within herself to give her what she wants and needs. She thought she did in P-Town. It seemed she was able to please her, despite her own hesitancy and awkwardness, and satisfy her, but maybe she wasn't, not completely. Maybe Cryssie's hoping she has more to give emotionally and sexually and is just being patient with her. She doubts she does or that it will ever be enough. She stares at the evening sky. She's lived in an emotional cocoon so long, feeling safe, as if protected by the closed petals of a flower. The petals suddenly opened in P-Town, but she's felt them slowly closing again ever since and now she doesn't know if she wants them to continue closing or open again.

"I'll let you get back," Cryssie says softly.

Jenn can hear her reluctance to let her go and sadness at having to and feels awful for her. "Sweet dreams."

"Love you."

"Love you too. G'night."

Cryssie puts the phone on the nightstand, rolls over, wraps her arms around the pillow and hugs it, imagining it's Jenn. She feels momentarily satisfied physically, but not emotionally and certainly not mentally. Her mind is churning. She's sure Jenn feels like she's being smothered. She could hear it in her voice. She's been worrying about that a lot lately in their phone conversations. It's the last thing she wants to do to Jenn, but she can't seem to help it.

Sharon, huh? Attractive…in great shape? Cryssie pictures an Amazon with sparkling blue eyes and creamy white skin and flowing blonde hair every bit as beautiful as Jenn. It just isn't fair. Here she is three thousand miles away and Sharon can see Jenn anytime she wants.

She's a lucky girl. She has no idea how lucky. They've only just met. Of course, they're just friends. Still, Cryssie knows she'll obsess about Sharon. She's too tired to now and just wants to fall asleep with her arms around Jenn, or what passes for her.

Cryssie pictures herself and Jenn sitting by the window that last night in P-Town, holding hands and watching the full moon disappear in a blaze of light. It really was a magic moment, and she's lately convinced herself it was a sign they belong together. She's always resisted hoping about people, but not now, not about Jenn. Hope is all she has.

CHAPTER 16

Dee Dee Learns to Surf

Matt and Dibs wait in their wetsuits on the wall by the beach volleyball courts by Huntington Beach Pier, their surfboards propped up beside them. The gray marine layer hugs the coast and Matt notes with a photographer's eye how one-dimensional the two couples in bathing suits and tee shirts playing volleyball look in the flat light. One of the women dives to make a save and manages to pop the ball up for her partner, who spikes it into their opponents' court.

"Gnarly," Dibs says.

Matt smiles. Dibs's comment sounded as flat as the light, but that's about as enthusiastic as Dibs ever sounds. He was clearly impressed.

"Older is good," Dibs says.

"She has her act together," Matt says.

Dibs nods. "Nice change of pace."

"I'll say," Matt says and hears Dee Dee say, "Hi, Matt!" and turns and sees her walking toward them. "Hey!" he says and waves. She's wearing flip-flops and a hoodie over her wet suit and has her braids fastened at the top of her head to keep them off her face when she's in the water. He sees she's eager and ready. Kate's right behind her, dressed in a tee shirt and shorts and wearing running shoes. She has her hair pulled back in a ponytail through her blue sailing cap and looks younger and even more attractive with her hair that way. He and Dibs stand and Matt smiles as he sees Dee Dee eyeing Dibs curiously, which isn't surprising given Dibs's appearance. His body is pear-shaped, his skin is so pale it's almost white, his eyes are pale blue and he wears round wire rim glasses. The sides of his head are shaved and the curly blonde hair on top of his head spirals out in all directions. He's a curious sight, all tight.

Kate admires Matt as she approaches. That body of his looks even better in a wet suit. "Hi, Matt."

"Hey! This is Dibs."

"Hey," Dibs says with a lazy wave.

"Nice to meet you," Kate says and looks at Matt. "I thought I'd go for a run while you guys surf. Okay if I'm back in, say, an hour?"

"Sure."

Kate gives Dee Dee a hug. "Have fun!" she says and jogs off toward the boardwalk, waving back at them.

Matt watches her go, admiring the movement of her body and the way her ponytail sways behind her.

Dibs leans close to Matt's ear. "Dude, she's totally hot."

Matt smiles. That was pretty much off the "Dibs chart" for being impressed. He picks up his board and turns to Dee Dee. "All set?"

She grins up at him and nods.

"Good. Let's go." He puts an arm around her shoulder and looks down at her as they walk across the beach toward the water. "I know most of the guys out there. They're good guys, but you're a newbie, so they're probably going to razz you. Don't let it get to you."

"I won't," she says firmly and feels a pat on her back and looks up to see Dibs smiling down at her. She likes him and the way he looks, kind of goofy, reminds her of someone, but she can't put her finger on whom.

Matt stops at a spot near the water's edge but safely out of reach of the surf. "Leave your stuff here. It'll be okay."

She steps out of her flip-flops and removes her hoodie and tosses it on the sand.

Dibs heads toward the water with his board and Matt kneels and fastens the Velcro strap around his ankle, tethering him to the board. He stands and looks down at Dee Dee and grins. "Read, surfer girl?"

"You bet!"

They wade out into the surf and he puts the board in the water. "You lie down in front as far up as you can get and paddle," he tells her. "Spread your legs, so I've got room."

She climbs onto the board and Matt lies down behind her and they begin paddling out. The smell of salt in the air fills her nose and she can taste it. The water feels cold on her hands and feet, but she's pleased to find that the wet suit really does keep her body warm. She had her doubts. They come up on a couple of guys sitting on their boards, chatting and bobbing on the waves.

"Hey, Matt! Who's your new girlfriend?" one of them asks, grinning.

She smiles at him and waves and looks back over her shoulder and sees that they're far from the shore now. It feels like another world out here. She looks up and sees the people above them on the pier, some walking, some standing, leaning on the railing, watching the surfers, some just staring out at the ocean. The world now seems divided into two groups of people: those on the water and those on land. Most people prefer to stay on land and never venture out on the water. She used to be one of them, but now here she is, a member of that small group of people who are excited to be in water well over their heads. The feeling is thrilling and also a little scary, but it's a fun kind of scary. When they're far enough out, they sit straddling the board facing each other.

Dee Dee's expression looks wonderful to Matt, filled with excitement and anticipation and he wishes he had a camera with him. "Pretty cool, huh?

"Yeah." She looks around at the surfers. "Why are there only guys out here?"

"Lots of girls surf but, yeah, mostly guys. It's good that you're learning. This is your home beach now. We need more girls in the water. Okay, there are a few rules that are important to remember. Surfing can be dangerous. You've got all these people in the same spot. They could be experts or newbies, like you, but they're all on surfboards and I guarantee you don't want to get hit in the head by a surfboard and you don't want to hit anyone. So, it's really important to be aware of other surfers and look out for them."

She nods. "Got it."

"The most important rule is don't take off in front of someone else. The person who takes off nearest the peak and catches the wave first has the right of way. I've seen some pretty ugly fights happen because someone broke that rule."

She nods again. "Got it."

"You noticed when we paddled out, we stayed away from other surfers. Always do that until you're more experienced. Remember, you're a newbie. See all those guys over there?

She looks at the spot Matt nodded toward, where most of the surfers are.

"That's the best break right now. We're gonna stay away from the crowd while you're learning. So, here's what you do. Lie in front of me on the board and when we catch the wave, stand up and put your arms out. I'll hold you. Just concentrate on trying to maintain your balance." He grins at her. "Okay, let's do it." He turns the board around facing shore and they both lie flat, looking back over their shoulders. "See it?"

She sees a wave a few waves back, higher than the others and feels a thrill. "Yeah."

"Let's catch it."

She watches the wave approach, rising higher as it does and now it's right behind them and begins lifting them up.

Matt jumps to his feet and they begin moving forward along the face of the wave. "Okay!"

She jumps to her feet and loses her balance and before Matt can catch her goes head over heels into the water. She's submerged and the feeling of having nothing beneath her with the bottom a long way down is terrifying. Her instinct is to begin clawing her way to the surface as quickly as possible, but she fights it and holds herself back. She knows if she's going to surf, she can't be scared of this and has to get used to it. She feels the fear and panic subsiding and her body buoyed up by the water. There! She's not sinking, and she can swim to the surface whenever she wants. She can't see much under the water, but as she turns, she comes face to face with a harbor seal, suspended in front of her and staring at her. The seal's expression looks curious and a bit concerned. She feels

Matt's arm around her waist, pulling her to the surface and she watches the seal dart away and quickly disappear in the murkiness.

"You okay?" Matt asks. "I thought you could swim."

Dee Dee treads water and nods as she gasps for air and blows water and mucous out her nose. "I can. I was scared and didn't want to be."

He smiles. "Come up next time."

"I will," she says and looks toward the pier. "I saw a seal. It was right in front of me."

Matt scans the waterline beneath the pier and spots a seal with its head out of the water, looking at them. "That guy?"

"I think so."

"He's got your back now."

Dee Dee lies on the board, looking back over her shoulder, feeling frustrated as they wait for their wave. Once? Okay. Twice? Maybe. Three times? That's one too many. She was able to maintain her balance better and stay up longer each time, but now she's determined to ride the wave all the way in. She sees it rising up and coming closer and feels that same thrill of anticipation. She feels the board begin to rise as Matt jumps to his feet. He doesn't have to tell her when to stand now and as soon as she sees he's up and balanced, she jumps to her feet and holds her arms out. This time the board feels steadier under her feet and she feels Matt remove his hands from her waist. She's confident and knows she has it this time. It feels like she's flying and she beams as they ride across the face of the wave until it subsides and they settle in the water. She raises her fists over her head and shouts louder than she ever has, "Woohoo!"

She hears a shrill whistle coming from the pier and turns and sees the person whistling is a man with a red bandana around his head, wearing a white tee shirt and baggy blue shorts. He's leaning on the railing with one flip-flopped foot up and pointing at her, and when he sees he's made eye contact pumps his fist in the air and whistles again. She waves at him.

"Wow!" Matt says. "Props from 'Jet Ski!'"

Dee Dee looks back at Matt. "Who's he?"

"Big wave surfer."

"How big?"

"Fifty feet, more." Matt smiles as Dee Dee's eyes widen and her jaw goes slack and she turns and looks back at 'Jet Ski.'

Dibs wades up to them with his board under his arm. "Hey, surfer girl, caught your last ride. Awesome."

Hearing this from Dibs, who Dee Dee's seen is a really good surfer, fills her with pride and she feels her heart pounding. He holds out his fist to her and she bumps it with hers and beams at him. "Thanks!"

"Later," Dibs says with a lazy wave.

Dee Dee watches him wade toward the beach. "He's really nice. Is Dibs his real name?"

"Dilbert," Matt says. "His folks are engineers. They named him after the comic strip character."

That's who he reminds her of! Dilbert! They're a lot alike.

Matt glances toward the beach and sees Kate sitting on the sand beside Dee Dee's things with her knees up and hugging her legs, watching them. She smiles and waves and he smiles and waves back.

Dee Dee follows Matt's gaze to the beach and sees her mom sitting there, smiling and waving at them and looks back at him. "One more," she says.

They paddle out and she knows now just how far out they need to be to wait for the wave, and when they reach the spot she pulls herself up onto the board and straddles it, facing Matt. "Can I ask you something?"

"Sure," he says, curious why she's suddenly so serious.

"Do you like my mom?"

"Yeah. She's nice."

Dee Dee narrows her eyes a bit. "You know what I mean."

Matt knows just what she means, but is surprised by the question and searches for what he thinks is the right thing to say.

She studies his eyes as he struggles to answer. "I think you do. I know she likes you."

He's relieved Dee Dee spoke first. "Yeah? What makes you think so?"

"The way she looks at you when you're not looking, and acts around you. You act the same way around her. You're both a little goofy in your own ways."

He laughs. "Yeah, I guess we are."

"Why don't you ask her out? If you wait for my mom to ask, it'll never happen. She's shy, just like you." Dee Dee sees him smile and shake his head the same way her mom did. "What?"

"You," Matt says, "You're too much. Maybe I will."

"Good. Let's go."

Kate stands as they wade toward the shore, brushes the sand off the seat of her shorts and looks proudly at Dee Dee. "Wow! You were great!"

"Thanks," Dee Dee says. She picks up her hoodie and puts it on, steps into her flip-flops and walks between her mom and Matt toward the parking lot.

"She's definitely got the hang of it," Matt says. "She needs her own board."

"You'll have to tell me what to get her," Kate says. "I know nothing about surfboards."

"Sure." He looks down and sees Dee Dee looking up at him, rolling her eyes toward her mom.

"Thanks for teaching her," Kate says as they arrive at her car. "I really appreciate it."

Matt smiles. "It was fun. I'll email you some info."

"Great. I'll look for it."

He looks down at Dee Dee. "I'll let your mom know when I'm going out again. You're welcome to come anytime."

"Thanks," Dee Dee says and rolls her eyes toward her mom again.

"See ya," Matt says and turns to go, but turns back and looks at Kate. "I was wondering," they both say, startling each other. They freeze and stare at each other a moment. Kate puts a hand to her mouth and laughs and Matt laughs and glances down at Dee Dee and sees her smiling up at him and looking very pleased with herself.

Saturday, September 3, 2011

Dear Anneliese,

I went surfing for the first time with Matt yesterday! It was AWE-SOME!!! I knew it would be! I've wanted to learn to surf for so long and Matt was really nice to offer to teach me. We both used his board. It's called "tandem" and we were the only people surfing that way. It seemed kind of strange to me that I was the only girl there. Matt said lots of girls surf, but you'd never know it.

Anyway, the first time I tried to stand up on the board I fell off! I felt like such a dork! I got the hang of it after a while and by the end of the day I could stand on the board without Matt holding me. What a feeling! I felt if I could do that, I could do anything!

When I fell off the board I was really scared. I was surprised how scared I was. I mean, I know how to swim and I've swum in the ocean before. I guess it's just that I was so far out and the water was so deep. I figured that if I were going to be a surfer, I couldn't let that bother me, so instead of coming up right away I forced myself to stay under water. Believe me, it wasn't easy! But I did and I wasn't afraid anymore. And get this! While I was underwater, I turned around and there was a seal right in front of me! It was just looking at me like, "What are you doing here? Are you okay?" That was pretty cool.

There was a man on the pier watching us surf. Matt knows him. His nickname is "Jet Ski" and Matt says he surfs waves 50 feet high! Can you believe it? When we got home, I went online and watched videos of big wave surfing. Those people are CRAZY!!! I mean the waves we were surfing were maybe six feet, and they seemed big. It must be like surfing down a cliff! I don't know if I'm brave enough to do it.

Did you know there are rules for surfing? I was surprised to hear there are. I'd always thought of surfing as something wild and free, but I guess there are rules for everything in life.

Yours, Dee Dee

P.S.: I just realized you probably have no idea what I'm talking about, I mean about surfing. Did you ever hear about it or read about it? I think surfing was around back then. I'll do some research and let you know.

P.P.S.: Great news! My mom just told me that she and Matt are going on a date the Saturday after next! She's going to use two of her vacation days so she can have the weekend off! Can you believe it? Am I good or what? I knew they liked each other!

I'm really happy for my mom. She needs to have more fun and Matt's a really a nice guy. Did I mention that he's younger? I can't remember. Anyway, he is. My mom asked me if I thought it made a difference, and I told her I didn't. Really, I don't. What difference does it make if two people like each other? I like Pauly and he's four years older.

* * *

The restaurant was Kate's idea, a trendy new one in Los Angeles she'd read about and has been wanting to try that specializes in gourmet dishes featuring locally raised meat and locally grown produce. The portions are small and expensive, but she and Matt decided to treat themselves on their first date and they both agree it's well worth it. She savors another mouthful of the pork belly, kimchi, peanuts and chili soy dish and watches Matt take another bite of the quail fry with grits, maple jus, cooked chard and slab bacon dish.

The Huntington Museum in San Marino was Matt's idea, which she welcomed. She'd been to The Huntington once before long ago and looked forward to revisiting it. She was impressed by Matt's knowledge of fine art as they walked through the galleries and he commented on the paintings.

They strolled through the Japanese garden and visited the Botanical Garden to look at the titan arum, the gigantic pitcher-shaped plant with an enormous phallus-like spathe sticking up out of it. It's indigenous to the rainforests of Sumatra and is called the "corpse plant" because it smells like rotting animal flesh when it's in bloom, which it isn't now, so no putrid smell. Apparently, when the first one bloomed at The Huntington in August of 1999, nearly seventy-six thousand people lined up to see it. There are several offspring now and more chances to see one in bloom. They agreed to keep an eye on the blooming schedule and come back with Dee Dee when one is.

Kate shared with Matt on the ride up from Orange County a bit about what's going on in her life, mainly her concern about Ed and Rita's relationship and the affect it's having on Dee Dee, who no longer wants to stay at her dad's, at least not for now. Kate was reluctant to talk about herself at first and it felt strange doing so. She's always been a private person and realized how used to being alone she's become and how little she shares about herself with anyone, and it felt good to open up and unburden herself. Matt's a good listener.

"More wine?" Matt asks.

Kate glances at her almost empty glass and nods.

He looks for their waitress and sees she's occupied at the moment. He'll keep an eye on her and looks back at Kate. "Marriage just didn't work out, huh?"

She could let it go at a simple no, but it seems like a good opportunity to share something important about herself with him. "He was unfaithful."

Matt sips his beer and thinks of Cyn and her husband. "Some people don't seem to have a problem with it."

"I'm not one of them," Kate says and sees him smile and nod. "So, what was your girlfriend like? Amber, right?"

"Spoiled rotten. I think she hates men."

Hearing this so surprises Kate that she laughs and covers her mouth with her napkin and shakes her head. "Sorry. I didn't mean to laugh. So, what were you doing with her then? I mean I know she's beautiful."

Matt catches the waitress's eye and signals for another round. "I dunno. I'd never met anyone like her before. I was intrigued."

"How long were you together?"

"Not long, three or four months."

Kate studies him. He's young and a little naïve about women, but she knows that his having been intrigued by Amber doesn't really have anything to do with his age. What is it about men and women like that?

Look at Ed. Rita's not spoiled rotten and she doesn't hate men, but she's trouble in her own way. Kate saw it the first time she met Rita and she's certain Ed saw it too. She'll never understand what makes men want to punish themselves by getting involved with women they know aren't good for them. Well, enough about that. "Brothers and sisters?" she asks.

"A sister, Jenn. She's at Stanford. Going to be a doctor."

"Good for her."

"You?"

"Only child."

"Did you miss having siblings?"

"Not really. I liked being the center of attention." She sees he's surprised to hear this for some reason and is curious why and looks at him questioningly.

"Seems out of character," he says.

"Really? That's interesting."

"You don't strike me as the type of person who needs a lot of attention."

"I don't? How do I strike you?"

"I dunno, reserved, a little guarded."

"Huh." Just how she views herself. She remembers Dee Dee saying that Matt's shy and that if she waited for him to ask her out it would never happen. He is shy. They both are. In fact, their personalities and temperaments strike her as very much alike. She thinks she has a pretty good idea now how he perceives her, perfectly content being alone, not needing anyone else in her life. If that were really case, she wouldn't be sitting here across the table from him, but he doesn't know that and has no way of knowing unless she shows him. She's not sure how to do that yet. Then there's the age difference. She's not sure how he feels about that. He's very respectful of her, perhaps a bit too respectful. Is it because he feels like he's on a date with an older woman friend? "I don't sound very exciting."

He smiles and picks up his menu. "Let's get a couple more dishes."

She picks up her menu and stares at it without reading and thinks about lying in bed, masturbating and fantasizing about him. It was so easy to give expression to her feelings then, alone in her bedroom. It's not so easy now, sitting across the table from him.

"The rock cod dish looks interesting," he says without looking up.

"It does...," she muses. She's never pursued anyone. She's always been the one pursued. It's not that she's proud of the fact, it's just that she's always considered the idea of a woman pursuing a man to be unseemly and a man pursuing a woman to be the way things naturally should be. She studies him over the top of her menu as he studies his. She's not so sure now. Looking at him feels a lot like looking at herself. He's no more a pursuer than she is. It's clear that if she doesn't give him some sign of her interest in him beyond friendship, that's how they'll remain, friends. There's nothing wrong with friendship, but she wants more. She's not sure what, but more.

"What about the foie gras?" he asks, glancing up.

"Let's try both," she says, puts down her menu, drains her glass and looks at him and smiles. "I'm so glad you offered to teach Dee Dee to surf. When you told me you were leaving the store, I was afraid we might not see each other again." There's that easy smile of his and that brightening of his eyes again. It's such a sweet expression and when she sees it, she wants to take him in her arms and cuddle, for starters, anyway.

"You're the reason I left."

She's surprised to hear this. "I was? Why?"

"I knew you wouldn't have gone out with me as long as I was working there."

"You were thinking of asking?"

"I was, toward the end."

She's flattered and delighted to hear this and feels herself blush. She looks at him a little sadly. "You're right. I wouldn't have. It would've been a shame, huh?"

He nods. "Yeah, a real shame." The waitress places Kate's glass of wine and his glass of beer on the table and collects the empty glasses. Matt picks up his glass and holds it out to Kate and smiles. "Cheers."

She smiles warmly and picks up her glass. "Cheers," she says and wants to add, "Here's to us," but doesn't.

She listens on the ride back to Orange County as Matt describes the campground in Ensenada. The place sounds beautiful, on a hill, overlooking the Pacific. It's a great idea. "I'd love to go!" she says. "I haven't been camping in ages! It'd be fun!" It would be fun. They'd stop at Trestles on the way down so he and Dee Dee could surf. Kate's heard about Trestles and knows it's a Mecca for surfers in San Clemente. She's never been there. It would be nice to finally see the place. She used to go camping with her family and always enjoyed it and Dee Dee loves camping too. Dee Dee's never been to Ensenada, but Kate was once, with Ed on a cruise from Long Beach before Dee Dee was born. They walked all over the city and ate in some great seafood restaurants and danced in bars to live music in the evenings. It was fun, but she knows it would be even more enjoyable and a totally different experience with Matt.

She remembers the look on his face when they left the restaurant and were out on the sidewalk and she held out her hand to him. His expression was a mixture of surprise and relief that she'd made the first move. She used to love walking hand in hand with her dad when she was a little girl, and when she went on her first date with a boy when she was twelve, she did the same thing, held out her hand to him. The boy took it reluctantly and was so uncomfortable that she politely let it go. Bobby liked holding hands and they used to walk that way all the time. She thought Ed would be a hand holder and was surprised to find he isn't. She hoped Matt would be and was delighted when she saw that easy smile of his and that brightening of his eyes when she held out her hand and he took it and held it firmly, proudly it seemed as they walked to his Jeep. It sure didn't feel like he was just being deferential to the wishes of an older woman friend.

He pulls into her driveway and she can hear Sharianna's voice in her head urging her on: "Do it, girl!" She doesn't want the evening to end and with Dee Dee at Rosa's, it doesn't have to. How to keep it going is the question. She drank more wine at dinner than she has in years and a port afterward and the espresso they had before leaving had no affect on her whatsoever. She feels elevated and uninhibited. She could throw herself at him, if it comes to that. She doesn't think it will and looks at his hand on the gear shift as he puts the Jeep in park and then at his lips and then his eyes and sees him looking at hers. "Well," they both say, startling each other and sit laughing and shaking their heads. "Would you like to come in for a beer?" she asks.

"Sure."

The handful of bottles of Dos Eques in the bin at the bottom of the fridge have long been reminders of Ed she's been meaning to get rid of but hasn't gotten around to and now she's glad she hasn't. She takes out two bottles, opens them and hands one to him.

They walk to the couch in the living room and sit, Matt at a respectful distance, which she finds disappointing and gazes thoughtfully at the framed black and white portrait of Dee Dee, looking dreamily inspired and confident, hanging above the fireplace as she sips her beer and considers what her next move should be. She tries to bring the two images she sees of Dee Dee, one slightly above the other and both drifting, together and is finally able to, but with difficulty. She's tipsy, all right. She can't remember the last time she had this much to drink.

She's not sure what to do next and notices out of the corners of her eyes that Matt's taken something out of his shirt pocket. She looks at him and sees his questioning expression and is surprised to see he's holding up a joint. It brings their age difference to mind again. The last time she smoked pot was with Ed, years ago, shortly after they were married. Matt would have been just a little older than Dee Dee then. Ed brought a bag of it home, saying that a buddy at work had given it to him. She always suspected it was purloined contraband. Cops will be cops. It was her first time doing drugs of any kind. She was afraid of them when she was a kid and, ironically, the fact that Ed was a police officer gave her the courage to try. She discovered to her and Ed's surprise and his delight that smoking pot made her incredibly horny. They had fun working their way to the bottom of the bag, but he never brought any home again and she never asked why.

"Smoke?" he asks.

"Sure. I haven't in a long time." She smiles and narrows her eyes. "I have to tell you, though, if I do, I can't promise I'll behave myself." No sooner has she said this than she can't believe she actually did and knows that it's only because of the alcohol and her suppressed inhibitions. She sees him smile and feels happy she did now.

"Why on earth would I want you to?"

Hearing this and seeing his expression, she feels relieved and delighted and excited and proud of herself that she managed to pull it off. She's a rookie seductress and had her doubts that she'd be able to. She watches him take a lighter out of his shirt pocket, light the joint and offer it to her. She takes it and draws the smoke deep into her lungs and hands it back to him. She holds her breath and feels her tipsiness replaced by a feeling of expansiveness and growing horniness.

They pass the joint back and forth and now she can't take her eyes off his lips. He looks at what's left of the joint in his hand and around for something to put it on and gets up and walks to the kitchen.

She watches him go, staring at his butt and then the empty kitchen doorway until he reappears, holding a small plate, and then his crotch as he walks toward her. She sees he sits closer to her now and watches him put the plate with the joint on it on the coffee table, sit back and turn toward her and put an arm on the back of the couch behind her. She gazes at his lips and puts her hand on his forearm and squeezes it gently. She leans slowly toward him as he does toward her and she feels his lips on hers, softly at first, then harder as she presses harder.

Bobby and Ed were both good kissers, but there's something about Matt's kiss that feels different. It's as though he can read her completely through her lips, see and understand everything about her. It's a curious and wonderful feeling. She draws back her head and sees that easy smile appear and that brightening of his eyes and takes him by the hand and leads him to the bedroom.

She kneels, naked, rummaging through the bottom dresser drawer where Ed used to keep his sweaters and she now keeps hers, together with other miscellaneous items. She knows they're in here somewhere. She remembers seeing them but where are they? She can feel Matt's eyes on her back the same way she did the first day they met when she was walking away. She must look ridiculous, and he must find this pretty amusing, watching her searching frantically for a condom. He should have had one with him.

There they are! She takes one, closes the drawer, stands and turns and sees him grinning at her. She shows him what she hopes looks like a stern expression, walks to the bed, sits next to him and looks down at him as she tears open the wrapper. She's never put a condom on a man before but wants to put this one on Matt. "Bad boy," she says. "See what you put me through?"

"Sorry about that."

"Humph. Don't let it happen again."

"I won't. Promise."

She nods and shows him the hint of a smile. "Good." She takes out the condom, tosses the wrapper on the nightstand and places it on him and tries to unroll it but it won't. She glances at him and sees he's enjoying watching her bungling.

"Turn it over," he says softly.

How stupid. She turns it over and unrolls it. She doesn't feel like an older woman now. She feels like an inexperienced schoolgirl encountering a man for the first time. She's never wanted a man the way she now does Matt and never taken matters into her own hands the way she is now. She realizes she's been unrolling the condom for some time now. She got lost in gazing at his penis and feeling its firmness and warmth as she stroked it. It reminds her of the titan arum's proud-looking spathe, which, not surprisingly, has been on her mind ever since she saw it.

It occurs to her that she's only made love in the missionary position and wonders if she's been a boring partner in the past, if Bobby and Ed really found sex with her satisfying. They seemed to but why not begin things with Matt by experiencing something new? She straddles him and eases him into her, settling down on him. She brings her lips to his and feels again that he's reading her completely and that there's nothing about her he can't see, and it's joined now by the feeling that there's also nothing about her he wouldn't accept or forgive. As strong as her feelings for Bobby and Ed were, she didn't feel with them the same desire to share herself completely, to give herself over entirely that she does now with Matt.

* * *

Kate wakes with a headache, which isn't surprising, given the amount of alcohol she drank and the pot on top of that. She looks at the clock and turns off the alarm just before it sounds, as usual. She looks over her shoulder at the other side of the bed and sees Matt's not there. Did he leave during the night? She doesn't think he'd do a thing like that and if he did, it would be a big disappointment. She's relieved to hear sounds in the kitchen and smell coffee brewing. She hasn't smelled that since Ed left and is happy she kept the can of coffee and box of filters in the back of the cupboard for guests.

She gets out of bed, puts on her robe and shuffles to the bathroom and looks at herself in the mirror. Her eyes are red, her face is a bit puffy and her hair is a tangled mess. She's not so sure now about wanting him to see her like this. She sighs and runs her fingers through her hair and sits on the toilet. Last night felt so good and their lovemaking was so wonderful, their age difference never crossed her mind, but now she's thinking about it again. Well, she is who she is, and this is how she looks in the morning and if seeing her like this doesn't scare him off, they might have a future together.

She shuffles into the kitchen, still running her fingers through her hair, combing out the tangles, and finds him leaning against the counter with a mug of coffee in his hand, waiting for her. She smiles, relieved and happy to see that expression of his she was hoping to see and has come to love.

"Mornin', beautiful," he says.

"Morning," she says, smiling shyly. She shuffles over to him, puts her arms around his waist and looks at him tenderly, watching his bright eyes come closer as he brings his lips to hers. She's never been greeted and kissed like this in the morning. It's wonderful and she imagines what life would be like if every day began this way. She knows it's fanciful but still....

Sunday, October 2, 2011

Dear Anneliese,

I had fun at Rosa's this weekend. Her friends Ana and Flora came over on Saturday afternoon and we hung out in Rosa's bedroom listening to music. I've met them before. They're both nice. Ana's 14 and Flora's 13.

Ana said she's going steady with someone (I can't remember his name) and that she and her boyfriend have smoked pot, marijuana. I don't know if you ever heard of it. It's like tobacco only it makes you feel high. I don't know what it feels like because I've never smoked pot, but I hear it makes you feel kind of goofy and giggle a lot and want to munch on stuff like ice cream and cookies and potato chips and popcorn.

Anyway, lots of older kids and adults smoke it, but fourteen-year-olds? I'm sure Ana's mom doesn't know about it. I'd be really surprised if she did and is okay with it. Ana seems to me to be the type of kid who's just looking for trouble.

We watched "The Incredibles." It's an animated movie about this family of superheroes, each with a different superpower. The dad's called Mr. Incredible and he's really strong. The mom's called Elastigirl and she can stretch her body. The daughter's name is Violet and she can make herself invisible and form this bubble around herself and others for protection. The son's name is Dash because he can run really fast. I've seen the movie before but didn't mind watching it again. It's one of my favorites.

We asked each other what superpower we'd like to have. Rosa thought Violet's was pretty cool. Ana said she'd want to fly and Flora said she'd want to have X-Ray vision, like Superman. I said I'd want to be able to travel through time and they all said that's not a superpower. Well, if that isn't, I don't know what is!

Anyway, they asked me where I'd travel to first and I told them to the Secret Annex, to be with you. They said I was crazy! Why would I want to do that? Rosa's read your diary, but Ana and Flora haven't. They know about you, though, and what happened to you. I honestly didn't know what to say. I didn't know where to begin. But it's true. If I could do it, I'd travel back to be with you. That's what friends are for.

Okay, so here's the REALLY JUICY NEWS!!! When my mom came to pick me up at Rosa's, guess who was with her? Matt! I guess they had a sleepover too! WOOHOO!!!

They told me about their date on the ride home and it sounded like they had a great time together. I can't wait to see this plant they told me about. It's called the "corpse plant" and when it blooms it smells like rotting flesh. GROSS!!! It can't be that bad, though, because thousands of people go to see it. I also can't wait to go on this camping trip to Ensenada, Mexico! Matt said we'd surf at a beach called Trestles on the way that's supposedly one of the best spots around here. That will be SOOO COOOOOL!!!

Yours, Dee Dee

P.S.: I almost forgot to tell you. I saw Pauly at Rosa's and we talked a little bit. It was the first time I'd seen him since Consuela's Quinceañera. I think about him a lot but don't know how he feels about me or whether he thinks about me at all. We had such a good time together at the party. It seems to me he should feel like I'm more than just a friend. Maybe that's just wishful thinking. We'll see.

CHAPTER 17

Therapy

Rita tries to stay focused on her case notes as she waits to see her therapist, but it's difficult. Staying focused has been a challenge ever since meeting with Dr. Kline, her pediatrician, six or so weeks ago. Everything about life has been more difficult, the way she imagines walking through a swamp wearing rubber boots would be. She's never even been in a swamp or worn rubber boots, and maybe that's why the image is stuck in her mind, because it's so improbable, but she knows just how it would feel, the water spilling over the sides of the boots, filling them up and weighing her down, making it almost impossible to move.

"If you weren't pregnant and in the first trimester," Dr. Kline said, "I'd prescribe disulfiram, Antabuse. It has a fifty-percent success rate. It's only prescribed during pregnancy as a last resort, if the benefits to the mother and fetus outweigh the risks to the fetus. Why don't you give AA a try or see a therapist?" Dr. Kline wrote down the name and contact information of a therapist friend on her notepad, ripped off the sheet and handed it to Rita. "Deborah Mattheson's good," she said. "Give her a try."

Rita reluctantly gave AA a try first, just to get Ed off her back. He knew nothing more about it than she did, and she knew he was urging her to try it for the same reason most people faced with having to deal with an alcoholic do, because he was at his wit's end. The experience was every bit as awful as she anticipated it would be.

She was only one of two women present at the meeting. The other woman, Beryl, was an obese, white middle-aged cosmetologist who looked like the Pillsbury Doughboy's twin sister and sat through the meeting with her arms crossed and a sullen look on her face. One of the men was in a rumpled business suit but the others looked scruffy, and most were there by court order for DUI convictions. Rita listened as one by one the group members introduced themselves, admitted to being alcoholics and shared how it had destroyed their lives and why they wanted to stop drinking and stay sober. Listening to the dreary details of these people's shattered lives was depressing. She knew the public confessing was supposed to be therapeutic, but everyone present admitted to having fallen off the wagon, so what was the point, to add humiliation to self-loathing and hopelessness? It didn't make sense to her. When her turn came, she got through the obligatory "My name is Rita and I'm an alcoholic" part of the ritual as quickly as possible and shared as little as possible about herself, and when she left the meeting she was done with AA.

She's met with Deborah a few times, once a week after work. Deborah's nice enough, but Rita doubts her brand of talk therapy will prove any more helpful than AA's. The office door opens and a worried-looking young woman leaves hurriedly without making eye contact. Deborah appears in the doorway and looks at Rita with that now familiar benign expression of hers.

They sit facing each other, Rita with her hands folded in her lap and Deborah with a yellow legal pad and pen in hand. Rita's struck again by how different she and Deborah are in appearance. Rita's so conscious of making herself look as attractive as possible and Deborah, apparently, as plain as possible. The wire rim glasses make her look easily ten years older. She wears no make up or nail polish. Her shoulder-length salt and pepper hair is frizzy and her white shirt and long navy blue skirt look professional, plain and unflattering. The clunky black oxfords don't do anything for her, either. The one thing about Deborah's appearance that intrigues Rita is the small Grateful Dead logo tattooed on the outside ankle of her right leg. She can picture Deborah when she was younger, stoned out of her mind on pot or acid at a Dead concert. Maybe she's still wild and crazy when she isn't sitting here helping people try to get their cloud back in the bottle. She sees Deborah raise her eyebrows slightly, which she always does before asking her first question and the question is always the same.

"So, how was your week?" Deborah asks.

"Busy, as usual."

"How are you feeling?"

"Like shit."

"How's your drinking?"

"In the evening, after work." Why humiliate herself further by mentioning the nips during the day? "Not enough to do any damage, I don't think."

"Well, I'm sure Doctor Kline explained the potential harmful affects to the fetus. You shared with me last week that your drinking began to increase during your first marriage. Let's talk about that a bit more. You and your husband were having difficulties?"

"Yeah."

"Tell me about it."

"I wanted to have children. He said he did but he didn't. He always had an excuse why the time wasn't right. It was a painful realization. Alcohol didn't take the pain away, but it dulled it. It made life bearable."

"So, having children is important to you."

"Yeah. I thought so, anyway. I'm not so sure about having a kid now, though. I can barely take care of myself."

"Did you and Ed plan to have children?"

"It's funny. We never really talked about it. We were hot and heavy into sex. That's how our relationship began and the marriage thing just sort of happened."

"Was the pregnancy planned?"

Rita shakes her head and stares at one of the framed diplomas on the wall behind Deborah. The ornate title and calligraphic lettering seem so artful and precise, so skillfully executed, the work of someone who knows what she's doing, who has her act together, the opposite of her. She shrugs and looks at Deborah. "We stopped having sex, so I stopped taking the pill. I figured why bother? I've gotten sloppy in my personal life."

"How did Ed react to the news?"

There's Ed in her mind's eye, sitting across the kitchen table. She remembers the feeling of relief and surprise at the hopefulness in his eyes and happiness in his smile and gentle encouragement in his voice when he stood behind her and held her and said she had to stop drinking. She's still amazed and mystified by his reaction. "Not at all the way I expected. I thought he'd be angry. It seems he couldn't be happier."

"You mentioned that Ed has a daughter from his first marriage."

Rita nods.

"What's your relationship with her like?"

She wants to lie, but lying to her therapist seems beyond pathetic. "Not good."

"How so?"

"I resent her."

"Why?"

"She's a tie to his ex."

"What's Ed's relationship with his former wife like now?"

Rita searches for the word. "Civil…strained at the moment."

"Do you think he still loves her?"

"I wonder about it. It seems so sometimes."

"You say he's happy about your being pregnant."

"Yeah. It's a funny thing."

"Do you think you'll feel more secure in your marriage if you have the baby?"

"I'd like to think so. I dunno. I don't think Ed's happiness has anything to do with me. It's about the baby, starting out fresh with a new kid. I know he feels guilty about what he's put Dee Dee through."

"She's his daughter?"

"Yeah. Deirdre. I think he sees the baby as a chance to redeem himself."

"That's understandable, don't you think?"

Rita narrows her eyes slightly and studies Deborah's. "Yeah, I guess so," she says, but she's not sure she understands anything anymore, certainly not since receiving the death threat. The world seems like a crazy random place where bad things can happen at any moment, and she imagines those bad things to be big black birds, circling overhead and coming closer all the time. Whenever she tries to make sense of it, she can't and drinks to stop thinking.

* * *

Rita finishes the nip in the car and begins the drive home. At her first meeting with Deborah, Rita felt like a wounded animal that had been dragged into the vet's office and was being poked and prodded by questions, and all she could think as she sat there looking at Deborah was how little Deborah really cared about her well-being, that listening to people talk about their problems is Deborah's job and that if Rita stopped meeting with her, Deborah would simply fill her time slot with another patient. It was unfair and her opinion of Deborah has changed. Deborah's all right. She's only trying to help. Of course, what's at the bottom of it all is Rita's inferiority complex and why she doesn't just tell Deborah that and be done with it she doesn't know. Well, she does know. Deborah would want talk about it, which she can't bring herself to do, which she knows defeats the entire purpose of meeting with Deborah. She's wasting her time and paying Deborah to do it and why she's continuing to do so is beyond her.

For as long as she can remember she's felt like an alien, an outsider, like she's in the wrong color skin. Most of the kids at the grade school she attended in Santa Ana were Hispanic like her. The few White kids were from low-income families. Still, she wanted to be friends with them more than anything. Even though she grew up in a community where most of the people in positions of power were and still are Hispanic, she learned early on who really runs the show in the country: Whites.

She made her first White friend when she was ten years old and her aunt enrolled her in a Saturday modern dance class. "It will be good for you," her aunt told her. Most of the girls were White and none of them attended her school. Daphne was one of them. Rita had never heard the name before. It sounded like the name of a princess in a fairy tale, and she wasn't surprised to learn from Daphne that her namesake was a nymph who was turned into a laurel tree in Greek mythology. Daphne was pretty, blonde and blue-eyed like Dee Dee and extremely shy. One thing Rita's never been is shy and she's always been calculating. She was shameless in her fawning over Daphne, heaping praise on her awkward attempts to execute dance moves, and it had its desired effect. Daphne was overjoyed and thrilled by the attention, and they became best friends in the class.

Rita was surprised and delighted when she received an invitation to Daphne's birthday party. She knew Daphne's family lived in the part of town where people with money live, and she felt like she was being invited to visit another world. When she arrived at the party, she discovered that Daphne had invited only her girlfriends and that she was the only Hispanic. It wasn't anything that someone said or did that made her feel uncomfortable and excluded. It was more what wasn't said or done. After she was introduced to everyone, the other girls paid little attention to her, except to glance at her now and then. She knew what they were thinking. What's she doing here? Daphne was too busy with her party to pay much attention to her, so she was on her own and felt isolated, like she was in a bubble, watching the other girls play games and laugh. She thought of where she lived and her family and friends and community and that all seemed like a bubble too, just a bigger one and she longed to escape it.

She and Daphne remained friends while the dance class lasted, but when it ended so did their friendship. They told each other they'd keep in touch, but she didn't have the courage to call first and told herself that if Daphne really wanted her in her world, she'd call. She never did and Rita's never forgotten how painful it felt to be dumped and how resentful it made her feel toward Daphne and her kind, and she's never gotten over it. The feelings are still there deep inside her, poisoning her.

They were the reason she blamed herself for her marriage to Dan not working, because she wasn't good enough, even though he was a drunk like her and a liar as well. They were the reason she retreated to Ed, one of her kind, and proceeded to make his life a living hell. Why he didn't kick her out long ago is beyond her. She knew he'd gotten to the point where he resented and hated her being in his life, but now she's pregnant and he seems to have had a change of heart. She still doesn't know how she feels about the baby, or thought she didn't. She surprised herself when Deborah asked how she felt about it and said, "I guess it's important to me. Why else would I be here?" It felt like she meant it.

* * *

Ed sits in the unmarked car and eyes the warehouse in the darkness. It doesn't look like the distribution hub of an international drug smuggling operation, as DEA and FBI are now certain it is, but then, that's the point. The agencies don't want to move in yet. They want to let the ants do their work so they can map the network throughout Southern California.

Surveillance can be mind-numbing work, long hours spent sitting and watching and waiting while nothing happens. The point is to be ready if and when something does, so he keeps himself alert, thinking. He pictures Rita, lying on the bed in her red robe, propped up on pillows, watching TV. She undoubtedly has a drink in her hand. It's a familiar picture, one that used to madden him, but he thinks of it differently now, fondly. She's at least trying to curb her drinking, and she is seeing the therapist. She's a proud woman and it took a lot of courage to admit to herself that she needed to seek help. He's proud of her for having taken that step.

It's amazing how her being pregnant has changed his feelings for her and the way he views her and their life together. He'd written off their relationship, but now the prospect of being a father again fills him with hope. He's still having a hard time picturing her as a mother. She'll probably be a good one, though. Boy or girl? Does he have a preference? Not really. He knows what having a daughter is like and Dee Dee's a great kid, but girl's can be a handful when they get to be teenagers, and if it's a girl and she's as headstrong as Rita, there could be real fireworks between them. Well, either way, it doesn't matter to him. All that matters is that the baby is born healthy and Rita's trying her best.

It's funny how the pregnancy has changed the way he thinks and feels about Kate too. He'll always feel guilty about being unfaithful to her and responsible for ending their marriage, but he no longer feels the lingering hope that she still loves him and wants him back, or that being with Rita is settling for second best and that their marriage is a refuge for damaged goods. They have a lot to look forward to now and he's looking forward to their future together as parents.

He had no idea Rita wanted children that badly. When they were dating and talked about having kids, they both said they wanted them, but they haven't talked about it since and having kids has been the farthest thing from his mind lately and hers too, or so he thought. Could he have done what she did, stop taking the pill without telling him to get pregnant? It was a bold stroke, risky and dangerous and he admires her for having had the courage to do it. Thinking about it makes him smile.

He sees headlights on the face of the buildings across the street at the end of the block and a van turns onto the street and comes toward him. It turns into the warehouse parking lot. He sees it's a white windowless van but can't read the license plate. It pulls up to the warehouse door and stops and the door opens. The van pulls inside and the door closes behind it. The Feds know where he is. They're monitoring him by GPS but maintaining radio silence. If he needs backup, which he doubts he will, he'll call for it.

He eyes the warehouse door and thinks about what happens next. It's anybody's guess. This is what he loves about the job, being on the street, in harm's way. It's what attracted him to police work in the first place. He'll miss it when he begins the new desk job, but it's a promotion and better pay and it's all for the best. Anything can happen on the street, and he has a new kid on the way.

The warehouse door opens and the van backs out. He watches it pull out of the parking lot and turn onto the street and waits until it's at the end of the block, then follows it with his headlights off. When they're heading north on Grand in traffic, he turns on the headlights and pulls up close enough to the van to read the license plate, then falls back again and remains at a distance. He follows it heading east on McFadden toward the 55. That's probably where these guys are headed. They're either returning to Los Angeles or on their way to San Diego. Either way, once they leave Orange County, they're someone else's problem.

He sees the entrance to the 55 up ahead and feels the skin on the back of his neck begin tingling and his pulse quickening as the van slows and turns onto a side street a block before it. He knows this feeling. He's been in situations like this before. The important thing is to stay calm and proceed with caution. He follows the van at a distance and when they're mid-block the van's brake lights come on and it slows and pulls to the curb and stops. He stops a couple of car-lengths behind it, grabs the radio handset and calls in a description of the van and the California license plate and requests backup. He eyes the van as he listens to confirmation of all three.

He notices headlights in the rear-view mirror and knows instantly they're not his backup's. He watches the vehicle approach and pull to a stop by the curb behind him. He unfastens his holster, removes his gun and takes it off safety. The best thing to do is sit and wait. If he steps out of the car before backup arrives, he's almost certainly a dead man. He's relieved to see flashing blue lights at the end of the block in the rear-view mirror and can see the heads of two men silhouetted in the car behind him as the police car pulls up behind them. Would they open fire on him now? They'd be crazy to, but maybe they're crazy. They're drug traffickers, after all. He opens the door, steps out and sees the doors of the police car and the car behind his opening and silhouetted figures stepping out. He feels his heart pounding as he turns, gun in hand, toward the van.

* * *

The ringing phone rouses Rita. She opens her eyes and tries to focus, but the room's a spinning blur. She notices she still has the remote in her hand and turns off the TV. She peers at the clock on the nightstand, 1:17 pm, and glances at the other side of the bed. Ed should be home by now. Maybe it's him. She picks up the phone and looks at the screen. Why would Ricky be calling at this hour? "Hi, what's up?" she asks groggily. "Ed's been shot, Sis," she hears Ricky say and the rush of adrenaline clears her head and stops the room from spinning.

"I'm at the hospital," he says. "They're operating on him now. They're not sure he's gonna make it. There's a car on the way."

"I'll be ready," she says. She knows she's still drunk but feels stunned and numb as she gets off the bed, pulls off her robe and tosses it on the chair. As she pulls on clothes, all she can think about is Ed gone and her alone with a baby.

She's unsteady on her feet and moving too fast as she crosses the living room, heading to the front door. She bangs her leg against the corner of the coffee table, stops and looks down at the leg of her jeans. She doesn't have to check to know there's a bleeding gash in her shin and wishes she could feel the pain.

She sits beside Ricky in the Emergency Room waiting room, hunched over, her face in her hands and Ricky's hand on her back. He shared with her what he knows about what happened, that Ed was shot in the head and it's unclear by whom. Apparently, there was a lot of shooting going on. There's really nothing more to say while they wait for word from the doctor. It's been a long wait. Finally, the door swings open and she looks up at a young grim-faced doctor in scrubs, Indian she thinks. He pulls up a chair and sits in front of her.

"I'm Doctor Dhanidina, Missus Beyer. Your husband is alive, but just barely."

She stares at him blankly.

"He has a very severe head wound and he's on life support. We have him stabilized and in an induced comma. I'm sorry to say his chances of recovery are not good."

"What are his odds?" Ricky asks.

The doctor glances at him, shakes his head and looks back at Rita. He wishes there was something he could say to encourage her, to give her even a shred of hope, but there isn't. It would have been better for everyone if his patient had died at the scene. "Missus Beyer, have you and your husband discussed what he wants done in a situation like this?"

She shakes her head slowly.

"Give it some thought. I don't want to upset you anymore than you already are, but would you like the Chaplain to administer Last Rites?"

Last Rites? This can't be happening. She should be crying, howling, shrieking, but she feels nothing. This must be a nightmare. Any moment now she'll wake. She nods and puts her face in her hands again.

* * *

Kate stares at her phone's screen until it dims. One of the men she loved is dead and according to Rita's brother the other probably will be soon. This is not the way life is supposed to be. She dreads telling Dee Dee. She stands and walks to the hall. "Dee Dee, honey," she calls, "would you come here please?" Dee Dee comes from her bedroom and Kate can see her concern and knows it's from hearing her tone of voice when she called her. She's just not very good at hiding her emotions. She puts an arm around Dee Dee's shoulders and leads her to the couch in the living room and they sit close together facing each other.

Dee Dee's never seen her mom look this way, but she knows by the sound of her voice when she called her and her expression and the way she's sitting with her knees together and her hands on her knees, clasped tightly, her knuckles white, that whatever she's about to hear is very bad news. "Did someone die?" she asks.

"No, sweetheart. Daddy's been hurt."

"How?"

"He was shot."

"Who shot him?"

"They're not sure, honey. He's in the hospital."

"Can I see him?"

Kate knew this question would come and is still wondering how to answer it. Ed's in a coma on life support and she doesn't know when they'll be able to see him, or if they will again while he's still alive. He's only alive now because of the machines and if he stays on them, he'll probably remain in a vegetative state. She doesn't want to deny Dee Dee her right to see her father, but she also doesn't want her final memory of him to be lying there looking like that. She wants to be truthful with her and prepare her for the worst but doesn't want to frighten her any more than she probably already is. She takes Dee Dee's hands in hers. "Daddy's hurt badly, honey. He may not live." She sees Dee Dee's fighting back tears now and trembling. "It's okay to cry, sweetheart. I sure want to."

Dee Dee squeezes her eyes shut and grimaces and feels her mom take her in her arms and slowly rock her. Ever since she was old enough to understand the danger involved in her dad's work, she's been worried that something like this would happen to him. They had a conversation about it once and he assured her there was nothing to worry about. "There's a right way to do things and a wrong way," he said. "If you do things the right way, bad things don't happen." She believed him, although it didn't stop her worrying. She's sure her dad did everything the right way, but this happened anyway. Now she doesn't know what to think or if she can believe anything anyone says anymore. She feels the way she did that first time she fell off Matt's board, in over her head with the bottom a long way down. She wipes her eyes and sniffs.

Kate sits back and looks in Dee Dee's eyes and shakes her head. "It's awful, just awful. Why don't you stay home from school today, honey? You know, just take it easy."

Dee Dee searches her mom's eyes. "Are you going to work?" she asks and sees her mom nod. She remembers that moment when she was submerged, panic-stricken and wanting to get to the surface for air. She knew then that to be a surfer she had to conquer her fear of being in deep water and she knows now that to be a strong person she must conquer her fear of seeing her dad the way he is and possibly losing him. She pictures the seal's face and remembers Matt saying the seal has her back now. "I'm going to school. I want to see Dad."

Tuesday, October 4, 2011

Dear Anneliese,

Really bad news. You know my dad's a police officer. Someone shot him in the head last night and he's in the hospital and the doctors don't know if he's going to live. I can't begin to tell you how awful I feel. I really can't. The thought of not having my dad here anymore is horrible. I just can't imagine it. I want to visit my dad so badly, but my mom says he can't have visitors yet. What if he dies before I see him again?

My mom asked me if I wanted to stay home from school today. I know she wanted me to, but I went. I knew it was the right thing to do. I didn't tell anyone at school about what happened, not even Rosa. I thought the day would go by really slowly, but it was over before I knew it. I hardly remember anything that happened.

I haven't told anyone this, but I'll tell you. I'm really scared and worried about my dad. I mean really, really scared and worried. I've never felt like this before. I know you know how I feel.

I kept thinking today about the day the planes flew into the World Trade Center Towers in New York City. I was a baby then, but I know a lot about what happened. There are lots of videos on YouTube and people still talk about it. It was a beautiful morning and people went to work in the buildings the way they always did. There were people having breakfast in a restaurant at the top of one of the buildings and they had no idea what was about to happen. It was just another day to them. Well, now I know how they felt, sort of. I was in my room getting ready for school when my mom called me. We sat in the living room and she told me about my dad. I felt like the whole world was collapsing around me, the way those people felt the buildings collapsing around them. I don't know what else to say right now.

Yours, Dee Dee

P.S.: Honestly, I didn't really feel like writing to you about this yet. I didn't think I could, but I'm glad I did. You know I'm not very religious but I'm praying for my dad. I know you are too.

* * *

Kate turns the corner and is surprised to see a police officer from the department posted at the door to Ed's room. She's forgotten how things work in the police world. It's not standard procedure for the department to post an officer, but if it feels there might be a further threat to the wounded officer's life, it may choose to do so. Obviously, it does, although given Ed's grave condition she doesn't really see the point. She studies the officer's profile as she approaches. Does she know him?

He's an older man and looks vaguely familiar. She probably met him at one of the department functions she attended with Ed. The officer turns his head and looks at her sympathetically.

"I've very sorry, Missus Beyer," he says. "You hope this kind of thing never happens. Ed was a good man."

So, there it is. He's as good as dead. "Thank you. Is Ed's wife here?" The officer nods. Kate enters the room and is surprised that the scene reminds her of those in some of the early religious paintings by Italian artists at the Getty, the ones depicting Christ being mourned after his crucifixion. There's Ed, lying on his back in bed, eyes closed, looking lifeless, and there's Rita, sitting at his bedside with her hands folded in front of her on the bed, staring at him. Rita looks like she's praying and maybe she is. Kate pulls up a chair beside her and sits. "How're you doing?" she asks and sees Rita shrug listlessly.

Kate studies what she can see of Ed's face that isn't obscured by the oxygen mask and tubes and tape. His skin color is bluish-gray and the only sign that he's still alive is the steady rising and falling of his chest. There's a tube taped to his cheek that's probably running into his stomach to feed him and needles taped to his arms. She can't think of anything to say to Rita, so she just sits quietly, watching Ed's chest rise and fall and listening to the clicking, hissing, whirring, beeping sounds of the machines he's connected to that are keeping him alive. There sure are a lot of them. "Any news?" she finally asks. "How's it look?"

Rita shrugs listlessly again, keeping her eyes on Ed. "I have to decide whether to turn off the machines. He's not coming back."

"They're sure?" Kate asks and sees Rita nod. What would she do if she were Rita? It's an awful thing to have to decide if someone lives or dies. She'd probably have the machines turned off and just let Ed go. That's probably what he would have wanted. If there's anything good about the situation, it's that Rita and Ed don't have children. It'll take time, but Rita will get over it and begin again with someone new. "How's Ed's family taking it?"

"Not well. I thought they knew about the baby."

Kate's astonished. "You're pregnant? I didn't know!"

Rita looks at her. She's not surprised Kate didn't know. Ed didn't tell anyone. Maybe he was hedging his bets. They didn't discuss the baby much, but he must have sensed her indecision about having it.

Kate has the feeling that anything she says about the baby will be wrong. She's happy for Rita, but there isn't much to be happy about. She's bringing a new life into the world, but she's going to be burdened with raising it alone. Kate knows the odds of Rita meeting a man who'll want to take on the responsibilities of another man's child. Would Ed have been interested in her if she'd kept her first baby? She doubts it. She puts her hand on Rita's forearm and Rita looks at her. "Whatever you decide to do about Ed is the right decision," Kate says and sees Rita's eyebrows rise slightly.

"How would Dee Dee feel if she knew I was the one who decided to let her father die?" Rita asks.

"I think she'd understand."

"Think so? I'd hate me," Rita says and looks back at Ed.

Kate studies Rita's profile. Her eyes look lifeless and the side of her face, like the rest of her body, looks sagged, as if burdened with an unbearable weight. How life changes us. There's no trace of that fiery woman Kate once considered an adversary. Rita looks utterly devastated and Kate feels deep sympathy for her and profoundly sad about her situation. She wants to reach out to her and help her. "Dee Dee wants to see him," Kate says, and Rita looks at her.

"Like this?"

"She has a pretty good idea what to expect."

"She better do it soon," Rita says, looking back at Ed. "I'm not sure I want to keep it."

"You don't have to decide right now. You're dealing with a lot. Give it time."

Rita knows Kate means well, but time is hell and it's all she has to look forward to. Speaking of time, it's time to go to the ladies' room and drink a couple of the nips she has in her bag. She's craving a drink and looks down at her trembling hands and glances at Kate. Does she notice them? How ridiculous. How could she not? What would Kate think if she just drank them here? She'd probably understand and pity her. How could she not?

* * *

Thursday, October 6, 2011

Dear Anneliese,

I went to see my dad in the hospital today. My mom told me that he wouldn't know we were there and that there would be all these machines, and that the machines are keeping him alive, and if they're turned off, he'll die. The most important thing she said is that he's not going to get any better.

I have to admit I was a little scared to go into his room. My dad was lying in bed with his eyes closed with a mask over his nose and mouth and all these tubes (even one in his throat!). It was creepy. Rita and her brother were there. We sat with them for a while and then they decided to go have a cup of coffee so we could be alone with my dad. My mom and I just sat there looking at him and it was so sad. My dad looked so weak.

He's a really strong man. When I was little, he used to pick me up and hold me over his head with one hand. I remember the first time he took me to the beach (I think it was the first time). He put me on his back and swam out in the ocean and I was between his shoulders with my arms around his neck, and I remember how big his muscles were and how hard they felt. He can't even move now.

I wanted to cry, but I couldn't. I asked my mom if he was just going to stay that way and she said that the doctors were probably going to turn off the machines. I should have felt horribly, but I didn't. I knew it would be better for him. Do you think that's awful?

Here's the thing. The person in the bed isn't my dad. It's just my dad's body. My dad is gone and he's never coming back. What's the point in keeping his body alive if he can't enjoy life anymore and all the things that people love about him are gone, all the things I love about him? They're all gone now. I never in a million years would have thought I would wish for my dad what I do. It feels so strange and makes me very, very sad.

Yours, Dee Dee

P.S.: Even though I knew my dad didn't know we were there, before we left, I gave him a kiss on the cheek and told him I loved him and would always be thinking of him. I like to believe he heard me.

* * *

Dee Dee stares at the flag-draped casket in the aisle by the altar rail. She only visited her dad in the hospital that one time. After that there was really no point in visiting him again. When her mom told her he'd passed away, she wasn't surprised and felt sad and relieved. Good, she thought, he's not suffering anymore. She tries not to think that it's her dad lying in the casket and when she does, she reminds herself that it's just his body. She remembers her conversation with Pauly at Phantom Ranch. He doesn't believe people's spirits go anywhere when they die and now she feels certain they don't, as certain as she can be.

She feels stupid staring at the casket, it's just a metal box, but she tired of watching the priest at the altar celebrating mass. "Celebrating"? What is there to celebrate? She looks discreetly over her shoulder and around at the people in the church. She's never seen so many police officers. Some of them knew her dad, but most probably didn't and are just here out of respect. She looks at her mom beside her, whose eyes are on the priest. Her mom looks sad and tired but seems to be holding up pretty well.

Dee Dee leans forward a bit and looks down the row of people at Rita. She's worried about Rita. She doesn't seem to be holding up well at all well. She looks like a ghost. Well, he was her husband. Maybe that makes her loss greater somehow, although she doesn't think so.

She sits back and looks up at the altarpiece behind the priest. At the top are the letters "HIS", which she knows stand for Jesus, in a circle with a cross behind them and lines radiating downward from the bottom half of the circle. It seems stark in comparison to the altarpieces at the Getty, which are much smaller but much more artful and colorful. Everything about this place seems stark. The world seems stark.

Being in church reminds her of Consuela's Quinceañera and her desire to have her own. She remembers thinking about her First Waltz with her dad. She pictures herself and her dad dancing together, the only people on the dance floor. She's wearing her tiara and necklace, her white dress and gloves and stockings and heels, and her dad's dressed in a black tuxedo. They're smiling at each other as they swirl round and round. She looks at the casket. That's not going to happen now. There are so many things her dad will miss in her life; seeing her off when she goes to her prom; attending her high school and college graduations; celebrating her wedding and the birth of his grandchildren, so, so much. It's so sad. He'll always be there, though, in her thoughts, the way Annaliese is.

Dee Dee stands beside her mom at the gravesite, staring at the casket while the priest reads a prayer. She's not really paying attention to what he's saying. All she can think about is that when they leave, the casket is going to be lowered into this hole in the ground and covered with dirt and that'll be that. Her dad will be gone forever. Will she come visit his grave? Why should she? It would be better to just keep her dad in her thoughts. She knows just how his smile looks and hug feels. She'll never forget them.

The priest closes his prayer book and she joins everyone in saying "Amen," but notices that Rita says nothing. She watches Rita step forward and put her red rose on top of the casket, and then her mom and she do the same and they walk away slowly as three men standing at a distance dressed in kilts and holding bagpipes begin playing "Amazing Grace." She knows this is customary at funerals for police officers and firefighters. She's always wondered how it came to be and what the Scottish connection is. She thought to ask her dad but never did. She knows as time goes by there'll be many more questions she would have liked to ask him that she won't be able to now. It's so sad.

* * *

Rita stares down at the now cold coffee in her cup, which she hasn't touched since Estella put it in front of her.

"You going to be okay, Sis?" Ricky asks.

She looks up at the two of them, standing across the kitchen table, ready to leave and looking down at her with concern. "Yeah," she says softly. She will be too. As soon as they're gone, she'll have a stiff drink and feel better.

"Take care of yourself," Estella says.

Rita nods and watches them go and sees Ricky glance back at her over his shoulder with a worried expression.

"Call if you need anything," he says.

She nods again and listens to their footsteps and hears the front door close. It feels like she's being shut up in a tomb. She pours the coffee in the sink and puts the coffee cup in it. She makes herself a strong vodka tonic, sits at the kitchen table and takes a long sip. She notices her hands are still trembling, but she feels better already.

She looks around the kitchen. So, here she is, alone in a house filled with reminders of Ed. The clothes can all go to Good Will. The police uniforms will probably sell at Halloween. Should she keep his gun? She'll never use it even if she comes face to face with a burglar. Maybe she'll sell it or give it back to the department. The photographs? They can all go in a box.

She looks at her empty glass, makes herself another drink and sits and sips. It's shameful. She's just buried Ed and already she's thinking about erasing his memory. Sure, there's a lot she wishes she could forget about their marriage, but it wasn't all bad, and toward the end Ed's feelings for her really did seem to change. He seemed to genuinely care for her, maybe even love her. Who knows? It was because of the baby, of course, but still.... She drains her drink.

What about the baby, the ultimate reminder? She can't give that to Good Will or sell it or put it in a box.

She thinks of Kate and Dee Dee. Ed's hospital stay and death has brought the three of them closer together. They've both been very nice and very supportive. They seem more concerned about her feelings than their own.

Poor Dee Dee, losing her dad like that and at such a young age. Rita's feelings toward Dee Dee have changed. She's a sweet kid, thoughtful and polite. It says a lot about her character that she wanted to see her dad in the hospital, knowing the shape he was in. It took courage for her to walk into that hospital room. She's a brave kid and strong-willed, in a good way.

Rita looks at her empty glass, makes another drink and sits and sips. Of course, if she didn't have the baby, she'd have a better chance of getting into another relationship. It's shameful to think about that at a time like this and selfish too, but there it is. It probably doesn't matter one way or the other. What are the odds of her meeting someone, especially since all she does is sit at home and drink when she's not at work? Even if she did meet someone, it wouldn't be long before he'd find out she's a drunk. Who'd want to be with her? Another drunk? Once was enough.

If she did have the baby, she wouldn't be alone. She'd have a reason to be alive, something to live for other than drinking. Maybe she'll have an amnio. Does it matter if it's a girl or boy? She hadn't thought about it, and it probably doesn't, but thinking about it now, it would be nice to have a daughter, like Dee Dee.

CHAPTER 18

A Secret Life

You don't even have to watch the news anymore to know what's going on in the world: strife and suffering everywhere. Ira turns off the TV and glances at the picture of the dancing Thai goddess on the wall above it. She's young and beautiful and graceful, wrapped in a swirl of yellow and purple silk. Gazing at her takes his mind off the harsh reality of life, if only momentarily.

He loves his trips to Thailand and always looks forward to his visits. The first time he visited Bangkok and stepped out of the airport terminal and breathed in the air, he could smell it. It's a smell he's come to associate with the place. There was just the hint of it at first mixed in with noxious diesel exhaust fumes from taxis and buses, and the further into the country he went, the more distinct the smell became. It was there in the air as he toured the city and experienced the people, so beautiful and courteous and respectful, and visited the temples and saw the monks in their saffron robes. He discovered that it was a mixture of rice paddies and sugar cane fields, a sweet earthy scent that coated the insides of his nostrils and mouth and stayed with him for a long time after he returned to London.

This house in the quiet residential area of Raminthra once belonged to his old London School of Economics chum Ali, an Afghani whose father was a powerful tribal leader. They were an eclectic bunch at the London School. They came from all corners of the globe from families engaged in very different pursuits. Some owned restaurants, some large businesses and some ruled countries. Ali's family headed a tribe, and when the crowd would gather at a favorite pub for a few too many pints, Ali would tell them proudly about the family's lucrative opium business and his plans to expand the scope and profitability of its operations, which was why he was attending the school, to learn how to do it. He talked about the family business proudly and brushed aside questions of ethics and morality. "This is our life," he would say, "it is what we have always done and what we will always do. If the world did not want our product, it would not buy it. In fact, we cannot produce enough." Asking the family to voluntarily end its opium business, Ali would point out, would be like asking someone to cut off a perfectly good right arm for no reason at all. His logic was unassailable.

Ali maintained a flat in London after graduation but spent most of his time in Afghanistan. On one of his return trips to London, when the two of them were having pints, Ali explained that he'd been diligently working to establish an operation to export and distribute their own product. This had been the problem all along. As lucrative as the opium business is, his family was forced to give up the lion's share of the profits to middlemen. Now he had people in place to transport product out of Afghanistan to Lahore, Pakistan, and from there to strategic locations throughout Southeast Asia, Bangkok among them. What he needed was capital investment.

Ira studied Ali's business plan and, although illegal and risky, the return on investment was potentially so enormous that it proved irresistible. He and Ali would share equally in the profits as partners. Ira wouldn't be directly involved in operations. All Ali was asking was that he assist him in securing funding. In the great scheme of things, they weren't looking to raise all that much. The amount each investor would be asked to contribute "no questions asked" to the venture was relatively small compared to the prospect of a one hundred percent return on investment within a year. Ira worked his contacts, raised the money and off Ali went to Afghanistan and within six months he had the operation up and running smoothly.

Ira smiles, remembering their astonishing success. It was one of the sweetest moments he's ever experienced in life when a year later he and Ali sat in an expensive restaurant in London enjoying an excellent meal and toasting their success with bottles of champagne. They'd paid back the investors and had each made what seemed to them a staggering sum of money. It was a lot of money, all right, but nothing compared to what was to come.

It was fortunate that Ira took Ali up on his suggestion to accompany him on a trip to Afghanistan to meet his family, and to Lahore and Bangkok to meet the contacts in the network. Ali's family gave Ira the royal treatment. Ali assured him that his politely passing on the offer of a young boy for companionship was not viewed as a slight.

When Ali was murdered in Lahore, a crime unsolved to this day, Ira was knowledgeable enough about operations to be able to keep the business running from London. Ali's family designated his younger brother Ameen to handle things on their end and he's done an admirable job ever since. Ira misses Ali, though. He was a good friend and a sharp businessman and had a sexual appetite to match his own. They enjoyed some unforgettable times together in Bangkok.

Ira smiles as he remembers the first time he was out on the town with Ali and how all the women looked beautiful and exotic and young. He had a difficult time estimating the women's ages and still does with women in this part of the world. Twenty-year-olds look like fourteen-year-olds, forty-year-olds like twenty-year-olds and so on. He has the same difficulty telling the ages of Black women.

He remembers standing with Ali and a Madame in a brothel, looking through the window at the ten or so girls seated on a long bench, waiting to be chosen by customers. All the girls were in their early teens and he and Ali listened to the Madame's description of each girl's best attributes and qualities. Ira had never had sex with a girl so young and was excited by the prospect. One girl, the Madame told them, a fourteen-year-old with long black hair and a nice figure, was particularly good at fellatio and always received high marks from customers. Ira chose her and she more than lived up to her reputation.

When Ali met Rose, they stopped visiting brothels. Rose's girls are top quality, unlike the uneducated and unimaginative fare at the brothels, and she delivers them to her customers. As experienced in the business as Rose is, she'd never heard of breath play. No customer had ever requested it, and she listened and watched with a businesswoman's interest as Ira described what he wanted the girl to do. When he was finished, she narrowed her eyes and pursed her lips and nodded. "No problem," she said. She was true to her word. His experience with the beautiful fifteen-year-old girl Rose brought to him, well-trained and eager to please, almost equaled in enjoyment those he'd had with Leslie. Almost.

He has to hand it to Rose. She's a consummate professional and has never disappointed him, and she's grateful to him for having exposed her to his exotic taste. It opened an entirely new revenue stream, and business has never been better. He glances at his watch. She's running uncharacteristically late. At least he can count on her. He's confident that whomever she's bringing will be well worth the wait.

He doesn't think about Olga as often now, but the image of her face in the bag, frozen in a wide-eyed gasp, and of her body, lying on the bed in her own mess still haunts him. He'll never forget that smell, either.

The doorbell rings. He stands and walks to the door and opens it. Rose is there and next to her is a beautiful young girl with long shimmering black hair, wearing a floral print sarong and sandals. Rose and the girl place their palms together, hands pointing upward, bow their heads and touch their fingertips to their brows in the middle of their foreheads and he does the same.

"Hello, Mister Ira," Rose and the girl sing in Thai.

He smiles. "Greetings, ladies!" he says and waves them in.

Rose escorts the girl to the couch and they sit. "Sorry we're late, Mister Ira," Rose says.

"No problem." He sits in an armchair and studies the girl. She's more than beautiful. She's exquisite, like the dancing goddess on the wall.

"Her name is Carissa," Rose says. "It means 'sweet smelling flower' and 'sweet tasting plum.'"

He smiles at Carissa. "I'm sure she is. How old?"

"Fourteen," Rose says.

"Does she speak English?"

Rose squints one eye and pinches her thumb and forefinger together, indicating a little. "Say something in English," she tells Carissa in Thai.

Carissa smiles sweetly at Ira. "You handsome man!"

He beams at her. "Thank you, my dear." Her youthful eagerness to show off the little English she knows and her obvious pride in doing so is delightful. He stands and Rose and Carissa stand and he looks at Rose. "She's in good health I presume. You've checked as I asked?"

Rose nods. "Excellent health, Mister Ira, and she learned very well!"

He bets she did. She had a good teacher. He remembers the one session he had with Rose, which she insisted on having, so that she could understand exactly what this breath play business was all about. It was a delightful experience for him and he encouraged her to offer the service personally. She was flattered but demurred, saying she was too old and not as attractive as the young girls. He'll take old and experienced over young and attractive and inexperienced any day. "Good. I've had quite enough surprises. I'll call you in a few hours." He smiles at Carissa and holds out his hand to her. "Come, my dear." He sees Carissa glance at Rose, who nods at her. Good. There was not even a hint of apprehension in Carissa's expression. She looked at Rose the way a young athlete does her coach just before competing, as if to say she's confident in her abilities and ready to perform and Rose nods at her, knowing that she is and will. Carissa smiles at him and steps forward. He thrills at how eagerly she takes his hand. This girl couldn't be more unlike Olga, and he knows the experience will be sublime.

* * *

Ira rolls his suitcase out of Customs at LAX. All this security is just a nightmare. He remembers when he used to love to travel and looked forward to getting on airplanes, but no more, not since 9/11. Even First Class feels like riding in a cattle car. He just wants to get home and get a good night's sleep. He scans the signs being held up by the liveried chauffeurs, looking for his name. Ah, there it is. He nods at the driver, a middle-aged heavyset Hispanic, who lowers his sign and takes the roller bag. Ira follows the driver to the curb and climbs into the back of the Town Car. He calls Adele to tell her he's on his way as the driver puts his suitcase in the trunk.

They head out of the airport and get on the 405 South toward Orange County. Traffic is light this late in the evening. They'll make good time. They haven't traveled far when the driver pulls over into the exit lane. "Gas," Ira hears him say, which strikes him as odd, but he pays it no mind. He turns on the reading light, removes Steve's report from his attaché case and picks up reading where he left off on the plane. As always, Steve's ideas are very good. It's the only reason he tolerates his and now Cynthia's behavior. He keeps a watchful eye on them, so that he can take quick action to protect the company if need be.

He feels the limo slow and sees the slash of the gas station's cool overhead fluorescent light on the facing seat in front of him and then it's gone. He sees parked cars in the darkness in front of them. Why are they at the back of the gas station? Maybe the driver's pulling around to the other side, but no, the limo stops and his door opens and before he can look up he feels what he knows to be the muzzle of a gun pressing against his cheekbone, preventing him from turning his head. "Don't move," he hears a man say, also Hispanic by the sound of it, and now someone is putting a hood over his head.

How foolish. All the signs were there. He's been careless and his mother is certainly spinning in her grave. His pockets are emptied, he's put in the back of a van and his hands and feet are bound. Adele will know what to do. His instructions to her have been clear: cooperate and give them the money. They'll ask for a great deal of money and there'll be no guarantee that he'll be returned alive. Don't think about it. Just do it, as difficult as it might be. After all, it's only money and they have plenty and, for God's sake, don't call the police. It will only complicate matters.

Wherever they're headed, it's a long drive and finally he feels the van slow and stop. They unbind him, remove him from the back of the van and walk him a short distance. He knows by the smell of jet fuel in the air that he's at an airport. "Step," he hears a man say. He lifts his foot and places it on a narrow metallic step, then another, and another and he feels the plane dipping toward him slightly. He's guided to a seat and sits for a while, waiting. Finally, he hears activity and muffled voices. The door closes with a "thunk" and then there's the whine of jet engines starting up. The situation is more complex and dangerous than he thought. He's almost certain they're taking him to Mexico, but given the global scope of his illegal activities, they could be taking him anywhere and this Mexican connection could just be the first leg of the journey.

The flight isn't long. He estimates an hour and a half. He knows Mexico is the final destination when he's put in the back seat of a car and driven, still with the hood over his head, about forty-five minutes. He's taken out and led into a building of some sort and finally someone is removing the restraints from his hands and the hood from his head. Blinking, he sees he's in a bedroom and hears the door close and lock. He hears the sound of waves breaking on the shore and walks to the window, peers out at the darkness and when his eyes adjust can make out the shoreline and the ocean beyond. The few clues he has lead him to conclude he's in Rosarito and probably in Rios's residence. He heads to the bathroom to relieve himself and tells himself he must sleep. Whatever it is that's going to happen tomorrow, he needs to be rested.

He's awakened by a knock on the door, lifts his head from the pillow and sees a handsome young Hispanic man with a well-trimmed Vandyke standing in the doorway. "Get dressed," the man says politely, steps back and pulls the door shut. Ira does and waits by the window, gazing out. It's a gorgeous day and there are seagulls wheeling above the ocean and one gull in particular, near the shoreline has his attention. The gull has a clam in its beak and flies straight up to a height of about thirty feet, then drops it on the rocks to break it open. It does this time and again and he admires the gull's cleverness and persistence. Is it cleverness? That suggests thinking and free will. Perhaps the gull is simply programmed genetically to break clams this way and perhaps it's the same with people, with himself. Perhaps the idea of free will is simply a conceit to distract us from the fact that our actions in life are like those of falling dominoes, governed more by the laws of physics than logic. He thinks of the decisions he's made in his life that have led him to be standing here in this room, held captive and gazing out at the gull while he waits to see what happens next, and he does feel more like a domino about to be pushed over from behind than someone acting of his own free will. He knows it's the circumstances that are making him think this way and that he must stop. It's dangerous.

He hears the door open and turns. A squat burly man stands in the doorway and motions for him to follow. The man leads him to the dining room and indicates the chair he's to sit in at the table. It's the only one with a place setting in front of it. He's served a breakfast of huevos rancheros and coffee and then led outside to a large deck, where he notices a man with an AK-47 posted on the beach below and two men seated at a large round table under an umbrella.

The man on the left is casually dressed in a bright pink Brooks Brothers polo shirt, with a bright blue embroidered Golden Fleece logo on the breast. He has a swarthy complexion, a tangle of curly black hair and a neatly trimmed mustache. There's a scar in the clean-shaven groove of his upper lip that gives him a thuggish look. Perhaps he was drunk and fell face down on the sidewalk or was hit in the face with a frying pan one morning by his wife in a jealous rage. There's an ocelot curled up on his lap and he's stroking it gently, lovingly, as he would his mistress.

The man next to him has pale skin and his glistening black hair is combed straight back and held in place with brilliantine. He's wearing a Brooks Brothers navy pinstripe suit and a distinctively iconic BB #1 Repp Tie. Ira thinks of Henry, the associate at Brooks Brothers at South Coast Plaza who assists him with custom clothes. Drug traffickers sporting such a respectable brand — Henry would appreciate the humorous irony.

The two men talk in Spanish in lowered voices and keep their eyes on Ira as he approaches. The man in the suit indicates the chair across from them and Ira lowers himself into it, keeping his eyes on them. He notices the phone on the table in front of the man in the suit and it's being there strikes him as significant.

"Welcome, Mister Weiss," the man in the suit says and gestures toward the man next to him. "This is Mister Rios."

So, this is Rios. His expression is as serene as the ocelot's and their slightly hooded eyes look remarkably alike. Ira knows from Rios's reputation that he's every bit the animal the cat on his lap is.

"I am Enrique," the man in the suit says with a slight shrug. "Mister Rios speaks only a little English. I will translate."

How Ira wishes he'd learned Spanish, as he's been telling himself he should ever since they arrived in Southern California, and how he regrets that fact that his parents didn't teach it to him. They spoke the language, but saw no need to when they moved to Israel. As a result, he's at a real disadvantage here, not being able to pick up on the nuances of what Rios will be saying and having to rely on a translator, which is always risky.

Enrique nods toward the pitcher of ice water on the table. "Would you like something to drink other than water?"

"I'm fine."

"Let me begin by apologizing for any inconvenience we may have caused you."

Ira nods.

"I regret to say that Mister Rios is disappointed with your efforts so far to establish operations in Southern California. Your people have compromised the distribution center in Orange County and killed a police officer in the process. He feels they're bungling amateurs."

Ira never should have agreed to let Ameen move forward with the idea. It was too close to home. He wouldn't be involved, of course, but Ameen would be trying to run the operation from halfway around the world. It was too risky, no matter how great the potential profits. He definitely took his eye off the ball with this one.

"Frankly, Mister Rios is surprised and a bit offended that you didn't ask him to run the operation in the first place. Is there a particular reason?"

"No." The reason, of course, is that Ira doesn't want anything to do with Rios, who has a well-earned reputation for treachery.

"That was unfortunate and regrettable. In any event, Mister Rios feels it's in everyone's best interest that he controls things now. You will receive ten percent of the profits, a very generous and, I might add, gracious offer given the circumstances."

So, Rios now wants the lion's share. The businessman in Ira stirs and his back stiffens. He wants to say it's unacceptable but says nothing. He's an experienced and good negotiator but isn't here to negotiate and, anyway, is in no position to. He's here to have the terms dictated to him and he'd be surprised if they don't get harsher. Rios murmurs something to Enrique, who nods, picks up the phone and holds it out to Ira. He takes it and looks at the screen. It's filled with a picture of Adele, bound and gagged, sitting in a chair at their dining room table. He looks up at them.

"The price of not accepting Mister Rios's offer is your life and that of your wife. And, I might add, it's the same should your people in Afghanistan fail to supply product." Rios murmurs something and Enrique nods and motions for Ira to hand back the phone.

He does and watches Enrique place a call and hold out the phone again. Ira takes it, puts it to his ear and listens to the rings. "Ira?" he hears Adele ask. She sounds terrified. "Yes, dear," he says, as calmly as he can manage.

"They haven't asked for money!"

He rubs his eyes. "They don't want money. I haven't been kidnapped."

"When are you coming home?"

He covers the phone with his hand and looks at the Enrique. "When am I going back?"

"Today," Enrique says.

"I'll be home later today," Ira tells Adele. "Try not to worry."

"I love you."

"I love you too." He sees Enrique put a finger in the air, indicating that Ira shouldn't end the call. Enrique motions for him to hand back the phone and Ira does and watches and listens as Enrique says something in Spanish to the person on the other end, ends the call and places the phone on the table.

Rios murmurs something and Enrique's expression brightens. He raises his eyebrows and smiles at Ira. "Mister Rios would like to compliment you on your taste in clothing."

It occurs to Ira that he and Rios and Enrique have more in common that just a drug trafficking business. If you didn't know these two were thugs, you'd think they were models of civility. It's just how people who know nothing of his secret life view him. He looks from Enrique to Rios and sees Rios gazing at him serenely with those catlike eyes of his and it occurs to Ira that he's never seen him blink.

Ira's led from the porch and placed hooded but unbound in the backseat of a car and they drive away. This situation is not good, not at all good. To think that after everything he's accomplished it's come to this, to be at the mercy of a thug like Rios. The irony is bitter. His people beat Pharaoh, beat the British, beat the Egyptian and Syrian surprise attack on Yom Kippur and have thwarted for decades the misguided efforts of the Americans to establish a separate state for the whining, ungrateful and treacherous Palestinians, believing it would be in Israel's best interest to do so. How naïve. Well, he'll prevail, somehow. He has no choice. If left unchecked Rios, will destroy him. That's the man's modus operandi and his appetite is insatiable. Ira must kill him. It won't be easy, but it has to be done. Uri can handle it. When they worked together at Mossad, they orchestrated takedowns of bigger fish than this Mexican small fry. It only takes know-how and money, and between the two of them they have all of both they need.

Ira knows he'll have some explaining to do to Adele, though. She's been the perfect companion all these years, never questioning his comings and goings. He's managed to keep her in the dark about his clandestine activities. That no longer seems possible.

The hood is removed from his head and he sees they're entering Rodriguez International Airport in Tijuana. He sees the man sitting next to him is the handsome young man with the Vandyke, who hands him an envelope. He opens it and sees it contains his passport and an airline ticket.

"Your suitcase is in a cart at the curb," the man says politely. "Get out and walk to it and don't look back. Go directly into the terminal. Understood?"

Ira nods and gets out.

Arriving home, he's dismayed to see what he's sure is a gray unmarked police car parked at the curb in front of the house. Adele must have called them. What has she told them? Undoubtedly that she was bound and gagged in her own home. Well, his having been abducted isn't a crime. He gets out, takes his suitcase from the driver and rolls it up the front walk. He has the feeling things are spiraling out of his control. He hasn't felt this way since he was a boy and would be called on the carpet by his parents to explain some mischief he'd gotten up to and could see by their expressions that, despite his protests of innocence, they already knew he was guilty. He closes the front door. "Ira?" he hears Adele call from the living room. "Yes, dear!" he calls to her. She comes to greet him, throws her arms around him, presses her face against his chest and then looks up at him guiltily and worriedly.

"I was so frightened!"

"Everything is fine, my dear." They walk to the living room and he sees two men, the one on the left in a dark blue suit and the one of the right in a dark gray suit, both standing in front of their chairs, staring at him with blank expressions. He notices the cups and saucers and spoons and napkins on the coffee table before them. Adele's been a gracious hostess, as always. He leads her to the couch and they sit, Adele gripping his arm. The men sit and both remove their badges from their inside coat pockets and hold them up for him to see. The man in the dark blue suit seems to be in charge.

"Mister Weiss, I'm Agent Reynolds," he says, "and this is Agent Salazar. We're with the FBI." The men put their badges away and Agent Salazar holds his pen and notepad at the ready. "We'd like to ask you a few questions, Mister Weiss," Agent Reynolds says.

Ira nods.

"Missus Weiss contacted local law enforcement and they contacted us. Missus Weiss stated that two men entered your home early this morning and tied her up, bound and gagged her. She identified them as Hispanic. She stated that she spoke with you on one of the men's cell phone this morning and that after speaking with you, the men untied her and told her before leaving not to call the police or you'd both be killed."

"I know you told me not to, Ira," Adele says apologetically, "but I was so worried and frightened!"

Ira sees a slight rise in both men's eyebrows. He's seen this same look of barely concealed suspicion countless times on detectives' faces in movies. They must teach it at the academy.

"Mister Weiss, you arrived at LAX yesterday evening on a Royal Thai flight from Bangkok? Is that correct?"

Ira keeps his eyes on Agent Reynolds, but out of the corners of his eyes sees Adele glance at him. "Yes."

"You were picked up at the airport?"

"Yes."

"Who picked you up?"

"I thought one of the drivers with the limo service we use." Ira sees Agent Salazar flip a few pages and show the pertinent notes to Agent Reynolds.

"Your secretary Suzanna Lopez stated that you made your own flight arrangements."

"Yes, I sometimes do that."

"But that she arranged for the limo to pick you up."

"Yes, I asked her to."

"You're aware that her brother owns the limo service?"

In fact, Ira wasn't and how did this escape his notice. "Yes." Now his mind is racing. Is her brother working for Rios? Is Suzanna complicit in this?

"Her brother stated that the driver was delayed by a flat tire and when he arrived you weren't at the terminal. Did you recognize the driver?"

"No."

"Do you remember what he looked like? Could you identify him?"

"I think so."

"Did you leave the airport in the limo?"

"Yes."

"And what happened?"

"The driver stopped for gas somewhere just off the 405 and I was taken at gunpoint. They put a hood over my head and tied me up." Ira feels Adele's grip on his arm tighten and pats her hand.

"Where were you taken?"

Ira considers carefully how much to divulge in answering this and the questions he knows will follow about his whereabouts and what happened. The FBI might very well already know that he was in Tijuana simply by checking filed flight plans. "Mexico." Ah. He sees the two men glance at each other, so perhaps the Bureau hasn't begun digging and delving yet, which they certainly will. That's a given.

"How do you know?"

"The flight time and the fact that the people I dealt with were all Mexican, at least I assume they were."

"Do you know where in Mexico?"

"Tijuana. That's where I returned from."

"Where were you taken?"

"A house."

"Did you see your surroundings?"

"No. When they removed the hood I was in a room with no windows, and I was blindfolded before I left it." Good, no windows, blindfolded. Quick thinking.

"Who was there?"

"Five men that I know of. They're might have been more."

"What happened?"

"They asked for money. They said they'd kill me and my wife if I didn't give it to them."

"Who did the talking?"

Remembering it, Ira can't help but smile and is only too willing to describe Enrique to the agents for his own amusement, despite the fact that in doing so, he knows he's likely divulging incriminating information. He's mindful that his willingness to do so is more proof that he's slipping. "A man in his thirties with fair skin and slicked back black hair dressed in a navy blue, pinstripe Brooks Brothers suit." He sees the agents glance at each other again and Agent Salazar write on his notepad. Agent Reynolds looks at Ira.

"Did you give them the money?"

"Yes."

"You had the money wired from an account?"

"Yes."

"Here in the U.S.?"

"No."

"From?

"I'd rather not say."

"How much?"

"I'd rather not say that, either."

"Why is that?"

"It's a private matter and I'd prefer to keep it that way."

"Kidnapping is a crime, Mister Weiss, in this case a federal and international one."

"Being kidnapped isn't." Ira sees the two men glance at each other again and look back at him. Agent Salazar writes on his notepad and Agent Reynolds's eyes narrow slightly.

"Is there anything more you can tell us, Mister Weiss?"

"No."

"Thank you, Mister Weiss. I know you and Missus Weiss have been through an ordeal. I think those are all the questions we have at this time. We may contact you again. Thanks for the coffee, Missus Weiss."

Ira keeps his eyes on Agent Reynolds's as they stand. He knows from his own experience as an interrogator that Agent Reynolds isn't finished yet, that he's saving the most important questions for last.

"I do have one more question, Mister Weiss."

"Yes?"

"Missus Weiss stated you told her on the phone that you hadn't been kidnapped, and these people didn't want money. Is that correct, Missus Weiss?"

Adele glances guiltily at Ira and looks back at Agent Reynolds. "Yes," she says softly.

"Did you tell her that, Mister Weiss?"

"I didn't want to upset her anymore than she already was."

"One last question. Do you know Rodolfo Rios?"

So, here it is. "No. Why would I?"

"You know of him?"

"Vaguely, from the news."

"But you don't know him personally? Never met him?"

"No." Ira sees Agent Reynolds nod and Agent Salazar put his notepad and pen away. He escorts the two detectives to the door, closes it behind them and finds Adele sitting on the couch, hunched over with her face in her hands. Poor Adele, she panicked and wasn't thinking straight and called the police out of concern for him. He can hardly blame her. Anyway, the damage is done. He sits beside her and pats her knee. "It's over now, my dear. We're both safe and sound. We should be thankful for that." She looks at him and he sees the fear in her eyes.

"I don't feel safe anymore, Ira."

He puts an arm around her and draws her to him. He knows just how she feels.

* * *

The trawler out of Ensenada arrives at the drop point on a moonless night at two in the morning almost to the second, as planned. Uri and the three Chilean operatives he hired for the mission, all dressed in hooded wet suits with their faces blackened, make a final check of their gear and two of the men lower the inflatable over the side and climb down to it. They're a mile offshore and just south of the compound in Rosarito. The plan is simple: paddle in, make their way up the beach to the compound and take out Rios. Locating his house was easy. All it took was a generous payment to the chief of police. Once they kill Rios, they'll motor back to the trawler, return to Ensenada and then to their respective home countries.

The man still on deck with Uri, who goes only by Pantera, picks up the bag filled with night vision equipment and hands it over the side. "I hate using these things," Pantera says in Spanish.

"They're a pain but they work," Uri answers in Spanish. "We'll put them on when we get to shore."

Turning Fidencio was easy. Uri had the sense that the money was unimportant to him. There's obviously no love lost between Fidencio and his brother-in-law. Fidencio doesn't seem to want to take Rios's place. He just seems to want him dead. In any event, he was only too willing to provide information about security in the compound. There will be one man on the beach in front of the house, another on the deck overlooking the beach, another at the front door of the main house and another in the house, probably in the living room. Uri and his men are well armed with knives and Uzi pistols and submachine guns. As he told them, he doesn't care how they get to Rios or how they ultimately kill him. He just wants him dead. He knows by the way they looked at him as he explained the mission and the way they nodded solemnly when he was done that they understand the importance of what they've been paid to do and are prepared to do it, and he feels confident they'll succeed.

He and Pantera hand the last few bags down to the men in the inflatable. They're about to go over the side when a meteor streaks across the sky, leaving a brilliant phosphorescent trail in the darkness that lasts only an instant but whose after image lingers in Uri's eyes. "Bad sign," he hears Pantera say.

They climb over the side and down to the inflatable and the four of them begin paddling toward shore. Uri's concerned about Ira. He seems to be losing his grip lately. How he managed to allow himself to be abducted in the first place is beyond him. A limo stopping for gas — It should have been a big red flashing sign to Ira. Ira never would have missed it when he was younger.

Uri scans the shoreline. A few lights on here and there in the houses but otherwise the beach area is dark. Ira was right when he told him the flat in Mayfair was a mess. What a lousy job that was. Uri's no moralist and Ira's outré sexual practices are no business of his, but when they involve killing someone, albeit accidentally, well, that's going to far.

It was just plain foolish of Ira to allow Ameen to talk him into setting up a drug distribution network in the United States. The U.S. authorities are not like those in other countries. Money doesn't talk and once you're on the radar screen the authorities' pursuit of you is relentless. He should have known that Rios would come sniffing like a fox smelling chickens and soon be in the hen house.

Uri's had the feeling lately that it's only a matter of time before his own luck runs out and he's begun thinking about retiring. He's getting too old for this business. It's a young man's game. He has more than enough saved to live comfortably for the rest of his life. What he should do is marry Elsa, buy a nice house with an orchard near Tel Aviv and settle down, just relax and enjoy life. They've been together for years and he knows how much she wants to marry. Why not? She's been a good companion. It would make her happy and if she's happy, he's happy. "Happy wife, happy life," as they say.

They're about a half a mile from shore now and making good time. "Shit," Uri hears one of the men behind him say. He looks back over his shoulder and can just make out the ship, its silhouette a little darker than the darkness surrounding it, bearing down on them with no running lights. It's a Mexican Navy Durango class patrol vessel armed with, among other things, a 57-millimeter gun. Shit, all right. The mission has been compromised but by whom? Fidencio? Why would he do it? If not by him, then whom?

Uri can hear the low rumble of the ship's engines now and the sound of its bow plowing through the waves, and the water around them is suddenly illuminated by brilliant white light. It's so intense he can feel the heat on his back. He's a bit relieved. If they'd intended to kill them outright, they wouldn't have turned on the searchlight. They'd have just run them over in the dark. He wonders if he'll ever see Elsa again. He's doubtful, but the light gives him hope.

CHAPTER 19

Cabo San Lucas

Amber gazes through the picture window in the living room at the ship in the distance, slowly heading south. With no moon, all she can see of it are the green, red and white running lights. It's probably headed to Mexico, most likely Ensenada. Matt's photos of the wreck in Ensenada harbor come to mind and that place overlooking the Pacific where he said he likes to camp. He's a nice enough guy and he was an exception. She went easy on him. He has nothing and, so, nothing to lose.

Steve wants to take her to Cabo San Lucas. He thinks a change of scenery will work to his advantage, which shows how little he knows about her and this game. If he could buy Cabo and give it to her, it wouldn't make the slightest bit of difference. She'd still make him suffer. Of course, she told him she'd think about it. Maybe she'll go, maybe she won't. Either way it doesn't matter. Their relationship has become a dull routine of meeting once or twice a week in the evening. They eat out and end up back at her apartment. She's kept him on a tight leash where sex is concerned, not giving him what she knows he wants but hinting at her willingness to, maybe, if he's a good boy, just to keep him in the game and foolishly hoping.

His first present was a 24-karat charm bracelet, and he brings other charms to add to it. She wears the bracelet when she sees him to humor him, although she decided not to this evening, just to see what his reaction would be and how he'd interpret the fact that she isn't wearing it.

Expensive or not, charm bracelets are for teenagers. She expected better, something more imaginative.

She's bored with him now. She could let things go on as they are forever and he'd probably play along. It's time to up the ante. Would he leave his wife? If he doesn't, the game will be over and she'll find someone new to toy with. If he does, her victory will be sweet and she'll be done with him anyway and will relish sharing that fact with him. There's nothing more enjoyable than laying low powerful men. They play into her hands so easily and willingly. You'd almost think they want it to happen. Maybe they do. Maybe it's like a death wish. The buzzer sounds and she walks to the intercom. "Yes?" she asks coolly. "Hey," she hears him say. "Your late," she says and buzzes him in.

Steve gives Amber a kiss at the door, hands her the gift box and notices she isn't wearing the charm bracelet. What could this mean? He takes a beer from the fridge and a glass from the cabinet and watches her as he pours. She sits at the island in the kitchen and places the gift box in front of her. He sits across from her and doesn't like the way she's staring down at it, without a hint of interest in her expression and, really, why should there be? She knows what's inside. Still, it was a pretty good idea. The first charm was a sailboat, then an anchor, then a buoy. She picks up the box and undoes the ribbon and he studies her face as she opens it and removes the charm, two lanyards tied in a square knot. She holds it up and looks at it, her expression blank, and then at him and raises her eyebrows. He watches her drop the charm in the box and set it aside, her expression now one of supreme boredom. "So, what about Cabo?" he asks.

"What's the point? Things would be the same there."

"Any suggestions?"

"Why do you treat me this way?"

He eyes her as he sips his beer and puts down his glass. He knows what the "little girl" pout and voice mean, a continuation of the same tiresome conversation they've been having lately about their relationship, always initiated by her. "How's that?"

"It's always the same. Dinner out, back here for sex...."

"What little there is of it," he interjects.

She glares at him, catches herself and quickly has her "hurt" expression back on her face. "What kind of relationship is that? You can do that with anyone."

"What do you have in mind?"

"More."

"Like what?"

"A life together."

"It's not gonna happen. You know that."

"I'm tired of holding back."

This sounds interesting. She hasn't taken this tack before. "Waddya mean?"

"I know what you want, and I want to give it to you, but I can't unless I feel you love me as much as I love you."

He laughs nervously. "So, what, now you love me?"

She frowns. "What's so funny about that?"

He's impressed. She looks genuinely hurt. Is she? She's good, so he can't be sure. She's lying about being in love, though, that much he is sure of. She's incapable of loving anyone, including herself. Having spent time with her, he's sensed self-loathing lurking in the shadows of her personality. It explains a lot about why she is the way she is, and he's been wondering what caused it. There must be a man at the bottom of it or else she wouldn't hate men the way she does and be so intent on punishing them. "Nothing, if it were true. Why should I believe you?" He reads contempt in the slight rise of her eyebrows and there's that icy stare he knows so well. It's moments like this that make him wonder whether his continued pursuit of her is really worth the trouble.

"You don't have to," she says.

"And if I don't?"

"We're through."

He sips his beer and studies her eyes. The game they've been playing is a lot like chess and he imagines her eyes look the way a queen's would, having masterfully worked the opposing king into a corner of the board. She has him where she wants him, all right, checkmated. His better sense tells him that as beautiful as she is and as much as he desires her, he should get up and leave and be done with her, but he is who he is, and he's come too far, and has too much invested to quit now and knows she knows that. There's always the possibility that she's bluffing, but he doesn't think she is. He watches her expression change and isn't surprised to see her looking at him coquettishly now.

"Just thinking about being together makes me horny," she says.

She tosses her panty on the chair and turns and sees him still dressed, lying on the bed with his back against the headboard and his hands behind his head, gazing at her with that dopey grin on his face. Not this game again, posing for him the way she did in the photographs. She knows it's a big turn on for him, but she's done with it. He might as well be jerking off watching porn. "Get undressed," she tells him. She watches him scamper off the bed, quickly undress and plop himself on the bed again. She stares down at him and tries to hide her contempt. He's such a little boy. They all are.

As much as she enjoys playing chess, she prefers bridge, her father's favorite game. He's masterful at both and taught her well and the pleasure she derives from systematically picking clean men like Steve is the same she feels when making a Grand Slam. The only card he has to play is his refusal to leave his wife. She has a trump.

She sits on the side of the bed and stares down at his erection. She hates it and wants nothing to do with penises, but forced herself to and learned how to use it to her advantage by allowing it to enter her vagina and only her vagina, that unfeeling place where it's out of sight and, by imaging herself rowing on the open ocean, out of mind. As much as the idea repulses her, she knows what she must do now. She shows him her "sweet look" and wraps her hand gently around it. She watches him gaze delightedly at the sight and thinks again how like a little boy he is where sex is concerned. "Feel good?" she asks. He looks at her glassy-eyed and nods. "I know it does," she says and shows him her "naughty look." "I know what you've wanted," she says, leaning over and taking it in her mouth and closing her eyes.

She pictures herself gliding along on the perfectly flat surface of the water with no land in sight and no sound. She's like a machine, continuously in motion. She can row as long as she needs to, there's plenty of ocean, but knows from experience she won't have to long. As much as men crave sex, they seem unable to control themselves and it's usually over in a matter of minutes and sometimes seconds, which is a blessing. Steve's taking a bit longer than usual, but she finally feels his body stiffen and jerk and her mouth filling with his semen. Her mind is screaming to take her mouth away and spit it out, but she forces herself not to and swallows it. She sits up and looks at him and shows him her "pleased and grateful look." "Like that?" His eyes are even glassier now and hooded and he nods contentedly. Good. Time to play her trump.

She feels his relief and renewed confidence in the way he's holding and kissing her, like he's regained control over her and now has the upper hand. Good. He positions himself between her legs and she spreads them and strokes his chest lightly with her fingertips. She feels the head of his penis pushing against her labia and looks in his eyes and shows him her "naughty look" again. "I know something else you've wanted," she says and sees him raise his eyebrows and smile down at her as she pulls back her legs and presents it to him.

She's wondered how this would feel, if and when she ever did allow it to happen. She knew it would be painful, there's no way it couldn't be, but it's even more so than she imagined as he pushes the head of his penis into her and the pain increases the further in it goes. She looks up at him as he slowly pumps, his eyes closed, his expression blissful, oblivious to the fact that he's causing her excruciating pain. Her body feels like it's being split in two. She despises him and if she had a knife, she'd cut off his penis, then plunge the knife into his heart.

She feels the man in the shadows in the back of her mind move forward. She can control Steve and men like him but doesn't think she'll ever be able to control the man in the shadows, only keep him at bay. She forces him not to come closer, but given the situation doing so is more difficult than ever.

She feels Steve's body jerking again as he empties himself in her and winces as he withdraws. He rolls over and lies on his back with his eyes closed. She turns toward him, puts a hand lightly on his chest, slowly strokes it and shows him her "pleased and grateful look" again. "Enjoy that?"

He opens his eyes and looks up at her. "Hmm...."

"Imagine doing it every night."

This is crazy. Steve can't believe she doesn't know he isn't going to leave Cyn. If Amber really thinks he is because she finally gave him what he wanted, she's not as sharp as he thought she was. Maybe she's gotten other men to leave their wives and thinks she can make any man do it. If so, then her tragic flaw is hubris.

Even if he did leave Cyn he knows Amber wouldn't give it to him again and then where would he be? It was good, though. No, fantastic! The idea of having this icy beauty all to himself and available whenever he wants is tantalizing, not that it's going to happen. He lies there, feeling exhausted and satisfied and tells himself he's done with her and that he really means it.

* * *

Cyn sits on the couch with her legs tucked under her, sipping a glass of wine and looking at Steve, who's slouched back with his legs crossed on the coffee table and a bottle of beer in his hand, resting it on his stomach. She listens to his account of his evening with Amber without commenting or asking questions. It's good that they're open and honest with each other and can share every detail of their lives, but it can be painful sometimes, there's no denying that. What she feels now is mostly worry. She knows her man. Everything she's heard leads her to believe he's had it with Amber, but he hasn't come out and said it, which is what's troubling and worrying her. "You're not going to see her again, are you?" she asks when he's finished. "You can't, Steve."

He sips his beer and shrugs. He's still savoring the intoxicating feeling of finally having triumphed over Amber and can't get the tantalizing idea of having her all to himself anytime he wants out of his head.

"I told you she was dangerous," Cyn says. "I knew it wouldn't make any difference, but just for the record."

"Duly noted."

There's no better time than now to discuss her concern about Ira and come clean about Matt. She must. Steve's going to find out sooner or later, so better now and from her. "Ira knows." She sees that got his attention. "He knows about everything, about Westminster, every last detail, I'm sure."

"How do you know?"

"He told me at the party. We talked while you were chatting up Amber. I'm worried, Steve. You're a star at the company and my business is doing great, but it's all because of Ira and he could shut us down in a heartbeat. I don't like feeling beholden to him. Know what I mean?"

Steve shrugs. "There's not much we can do about it."

"Maybe not, but maybe we shouldn't keep giving him reasons. You can't see her anymore. I know you're still toying with the idea, but you can't."

He nods slightly and stares down at his beer bottle.

Cyn stares at him and feels her anger about to erupt. His nod was almost imperceptible and looked noncommittal, and she knows he's still thinking about Amber, despite everything she's just shared with him. "Get your brains out of your balls!" she screams, raising her arms and clenching her hands to hit him. He flinches and she manages to restrain herself, but only just. Her violent outburst startles her as much as it does him. If there's anyone to blame for all this, it's herself. She was the one who thought allowing him his dalliances was the way to keep them together. She was certain at the time it was the right thing to do, but now she's questioning the wisdom of her decision. For the first time she feels things coming apart, the way you sense there's something wrong with your car just before it ends up broken down on the side of the road. This business with Amber is like that funny sound you begin hearing under the hood. She closes her eyes and unclenches her hands and lowers them, holding them out in front of her with her fingers spread and pushing against the space between them, testing it.

"You okay?" he asks.

She opens her eyes and looks at him. "Yeah. Be right back," she says and returns with the album and the CD with Ira's message on it. She sits next to him and hands him the album. "Your birthday present, in advance." She watches him raise his eyebrows, smile and look down at the album. He opens the cover and study the first photo, then the next and the next, slowly turning the pages. She sees he's transfixed by them and that he's both turned on and curious about everything having to do with them. He's about halfway through, which seems a good time to ask, and she puts her arm on the back of the couch and strokes the back of his neck. "Like them?"

"Yeah. They're hot. That guy at Bloomingdale's take them?"

"Yeah." She watches Steve work his way to the photos toward the end where she begins interacting with Matt and she can see he's struggling to keep his emotions in check. He stares at the last picture with a hangdog expression, and she sees his shoulders sag and waits for his reaction.

"I probably don't have the right to feel jealous or angry, huh?" he asks without looking at her.

"No, you don't. It was fun."

He glances at her. "Don't rub it in."

She hands him the CD and watches his eyes as he reads what's written on it. "From Ira," she says. "Get the picture?" She hopes he does, but despairs when he sets the CD aside on the couch and picks up the album again and stares down at the last photo with that same hangdog expression. He's focused on entirely the wrong thing. What he needs to focus on is the issue of their lifestyle, the fact that they're in over their heads and that if they continue this way, they risk losing everything. She knew that if she was ever unfaithful, this is how he'd react, like a hurt little boy, the way all men do when the tables are turned.

"Have there been others?" he asks without looking at her.

She's never seen him like this and tries hard not to view him as pathetic. It would be so easy to punish him, but she pushes that thought from her mind. She knows he's better than this and feels it's up to her to bring out the best in him.

She's felt from early on that women are in one of two camps where men are concerned: "stand them up" or "pull them down." Her mom and Amber are in the "pull them down" camp. Cyn doesn't agree with her mom, but understands why she feels the way she does. As for Amber, she must have her reasons. Cyn doesn't have time to waste wondering about who's right and who's wrong. It's not important. What's important is that the skin on the back of her neck tells her, the way people's arthritic joints do, that there's a storm coming and she knows that if she and Steve are going to weather it, they need to stand together and trust each other completely. Now more than ever it's important to be honest with him. She strokes his cheek gently with her fingertips. "No, baby."

* * *

Steve and Chris stand in the tee box on the seventeenth hole of the Ocean Course at Cabo del Sol in Cabo San Lucas. It's the signature hole, a 178-yard par three over a sandy beach to a green perched on granite outcroppings and protected by bunkers with the Sea of Cortez looming in front and to the right of the green. It's spectacular, but treacherous. They're both good golfers and have 7 irons in their hands. There's a box of expensive cigars riding on the match and Chris is up a stroke, having birdied the last hole.

Chris walks forward to the championship markers and tees up his ball. He steps back and eyes the flag. He takes an easy practice swing and steps forward again and addresses the ball. He swings and sends the ball in a high arc straight toward the flag, cutting it to counteract the sea breeze pushing it left. The ball lands and sticks about five feet from the hole. Cyn and Chris's wife Jacquie clap in their cart and Chris turns and grins at Steve. He picks up his tee and walks back to him. "Pretty sure you need a hole-in-one here, buddy," Chris says.

Steve glances at him and walks to the markers and tees up his ball. He steps back and looks at the flag and tries to visualize his ball's flight. He hasn't played well today or since they arrived. He hasn't had his usual confidence in his swing and knows from experience that when that happens the results can be disastrous.

He takes a forceful practice swing, which is very unusual for him, and then another, which rattles him. He steps forward and addresses the ball and tries to focus his attention on it, but his mind is on Ira and the question of what's going on with him. Something is. He hasn't been himself lately. He seems distracted in meetings, like his mind is a million miles away. Even worse, he looks worried. The company's doing well, so it can't be about business. It's something else. Maybe Connell knows.

Steve bends his knees slightly and waggles his club. He glances at the flag one more time. He wants to do what Chris did but has been having difficulty cutting and drawing the ball and now has spent far too much time over it. He swings and hits the ball cleanly and looks up and watches its flight. It's headed in a high arc toward the left side of the green, as intended, but isn't cutting right enough and lands with a splash of white sand in the left greenside bunker. He picks up his tee, glances at Chris and sees his grin is even bigger now.

"I can taste those stogies now," Chris says.

Cyn knows the last place Steve wants to be is standing in the bunker one shot down, having to hole out on this shot to tie Chris. If he does it will be sheer luck, but luck seems to have deserted him as it tends to when he's not playing well. He's passionate about golf, but he's been preoccupied about work and what's going on with Ira and has been for weeks. She's sensed the storm clouds gathering and moving closer all the time. Whatever form it takes, when it hits, it'll be a doozy. She can feel it.

She's lately been thinking they should do more than just change their lifestyle, that what they should really do is change their lives, do something that doesn't have anything to do with Ira. She's prepared to do it but hasn't broached the subject with Steve. He hasn't been in the right frame of mind to have that conversation.

She watches him from across the green. He's been spending way too much time over the ball. He finally takes his club back and swings. She can see he's trying to baby the shot, just pop the ball up over the lip of the bunker onto the green and roll it toward the cup and, hopefully, in, but he blades it and the ball shoots out of the bunker, narrowly missing her, and lands with a splash in the Sea of Cortez behind her. She sees he's trying to remain calm as he rakes his way out of the bunker but knows he's disgusted with himself. It's time they talked.

* * *

Steve rolls over on his back and Cyn turns toward him and snuggles against him. That helped a bit. The end of the world could have begun and he wouldn't have noticed. She puts her hand on his chest and strokes it lightly with her fingertips and lets him relax a few minutes and enjoy the afterglow of their lovemaking. "I've been thinking…," she finally says.

He opens his eyes and looks at her. "About?"

"Things. What would you do if you left the company and did something else?"

"Why would I do that?"

"I dunno…. What would you do if you did? What would you be happy doing?"

His mind is blank. He's never thought about doing anything else. Why would he? He's doing what he's always wanted to do. He knows by the way she asked, though, that she did for a reason and that it's important, but he has no idea what to say. He closes his eyes and concentrates on the feel of her fingertips stroking his chest.

"Hmm?" she coaxes.

"I dunno."

"No?"

He thinks of her question again and "happy" stands out. That's why she asked, because she knows he's miserable. Those hot steamy summer days in the Bronx come to mind, playing stick ball with his friends in the street, hearing the Mr. Softee jingle and looking up and seeing the blue and white truck on the next block. It seemed to take forever to get to them and when it finally did, they'd gather at the window and one by one hand the driver in his white uniform and hat their money. He was a hero to them. He knew what each of them wanted and handed it to them without having to ask. They'd sit on the stoop, licking and twirling their ice cream cones and talk about Pee Wee Herman movies and the latest episode of *Mystery Science Theater 3000*, about their favorite computer games and how the Yankees were doing, about which girls they'd like to get alone in the dark and they couldn't have been happier. Steve opens his eyes and looks at Cyn and sees she's been gazing at him, smiling and waiting patiently. "Open an ice cream parlor," he says and isn't surprised she's surprised to hear it.

"Huh. I wouldn't have figured. I want you to be happy, Steve. If you're happy I'm happy. If selling ice cream makes you happy it's fine with me. Don't get me wrong. I like our lifestyle as much as you do, but there are more important things in life."

He could hear her biological clock ticking in the "more important things in life" part and it surprises him that it would be at a time like this, when so much about their situation is uncertain, but not really. He realizes how focused he's been on getting what he wants and how little attention he's paid lately to Cyn and what she wants and it sobers him. He's been selfish. They told each other they wanted to have kids someday. Why not now? He thinks he'd be a good dad and knows Cyn would be a great mom. He imagines what life with kids would be like. It would mean the ultimate change in his lifestyle, that's for sure. No more screwing around. He thinks of what he went through with Amber and how empty his experience with Thien is. It would be a relief and a welcome change to be done with all that. As far as making love to only one woman is concerned, he'll never get enough of Cyn. "Wanna have a kid?"

She looks at him tenderly, smiles and gives him a squeeze. "Yeah," she says and kisses him, then draws back her head and fixes her eyes on his. "Trust me, Steve. Nothing's going to come between us."

He does, now more than ever.

* * *

Ira sits alone in the conference area of his office, gazing out at the Pacific. Such a lovely view and beautiful day, but it's lost on him. He hasn't heard anything from Uri and can only assume he's either being detained by Rios or the Mexican authorities or dead. In any event, his flank is exposed, and he's never felt so vulnerable. The long knives are out for him. He doesn't know which direction they'll come from, but he knows they're coming. It's only a matter of time.

The thought crosses his mind that maybe it's time to pack it all in and move back to Israel with Adele and just relax and enjoy life. How foolish. There's no place on earth he can hide from his pursuers. He hears the intercom on his desk phone beep. "Steve's here for the eleven o'clock," he hears Suzanna say. An investigation of her brother's limo service turned up no link to Rios. He's sure there is one, though. Rios is good. Ira will give him that. He looks over his shoulder and sees Steve in the doorway with a report in hand. Ira waves him over and indicates the seat across from his.

Steve sits and studies Ira's face with concern. He doesn't like the way Ira looks, detached and far away. "You okay, Ira?"

"Fine, fine. How's your lovely wife?"

"Fine."

"How was Cabo?"

"Good. Golf was lousy, but otherwise good."

"It's a pastime I thankfully never took up. I don't know why people subject themselves to it. Life is frustrating enough as it is. I'm happy to see you broke things off with Court Brennan's daughter."

Steve shifts uneasily. He thought he was here to discuss his report, but it seems to be the farthest thing from Ira's mind and he's not sure where this is going.

"Westminster is one thing. There's no one of any consequence involved, other than you, of course. But the daughter of a Board member...."

"Can I speak freely, Ira?"

"Of course."

"I understand your wanting to protect the company's reputation and the financial implications of bad press and all that, but, honestly, I don't appreciate living under a microscope. Are you watching everyone this way?"

"Yes, although there's not much interesting going on with the others. Anyway, you're of particular interest to me."

"Why's that?"

"I don't know how much longer I'm going to be here, in this position."

"Are you ill?"

Ira shakes his head.

"Thinking of retiring?"

"I don't know...possibly. I want there to be an orderly succession, in the event I do leave."

"Isn't Connell the obvious choice?"

"One would think so," Ira says, tapping the arm of his chair thoughtfully. He looks at Steve. "You'd be a better one."

This idea strikes Steve as irrational, crazy. Still, Ira seems composed. Is it possible he's unhinged? "I don't have any operational experience."

Ira waves dismissively. "That's Bill Keane's department," he says, referring to the company's Chief Operating Officer. "Your job is to keep coming up with investment strategies that make us money."

"Have you discussed this with Connell?"

"No."

Steve holds up the report. "Did you want to discuss this?"

"Ah, yes, your report…." The intercom beeps again. "Yes?" Ira asks.

"Sorry to disturb your meeting," they hear Suzanna say. "An agent Reynolds with the FBI would like to see you when you're finished with Steve. He's waiting in the lobby."

Ira gazes at the Pacific, his eyes coming to rest on the horizon. "Ask him to come up and wait."

"He'd like you to go down and bring your things with you," Suzanna says.

Ira sighs. So, the Feds have gotten to him first. "Very well."

Steve stares at him, his mind racing. The FBI? He has no idea what's going on or what Ira might have done, but he isn't entirely surprised. He's had a sense of foreboding about the company for months. As hard as it is to believe, he now realizes that control of this clockwork operation Ira micromanages and works so hard to protect is slipping away from him, yet he seems perfectly calm and resigned to the fact. It's bizarre.

* * *

Steve and Cyn sit on the couch in the entertainment room, staring in amazement at the screen as they watch the evening news. It's the lead local story. Ira Weiss, the founder of PACBOND, a prominent businessman and a pillar of society in Orange County has been indicted as a co-conspirator on a charge of drug trafficking, has been arraigned and is out on bail. Also named in the indictment are Rodolfo Rios, the notorious Mexican drug lord, and Ameen Khan, a citizen of Afghanistan thought to be living in Lahore, Pakistan, but whose whereabouts are currently unknown. The prosecution argued that Ira posed a flight risk. The judge agreed and ordered him to surrender his passport. It seems surreal to Steve and Cyn to be watching footage of Ira, such a secretive man and so protective of his privacy, now surrounded by reporters and camera people, all pressing in on him as he slowly makes his way from the courthouse to the waiting limo. Of course, he answered none of the shouted questions, but his criminal defense attorney, one of the best in the country, made a brief statement before climbing into the limo, saying that his client was innocent and would be proven so at trail. Steve shakes his head and looks at Cyn. "Should I call him?"

Cyn stares at the screen and shrugs. She's not happy about what's happening to Ira, but has no sympathy for him. "Poor Adele. She must be a basket case."

"Maybe you should give her a call."

"Yeah, maybe I will."

His phone rings. He picks it up and looks at the screen. It's Connell. What time is it there? Three-thirty in the morning, something like that? "Hi, Connell. Heard the news?"

"Legal briefed me. I spoke with Ira a little while ago."

"Did you know anything about this?"

"No, but I've known he's had things going on in the shadows. He's been very preoccupied lately."

"Tell me about it."

"He told me he discussed succession with you."

"He brought it up out of the blue. Said he wasn't sure how much longer he'd be with the company and that he was considering me as a possibility. I told him I didn't have any operational experience."

"Right, well, as he told you, that's not the important thing. Ira's going to be lying low for the foreseeable future. He won't be entirely out of the picture. He'll keep in touch from home. I doubt he'll leave the house. He has it surrounded by private security. He fears for his life and with good reason. So, for the time being we want you to stand in for him there. You'll be Acting President and Bill will handle the operational end of things. We need you to concentrate on the company continuing to make money. Understood?"

"Yeah."

"PR is working on damage control. We'll get through this. Let's talk in the morning. Good night."

"Good night." He puts the phone on the table and looks at Cyn. "I'm Acting President now."

She raises her eyebrows. "Congratulations." She tried her best to sound happy for him, but her strong feeling is that the storm is now almost upon them.

* * *

Ira pours two more fingers of single malt scotch into his glass, places the bottle next to it on the desk in his study and massages his eyes. What a day this has been. A nightmare. He knows these press people are like savages, but he's never been on the receiving end of the Fourth Estate's particular brand of incivility. Notoriety is anathema to him and now he's the topic of conversation around the world, certainly among the business community and those who love news about the misfortunes of powerful wealthy people. *Schadenfreude* is simply the German word for the pleasure people derive from the suffering of others. Everyone delights in it, some secretly, others openly, and the more he's humiliated, the lower he's laid by this scandal, the more people will enjoy relishing the sordid details.

He takes a long sip and stares at the picture of Adele and him on the desk. He hasn't seen her since he arrived home. She's been upstairs in the bedroom with the door closed and he hasn't wanted to disturb her. Truth be told, he hasn't been able to muster the courage to face her. He knows how she feels: utterly betrayed. How could she not? The man she's been married to most of her life and who she believed to be a successful businessman and morally upright person is now charged with drug trafficking. Should he have shared his secret life with her? No, he couldn't possibly have. He made the decision at the outset to shield her from it. She's a moral person. She couldn't have abided living with a man involved in illegal activities, not to mention immoral ones. What she didn't know couldn't hurt her. Well, so much for that.

He drains the glass, pours another two fingers of scotch and stares at the picture of his parents. Thank God they're not alive. He can't imagine them being subjected to this. It's too awful to contemplate. He surveys his desk. His computer is gone and all the phones and the contents of his file drawers have been confiscated, as have those in his office at work, to be painstakingly gone through in the prosecution's search for incriminating evidence. How humiliating and degrading it must have been for Adele to have men in drab suits appear at the door, flashing badges in her face and waving a search warrant, forcing their way into their home and carting off equipment and boxes of documents. How can she ever forgive him? It doesn't seem humanly possible.

He sips his scotch. How much time will he end up doing? How silly to be thinking about that. Were he a younger man it would matter, but at his age any sentence might as well be a life sentence, a death sentence.

He stands and walks to one of the windows facing the street and pulls back the drape just enough to peak out. The walk lights are on and he can see the security detail sitting in the car parked by the curb. There's another posted at the back of the house. Rios is undoubtedly concerned that Ira will cooperate with the authorities and will try to kill him before he's able to.

He thinks of his decision to buy this house, with the ground in back sloping down to the golf course. At the time it seemed like a glacis, a bulwark against attack, but now it doesn't seem so secure. He's worried about all that open land, unlit and unpatrolled at night. How easily someone could approach the house from that direction. When they come, he's certain they'll come that way. He'll have to discuss his concerns with security.

He lets the drape fall back and walks back to his chair. He sits and drains his glass and puts it on the desk. It's best if he sleeps in one of the guest rooms tonight. He's still not ready to face Adele, even after a few drinks.

He walks up the staircase and sees that their bedroom door is now open and the room dark. He tiptoes down the hall and is just past the bedroom door when he hears Adele call, "Ira!" He walks back to the doorway and peers in. "Yes, dear?" He sees her under the covers with her back to him. She looks over her shoulder at him.

"Where are you going?" she demands.

"I thought I'd sleep in one of the guest bedrooms."

"Don't be ridiculous!" she says and lays her head back on the pillow. "Come to bed."

"Yes, dear." He can hear it in her voice. He'll have a lot of explaining to do in the morning. She'll insist he tell her everything and he will, in all its sordid detail. He owes it to her and wants to. Maybe she can find it within herself to forgive him. That's all that matters to him now.

CHAPTER 20

Andrew

Rita makes her way home from the court appearance in Los Angeles. Rush hour traffic is crawling on the 5 South out of downtown L.A. She's had a hard time keeping her mind focused on work ever since her most recent conversation with Aracelle and today was a particularly difficult one.

The case was routine. Her client, a young undocumented Salvadoran, was rounded up in an immigration sweep at the restaurant where he worked, cleaning up all night after banquets, doing alone the work of three people and being paid minimum wage. He's an honest, hardworking family man with a wife and three children back home and he's their primary source of income. He lives in L.A. in a 650-square-feet apartment with seven other men, which is the only way he and they can afford to live here and send money home. To her thinking, if everyone in the country was as hardworking and frugal and responsible as her client, it would be a much better place. The judge ordered him deported and he was taken into custody and then to jail to await deportation. More than once during the hearing her mind was elsewhere, and she was brought back to the matter at hand by the judge's, "Counselor?" and had to ask to have the question repeated. It was discourteous and unprofessional, but she couldn't help it.

When she first spoke with Aracelle and told her about the death threat, Aracelle said she'd ask her brother about it. That was weeks ago.

Aracelle called yesterday and said her brother had asked Rodí in passing about it and he said that he did indeed intend to kill the lawyer, but would do so at a time and in a place and manner of his choosing. Aracelle said this is very important to Rodí, that to him killing is an art and he takes great care in planning executions. Rita should be careful and try not to put herself in situations where there are no other people around. Of course, they both know Aracelle's advice is ludicrous. Rita could be standing in the middle of Times Square on New Year's Eve and if that were when and where Rios wanted her dead she would be.

She realized when she stopped seeing Deborah that she had no one else to talk to and Kate came to mind, which shows how much their relationship has changed since Ed died. She needed white dress shirts and usually shops at Nordstrom, but thought why not buy them at Bloomingdale's and have lunch with Kate? She's glad she did.

She was surprised to hear Kate's seeing a man so much younger than she. It struck her as totally out of character and nice and Kate looked and sounded so happy talking about him. Good for her! She should be so lucky!

Kate was delighted to hear she's decided to have the baby and also that she's begun taking Antabuse and wasn't at all judgmental when Rita said that, even so, she's still drinking despite the nausea and vomiting. Kate said she thinks it's courageous of her to try to stop or at least curb her drinking, and that she knows she has the health of her baby at heart and told her to just keep trying her best. Kate also said she understood her decision to stop seeing the therapist, if she felt it wasn't doing any good.

Rita was surprised to hear that earlier in her life Kate suffered from severe depression and that it took her a long time to recover from it. She'd always thought of Kate as this perfect being, just as she'd always viewed her as a threat when Ed was alive. How wrong we can be about people. Kate said if she needs any help, she just has to ask, that she'll be there for her. Rita was happy to hear it. She needs all the help she can get.

The black Mercedes E-Class sedan in front of her stops suddenly and she rear-ends it. "Shit!" she screams and thumps the steering wheel. They were only crawling along, so there's probably not that much damage, but still. She sees the blinking right taillight and the driver motioning for her to head over to the breakdown lane and it seems to take them forever to reach it. She glances at him as they get out of their cars: white, handsome, middle-aged, wavy blonde hair. She looks at the black paint marks on the front bumper of her red Camry and then at the red paint marks on the rear bumper of the Mercedes. "Doesn't look to bad," she hears him say. "No," she says and looks at him and notices the WestWave logo on his shirt. "I'll get my information," she says. She walks to her car and collects a pen, her license, insurance card and a business card. He has his information ready when she returns and they exchange.

"I'm really sorry about stopping so suddenly," he says. "The guy in front of me slammed on his brakes. I nearly rear-ended him."

"I was probably following too closely," she says.

He looks at her business card and grins. "Surprisingly honest for a lawyer."

She glances at him and frowns and looks at his license: Andrew Weston. She knows the name from the news. No wonder he's wearing WestWave clothes. He owns the company. It prides itself on manufacturing products in the U.S. The company is cited as a model of success by the City of Los Angeles in its efforts to attract manufacturing companies. WestWave's racy ads featuring beautiful young women showing lots of skin are everywhere. The company was once in the news for its practice of employing undocumented immigrants. So was Andrew when he and his then wife Pia Kesterling, the actress and human rights activist, were going through their divorce. She got something like twenty million as part of the settlement and Rita remembers thinking at the time, Good for her! "You own WestWave, don't you?"

He smiles. "Yeah. I hope you're a customer."

"I'm not exactly in your demo."

"Beautiful women are the sweet spot," he says and glances at her business card again. "I'm sure you know all about our problems."

"Yeah."

"We try, but it's really hard to verify people's status."

"I know. Listen, I don't think you're the Big Bad Wolf. I wish every undocumented immigrant that's here working hard and paying taxes were just left alone. It's hypocritical to persecute them and a waste of time and money to prosecute them."

He glances at her left hand and sees she's not wearing a ring. "Rita's my mother's name, Arithea, an old family name."

"Huh. Never heard that. It's beautiful."

He copies down her information on the back of her business card. "Married?"

"I lost my husband recently."

He looks at her. "Sorry to hear that. How?"

"He was a cop. He was shot."

"I wanted to be a cop when I was a kid."

"Count your blessings."

He hands back her license and insurance card. "Well, the least I can do for all the trouble I've caused you is buy you dinner."

She fixes her eyes on his. "I'm pregnant and an alcoholic."

He smiles and raises his eyebrows. "Then we'd have a lot to talk about."

She follows him to a steakhouse just off the 5 in Commerce. She recognizes the place as soon as she sees it. She hasn't been here since she was fifteen. A friend of hers had her Quinceañera in the banquet room. She thinks about the girl she was then and everything that's happened since. What would that fifteen-year-old Rita have thought had she known what lay ahead?

They order drinks and dinner. She desperately wants a vodka tonic but settles for the tonic. He says it must be hard work defending undocumented immigrants and she shrugs and says it's a job, like any other. He asks what type of people she typically defends, and she says all types and tells him about Aracelle and Leticia and he listens wide-eyed as she tells him about receiving the death threat from Rios.

"Have you told the police?"

"My husband knew about it. There's nothing they could or would do."

"So, what are you going to do?"

"Get on with my life." She sees he's puzzled. "What?"

"I'm trying to imagine myself in your situation. I'd like to think I'd be as calm about it as you are. I don't think I would be."

"What else can I do? Look at it this way. We're all going to die someday, someplace, somehow and we don't know where or when or how, so what's the difference if I get shot in a parking garage next week or die of pneumonia when I'm ninety-two?"

He shakes his head slowly and smiles. "You're really something."

"So, what about you? How'd you get into the clothing business?"

"My grandfather was a draper, a cloth wholesaler. My dad started a textile manufacturing company. His factory was in City of Industry. I used to work there during summer vacations. Learned how to run all the machines. My favorite was the frame."

"What's that?" She sees his eyes brighten.

"It's this monstrous contraption as long as a bowling alley. Once fabric is dyed it has to be finished with heat. So, you put these enormous rolls of material on one end and feed it through the frame and it passes slowly over jets of flame and is rolled up on the other end. I used to watch the fabric moving along and imagine it was disappearing into the mouth of a fire-breathing dragon."

"I can see it."

"The guys in the factory were great. They could've given me a hard time, you know, being the owner's son, but they didn't. They were really proud when I went off to college. I was like one of their own making it."

"Yeah. I can see that too. What did you major in?"

"Business management."

"Did you know you wanted to start a clothing company?"

He nods. "I guess it's in my blood."

She sips her tonic and looks at him over the rim of her glass and considers what he's shared with her so far about himself. He seems like a genuinely nice and sweet man, very easy-going and understanding. She's glad she met him, although she wishes it hadn't taken rear-ending his car to do it. "I think I'll have a drink," she says and sees his concern. "Don't worry. I won't turn into a fire-breathing dragon."

He laughs. "What would you like?"

She holds up her glass. "One of these with vodka in it."

He catches the waiter's eye. "A vodka tonic and I'll have another."

"What's it like hanging out with the Hollywood crowd?" she asks.

"I don't anymore. I only did for a short time when I was with Pia."

"I've seen a couple of her movies. She's good. Nice person?"

He nods.

"Just didn't work out, huh?"

"We never saw each other. She was always on location."

"I had that problem with my first husband, the never seeing each other part."

"I guess if you're with the right person it can work."

"I guess." The waiter returns and places their drinks on the table. She picks up hers and takes a long satisfying sip. There's plenty of time before the effects of the Antabuse kick in. She's noticed that he's not wearing a wedding band. "You didn't remarry?"

He shakes his head. "I date. Nothing serious."

"The models in your ads?"

"I've gone out with a few of them."

"They're beautiful."

"When's the baby due?"

"Late February," she says and sees that puzzled look again. "What?"

"I've gotta tell you, I wish I had half your courage."

"If I were so courageous I wouldn't be a drunk."

He shakes his head. "I think you've got it wrong. You know as well as I do, alcoholism is like any addiction. Some people are more susceptible to it than others and kicking it is never easy. It's how you deal with it that matters. You seem to be dealing with it pretty well. I used to be addicted to coke. I nearly let it kill me."

She sensed from his tone of voice and expression and the look in his eyes that he was speaking from personal experience, so she isn't surprised to hear about the coke. She views him differently now, more like a regular person and likes that. "How'd you stop?"

"Took a cold hard look at myself in the mirror."

She shrugs. "I do that every morning."

"All night in a hotel room in Manhattan."

She raises her eyebrows. "Huh." She tries to imagine what looking at herself in a mirror all night would be like. Could she do it, and if she could what would she see that she doesn't see now? Would she come face to face with that insecure kid and be able to talk sense to her?

They arrive at their cars, keys in hand and he turns to her. "Listen," he says, "you're going to end up paying most of the cost to have your car repaired and you'll get dinked on your insurance. Don't bother filing a claim. Just have it fixed and send me the bill."

"Thanks, but I'll take care of it. I'm the one who rear-ended you."

He smiles. "I'm glad you did. I really enjoyed meeting you. Can I see you again?"

"Sure. You've got my info."

He holds out his hand. "Well, take care."

She takes it. "You too."

"Drive safely."

"I will. Thanks."

She watches his taillights as she follows him south on the 5 past Angels Stadium and Disneyland in Anaheim toward the 55. What a day this has been. It was nice meeting Andrew, although not the actual running into him part. Dinner with him took her mind off her awful performance in court and the fact that she lost for her client, if not the death threat. He seems like a down to earth guy. They live in very different worlds, but hearing about his own struggle with addiction makes her feel they have a connection. Will she see him again? Will he call? It would be nice. She watches his taillights pull ahead as he continues toward Newport Beach, and she slows to exit the 55 in Santa Ana. She can feel herself getting nauseous and hopes she gets home before she begins heaving. She doesn't have far to go.

She runs into the house and the bathroom and kneels in front of the toilet. She lifts the seat and vomits dinner and the drinks into the bowl until there's nothing left in her stomach and dry heaves. She watches the strands of saliva and mucous sway as they lengthen. Her phone rings and she takes it out of her bag, grabs a towel and wipes her eyes and nose and mouth and looks at the screen. She doesn't recognize the number, gets to her feet, puts the phone on the counter and stands and looks at herself in the mirror. She's pale and her eyes are bloodshot. She rinses her mouth with water and spits it out in the sink and hears the call go to voice mail.

She picks up the phone and puts it to her ear and stares at herself in the mirror as she wipes her mouth and listens to the message. "Hi," she hears and recognizes Andrew's voice, "just checking to make sure you made it home all right. Really enjoyed meeting you. Talk with you soon. Good night." She puts the phone back on the counter. Should she stand here all night, staring at herself? She probably should but can't. Her head and stomach ache and she's tired and has to be up early. She looks down at the phone. Why is he interested in her? She wouldn't be. She looks at the mess she made in the toilet, flushes it and watches it swirl and go down the drain and wishes she could rid herself of the mess she's made of her life that easily.

* * *

Andrew sends off his reply to his marketing director's email. The plan to expand from surf, beach and boardwalk to business is coming along nicely. The clothes are targeted at women and men 18 to 25; young people just beginning their careers who need business dress, but want to maintain their generational identity. They'll need new models, maybe a new photographer. This campaign calls for a fresh new look.

He sits back, sips his beer and looks at the picture of Pia and him on the desk next to the computer in his study. They only vacationed a few times and this picture was taken in Barbados, where the baby was conceived. He was being honest when he told Rita that Pia's a nice person. If she'd had the baby, they'd still be together. There'd still be the issue of her schedule, but he would have gladly taken on the responsibility of raising their child single-handedly. He'll never figure out why, when they discussed having a family before they married, she said she wanted kids. She seemed sincere, but then she called him from England where she was on location and told him she was pregnant and wasn't going to have the baby. Just like that. He tried to talk her out of having an abortion, but she had one anyway in London and that was the end of the marriage. The press made it seem like she took him to the cleaners, but he gave her the money willingly.

Wanting to have a family wasn't the only thing he misread about Pia. Before they met, he saw *Lily in the Afternoon*, the remake of *Belle de*

Jour, and her portrayal of a fantasizing but frigid young wife, who works secretly as a prostitute during weekday afternoons and blossoms sexually was thoroughly convincing. He imagined she had a real appetite for sex and learned firsthand how good an actress she really is. He has no idea where she is these days or what she's up to but wishes her well.

Rita reminds him a lot of his mom. They're both strong women, although he can see Rita doesn't think she is. Addiction can do that to you. His dad was an alcoholic and he watched his mom deal with him. She loved him but wasn't about to be co-dependent. She gave his dad an ultimatum: if he stopped drinking, he could stay at home and if he couldn't, he should get his own place and visit when he was sober. His dad got an apartment near the factory and visited the house infrequently. When he went on a bender he really went to pieces. A doctor at the VA hospital finally prescribed Antabuse. His dad went through hell for a long time, taking the drug and going through a bottle of cheap scotch a day and spending hours in the bathroom puking his guts out, but he finally got sober.

His dad had been sober a long time by the time Pia arrived on the scene, and when she met him she thought he was the sweetest man in the world. That's the way it is with drunks, with all addicts, really. Their families suffer and are left with permanent scars and the people who meet them after they've kicked their addiction enjoy all the sweetness and light. It isn't fair, but that's the way it is and he doesn't hold it against his dad. He's done his fair share of making other people's lives miserable.

He has some idea of what Rita's going through, but this death threat business. It's difficult to get his head around it. He knows she's right when she says she has to get on with her life, but still.

He glances at Pia in the photograph and sips his beer. He remembers that moment, standing in the breakdown lane, when he asked Rita to have dinner with him and how she looked him in the eyes and told him she was pregnant and an alcoholic, just like that. He admires her honesty and her courage. It would be nice having a partner like that in life.

* * *

Rita's been to Catalina once before. She and Ricky were kids and their aunt took them over on the ferry and they spent the day walking around Avalon. As Andrew pulls back on the wheel and the nose comes up and they lift off the runway at John Wayne into a sunny partly cloudy sky she's uneasy about flying there in his twin-engine plane. She's always nervous when she flies, fearful that the plane will explode or experience catastrophic mechanical failure and fall out of the sky. And this is no commercial jet. There seems to be very little separating her from the air outside and the ground below, which is getting farther away by the moment as they climb.

On the other hand, the noise-canceling headset is pretty amazing. She knows the plane's engines are loud, but she can barely hear them. Andrew looks at her with a big grin, as if to say, "Isn't this the coolest thing?" She smiles and looks around as the plane begins to level off. It is pretty cool, and the view is spectacular. It's a view you don't get when you're sitting in Business Class. You can actually see where you're going. She understands now why people love to fly. It's a thrilling experience and having your own plane is a nice benefit of being wealthy.

She can see Newport Beach before her and Catalina off in the distance. The island seems a lot bigger and closer from up here than it does from the ground. Andrew mentioned that the distance between John Wayne and Catalina Airport, "Airport in the Sky" he said it's called, is about thirty-eight miles and that the trip won't take long.

She was surprised and happy when he called the day after the accident and invited her to go to Catalina. She was hoping they might see each other again, although she had her doubts that he'd actually call. But he sounded like he couldn't wait to see her and sure acted that way when he picked her up and gave her a big hug. His sudden interest in her has thrown her a bit and she's trying hard not to second-guess his feelings and intentions. "Know much about Catalina?" she hears him ask and looks at him. "A little," she says.

"First people who lived there were the Tongva, tribal people. They date back to 7000 B.C. They lived around San Pedro and Playa del Rey. They used to mine soapstone there. They called the island Pimunga."

Both the name of the people and the name they gave the island strike her as odd sounding and not very native Californian. "Pimunga?"

"No idea what it means. A Portuguese explorer named Cabrillo discovered it and claimed it for Spain. That was a little after Columbus arrived. The way the island got its current name is that another Spanish explorer rediscovered it a hundred years later, on the eve of Saint Catherine's day, so he named it in her honor. Aleuts used to come to the island from Russia to hunt otter. They got along all right with the natives, but they brought diseases and that was the end of the Tongvans. It was a Mexican land grant rancho for a while. It's been home to smugglers, whalers. The Union army had a garrison there for a while. The barracks is still there. It's the oldest building on the island. It's used by a yacht club now. The whole vacation spot thing started in the 1890s. Wrigley owned it for a while."

"That I do know."

"Do you know the Chicago Cubs used to train there?"

"No."

"Wrigley really put the place on the map. He built the casino and did all the major development. They closed the island to tourists during World War II. The Army used it as a training facility and the steamships as troop transports. The Brown Berets tried to reclaim it for Mexico in '72."

The Chicana in Rita stirs. "Their real agenda was the plight of Mexican Americans in this country. They wanted to make their voices heard. So, they were heard, not that it made a difference."

He smiles. He likes this fiery side of her that he occasionally sees flashes of. "Ever been zip lining?"

"No, and I'm not going to!"

He laughs. "There's an awesome one on the island now. We'll do it sometime."

"Over my dead body!"

"It's fun!"

"I'm sure it's a blast!"

He grins and gives her thigh a squeeze.

"Why'd they put the airport on top of a mountain?" she asks.

He shrugs. "Don't know. It's a little tricky, not recommended for inexperienced flyers. Don't worry. You're in good hands."

She surveys the island as they approach. Part of it is forested and part nothing but barren rock and sand and the only development seems to be Avalon, which is straight ahead.

"See the bison when you were here?" he asks.

"No."

"Let's see if we can find some." He banks and flies low along the shoreline and they scan the hillsides.

She spots three and points. "There!"

"Good eyes!" He climbs and banks toward Descanso Canyon. "There's the zip line," he says, nodding toward it and grinning.

She looks down and sees someone traversing the canyon at a high rate of speed.

"See? You're strapped in a harness attached to the line," he says. "It's perfectly safe." He banks and they head toward the airport.

She's heard stories of gondolas at ski resorts crashing to the ground. They were "perfectly safe," too. As they make their approach, things look and seem normal to her, but then she feels the crosswind and sees him working to counteract it and she barely feels the plane touch down on the runway. He knows what he's doing, all right.

He nods toward the main building as they taxi toward the parking area. "They serve 'Hundred Dollar Hamburgers' in the restaurant here."

"What?"

"Pilots fly over from the mainland just to have a burger at the airport. Expensive burger. Ever had bison?"

She shakes her head.

"I'll buy you a bison burger next time. They're the specialty of the house."

She looks at his bright eyes and big grin. He sure seems intent on there being a next time.

They take the shuttle into Avalon and poke around in the jewelry shops. She loves looking at expensive jewelry. When she sees something she really likes she tries it on and admires herself in the mirror and always hands it back. They walk into one of the shops and stop at a display case filled with rings, earrings, bracelets and necklaces. One in particular catches her eye and she leans over the case and admires it. There's a little white card next to it, as there is next to each of the items, and she reads that the filigree chain consists of yellow and white gold and that the large teardrop-shaped pendant is an emerald. All of the other items are priced in the hundreds of dollars, but this one's priced in the thousands. "How beautiful," she says softly and looks up to see a woman standing on the other side of the counter, smiling and ready to assist her.

"With your skin tone," the woman says, "that would look stunning. Would you like to try it on?"

"I would, thanks." The woman removes it from the display case and hands it to her. Rita stands in front of the mirror and fastens it around her neck. The filigree feels coolly alive against her skin, and she has to admit that the way the emerald lays just above her cleavage and points toward it looks pretty hot. "Let's see," she hears Andrew say and turns toward him and models it for him. She watches him as he looks admiringly back and forth from the emerald to her eyes.

"Wow!" he says.

She glances at the woman and sees she's wisely keeping her eyes on Andrew now.

"Very nice, isn't it?" the woman asks him.

Rita removes the necklace and hands it back to the woman. "Thanks."

Andrew takes out his wallet and hands the woman a credit card. "We'll take it."

The woman smiles and nods and takes the necklace and credit card to the register.

"What are you doing?" Rita asks, flustered and staring at him incredulously.

"Buying you a present."

"I only wanted to try it on, and I certainly didn't want you to buy it for me!"

He leans against the counter, crosses his arms and legs and tilts his head. "I know that."

"Please don't embarrass me."

He raises his eyebrows. "Embarrass you?"

"I could never afford that."

"It's the money."

"Of course, it's the money," she says angrily. "If I were here by myself, that necklace would be back in the display case now."

He grins. "But you're not. You're here with me." The woman returns and hands him his credit card and a pen and the sales slip to sign and Rita the necklace in a bag. He signs, puts the pen on the counter and his credit card in his wallet and turns to Rita and smiles. "Wear it."

She glares at him defiantly, but reluctantly takes the case from the bag, opens it, removes the necklace and fastens it around her neck. She feels like a wild animal allowing herself to be tamed and obliging her tamer by putting on the collar for him.

He gives her a long admiring look. "You're the best thing that ever happened to that necklace."

She glances at the woman and sees her wink.

They step outside and he takes her by the arm and they stroll slowly along the sidewalk. She's furious with herself for having lost her temper and now feels like a fool for having done so. All getting angry accomplished was to cause her to humiliate herself by revealing to him her sensitivity about his money and the class difference she feels exists between them. What must he think of her now? He stops and she stops and faces him, not knowing what to expect.

"Listen, don't hold the fact that I have money against me. I work hard for it, and I enjoy spending it. Okay?"

"I'll try," she says and sees he's not satisfied with her answer. "Okay, I will," she says and sees him smile. "I'm sorry I got angry."

"I'm not." He taps the tip of her nose with his fingertip. "Anyone ever tell you how cute you look when you're angry?"

She feels her eyes filling with tears and shakes her head. "You're the first."

"I'm honored," he says and leans forward, gives her a peck on the lips and takes her arm and they walk on.

The blackened albacore is delicious and it's no wonder this is his favorite restaurant. As he said, "No folderol. Just the fish." She sips her wine and gazes out the picture window at the boats in the harbor and the casino beyond. She looks around the restaurant and wonders if he's brought other women here on dates. Probably and they're probably all beautiful, and he's probably just as nice and sweet and generous with them. Why wouldn't he be? That's who he is.

The thing she's wondering about most is why he's interested in her. She's a prickly immigration lawyer who rear-ended him and he knows two important facts about her that would have sent most men running. It can't be sex. She doesn't think she looks sexy these days and she certainly doesn't feel sexy, just pregnant. He glances at her almost empty wine glass and refills it and his own. "Thanks," she says. She didn't take Antabuse today. She didn't want to risk being sick in his plane. She just wanted to enjoy herself and the wine has finally relaxed her to the point where she's stopped wondering why he's interested in her. She's here with him and having a great time and that's all that matters.

The view is spectacular as they approach the coast. She sees the shimmering lights of Newport Beach arrayed before her and beyond the lighted runways at John Wayne and the red and white lights of the traffic streaming on the 405 and the lights on the buildings at South Coast Plaza and far off in the distance the sweep of the dark hills. All her life she's felt the crushing weight of life on top of her and for once she feels on top of the world, as light as air and tries to put the idea that it could all come crashing down at any moment out of her mind. She smiles at Andrew and puts a hand on his arm. "Thank you," she says, "it's been a wonderful day." She sees him smiling back, his face illuminated by the glow of the instrument panel lights. She notices that one of them is now flashing red and feels her stomach muscles tense and tightens her grip on his arm. She sees him glance at the instrument panel and look back at her reassuringly and smile. She's certain he sees the terror in her eyes.

"Needs oil. Nothing to worry about."

She gazes at him, so calm and in control. The scare has laid bare her true feelings. She's been telling herself it doesn't matter that he dates other women, but it does. It matters a lot. She's been telling herself she's not in competition with them, but she is. She wants him all to herself. She's been trying not to get her hopes up, but she knows herself. The odds of her being able to do that now are no better than those of her being able to stop drinking.

CHAPTER 21

Yosemite

Cryssie sits with her arms crossed in the middle of the backseat of Sharon's car and studies Jenn's profile, as Jenn listens to Sharon tell her about her last boyfriend and why things didn't work out from her point of view. That's all Cryssie's been doing on this ride to Yosemite, staring at the backs of Sharon's and Jenn's heads and waiting to see Jenn's profile when she turns to listen to Sharon or say something to her. Every now and then Jenn looks back at her and smiles, nervously it seems, to let her know she hasn't been forgotten, which she feels she has been, and asks how she's doing and Cryssie forces a smile and says, "Great," and can see in Jenn's eyes she knows she's doing anything but.

From the moment Jenn and Sharon met her at the airport, nothing about this visit has felt right. Maybe she's just imagining things, but Jenn's hug felt hurried and half-hearted and so did her kiss. Was she embarrassed to kiss her in front of her new best friend here? How close are these two? That's what she's wondering now more than ever.

She visited Yosemite once on a trip with her family when she was kid and the idea of visiting it again with Sharon along was not what she had in mind. What she had in mind was to have Jenn all to herself in a room at a luxury hotel in San Francisco, where they could make love in a nice big comfy bed, but when Jenn suggested visiting Yosemite with her friend Sharon, Cryssie didn't want to seem selfish and said, "Sure, that sounds nice."

So here she is, sitting back here and the two of them up there, and she feels no closer to Jenn now than when she boarded the flight to San Francisco in Boston to be with her. Jenn wouldn't have made her come all this way to tell her it's over, would she?

"Look!" Cryssie hears Sharon say. She leans forward and sees El Capitan in the distance on the left and Half Dome farther up the valley on the right and, given her mood, her impression is that these grand natural monuments look small and crowded together, like a model of the park in miniature.

* * *

Cryssie looks at Jenn and Sharon, standing on the trail at the next switchback up ahead, as they have at every one, chatting and waiting for her to catch up. Why did she agree to come on this hike and up a mountain no less? For the same reason she agreed to come to Yosemite, to please Jenn. Okay, she smokes and drinks and does drugs and she's not in as good shape as they are, and certainly not that gazelle Sharon, who looks like she could sprint up the mountain without breaking a sweat. Cryssie has to take it slowly and gets winded easily, huffing and puffing as she plods along, stopping frequently to catch her breath. If it weren't for her, those two would probably be at Glacier Point by now, admiring the view. It's four miles to the top and they're just over halfway, and she's not going to make it. She's beginning to think this trip is the worst mistake she's ever made.

Sharon looks down the trail at Cryssie. "I feel bad. She's having a miserable time. We should go back. We can drive up to Glacier Point tomorrow."

"Yeah," Jenn says, "she should have said something."

Sharon smiles. "She wanted to do what you wanted to do. She'd jump off this mountain for you."

Jenn looks down at the valley floor far below and up at El Capitan in the distance. The view keeps getting more spectacular the higher they climb, but Sharon's right, they've come far enough. She's right about Cryssie's feelings for her too. Jenn thought she was prepared to see her again, but as her arrival date neared, she began worrying more and more about disappointing her and now that she's here, she's more afraid than ever. Disappointing Cryssie now seems like a self-fulfilling prophecy that she's powerless to do anything about. This is what comes from all those years spent keeping herself walled in emotionally. The irony in wanting to please Cryssie, while at the same time preventing herself from trying isn't lost on her. She also knows it's driving Cryssie crazy that she's paying more attention to Sharon. It isn't fair to her, but she can't help it. If Sharon weren't here, she doesn't know what she'd do. The situation couldn't be more awkward, and she feels awful about it.

Cryssie holds her sides and huffs and puffs her way up the trail, halfway to the switchback. At least it was nice finally being able to spend time alone with Jenn last night. They did cuddle and kiss, but the experience was nothing like their last night in P-Town. They spent the entire time getting reacquainted and maybe she's just imagining things again, but Jenn's touch and kisses felt tentative. What Cryssie wanted to do was cover every inch of Jenn's body with passionate kisses and then spend the rest of the night pleasuring each other, but she purposefully held back. She didn't want to overwhelm Jenn. Has she misread Jenn's feelings for her? Maybe Jenn really is a dyed in the wool asexual and felt pressured into being intimate in P-Town. It didn't feel that way at the time, but maybe she did. The possibility that Cryssie's been deluding herself makes her stomach feel queasy.

Jenn watches Cryssie coming slowly closer, struggling to put one foot in front of the other. She glances at Sharon and sees her looking at her with concern.

"You okay, Gwen?" Sharon asks.

"Yeah" Jenn says and looks back at Cryssie.

And what's with this "Gwen" business? When Cryssie heard Sharon — okay, so her real name is Shirin — call Jenn that at breakfast she nearly choked. And when she and Jenn stopped back in their room before leaving for the hike and she asked her about it and heard that it was Sharon's idea to call each other pet names, since they were the first friends they'd made on campus, that it would be "their little thing," she just stared at Jenn in disbelief. It's the dopiest thing she's ever heard, the type of thing ten-year-olds do!

And the handholding business! Well, that did it for her. They were walking to the car to drive to the trailhead and she was following behind the two of them, feeling very much like a third wheel on a bicycle. They were chatting about something or other and just like that Sharon took Jenn's hand, with her right behind them! Jenn seemed fine with it, and they just kept walking and chatting and holding hands. Cryssie wanted to strangle them both, but especially Jenn. Wherever her mind is it's obviously not on her. She looks at Jenn and Sharon, chatting and waiting for her as she approaches. If Jenn feels more than friendship for Sharon, she would have told her before she came, right? Jenn wouldn't have come all this way to tell her, would she?

"Hey, mountain goat," Jenn says.

Cryssie stands, holding her sides and catching her breath. "Probably...should...stop...smoking," she pants.

"Let's head back," Jenn says. "We've hiked over two miles. That's plenty."

"You...guys...go...on," Cryssie pants. "Meet you...at the car." She knows Jenn won't leave her and that Sharon knows it too, but she looks at Sharon to see if there's any hint of disappointment at not being able to continue on with Jenn. She doesn't see any and Sharon looks at her sympathetically and smiles and puts a hand on her arm.

"I was telling Jenn," Sharon says, "we can drive up to Glacier Point tomorrow, or do something else. Whatever you two want to do."

* * *

Cryssie tries her best at dinner to be part of the conversation, but all she's interested in is being alone with Jenn so they can talk. Sharon's not the issue. The issue is Jenn.

It seems the meal will never end, but finally they're back in their room. Jenn heads to the bathroom and Cryssie takes two bottles of beer from the fridge. She opens them, climbs on the bed and sits cross-legged with her back against the wall and waits for her. She hears the toilet flush and Jenn walks to the side of the bed and stands there looking down at

Cryssie, who holds out a bottle to her and pats the bed beside her. She can see Jenn doesn't want to talk. Well, she did embarrass her on the hike, and she hasn't done a very good job of hiding how she feels about the pet names and handholding business. Jenn takes the bottle, climbs onto the bed and sits cross-legged, facing her. They sip their beers and look in each other's eyes and Cryssie can see Jenn wants to look away. She pokes Jenn's knee with her finger. "Let's talk."

"Okay," Jenn says reluctantly.

"I missed you more than anything. I couldn't wait to see you. You don't seem very happy to see me."

"I am."

"Could've fooled me."

"It's just...."

Cryssie watches Jenn struggle to get whatever it is she wants to say out, and as much as she wants to help her, forces herself not to and just keeps her eyes on Jenn and sip her beer.

Jenn shrugs and looks down at her lap.

"Was it just a thing?" Cryssie asks. "Let your hair down on vacation?"

Jenn looks up at her and frowns. "It wasn't. You know that."

Cryssie puts a hand on Jenn's knee. "Okay, I'm sorry. That wasn't fair. I'm just frustrated. I get the feeling you're scared to death of me. I scare off everyone I get close to. I'm too intense. That's just who I am. I can't help it." She searches Jenn's eyes and sees she's no closer to being able to share with her what's on her mind and how she feels and sighs. "I've gotta pee," Cryssie says and climbs off the bed, heads to the bathroom and sits on the toilet, the pee gushing out of her, which isn't surprising since she had a couple of beers at dinner, the first to settle her nerves and the second to slow down her brain, and the third here in the room to numb herself. She finds Jenn just as she left her, with her head down, staring at the beer bottle between her legs. She Cryssie strokes Jenn's cheek and takes the bottle from between her legs. "C'mon," she says, "let's get some sleep. We're both exhausted."

* * *

Cryssie's not even trying to be a part of the conversation at breakfast. She had no appetite and shouldn't have ordered the omelet and home fries and toast, most of which remains uneaten on her plate. She glances from Jenn to Sharon and looks out the window at the birds fluttering in the tree and mulls over last night's brief awkward cuddling, and then lying back-to-back waiting for sleep. It feels like they're nearing the end, and now she's thinking that maybe Jenn's waiting to tell her it's over at the airport. She doesn't want to believe it and it's disappointing to think Jenn would do that, but she can't help it.

They leave the restaurant and walk to Sharon's car to drive up to Glacier Point. Cryssie's amused by the new walking arrangement, the three of them abreast with Jenn in the middle. If it's an attempt on Jenn's part to make her feel that she isn't favoring Sharon, it isn't working. In fact, at this point she'd rather be walking behind them. They arrive at the car and Jenn and Sharon get in front, but Cryssie stands there, staring down at Jenn, who looks up at her puzzled and opens the window. "You guys go on," Cryssie says. "I'm gonna walk over to Half Dome. I'll meet you back at the lodge this afternoon."

"I'll come with you," Jenn says and begins opening the door.

Cryssie blocks it, pushes it shut again and shakes her head. "See you later," she says and turns and walks away.

Sharon pulls into the parking lot at Glacier Point and she and Jenn get out and walk to the overlook. They stand side by side, looking down at the valley and El Capitan in the distance. The view is spectacular, but Sharon has the feeling it's lost on Jenn, who didn't say a word on the drive up and just sat with her hands folded in her lap, staring straight ahead, looking defeated. She feels badly for Jenn and Cryssie. They're both having an awful time, and whatever it is that's bothering Jenn, she's having a hard time dealing with it. "Want to talk?" Sharon asks softly.

"I'm not sure it would help."

"It usually does."

"I'm stuck. I don't want to lose her, but I'm pushing her away."

"Have you talked with her about it?"

Jenn shakes her head. "I tried to last night, but I couldn't get the words out."

"Still afraid of disappointing her?"

"Yeah."

"Well, Gwen, you already know my advice."

Jenn looks at her and smiles. "You know I'm never going to get use to that, right?"

"I'll stop, if you like."

Jenn shakes her head and looks back out at the view. "It's okay."

"I can see how much she loves you," Sharon says. "Don't you think she's the one who should decide if she's happy with you? I think you owe it to both of you to at least try."

"Yeah, I guess you're right."

"You're fortunate to have found someone who feels about you the way she does. You might never again. I have the feeling you're going to be very unhappy if you let her go."

Jenn narrows her eyes and nods. "Yeah, you're right about that too."

* * *

Jenn searches in the lodge and checks in their room, but can't find Cryssie, who's probably still on her walk. Jenn can't wait for her. She needs to be with her and sets out walking quickly toward Half Dome. She feels miserable about having put her through this, but she couldn't have done otherwise. She wasn't there yet. She hopes Cryssie still loves her, although she wouldn't be surprised or blame her if she finds she's finally had enough of her. It would devastate her, but she's prepared for a chilly reception and Cryssie's decision to end the relationship. At least she thinks she's prepared, but the prospect of it actually happening has her stomach muscles knotted and her stomach churning.

The fact that when they were separated by geography, it didn't bother her before, or she made herself believe it didn't, but it does now, a lot, and it's going to be hard not being able to Cryssie that often, if at all. She's getting ahead of herself.

Her parents will welcome Cryssie into the family and be fine with the two of them being partners. They're understanding people. That's why she loves them. She's getting ahead of herself again.

She rounds a bend in the path and sees a woman walking toward her in the distance and knows instantly it's not Cryssie. Sharon's right. It's not up to her to decide whether Cryssie's satisfied with her. It's up to Cryssie to decide. In fact, she's been acting selfishly.

She watches Half Dome draw nearer and rounds another bend in the path and sees Cryssie in the distance, walking toward her. Jenn feels her eyes filling with tears and breaks into a run. She sees Cryssie stop and stand staring at her. It seems to take forever to reach her and when she finally does, she leaps at her and throws her arms around her neck and feels Cryssie wrap her arms around her and hold her tightly. "I'm sorry!" Jenn says. "I love you! Forgive me!"

Cryssie holds Jenn until she stops shaking, then steps back and looks at her tear-filled eyes and tear-streaked cheeks and smiles and shakes her head. "You are one tough nut," she says and takes Jenn's hand and glances back over her shoulder at Half Dome. Not a half hour ago she was imagining standing on top of it, ready to jump off it if that's what it would take to win Jenn's love, and now here she is with Jenn by her side. It's been a long hard struggle, and she feels good about herself for not having given up on Jenn. It's the first time in her life she's fought hard to win someone's love, and it's changed her, maybe not softened her but settled and strengthened her, and she feels she finally has the courage to confront her hypocritical relationship with her parents. It's been a long time coming and it won't be easy, but it's something she knows she has to do. She squeezes Jenn's hand. "I like Sharon," Cryssie says. "She's nice."

* * *

Cryssie closes her eyes and enjoys the waves of pleasure washing over her as they slowly subside. Now, this is more like it, lying with Jenn in her arms, the two of them bathed in moonlight and the afterglow of their orgasms. It was different this time. P-Town was wonderful, but this was amazing. She felt Jenn open up and give herself to her completely and the passion in her lovemaking left her breathless. She opens her eyes and looks at Jenn and sees her gazing at her and smiling. "Let's get married," Cryssie says.

Jenn laughs and shakes her head.

"What?"

"You."

"Let's have kids, you know, when the time is right, and we can afford them."

Jenn's thought about the idea of adopting. It's always seemed to her the right thing to do, having been adopted. "There are plenty to adopt."

"I mean our own. We'll each have one."

It dawns on Jenn what Cryssie's proposing and she laughs and shakes her head again.

"What?"

Jenn props herself up on an elbow, smiles down at Cryssie and strokes her cheek with her fingertips. "You're crazy."

"I'll have yours and you'll have mine."

Thinking about it, it seems like the sweetest, most tender, most loving idea imaginable.

"We don't want just anybody to be the donor," Cryssie says.

"I guess not," Jenn says and watches Cryssie's eyes as she considers the question of a suitable sperm donor and sees them slowly widen.

"Matt!"

Why doesn't this idea strike Jenn as ridiculous or absurd? Why does it make perfect sense? It's a strange new life she knows she's beginning with Cryssie. She feels like she's been shot out of a canon and is tumbling head over heels through the air. It's scary but the kind of scary that makes her feel like a kid and fills her with joy. She kisses Cryssie, rests her cheek against her shoulder and feels Cryssie slowly stroking her hair. "We'll have to run it by him," she hears her muse and smiles.

* * *

Kate studies Jenn and Cryssie as she listens to them talk about their trip to Yosemite. They strike her as an interesting pair. Jenn's gorgeous, wears no makeup or jewelry and has no tattoos, at least none that she can see, and Cryssie's edgily attractive and sports tattoos and piercings. Kate knows from Matt that Jenn's smart, is attending Stanford, plans to go to Med School and is a talented violinist. She's looking forward to hearing her play. Apparently, Cryssie's hasn't heard her play yet either and Jenn brought her violin home at Cryssie's request to play for her. What Matt didn't mention is that Jenn's adopted, and that discovery has Kate discreetly searching Matt's and his parents' faces for a family resemblance.

She glances at Matt, sitting beside her, holding her hand and looking at Cryssie with a bemused expression as she tells them about her struggle to keep up with Jenn and Sharon on Glacier Point Trail, and then at Carl and Dot, Carl sitting back in his chair with his arms crossed and Dot sitting forward with her arms on the dining room table and her hands clasped, both looking at Cryssie with sympathetic expressions. There really isn't much of a resemblance and what Kate thinks she sees of one she could just be imagining.

She looks at Cryssie. What she knows about her is that she's at Wellesley in Massachusetts, is Amber's older sister and that she and Matt hooked up around the time when he was breaking up with Amber, so it's curious. She can't see Cryssie's or Jenn's hands from where she's sitting at the table, but she's pretty sure they're holding each other's, and judging from the look in their eyes when they gaze at each other, she's also pretty sure they have strong feelings for each other. It's been an interesting Thanksgiving so far.

Carl steps out into the backyard and closes the door behind him. Dot and Jenn and Cryssie are cleaning up in the kitchen and Matt and Kate and Dee Dee are talking at the dining room table, and Carl needs a little time to himself. He walks to the patio table and sits and slowly unwraps the cellophane from his cigar. He nibbles off the end, spits it out, puts the cigar between his lips and lights it, turning it as he puffs and gazes up at what stars he can see in the nighttime sky.

It's been an eventful day in the Tildon family. As much as he and Dot love Matt and Jenn and consider them their own, they've always been mindful of the fact that they're guardians of other people's children and never more so than today. They've always felt their role as parents to be to bring Matt and Jenn along to the point where they can think and decide for themselves, as they have where religion is concerned. He and Dot are churchgoing Baptists, but neither Matt nor Jenn showed any interest in religion beyond learning about it and that's fine with him and Dot. All that matters is that they're decent moral people. What he and Dot have been more concerned about is instilling in them qualities such as curiosity about the world and understanding and compassion toward others and values such as the importance of realizing their full potential and doing anything worth doing to the best of their abilities. They're proud of the people Matt and Jenn have become, but he'd be lying if he said he isn't concerned about the decisions they've made about their personal lives lately, and he knows Dot feels the same way. They'll be supportive, as they always try to be, but they're concerned.

On the face of it, there's nothing wrong with the fact that Kate's some twenty years older than Matt. Relationships like that happen all the time, although it's usually the other way around. Maybe he's just being too parochial in his thinking. Matt's taking on a lot of responsibility. It isn't easy raising a young girl, whether or not she's your biological daughter. Dee Dee's a great kid, though, very polite and smart and perceptive. He smiles at how uncomfortable she was at first, calling him and Dot by their given names, as they asked her to. Kate explained that it was the first time Dee Dee had been asked to do that. It didn't take her long to warm to it, though, and he and Dot can see that it makes her feel less like a kid and more like an adult, which is the point. It's important that kids her age be allowed to feel and act grown up.

He puffs and blows the smoke out slowly. He likes Kate. She hasn't had it easy in life, despite which she's calm and optimistic and determined to provide the best she can for Dee Dee. He can see Matt's happy and proud to be with her. They seem good for each other and Matt and Dee Dee have a great relationship. He's happy for the three of them.

The news that Jenn and Cryssie feel the way they do about each other and are now partners came as a surprise. He probably should have seen it coming. For as long as he can remember, Jenn had no interest in becoming involved romantically with anyone, male or female. In fact, she seemed entirely uninterested in sex. When she left to visit Cryssie in New England, she seemed to him to be off to visit a friend and no more than that, but she was different when she returned. He could tell something happened between them on that trip and that Jenn had a lot on her mind. Neither he nor Dot asked her about it and Jenn didn't share anything with them. That's the way she is about her personal life, very private. Then she and Cryssie took that trip to Yosemite and when Jenn called afterward to say that Cryssie would be joining them at Thanksgiving, he could hear it in her voice, a kind of happiness he'd never heard before. He smiles. Yes, he should have seen it coming.

This idea of theirs — he wasn't surprised to hear it was Cryssie's — to have each other's baby with Matt being the sperm donor was a shocker. It took his and Dot's breath away, although Matt took it in stride and said he'd be honored. Dee Dee was amazed by the idea and Kate seemed stunned by it, which is understandable. It is pretty unusual. He and Dot consider themselves open-minded people and for a moment they thought the girls were joking, but when it was clear they weren't, they just looked at each other in amazement, not knowing what to say. They both knew what they were thinking, that Jenn needs them now more than ever. They've always wanted her to be her own person, and now she's trying to be and wants their approval and support and she'll have them. He was relieved when Dot finally told them she thinks it's a very loving thing to want to do. If it had been up to him, they'd still be staring at each other.

It's not every young woman and man who'd have the courage to follow their hearts the way Jenn and Matt are. He and Dot are proud of them, concerned for them too, but proud.

He puffs on his cigar and thinks of his parents and wonders what they would have made of all this. They were open-minded people too, and instilled their values in him, so he figures they would have reacted just as he and Dot did and supported their grandchildren. It's not that life was any simpler in his parents' day, and this type of stuff happened all the time back then. Maybe not Jenn and Cryssie's idea of having each other's baby. That just wasn't possible, although he's sure that had it been, people would have done it.

He was young at the time, maybe nine, but he remembers what his mom did for Marla Ewing. He never learned why Marla's husband left her, but he did one day, leaving her in mean circumstances with five small children to support. Marla was a plain woman and childhood polio left her with one leg slightly withered and lame. She was a housewife and had never worked, so she struggled to make money the only way she knew how, as a seamstress and laundress. She had a few women customers in town that gave her work out of charity. People began noticing men arriving at her door during the day when her kids were at school and that they'd stay a long time in the house too long just to drop off or pick up clothes that needed mending or cleaning. Pretty soon the rumor began going around that she was a loose woman, and no one would have anything to do with her except his mom. She knew Marla from church, not all that well, but she made a point of befriending her. She'd go over to Marla's and they'd sit and have coffee and chat. A few months later his mom mentioned at the dinner table that Marla had met a man named Bevis and that she and her kids and Bevis would be joining them for Thanksgiving dinner.

Carl remembers that Thanksgiving dinner well. Bevis was big and handsome and polite and soft-spoken and couldn't take his eyes off Marla. He'll never forget the way Bevis looked at her and listened to every word she said and didn't once interrupt her. He wasn't surprised when his mom told the family a few months later that Marla and Bevis were getting married. "'Love conquers all,'" she said, as she was fond of saying when she'd heard or read some story about people like Marla and Brevis, and she always added, "'let us all yield to love.'"

He hears Jenn tuning up her violin and turns and sees her through the window, sitting with it tucked under her chin, drawing the bow across it and everyone watching her, Cryssie intently, waiting to hear her play. His mom would have understood all this, and she would have attributed it to the power of love. He's happy for his children that they've found it. The Tildons have a lot to be thankful for.

Thursday, November 24, 2011

Dear Anneliese,

Today is Thanksgiving Day and it's been a BIG one! My mom and I and Matt had dinner at Gramma Mary and Grampa Gordon's. It was the first time Matt met them and they like him a lot, which

I knew they would. After dinner we went to Matt's parents'. It was the first time we met his mom and dad and his sister Jenn and her friend Cryssie (I think that's how it's spelled). I'm pretty sure Cryssie's more than a friend, but more about that in a minute!

Jenn brought her violin home with her from college because Cryssie asked her to. She'd never heard Jenn play. Jenn asked her what she wanted to hear and Cryssie said, "Play something romantic! That's what the violin's for, right?" Well, it sure sounded romantic to me, and I watched Cryssie's face while she listened to Jenn play and I thought she was going to cry! When Jenn was finished Cryssie asked her what the song was called and Jenn said she didn't know. It's a Gypsy song she heard a famous Gypsy violinist play on YouTube and learned it by ear. She's really good! She and Matt are both so talented. I guess it runs in the family.

Here's the really interesting news. Jenn and Matt were both adopted! Jenn's Asian so, I knew she had to be adopted. She was born in China and Matt's parents adopted her when she was a baby. She doesn't remember anything about China or her real parents and said it doesn't bother her, and she isn't interested in finding out anything about them. I guess I know how she feels. If my parents gave me up for adoption, I guess I'd feel they didn't love me and I wouldn't care about them much, either. It must hurt, though, knowing your real parents didn't love you. Jenn said maybe they couldn't keep her and had to give her up for adoption. I guess that would make it feel a little better.

It turns out Matt was born around here and doesn't know anything about his parents and isn't interested in finding out anything about them, either. He said Dot and Carl are his parents, end of story. My mom and I were surprised to hear that he was adopted, and she seemed really interested when he said his birthday is on summer solstice. I don't know why, but she was.

We got talking about birthdays and everyone said they understand why I feel the way I do about mine being on New

Year's Eve. I guess the only worse day to have your birthday on would be Christmas!

Anyway, back to Jenn and Cryssie. When Jenn finished playing, Cryssie put her arms around her and they kissed on the lips and they meant it! I'd never seen girls kiss like that before! Those two really like each other! They said they were thinking about having each other's baby and thought Matt would be the perfect sperm donor! At first I thought they were joking! Everyone else did too, except Matt. He just smiled at them and said he'd be honored. They're serious! I tried to figure out how it would work but couldn't. Thinking about it makes my head spin! I thought about asking my mom about it on the ride home but didn't. She seemed to have a lot on her mind.

Dot and Carl are really nice. When we first arrived, they asked me to call them by their names. I've been taught to call elders "Mister" and "Missus" and "Sir" and "Ma'am" so it felt a little weird at first, but I got used to it and it felt nice. That's what I liked about Cryssie too. She didn't treat me like a kid at all. She asked me all kinds of stuff about myself and what I thought about this and that. I really enjoyed talking with her. It's too bad she and Jenn live so far away and don't get home very often. I'd like to see more of them.

Yours, Dee Dee

P.S.: I'm really looking forward to the trip to Ensenada and surfing at Trestles! That will be SOOO COOOOOL!!!

CHAPTER 22

Christmastime in SoCal

The parade of boats makes its way slowly around Newport Harbor. *Raptor* is festooned with lights, as is *Spare Change,* following behind. Up ahead is *Wet Dream,* a big power cruiser with a dingy named *Clean Sheets* hanging from the stern. Steve knows the waving Santa at the wheel, a partner in a local investment banking firm and a player. He's surrounded by some hot-looking elves, waving at the people lining the shore. Ahead of *Wet Dream* is a trawler with its rigging ablaze with green and red flashing lights. And so it goes, about a hundred and fifty boats in all, from kayaks and canoes and Duffy electric boats to the behemoth in front of *Raptor,* all decorated with lights and some turned into elaborate Christmas-themed displays. The parade's come a long way since 1907 when John Scarpa, an Italian gondolier took a group of tourists from Pasadena across Newport Bay in his gondola decorated with Japanese lanterns.

Steve looks at the multi-million-dollar waterfront homes on Balboa Island with their private docks and yachts. This place has come a long way too. Back in the 1860s, the bay was used to load export goods — hides, tallow, hay and the like — and it wasn't a true harbor then. Apparently, the entrance was pretty treacherous and there were sandbars that were difficult to negotiate. Up until 1905, when the Pacific Electric line began operating from Los Angeles — "Red Cars" they called them — Newport was a small company town, home to workers in the local commercial and shipping industries. William Collins, a land developer, saw the resort and recreation potential in the area and enlisted Henry Huntington, who owned the railroad, to help promote it to people in L.A.

With the advent of the railroad the picture changed dramatically. Soon real estate developers were sending salesmen to L.A. and Pasadena, both connected to Newport by the railroad, to promote property around the harbor, which Collins decided t.o finally turn into a proper one. He dredged the harbor and Balboa Island was created using the sand. While Collins was offering lots on the island for sale at $350 to $750, he actually let them go for as little as $25. Steve eyes a particularly grand palazzo, shakes his head and smiles. In another hundred years God knows what it will be worth.

He looks at Cyn, sitting across from him in the cockpit dressed in a Santa costume and chatting with Bill Keane's wife. Talk about pictures changing dramatically. Ever since she shared the news with him that's she's pregnant he's felt concerned about her in an entirely new way. Call it sappy but he can't stop wondering how she feels, whether she needs anything, if she'd like her back or feet massaged, her pillow fluffed, breakfast in bed? He's asked her how she's feeling more times in the last twenty-four hours than the last twenty-four months. He loves the way she smiles when he does and looks at him, curiously with a slight tilt of her head. He can see she's wondering where this sweetly silly side of him has been hiding all this time and that she likes it. It feels great expressing it. He has a lot to be thankful for: a baby on the way, the company making money in a difficult market despite the scandal, shareholders happy. Life is good. He hears a blast from an air horn and looks up at the crowded restaurant deck where the sound is coming from.

Dee Dee grins at Dibs and he grins back and gives her the thumbs up. She blasts the air horn again and Kate presses her hands over her ears, shielding them from the eardrum-rattling noise. She wishes Dibs hadn't brought that thing along and given it to Dee Dee and encouraged her to use it, but she's having fun and everyone's enjoying the fact that she is and Kate doesn't want to spoil it. It's just been a trying day, and she's worried about what's going to happen to Randy now that he's been terminated. He's a young gay Black man who was the top producer on her staff and loved by his co-workers and customers.

Kate was disappointed when security informed her that he'd been ringing purchases off the clock, a practice that's against store policy and grounds for termination. She wasn't really all that surprised, though. She knows about his situation, that he has student loans to pay off and his mom's a single parent with four kids, the youngest, six, and relies on him for financial support. He simply needed the money. She sat him down and explained to him that if he did it again, he'd be terminated. She asked if he understood and he said he did and signed the document, but he didn't stop.

So, now he's out of work in a lousy job market and Kate can't help worrying about him. He can always lie on job applications and say he resigned from the company. All they're required to disclose to prospective employers, if they bother to inquire, are the beginning and end dates of his employment. The HR manager said Randy wept in her office when she told him they were terminating him. She said he told her his co-workers were like family to him and Kate believes him. She felt like a mother to him.

He'd poured out his heart to her at times and she'd listen sympathetically and try to advise and encourage him. He used to tell her how gorgeous he thinks Matt is and how it's too bad Matt's straight. It always made her laugh, but it doesn't seem funny now. It's sad and all these boats decorated with lights and the people on them wearing Santa hats, smiling and waving, aren't lifting her spirits. She feels Matt give her shoulder a squeeze and looks at him.

"You okay?" he asks. "Warm enough?"

She nods and hears her phone's message tone and fishes the phone out of her bag. She looks at the screen. It's from Sharianna, who's closing at the store this evening:

Omg! Randy's dead! Jumped off the Westin!

Kate stares down at the message and hears the blast from the air horn and doesn't bother to shield her ears. The noise sounds like it's coming from somewhere far off in the distance. She wonders when it happened. This evening? She wonders if Randy visited Bloomindales to see his old colleagues. Maybe being in the store and seeing them depressed him, to the point where he decided to cross over Bristol Street and somehow manage to get himself on the roof of the Westin Hotel. What a horrible thing to have happen, and she can't avoid feeling guilty. After all, she played a role in his termination, so in a way, she's partly responsible. She doubts she'll get in the Christmas spirit this year.

Rita and Andrew sip their wine and watch the junk slowly approaching again. It's a few boats back and they agreed it's their favorite in the parade because it looks so exotic and out of place. It has an enormous white star with an arcing comet tail of twinkling white lights rigged atop its masts. "That is the coolest-looking thing," she hears him say, just as he did the last time it passed by. She looks at him and sees him gazing out the restaurant window at it with that same expression of childlike delight and wonder. He looks at her wide-eyed and grins.

"We should do it!" he says.

She has to admit, the idea of vacationing on a junk in the South Pacific does sound exciting. It would be quite an adventure. Of course, it's not going to happen until the baby's old enough to be left in someone's care. They watch the junk pass, sit back and pick up their wine glasses.

"I know him from shareholder meetings," he says. "He seemed like a nice guy. Pia and I went to one of their Fourth of July parties. He was the perfect host. I guess you just never know about people."

"Do you really think that's true? You know everything there is to know about me. Do you have a secret life I don't know about?"

He smiles. "I'm a pretty simple guy. What you see is what you get." He sips his wine and shrugs. "Sometimes you find out things about people."

She knows he's referring to Pia and the abortion. She's come to understand how profoundly affected he was by Pia's decision to have one. He said he felt violated when she told him what she'd done. Rita's also come to believe that her pregnancy is part of her appeal to him. He hasn't said as much, but she knows it is and that he feels as much like an expectant father when he's with her as he would were the baby his own. She sees him looking past her toward the restaurant entrance and hears clapping and a man's booming voice saying, "Merry Christmas!" She turns to see a pretty convincing Santa Claus slowly making his way through the tables, greeting people, patting them on their backs and shaking their hands. She looks back at Andrew and sees him watching Santa with gleeful anticipation and it dawns on her that this is his doing. "Ho! Ho! Ho! Merry Christmas!" she hears Santa boom as he arrives at their table.

"Have a seat, Santa," Andrew says.

She watches Santa sit, fold his white-gloved hands on the table and smile at her. His eyes really do seem to be twinkling, although that could be because of an application of Liquid Tears in the men's room, and his curly white shoulder-length hair and thick moustache and beard look real, as does the ruddiness of his cheeks, although the hair could be fake and his cheeks rouged.

"Can't stay long," Santa says, "still have lots of work to do. Well, my dear, it seems you've been a very good girl."

She glances at Andrew and looks back at Santa. "I try my best, Santa."

He takes a small gift box out of his coat pocket and places it on the table in front of her. He looks from her to the gift box and back at her and raises his eyebrows. "You're not going to wait until Christmas to open it are you?"

"I guess not." She knows what's in it. She just wasn't expecting it. She's known Andrew a couple of months and they haven't even been intimate, and as much as she hoped things were moving in this direction, she resisted believing it and tried not to think about it. She searches Andrew's eyes and knows he knows her question: Are you sure? She sees his eyes and smile widen slightly and he nods slowly and there's no doubt in her mind about his answer: Never been surer.

"Don't hold us in suspense," she hears Santa say. She looks down at the box picks it up and unwraps it and opens it to see a dazzling array of diamonds set in a platinum band. "Very nice, indeed!" she hears Santa say. She looks at Andrew and sees him looking at her expectantly, but she's stunned and her mind is blank and all she can do is gaze at his eyes.

Santa pushes back his chair and stands. "Well, Merry Christmas to you both," he says and walks away booming, "Ho! Ho! Ho! Merry Christmas!"

She watches Andrew take the box from her hand remove the ring and put the box on the table, then take her hand in his and slip thße ring on her finger.

"The Egyptians believed this finger has a vein that goes directly to the heart," he says.

Yes, it must, because hers is pounding now.

* * *

Sunday, December 18, 2011

Dear Anneliese,

We went to the annual Christmas Boat Parade in Newport Harbor yesterday. My mom and I go each year, but this time we sat outside on the deck at a restaurant with Matt and his friends and we had the best view of the boats! My favorite boat was the junk. It didn't look like any of the other boats. It was really weird looking. I read about junks online. It's the type of boat they use in the South Pacific and Asia to haul stuff around.

Matt's friends are really nice. It turns out the girls all surf too, and they invited me to go with them sometime. It would be SOOO COOOOOL to go surfing with other girls! Matt's right, we need more girls in the water. They were really excited for me when they heard we'd be stopping at Trestles on our trip to Ensenada. I've heard so much about the place from Matt and now his friends that I feel like I've already been there! I can't wait to surf it!

My mom got some awful news from a friend of hers at work. A man named Randy who worked in my mom's department killed himself! My mom said he was fired yesterday and that's probably why he did it, because he was really depressed. He went up to the hotel across from South Coast Plaza and jumped off the roof!

I don't know how people can kill themselves. I held my breath once to see if I could hold it long enough to pass out and I couldn't do it. As hard as I tried my body wouldn't let me. It didn't care what I wanted. If I tried to kill myself I think it would do the same thing again, just not let me do it. But people do. I don't think their bodies are any different than mine, so their minds must be stronger than their bodies. I guess that's it. Or maybe they're just not thinking.

It must be horrible to feel so badly that you don't want to live anymore. I can't imagine what it must be like. I mean I've felt sad in my life sometimes, but I never thought about killing myself. Anyway, it doesn't solve anything. My mom said Randy was fired because he was stealing from the company. She said his family really needs the money. So now he's dead and they still need the money and he's not around to help them anymore. I guess he could have gotten another job. Don't you think? Everyone deserves a second chance. Maybe that's why he killed himself, because he was afraid he wouldn't get a second chance. What an awful feeling that must be.

Christmas is almost here! I've got to get my mom a present. I'm getting one for Matt too. I've been thinking about my dad and miss him a lot lately, I think because of the holidays. It's hard to imagine Christmas without him.

Yours, Dee Dee

P.S.: Hanukkah begins at sundown on the 20th this year, just a couple of days away. I'm all set with my Menorah. I can't wait to light it. I think of how hard you and the others in the Secret Annex struggled to stay alive and how people like Randy can want to die so much they kill themselves and, well, it just doesn't make any sense to me how people can be so different.

* * *

Amber holds up a long-sleeve, V-neck, navy wool sweater. "Waddya think?"

Cryssie glances at it. "He has tons of 'em." She continues browsing through the rack of designer men's sports shirts, but nothing looks all that appealing. "Why are we even looking at clothes? They have closets full of clothes. This is silly."

Amber frowns and tosses the sweater back on top of the pile. "Any suggestions?"

"No. Well, yeah. Let's give them a gift basket. At least it'll get eaten."

"Tacky."

"Maybe I'll get him a photography book."

"Not Maplethorpe."

"Why not? His mind needs expanding." Cryssie glances up at the speaker in the ceiling. "Ugh! I don't know how people in retail maintain their sanity."

"What," she hears Kate say and turns to see her grinning at her.

"You don't like 'Holly Jolly Christmas'?"

"Hey!" Cryssie says and gives her a hug. "I was gonna come find you and invite you to lunch. They said you were here today."

"Seems I live here during the holidays."

"This is Amber."

"Nice to meet you," Kate says and sees Amber force a polite smile. So, the infamous Amber. She's beautiful, all right, and Kate can see through Amber's open jacket that her perfect body is accentuated by a pink tube top and tight-fitting white jeans. Kate remembers a brief discussion about Amber at Thanksgiving at Matt's parents' and Cryssie saying she's a siren who loves luring sailors onto rocks. Looking at Amber, she can easily picture her sitting on a rock in the ocean with the remains of sailors and their ships strewn at her feet. Kate lingers on Amber's eyes a moment, so icily blue, and her eyebrows, arched slightly. Her look is a mixture of condescension and disinterest and Kate imagines Amber shows it to everyone. In fact, Kate does know why men willingly get involved with women like her. They're blinded by beauty and the desire for conquest. She's sure Matt was just a passing plaything, that Amber's really only interested in men who have a lot to lose. Amber turns her attention back to the sweaters and Kate turns hers back to Cryssie. "How's Jenn?"

"Great! Got home yesterday. My parents are having a party Saturday and we're going. That should be interesting. No chance of joining us for lunch, huh?"

"Afraid not. Enjoy the holidays," Kate says and waves as she walks away.

"You too!" Cryssie says.

"How do you know her?" Amber asks.

"She's Matt's girlfriend."

Amber looks up from the sweaters and stares wide-eyed at Kate's back. "You're kidding! She's old enough to be his mother!"

"So what? It's okay for a man to be older but not a woman? Your mind needs expanding too."

* * *

Cryssie hands the waitress her menu. "I'll have the same." She sits back, crosses her arms, tilts her head and studies Amber. "So, like, what happened to you, Sis? I remember you were a happy kid once. You used to smile and laugh a lot. Where did that kid go?" Predictably, she sees Amber's I-haven't-the-slightest-idea-what-you're-talking-about look, one of her favorites. "Why do you treat people the way you do? You couldn't have been ruder to Kate. It's like you couldn't give a shit about people and especially men. You've treated every guy I can think of like absolute shit. Why they put up with it is beyond me. It's like you enjoy punishing them. What have you got against men?"

Amber glances around the restaurant. "Let's change the subject."

"Let's not."

Amber glares at her. "Let's."

It's the same expression Cryssie used to see when they were kids and she'd try to talk with Amber about why she seemed so unhappy. How old was her sister then? Ten? Amber seemed to withdraw into her own little world. Cryssie assumed it was to avoid going through what she did with their parents and admired the way Amber was able to manipulate them and especially their father to get whatever she wanted. There's always been a thing between those two. She can't put her finger on what, but there has been and still is.

It's always mystified her why her parents sent her to see a shrink, since Amber was the sullen and uncommunicative one. Of the two of them, her sister was the one who clearly had problems and needed help, but instead she was the one who had to sit there week after week and struggle to answer her shrink's endless questions about herself and her relationship with her parents. She remembers her shrink saying at one point that she thought her "problem" might be the result of her being stuck in the phallic stage of her psychosexual development, which she considered complete bullshit at the time and still does. She might not have understood why she was the way she was, but she was perfectly happy with herself. She just liked girls and boys. It was that simple.

She's not sure what's going on with her sister, though, who doesn't seem to like anyone and least of all herself. As sexy as Amber looks, she seems sexless. Jenn might not have been interested in sex with other people, but she did enjoy pleasuring herself. Cryssie would be surprised if Amber ever feels the need, let alone the desire. She seems detached from her body, or resentful of it. "Talk to me," Cryssie says. There's a subtle change in Amber's expression, a slackening of her features and her eyes look unfocused now, like what she's really looking at is in her head.

"Don't do this to me," Amber says weakly.

Cryssie can barely hear her, but there's no mistaking the pleading in her voice. Her sister? Pleading? "Do what?" The waitress arrives with their orders and places them in front of them. Cryssie eyes the enormous burger and mound of fries on her plate and glances up at the waitress. "Thanks," she says and looks at Amber, who's still staring at her with those unfocused eyes and seems now to be someplace deep within herself. Cryssie leans forward and puts a hand on Amber's. "What's wrong, Sis? Tell me. It's okay." She sees Amber shake her head. It's more a slight twitch, so slight Cryssie almost didn't notice.

"It's not okay. It's ugly."

It dawns on Cryssie that her questioning has led Amber to a dark secret she's been keeping all these years. Cryssie wasn't that hungry to begin with and now it feels like her stomach is in her mouth. Why did the thought never occur to her? Maybe her subconscious has been shielding her from it. Anyway, it's in her head now and as disgusting and shameful as what she suspects happened is, she has to know if it's true. "Dad?"

Amber nods.

"Did he touch you?"

Amber shakes her head.

"What happened?"

"He made me touch him."

The son of a bitch! "How? Where?"

"He'd come into my room and make me sit on the side of the bed and he'd stand next me and take out his thing. He showed me how to stroke it and hold the tissue and when he was done, I'd fold it and take it to the bathroom and flush it down the toilet. He said he was so proud of me and called me his 'best little girl.'"

Cryssie stands, walks around the table, pulls a chair next to Amber's, sits and puts her arm around her shoulder. "Did it ever go beyond that?"

Amber shakes her head slowly.

Cryssie draws her close and rests her forehead against Amber's. She sees her eyes filling with tears and the tears begin trickling down her cheeks. She picks up a napkin and hands it to her and Amber wipes her eyes and blows her nose. "How long did it go on?" Cryssie's startled by Amber's sudden look of hatred.

"Until Mom caught him."

As if this story couldn't get worse. Cryssie isn't surprised to hear their mother knew, though, the spineless bitch. "What happened?"

"The door opened and there she was. I was holding his thing and just froze. She stood there staring at us for the longest time and finally told Dad he had a phone call and walked away, just like that, as if nothing in the world were wrong. He put his thing back in his pants and zipped them up and left."

"Did anything happen after that?"

Amber shakes her head. "He tried, but I told him if he didn't leave me alone, I'd tell my teacher. That worked."

"I'm so sorry, Sis. Had I known I would have done something."

"I know."

"Have you told anyone else about this? Talked with anyone?"

Amber shakes her head.

"Well, I'm glad you finally told me."

"So am I," Amber says, glancing at Cryssie's eyes and smiling slightly.

Cryssie's aware of the waitress standing across the table from them and looks up at her.

The waitress eyes the untouched food, glances at Amber and looks at Cryssie. "How is everything?"

"Fine," Cryssie says.

"Want to take it with you?"

Cryssie looks at Amber, who looks pale and shaken, then down at the plate heaped with untouched food. It reminds her of her parents' excessive lifestyle, the oversize house and all the things in it they don't really need and seldom use and the fact that while she despises everything her father stands for and now him, she's been perfectly willing to feed at his trough. She doesn't know which is more disgusting and shameful, her own spinelessness or what her parents have done to her sister. "Just the check, please."

* * *

"Wasn't it?" Cryssie hears Jenn ask. She glances at Jenn and the faces of the young couple they've been chatting with, although Jenn's been holding up their end of the conversation. "What?"

"Yosemite, spectacular?"

"Yeah, breathtaking," Cryssie says and looks back through the crowd of people in the living room at her father, standing outside on the patio surrounded by a group of listeners. His face is flush and he has a drink in his hand and she watches him gesticulate with it as he holds forth and the questions begin streaming through her mind again. Why did he do it and why with Amber and not her? Was he abused as a child? As she remembers her paternal grandfather, he didn't seem like the child abusing type. He was a flinty, hard drinking Irishman, but then, so is her father.

She looks at her mother, standing with a group of women on the far side of the living room. Based on Amber's description of their mother's reaction when she opened the bedroom door, she knew what was going on and tolerated it. How could she have? Was she too frightened to confront him about it or did she just not care? Cryssie can't believe her mother didn't care. "Think she'll come," she hears Jenn ask and glances at her. "She'll be here," Cryssie says and looks back at her father and sips her wine.

Amber stands on the sidewalk, staring up at the windows of her unlit bedroom and the nighttime sky reflected in the panes of glass. She watches a glowing cloud pass in front of the full moon and then sees the moon reappear and look down at her with its worried expression, but only for a moment and then it's obscured again by another cloud. That's the way she's been remembering what happened ever since she told Cryssie. She glimpses it and then it's gone. She wishes she could rid herself of the memory and somehow make the man who's always standing in the shadows in the back of her mind go away for good. She knows the memory will always be there, though, and that the only way to deal with it is to force him to come forward and finally confront him. She feels weak and wants to leave but takes a deep breath and heads up the front walk toward the house.

She sees her mother in the living room, and they nod coolly at each other as she passes. She sees Cryssie and Jenn through the crowd and makes her way toward them. It was nice meeting Jenn, nice spending time with her and Cryssie, and nice seeing how much in love they are. Amber's happy for them and wonders if she has it in her to feel that way about someone. She hopes so. She understands why Cryssie wanted to share with Jenn what happened and she's fine with it. As Cryssie told her, she and Jenn are partners and it's important that partners share things with each other. Amber's never had a partner and never been one to share, but she understands.

She sees her father on the patio and Steve and his wife standing in the group listening to him. She figured they'd be here. With the Weisses out of the picture, her parents' party is the "must attend" social event of the season. She regrets now what happened with Steve and feels too embarrassed to approach them. She arrives at Cryssie's side. "Hi," Amber says softly.

"Hey, Sis," Cryssie says and gives her a hug. "How're you doing?"

"Okay, I think. I need a drink."

The bartender hands Amber a glass of red wine and she takes a long sip and looks at Cryssie and Jenn. "Come with me," she says and makes her way through the crowd in the living room with Cryssie and Jenn following behind. She and her mother exchange glances again as she passes, her mother looking concerned now, and she walks up the staircase and down the hall to the closed door to her bedroom. It's been a long time since she's been in this room. She wanted never to reenter it and didn't think she ever would but has to now. She feels Cryssie's and Jenn's hands on her back, opens the door and turns on the light.

It looks like any girl's bedroom, any girl's whose parents are wealthy. It all looks so innocent. Anyone looking at this room would think it belongs to a normal happy kid. She walks to the side of the bed, stands looking down at it, slowly turns and sits, putting her elbows on her knees and burying her face in her hands.

Jenn sits beside her and puts an arm around her shoulders and Cryssie crouches down in front of her and puts her hands on her knees.

"I'm so ashamed," Amber says weakly.

"You're not the one who should be ashamed," Cryssie says. "They are, the one for doing it and the other for allowing it." She doesn't think she'll ever be able to forgive her parents, and she doesn't see how Amber can.

"Is everything all right?" Alicia asks.

Cryssie looks up at her mother, standing in the doorway with her hand on the doorknob, staring down at them. "Doesn't Dad have a phone call?" Cryssie asks and sees fear flash in her mother's eyes as she steps back and pulls the door shut.

Court's arrived at the time in the evening when he's feeling expansive and is delighting in telling the group of listeners about his upcoming trip to South Africa to hunt big game at the invitation of a financier friend of his in Johannesburg. He knows most people disapprove of the sport and think it's anachronistic and cruel and out of touch with modern values, but as he points out, if we did what most people wanted us to do, we'd still be living in the Stone Age and the world would be a bland and dreary place where progress would be impossible.

Progress comes from not giving a damn about what people think. As Thoreau said, although Court's always been suspicious of Thoreau, who he considers a queer duck, "Most men lead lives of quiet desperation and go to the grave with the song still in them." Well, hunting big game is a lyric in his song, just as collecting fine aged whisky and single malt scotch and sailing big boats and deep-sea fishing and gaming the markets are. He sings his song as loudly as he can and anyone who doesn't like it be damned, as his father used to say.

His Father. Now there was a man, the type of man who built this country into the greatest power the world has ever known. His father's father came from Ireland without a pot to piss in and settled in Pennsylvania, working in the coal mines. He didn't give a shit what anybody thought, either. Court's father worked beside his grandfather, but wanted better in life and got a job in a foundry, learned the trade, worked his way up through the ranks and ended up owning the company, making it a major weapons supplier during World War II.

His father married the daughter of an old Lithuanian mining family in Hershey and Court's their firstborn and oldest son and the first in the family to attend college. He could have gone to Penn State, a fine school, but his dad sent him to Harvard and on to the Business School, and when he graduated, got him situated in a firm on Wall Street. All of his siblings are college educated and successful, a fact his father was proud of to his dying day.

Court brandishes his glass. Could his father drink? People these days, certainly in this country, don't understand anything about drinking. Men drink for strength. It's an age-old practice. Real men get up early and work hard all day, whether it's in a field, or in a mine shaft thousands of feet down, or on a girder hundreds of feet in the air, or on a trawler in the dead of winter with the wind howling and the rigging encased in ice, and by noon they need sustenance to replenish their strength. Drink gives it to them, gives them the strength to get up and go back to work and work hard until day's end, and at the end of the day drink takes the pain of backbreaking labor away, relaxes them and puts them in a good mood and lets them sleep soundly, so they can get up before dawn the next morning and do it all over again.

Nobody works hard anymore. People have become soft, and their brains turned to mush. They lack discipline. His father didn't hesitate to use the belt when he thought it necessary. Court remembers many times being bent over a chair or the bed and having his ass whipped until it was black and blue and if he made a sound, he'd get ten more. He learned, all right. He sees kids today and thinks we're lost. These people are unfit to run the country. They look like hell and know nothing and care only about themselves and what the government can do for them. Their parents should be shot for gross negligence.

His daughter Amber is different. She has a good head on her shoulders. He's about to share with his audience her desire to follow in his footsteps into finance and be a successful broker when he notices Alicia making her way toward him through the crowd and doesn't like the look on her face. He dials up his smile and looks around at his audience. "Excuse me a moment," he says and steps away.

Cryssie sees her father approaching through the crowd in the living room. He's a little unsteady on his feet and his eyes are watery, a familiar sight. He arrives behind Jenn and Amber, but he's keeping his eyes on Cryssie's.

"Enjoying the party, ladies?" Court asks, glancing at what's-her-name, the attractive young Asian woman Cryssie introduced as her partner. He'll deal with that another time. First things first. "Mind if I borrow my daughter for a moment?" He nods toward his study and Cryssie follows him through the living room. She follows him in and he closes the door behind her. She turns and they stand facing each other, Court no longer smiling and barely able to contain his anger. "This probably isn't the best time or place to have this conversation," he says, "but it seems you've left me no choice." He sips his drink and narrows his eyes. "What happens in this family is no one's business but our own. Understood?"

"That's bullshit."

He slaps her face hard and she throws her wine in his. He raises his hand to strike her again but catches himself. It wouldn't do any good.

She's always been a thorn in his side this one and stubborn. He sneers and turns and takes a tissue from the box on the desk and wipes his face.

She glares at him. "How could you?"

"It's a father's prerogative."

"I can't believe I'm hearing this."

"You've got a lot to learn about life, missy. You've been living in a bubble." He wads up the tissue, tosses it in the wastebasket, sits on the edge of the desk and glares at her. "I was an altar boy. My priest liked to assist boys out of their cassocks after Mass. I didn't blab about his wandering hands. You'd do well to keep your mouth shut too."

"She's scarred for life."

"Who isn't?"

"Why? Why did you do it?"

"Your mother had little interest in sex after you were born and none after your sister was. Family takes care of its own."

She can't believe she's hearing this, either. It strikes her as something one of her ancestors would have said at the time when her people were peasants living in peat-roof hovels in Ireland, when every man, no matter how ignorant and impoverished and powerless, was lord in his home. She can easily see that man having his way with his daughter. Maybe his wife was sickly and lay with her back to them and her face to the wall. Maybe he was a widower. Could it be that her father's way of thinking is the result of a vestigial gene? She doesn't want to speculate. He's a monster and what he's done is unforgiveable. Her cheek hurts and feels swollen and her jaw aches. She wants to rub the side of her face but won't give him the satisfaction. "Why didn't you just jerk off, or pay for it?"

He looks at her haughtily. "It would have been beneath me."

"But abusing your daughter wasn't. I don't know about Amber, but I'll never forgive you."

"I don't want or need your forgiveness. Just keep your mouth shut."

She understands now why her parents treated her the way they did, why they made her feel like she was a freak. They viewed her as a threat and were afraid she'd discover their dirty little secret and expose them. They knew that if they gave her enough reasons to believe she was the problem in the family she'd be too preoccupied worrying about them to give much thought to what was going on with her sister. It worked, but now the secret is out. She doesn't know if Amber will ever be able to repair the damage they've done to her. She hopes she will somehow. For herself, she's done with them. She studies her father's face. It might be the last time she sees it. She doesn't know how she'll manage on her own, but she will. She must. She won't be able to live with herself if she doesn't.

* * *

Rita gazes at the peek-a-boo full moon as they ride along Pacific Coast Highway toward Andrew's. They didn't witness the incident. They were talking with that nice couple Cyn and Steve on the patio when it happened, but they heard the commotion and turned to see Court standing at the bar, rubbing his cheek, and heard someone say that his daughter Amber had walked up to him and slapped him and threw her glass of wine in his face and the glass at his head, just as Rita had at Ed's that time, and stormed out of the house with her sister and her sister's friend. Court's reflexes must not be as good as Ed's were because the glass hit him in the forehead and broke and cut him badly. That did it for Rita. She was feeling exhausted anyway and being pregnant gave them the perfect excuse to leave early, and when they did Court said good-bye to them pressing ice cubes wrapped in a towel against his forehead. He looked every bit the ridiculous fool she thinks he is.

She's not sure she'll ever be comfortable in Andrew's world, a world run by people like Court Brennan. What a pompous ass! She doesn't care how successful or influential in the business community around here he is. She has no idea why his daughter slapped him, but she's sure he deserved it. She felt like slapping him herself just to shut him up. She doesn't know what Andrew thinks of him. He just smiled politely and listened to Court go on and on about his hunting trip to South Africa and his family's rags to riches story and how the country's going to hell in a hand basket. Maybe it's because she's an alcoholic, battling her own demons, but his rant about the benefits of drink struck her as absurd and pathetic. The guy's a drunk, just like she is, plain and simple. She watches the moon disappear behind a cloud and looks at Andrew. "What do you think of Court?"

"He's a pompous ass."

She puts a hand on his thigh and gazes at him. He's brought calm to her life. She didn't think it was possible, but he has. It seems like such a small thing, but to her it's the most important and precious thing and what she loves most about him. She watches the moon emerge from behind a cloud and for once the worry she always imagines she sees in the Man in the Moon's expression seems to be about the world below in general and not her in particular.

CHAPTER 23

Matt's Big Break

Andrew swipes his badge through the reader at the employee entrance at the rear of WestWave's facility in downtown Los Angeles. All the white-collar employees and visitors enter through the showroom in front, but he always uses the back entrance, which opens onto the manufacturing floor. Beginning his day with a walk through it, greeting people by name and stopping to ask how they and their families are doing keeps him in touch with the bread and butter aspect of his business.

He's proud of the fact that his company manufactures its products here in the U.S. His dad had to close his fabric business because it got to the point where he couldn't compete with the low-cost goods from Asia, but WestWave manages to do it and still pay its workers a good wage and provide them with good benefits. The company's customers appreciate it and are willing to pay a premium for the products to support it. It's more than just the clothes. The WestWave logo means something. It's a positive brand whose message is that you can still manufacture quality products in the U.S. and compete globally and treat your employees well.

He watches the workers skillfully running fabric through the machines and remembers, as he always does, the time when he was a kid, and his dad showed him the trick of walking a nickel back and forth across the backs of his fingers. It looked easy, but then his dad handed him the nickel and said, "Try it." Try as he might, he couldn't do it and he learned that lesson well. So much in life looks easy until you try it yourself.

All these people who go on and on about how undocumented immigrants are taking jobs away from U.S. citizens are hypocrites. He could call an employment agency right now and say he has jobs available for skilled sewing machine operators and wouldn't get a single applicant who was born and raised in the U.S. and certainly not a White one.

He's pretty sure all the current employees are legally documented, but you never know. All you have to do to get a Social Security card or California driver's license is take a walk down the sidewalk at MacArthur Park. Even with E-Verify it's sometimes difficult to determine someone's status. He agrees with Rita. Anyone who wants to come here and work and pay taxes should be allowed to. He'd be surprised if Court doesn't have most of his money sheltered offshore to avoid paying taxes on it.

He sits at his desk, wakes up his computer and opens the folder of Matt's photos and reviews them again. He feels the same way about Amber this morning. She'd be perfect for the new campaign. He singles out the same photo of her he did yesterday evening and studies her face, and particularly her eyes. He still can't put his finger on what it is about her look he finds so appealing. She's beautiful, but all the models are. It's something else, her aloofness and detachment, her standoffish allure. Well, whatever it is he's glad he ran into Matt. He hadn't been surfing in a while and hadn't seen Matt in almost a year. He knows Matt is a good photographer and studying at Long Beach, but his portfolio and these photos of Amber really took him by surprise. Matt's as good as any of the photographers they use and better than most. Andrew will go to bat for them both. Everyone on the design team has a vote, but it's like *Animal Farm:* "all animals are equal, but some animals are more equal than others."

* * *

It strikes Amber as an amazing coincidence. Matt never mentioned that he knew Andrew Weston, and what are the chances that they'd run into each other and get talking about his photography just when the company's planning a new ad campaign and looking for a new photographer and new models? She was relieved when Matt said he didn't tell Andrew the black and white nudes in his portfolio are of her. Those pictures didn't mean anything to her then, but they do now. It's her body on display and she feels differently about it now, connected to it, still a bit uneasily but more the way she used to when she was that happy smiling kid Cryssie remembers.

It's hard to believe they're offering her the job, knowing she's not a professional model. She's knows that's Matt's doing, that he told Andrew she's a natural. The money's certainly good and she can use it, since she won't be using any of her father's anymore. It'll be hard making ends meet — she's begun looking for a smaller and much less expensive apartment — but she's not complaining. On the contrary, she's looking forward to severing her financial ties to her father, as Cryssie plans to do. It's an important step, scary but important.

She studies the ad layouts and listens to Matt explain the concept of the campaign and how the set ups will be shot on a stage they'll build on the beach with Banzai Pipeline in the background. It seems like an enormous expense to shoot this on location on Oahu when they could just as easily create these scenes using Photoshop, but she's familiar with WestWave's series of ads featuring famous surfing spots and knows they pride themselves on authenticity. As Matt says, they feel they owe it to the people who put the company on the map in the first place: surfers.

Apparently, a lot of time was spent in this design meeting trying to describe what they found so appealing about her look. She reads the string of adjectives they came up with and it all seems to her to be nibbling around the edges. She's reminded of the story of the blind men trying to describe an elephant by feeling it. She knows just what they want and there's only one problem. She isn't that person anymore.

She studies Matt as he looks down at the ad layouts and explains the scheme he's come up with to shoot the different scenes. There are a lot of them, the idea being to represent every aspect of these young professionals' lives. It involves set pieces being flown onto and off the stage using cranes. It sounds elaborate, but she hears the confidence in his voice and knows he'll pull it off.

How dismissive she was of his wanting to make a career of photography. It seems foolish and stupid now. Here he is, going off to Hawaii to shoot an ad campaign for WestWave and she's sure he'll do a great job and that it will lead to others and his career will be launched and where is she? Her heart's gone out of wanting to be a broker and she doesn't know what she wants to do and hasn't begun to think about it. It's too ironic.

Her reaction to hearing that Kate's his girlfriend seems equally foolish and stupid now. What difference does it make that she's older? Amber's happy for Matt, in fact, envies him. She wishes she had a partner in life the way he and Cryssie do, someone to share things with and confide in, someone to care for and care for her.

She's been wondering if he knows. She doesn't think so, but worrying about that seems foolish and stupid too. What difference does it make? It's who she is, forever a part of her now, like an indelible stain on her soul. She must learn to live with it and move on. The problem with this modeling job is that they want the person she used to be. She puts her cup of coffee on the table and clasps her hands in front of her. "Listen," she says and he looks up at her, "what if I said I don't think I can do it? I mean, you're getting this job isn't contingent on my being the model, is it?"

"No, but they're sold on you. Why don't you think you can do it?"

"I know what they want." She looks down at the string of adjectives on the paper again. "That look, that attitude." She looks at him. "I'm not that person anymore. I don't want anything to do with her."

He leans back, crosses his arms and tilts his head and studies her. He's noticed the marked change in her personality and demeanor and has been wondering about it. "What happened?"

She can tell by his expression, curious and concerned, that he doesn't know. "It's a long story."

He's interested in hearing it but can see she doesn't want to talk about it. "I wouldn't worry about it." He nods at the paper. "People see what they want to see. Just be yourself and I'm sure they'll love it."

Just be herself.... It sounds so simple. The question is who is she? She's not sure and feels like she's inching along on the frozen surface of a pond, testing the ice and expecting to fall through at any moment. "Let me think about it."

* * *

Sunday, January 1, 2012

Dear Anneliese,

It seems like ages since I've written to you. The holidays are such a busy time of year. There's always something going on. I just didn't have time to write, but today's New Year's Day, a quiet day, as usual, so I have plenty of time and I'll bring you up to date.

I lit a new candle in my Menorah each night during Hanukkah and thought of you and the others in the Secret Annex. It made me think about miracles. Maybe it's because it's such a religious time of the year and miracles seem to be in the air. Did the Jews really only have enough oil for one day? Did it really burn for eight or did they make that up, you know, to make what happened seem more important? Was Mary really a virgin when she had Jesus or did the Christians make that up too? I don't know. I guess we'll never know. The real miracle would have been if you and the others had survived. You came so close.

Christmas was great! I got clothes from my mom, a pair of jeans and some tees and a sweater and a really cool hoodie. She also gave me some books I wanted, best of all "A Canticle for Leibowitz." Can't wait to read that!

My mom loves romance novels and I gave her the latest by her favorite author. Another is chocolate so I gave her a box of her favorite, See's California Brittle. That stuff is expensive! $36! I also gave her some Japanese hair sticks. She has really beautiful long hair, but she usually wears it in a ponytail. I keep telling her she should wear it up more often. I think she looks beautiful with her hair up. I figured if she's going to, why not wear it like a geisha! She tried them out and her hair looked great! Matt really liked it. I gave him cologne. My mom picked it out for me, so I know she likes it. I want him to smell nice for her.

Matt gave me a surfboard! I had a feeling he was going to, but I didn't want to get my hopes up. He also gave me a DVD documentary called "Heart of a Soul Surfer." It's about a girl named Bethany Hamilton who grew up in Hawaii and has been surfing all her life. A shark bit off her left arm, but she found the courage to go back in the water and learn to surf with one arm. I can't believe how brave she is. If a shark bit off my arm I'm not sure I'd ever go back in the water. She felt the same way for a while and then decided she loves surfing so much she wasn't going to let a shark take it away from her. I'd like to think I'd have that much courage. I guess that's the point of her story. If she can do it, I can. And can she surf! It's like she was born on a surfboard!

On Boxing Day, the day after Christmas, I gave my mom a gift-wrapped box, just the box, nothing in it. I've done that for the last few years just for fun, as a joke. When I first heard about Boxing Day I thought people actually boxed, you know, with gloves in a ring. Silly, huh? I finally read online that it's called that because people in England used to give servants and tradesmen "Christmas boxes" with money in them. Now it's pretty much just a big shopping day.

December 26th is also Saint Stephen's Day. He was stoned to death! Nice, huh? They still do that in some countries, if you can believe it. It makes me wonder if the world is really getting any better or if we just like to think it is to make ourselves feel better about things. Sorry for sounding so pessimistic.

And now for the really big news! I had a surprise 13th birthday party! My first real birthday party on my actual birthday! YIPEEE!!! I knew it was really my mom and Matt's New Year's Eve party, but that was okay. I made out like a bandit with presents!

I knew most of Matt's friends, but a few I'd never met before, like Eli. He's Jewish (DUH!). He told me all about how important the number 13 is. He was really interesting and I tried to understand what he was talking about but, boy, is it complicated!

I'm sure you know all about this, but he said that Hebrew words are made up of letters and each letter has its own meaning and number value and the really important words add up to 13. He said there are twelve things that make up everything having to do with God and that those twelve things are all tied together by a thirteenth thing and that's why 13 is so important. Something like that. I haven't read about this online yet, but I will. It's a little like trying to figure out how Jenn and Cryssie are going to have each other's baby!

It just seems freaky to me that things have so many different meanings and you could live your entire life not knowing about them. I wonder about everything I see now and ask myself if what I'm seeing is all there is or if there's more to it? I'm looking at the words I've written on the page and wondering if there isn't some secret message here staring me in the face that I can't see. See what I mean? Freaky!

I really enjoyed talking with Amber. It turns out she used to be Matt's girlfriend! She said Matt's a great guy, but things just didn't work out between them and she's glad they're still friends. She is BEE-U-TEE-FUL!!! She's going to be the model in these new ads for WestWave and Matt's going to be the photographer. They're going to shoot the photos in Hawaii with Banzai Pipeline in the background. It's a famous surfing spot on the north shore of Oahu that produces these amazing curling waves. It has to do with the reefs offshore. I watched videos on YouTube of people surfing it. Awesome! It's on my list!

Anyway, I told her about my plan to have my own Quinceañera and she thought it was the coolest idea! She asked if she could be one of my Maids and I said sure, although I'm not sure I'll have Maids. I'm still thinking about it. I know I won't have a Thanks Action Mass, not being Catholic. I'm not even much of a Protestant. I'm thinking it'll just be a big party with me the center of attention in a beautiful dress. That works for me! Rita said she knows a store in Santa Ana that has beautiful dresses. She got her dress there when she had her Quinceañera and said she'd help me with mine. It was really nice of her to offer.

Rita's changed so much since my dad died and seems so happy with Andrew. It's nice to see. And, boy, is she pregnant! It turns out she's going to have a girl. Rita said she'd be my half-sister, which sounds weird to me. It's sad that she'll never know our dad. I'll tell her about him, if she wants. She might not. Andrew seems like he's going to be all the dad she'll need.

I keep thinking about Amber. We spent so much time together talking. She was so interested in what I had to say about my love of reading and surfing and wanting to have my own Quinceañera and how close I am with my mom and how much I like Matt, even though I love my dad and miss him. She said she envied me. Can you believe that?

Yours, Dee Dee

P.S.: Matt stayed over last night (he kind of lives here now). I didn't go to bed until late and I had a hard time falling asleep, I guess because of all the excitement. I listened to them cleaning up and then getting ready for bed and then talking in their bedroom. I couldn't hear what they were saying, just the sound of their voices. After a while I heard my mom giggling! She never giggled when my dad lived here, at least not that I ever heard. I don't know what they were doing in there (well, I kind of do) but it sure sounded like they were having a lot of fun! I'm happy for them.

I almost forgot: Happy New Year!

CHAPTER 24

New Beginnings

Uri checks the departure time of his flight from Tijuana to LAX and settles into a seat in the gate area to wait. He's been in some tight spots before, but the fact that he's now on his way back to Israel seems miraculous.

When he and his team were taken into custody up by the Mexican Coast Guard and detained at a military facility near Tijuana he thought that was it, that they'd be tried by military tribunal and incarcerated for a very long time, perhaps even executed. As it happened. the next day he was led to a room where Fidencio and two men in dark suits, one Mexican, the other American, were waiting for him. On the table in front of them was a dossier thick with information about him. The two men in suits introduced themselves only as representatives of their respective governments, but he's certain the American was FBI and the Mexican CISEN, the Mexican equivalent agency, and that Fidencio has been CISEN all along. The CISEN agent explained that the decision to terminate the operation was purely political. They'd learned of the plan late in the game and were insufficiently prepared with one of their own. It just wouldn't do to have Rios killed by a band of rogue foreign operatives. The government wanted to use Rios's execution to send a strong message to narcotraffickers and to the general public that it's serious about waging war against the cartels, and to those young people who idolize people like Rios, that if they're thinking of getting into the business they can expect the same treatment. The price of Uri and his colleagues' freedom the CISEN agent said was to work with Fidencio.

Uri was unfazed by the high degree of cynicism in all this. He knew the only reason the government moved against Rios was to try to quell the increasing public outcry, fueled by the clergy and NGO human rights organizations, about its having done nothing to try to end the collateral killing of innocent civilians — the dead already number in the tens of thousands — by the cartels in their battle for turf. The simple fact of the matter is that he and his men had been commandeered as a team ready in place to do the government's dirty work. They were expendable and should anything go wrong their mission deniable.

It went off like clockwork. They waited in the dark at a sharp turn in the road leading to Rios's house where it's necessary to slow down. They stopped the SUV with a grenade and killed Rios and the men with him. Uri and his men were taken from the scene as members of the Mexican security forces posed with Rios for the cameras. They were driven to the airport and handed tickets and their passports and now he's thinking of orchards and olive trees and balmy breezes and how nice it will feel to hold Elsa in his arms again and enjoy what's left of his ninth life.

* * *

Rita gathers up the folders from the respondent's table and stuffs them into her briefcase. She tried her best to get the judge to allow her clients, a young undocumented Mexican couple whose three-year-old son was born in California, to stay and continue on a path to citizenship, but she lost, despite the fact that both parents are employed and paying taxes and now the three of them will be deported. She's lost track of the number of times she's been unsuccessful in representing people just like these. Her clients are disappointed, but she explained to them at the outset that they had very little chance of avoiding deportation and they were prepared for the ruling. She shakes their hands and wishes them the best of luck and leaves the courtroom, rolling her briefcase behind her. That's it. It's time to have the baby.

She's exhausted and feels like the effect of gravity on her has doubled and it's an effort to put one foot in front of the other. Andrew wanted her to stop working a month ago and relax and rest at home until the baby was born but she couldn't just sit around all day watching TV or staring at the walls, which is pretty much the same thing. She had to stay active. She hasn't slept well lately and when she does doze off, she's often awakened from a bad dream in which something awful is about to happen to someone, not her, but an anonymous faceless someone, although there was that one dream she appeared in.

She's never been to Rio, so it's odd she dreamed about it. Maybe the reason her subconscious chose it as the location is because Rio and Rios sound so similar. She was standing in the street surrounded by people in feathery costumes and knew in the dream that it was Carnival. The people were dancing around her and the mood seemed festive, but then she felt a sense of foreboding and the expressions on the dancers' faces grew more and more menacing. Then skeletons, not dancers in skeleton costumes but real skeletons, came dancing toward her with their arms raised over their heads, each skeleton holding a bottle in one hand and a baby in the other. Behind the dancing skeletons came a gigantic float, shooting flames in the nighttime sky, and sitting on a throne high atop the float was the Devil, wearing sunglasses and grinning down at her.

That much of the dream makes at least some sense to her as being an expression of her anxiety about her drinking and the health of the baby, but she's still trying to figure out the significance of what came next.

She was standing on the shoulder of the statue of Christ the Redeemer on Corcovado, looking out over the city and islands in the bay, and she felt the statue slowly tipping forward, further and further, and she realized the statue was about to fall off the mountain with her on it and at the moment when she was unsure whether the statue would continue falling or begin flying she sat up in bed, panic-stricken.

She doesn't know how she would have gotten through this pregnancy without Andrew's support. When she wakes in the night he does too and takes her in his arms and holds her and comforts her. She feels badly that he has to drag himself through his day on so little sleep, but he never complains. He's always there for her.

She arrives at the elevators pushes the down button and stands waiting at the elevator door, feeling happy to be showing her back to this floor for a while. Finally having the baby will be a relief physically, mentally and emotionally.

As awful as it is to contemplate, she hopes that if Rios does kill her, it will be after she gives birth. At least the baby will have a loving father in Andrew. Then again, it would be just like him to kill her while she's carrying the baby, taking both their lives. Trying to second-guess the mind of a monster makes her head ache.

She glances at the faces of the people around her as the doors open and they walk into the elevator. She turns and stares at the blurry reflections of the people on the metallic doors. They look like a gathering of ghosts. She's suspicious of everyone now. When she looks at people's faces it's to see if she can recognize her assassin. What a miserable way to live.

The elevator stops on a lower floor, the doors open and people step out and two big men in suits carrying briefcases step in and she quickly dismisses them as suspects. She's certain that if and when her assassin appears, he won't look anything like them.

The doors close and the baby begins kicking. She puts a hand on her belly and rubs it, shifting her weight to try to get comfortable. She knows everyone in the elevator is discreetly watching her with that now familiar expression, a mixture of reverence and hope. People seem to naturally view a pregnant woman as being in a state of grace. She reminds herself that Rios isn't like most people.

The elevator arrives at the lower parking level and the doors open. She and a man exit and her anxiety grows as she sees him head in the opposite direction toward his car. She wants to call out to him and ask him to escort her to hers, but walks on. This dimly lit cavernous place has come to seem like a chamber of horrors to her in which the unimaginable is always about to happen. She scans the rows of parked cars on either side and the dark recesses of the garage as she walks along, keys in hand, listening to the sound of her briefcase rolling behind her and the blood pounding in her ears.

She arrives at her car and presses the key to unlock the doors. She sees the lights flash and hears the click of the doors unlocking and then the sound of a car door closing behind her. Her skin is crawling as she turns and sees a man dressed in black wearing sunglasses approaching. She feels weak and her legs feel wobbly. The man is close now and looking directly at her and she notices his well-trimmed Vandyke.

"Abogado," the man says.

She sees him reach inside his leather jacket and she drops the briefcase handle and puts a hand on her belly to protect the baby. She holds out the other in front of her as she backs into her car. "Please," she pleads in Spanish, "don't kill my baby!" She sees it's an envelope he's taken out and he stands in front of her and hands it to her without saying anything. She can't see his eyes behind the dark lenses, but knows they're fixed on hers and after a moment he turns. She watches him walk away and get in his car and drive off. She looks at the envelope in her shaking hand and feels the baby begin kicking more urgently.

There's no mention of the story on the English-language news but it's the lead story on the Spanish-language stations. Rodolfo Rios is dead, killed, the Secretary of the Interior explains to a crowd of reporters, by security forces in Rosarito that were attempting to arrest him peacefully, but came under fire and returned it. Rita watches the brief clip of Rios being played over and over, probably because it's the only footage that exists of him. He's smiling and walking with several other men and waving to the camera as he turns away.

She looks down at the photos spread out on the coffee table. They were taken from different angles and show him hanging upside-down out the open front passenger side door of a black SUV, the front of his white shirt and one side of his face covered with blood. She wants to feel relieved but isn't sure this is the end of it. It's possible the person charged with carrying out Rios's order is still determined to do it.

She has a strong feeling the man in the garage was Aracelle's brother. She'll ask her to describe him when she calls to convey her condolences. Rios was a monster, but he was also the father of Aracelle's child and Rita remembers her saying that he was the sweetest man imaginable and a loving father early in their marriage. That's probably the way she'll always remember him.

The contractions are intense and about five minutes apart now. Rita looks at Andrew, who's studying one of the pictures. "It's time," she says.

* * *

Rita's Ob Gyn is usually a mild-mannered young woman, but she's a different person here in the delivery room, like a demanding personal trainer positioned between her legs.

"That's it! Push!" the doctor says.

Rita can feel the doctor's hands inside her, holding the sides of the baby's head. The doctor glances up at her and frowns slightly, obviously dissatisfied with her effort. Rita didn't want an epidural. She's felt numb for so long that she wanted to feel the pain of natural childbirth. She's determined that her daughter's birth will mark the beginning of a new life, not only for daughter but also for herself, an unfoggy and feeling life filled with new purpose and responsibility. Her new life isn't beginning easily or comfortably, though.

"Push hard! You can do it!"

The pain Rita's experiencing is excruciating. She's pushing as hard as she can and can't help feeling resentful of the doctor's insistence and glares at her. She closes her eyes, clenches her teeth and squeezes Andrew's hand and pushes with all the strength she can muster and the sound she's making now, a mixture of grunt and howl and shriek, seems more animal to her than human. She feels the baby's head emerge and the rest of her sliding out, and then an enormous emptiness inside. She opens her eyes and sees the doctor aspirating the baby and is relieved when the baby coughs and begins breathing.

The doctor smiles down at the baby. "Welcome to the world," she says.

Rita watches her give the baby to the nurse and the nurse swaddle her in a blanket as the doctor clamps the umbilicus and cuts it. The nurse beams as she brings the baby to Rita and places her in her arms and Rita looks anxiously at the baby's face for any sign of fetal alcohol syndrome but sees only a healthy baby's face with what look like Ed's eyes and her cheekbones and chin. She kisses the baby on the forehead.

"Does she have a name?" the nurse asks.

She doesn't but gazing down at the expression of wonder on her newborn daughter's face, it seems a miracle that she's here, alive and well and Rita nods and smiles. "Mira."

* * *

Amber glides through the water in Long Beach harbor in her open water shell, maintaining a steady pace and watching the man in the shell about a hundred yards behind her slowly and steadily close the distance between them. She isn't sure if he's trying to catch up with her or if he's even aware she's in front of him. She hasn't seen him turn and look at her. He just keeps doing as she does, putting his oars in the water and pushing off as he pulls, gliding back and forth in his seat in a smooth continuous motion. Unlike her, though, he seems to know where he's headed, as everyone else does too, Matt toward a successful career and happy life with Kate and Cryssie and Jenn toward their degrees and careers and marriage and kids. Even Dee Dee is full of purpose. There seems to be no end to what she plans to do in life.

Matt was right about the photo shoot. Everyone thought she did a great job and gave them just the look they were after, whatever that was. It still feels weird seeing that gigantic picture of herself on the billboard beside the 405 in Long Beach. Matt says there are pictures of her on billboards all over L.A. That nice young Brazilian art director Gui tried to convince her at dinner the evening before they left the island that she should make modeling her career, just as Matt thinks she should, but it's not in her. It was a one-time thing and, really, she only did it as a favor to Matt. When she lost interest in wanting to be a titan of Wall Street, it left an empty space inside her and so far, nothing has filled it. It's an awful feeling having no direction in life. Out here on the water she's at least in motion.

The man is about fifty yards away now and she pulls a little harder on her right oar to move over and make room for him to pass. She watches his shoulders and back and arms as he rows and can see he's in great shape. Is he on the crew team at Long Beach? She watches him close the final distance between them and pull abreast of her and slow his pace to match hers. She glances at his profile and sees the high forehead and aquiline nose and full lips and wreath of curly black hair and thinks French, maybe Spanish or Italian but probably French. He looks at her and tilts his head back slightly and raises his eyebrows.

"May I join you?" he asks.

She guessed right.

* * *

Amber sips her beer and is content listening. He already knows she's a rower and she can't think of anything else to say about herself that could be of interest to him. She knows he'll eventually ask for more details, and she'll have to say something, but for now she's content just listening and enjoying doing so. The fact that she's the one hiding in the shadows now isn't lost on her.

He introduced himself at the dock as Phillipe Devereux and now she learns he's a physician with a practice in Paris who does volunteer work with Médecins Sans Frontières. He's here to attend a conference in L.A. and staying with a physician friend who lives in Long Beach. The shell is his friend's, and he borrowed it to get some much-needed exercise. He fell in love with rowing when he was in secondary school and doesn't often have the opportunity to get out on the water because he travels so much, so this was a treat and how fortunate he is to have met her. "What's your specialty?" she asks.

"Eyes," he says, pointing at hers. "I'm an ophthalmic surgeon. I see a lot of eyes. I must say yours are very beautiful."

Is he commenting as a physician on the healthiness of her eyes or paying her a compliment? The way he said it could be either and she assumes the latter. "Thank you," she says and sees him studying her eyes with keen interest now.

"They say the eyes are the window to the soul," he says.

She's surprised that his saying this should make her blush, but it's the way he said it and is looking at them, kind of dreamily.

"I've always been fascinated by the eye," he says. "It's such a marvelous and complex adaptation. I don't believe in creationism, but I understand why those who do use it to make their case. It's a compelling one. How could such a thing be the result of evolution? It doesn't seem possible." He sips his beer and looks over her shoulder through the plate glass window at the big expensive boats moored in the slips. "You wouldn't believe the diseases I see, most of them preventable, the result of poverty and hunger, of corrupt government. It's appalling, but that's the world and it isn't going to change anytime soon. We do what we can."

"Are you from Paris originally?" she asks, wanting to know and also keep the conversation focused on him.

"Bordeaux."

"I've been there. It's beautiful."

He nods. "I think of it when I'm in some village where the people have only contaminated water to drink and are slowly going blind because of the stupidity and greed of their government."

"You sound bitter."

He shrugs. "If you'd been where I've been and seen what I've seen, you'd be bitter too."

She's curious about his status, given that he travels so much. He's handsome and fit and intelligent and polite. She'd be surprised if he isn't in a relationship and possibly married, although he's not wearing a wedding band, which she's learned is no indication of anything. She's met married men who don't wear one for one reason or another. "Married?"

He shakes his head. "Divorced. My former wife is also a physician in general practice in Paris. We're on good terms. In fact, our relationship is better now than when we were married."

It's nice to hear him refer to her as his "former" wife and not as his "ex." It says a lot to her about the type of man he is. "I hear that often happens. What's her name?"

"Lisette."

"It's lovely. Things just didn't work out, huh?"

He shrugs. "I was away a lot." He could leave it at that but there's something in her eyes, genuine curiosity, yes, but something else that makes him want to be truthful with her. "I was unfaithful. She suspected and asked and I answered honestly. Perhaps that was a mistake."

"I'm not sure being honest is ever a mistake. Couldn't forgive you, huh?"

"Sadly, no. I understood."

"Yeah, Some things you just can't forgive. Kids?"

He nods. "A daughter, Giselle."

"Also a lovely name. How old is she?"

"She just turned nine."

"I bet she's beautiful." She sees his expression brighten.

"She is and very smart. She takes after her mother. So, what do you do when you're not a Nereid?"

Well, she held him off as long as she could. She thinks about what there is to say about herself, and it doesn't seem interesting to her and she can't imagine it will to him, either. "I'm a finance major at Long Beach State."

"Ah! And what do you plan to do?"

"I wanted to follow in my father's footsteps and make a ton of money on Wall Street. Now...." She shrugs.

He leans forward and crosses his arms on the table and studies her eyes again. "You'll think it fanciful, but I can see people's stories in their eyes."

She looks down at the beer bottle beside her glass and runs her fingertip through the beads of moisture coating its sides and stares at the amber liquid inside. She pictures herself a tiny Nereid, swimming in endless circles on its surface. "I guess when you've examined as many eyes as you have you can."

"Not the details of the story, but that there's one there." He holds out an upturned hand. "It's a little like reading palms."

She looks at his hand and then in his eyes. She has the feeling by the way he's looking in hers that he really can see her soul. She puts her upturned hand on his and watches him study her palm and place his fingertip on it and begin slowly tracing one of the lines, the heart line if she remembers correctly.

"I was examining a Bantu woman's eyes in Kenya," he says, keeping his eyes on her palm. "She seemed so calm and composed, but I saw horror in her eyes. I asked through the interpreter what had happened, and he said the woman fled Somalia with her daughter after men came to her house and killed her husband and raped her daughter while she and her son stood watching, and when the men had all taken their turns, they left and took her son with them."

Amber listens, gazing at his eyes as he slowly traces the line with his fingertip and her entire being is focused on the feel of it against her skin. Given what he just shared with her it doesn't seem right that she should be thinking about how nice it feels, but she is and realizes it's the first time in her life she's enjoying being touched by a man. She sees him glance up at her eyes and smile and look back down at her palm and begin tracing her lifeline. That one she's sure of.

"There was a tribal chief in Mali, a powerful man who was much feared. He presented with advanced age-related macular degeneration, but I also saw sadness and remorse in his eyes. I didn't ask him about his story. I was told later by one of his men that the chief learned his eldest daughter was having sexual relations with a married man from another tribe, bringing dishonor on himself and his family, and that he had no choice but to have her stoned to death." Phillipe looks up at Amber and smiles. "What's your story?"

She looks at his smile and then in his eyes and feels them drawing her out of herself, inviting her to be something more than a traumatized ten-year-old. He's been open and honest with her and it's the only important thing about herself she feels there is to share with him. "I was abused by my father when I was a child." She waits to see what his reaction will be, but there isn't much of one. He just gazes at her eyes and then slowly raises his eyebrows and lets go of her hand, the way she imagines he would a bird, gently and carefully. She wonders if he sees her profound feeling of relief in her eyes. He probably does. He seems to see everything and now he's looking at her with surprise.

"It's you, on the billboard! Isn't it?"

She nods.

"Why didn't you mention you're a model?"

"I'm not really. I did it as a favor."

"Ah. When I saw it, I was struck by the contrast between the model's beauty and the look in her eyes, so cold, icy. I have to say that having met you, you don't seem anything like her."

"I'm not," she says and now she's certain he can see her soul.

* * *

Amber sips her coffee and looks around the apartment at the empty walls and still unpacked cardboard boxes. He was probably just being nice when he said his apartment in Paris is even smaller. This place is a far cry from the apartment on Oceanfront with its spectacular view of the Pacific but, it's what she can afford now.

He looks good in yesterday's clothes, sitting across the small table from her with his phone to his ear. He sounds good too. She listens to his side of the conversation he's having in French with someone at MSF, enjoying the music of the language and catching a word and phrase here and there. She used to think her French was just a little rusty, but listening to him she realizes she's been kidding herself. She couldn't hold her own conversationally in French if her life depended on it. It would be nice to finally become fluent. She's getting ahead of herself.

Was he so tender in his lovemaking because of what she'd shared with him? She doesn't think so. That seems to be who he is. In any case, making love with him was a wonderful new experience. She didn't want to be anywhere else but in his arms and thrilled at his touch and wanted to please him as much as he was pleasing her.

She looks around the room again. It seems that for years her life has been funneling down and has finally arrived in this cramped apartment with a view of the rear of the apartment building across the parking lot. It feels more like a point of departure than a final destination, like a gate area at an airport. She knows where she'd like to go from here. He ends the call, puts the phone on the table, sips his coffee and looks at her over the rim of the mug. "When are you leaving?" she asks.

"Day after tomorrow."

"For Paris?"

He nods.

"How long will you be there?"

"A month, then off to Somalia."

"For?"

"Three months."

"And then?"

"Back to Paris."

"And then?"

He shrugs. "I'll go where I'm needed."

She gets the picture. She pulls her robe tighter around her and puts her feet up on the edge of the chair, her arms around her legs and her chin on her knees and looks down at her toes and wiggles them. There's the money in her savings account and she still has the credit cards. Her father would love it if she used them. It would make him feel like she's back under his thumb. How ironic it would be. He should pay for her new life. He owes her that and so much more. She looks at Phillipe and sees him gazing at her in that way of his. She knows he knows what she wants to do, that he can see it in her eyes.

"You'd like to come?" he asks.

She nods.

"Do! You can't accompany me on assignment, but it's only three months," he teases and grins. "Anyway, I'm sure you'll be very busy redecorating the apartment." He sees she's in no mood to be teased or trifled with.

She looks back down at her toes, wiggles them and considers. She does want to go. Phillipe's the first man she's wanted to be with. She's known him less than twenty-four hours but feels completely at ease and comfortable with him. Her only reluctance is the fact that he was unfaithful. She's not judging him and who knows what the state of his marriage was at the time, and it's to his credit that he was honest with his wife about it. It seems silly that it should bother her, but it does. As controlling as she was with men, she never cared what they did when they were out of her sight, but she cares what Phillipe does. A lot. She knows it's foolish. You can't make someone be faithful, but she wants him to know how she feels. It's important. She looks at him. "If I do you won't be sleeping with other women."

It's curious. Her statement didn't sound so much like an ultimatum as a request and his impression is that she hasn't felt vulnerable in a very long time and is happy to be able to again. He nods solemnly. He sees something now in her eyes that he remembers seeing in the eyes of the woman on the billboard, the haunting memory of a past life, perhaps as *une sirène*. He smiles. "*Très bon! Allons-y!*" he says and holds out his hand

and watches her expression change to one of excited hopefulness as she reaches out her hand and takes his.

She remembers Lao Tzu's observation from her study of philosophy: "A journey of a thousand miles begins beneath your feet." *"Oui!"* she says with all the nasality she can muster.

* * *

Steve can't fault Hue for keeping good records, but it was a bad idea for everyone concerned to employ underage girls. He knew Thien was young, but not seventeen. His attorney spoke with the assistant D.A. assigned to the case and was told they only plan to prosecute the men rounded up at the club that night. The names of the other clients they found in Hue's records will be released to the press and the Fourth Estate will do what it does best: public shaming. Having weathered one scandal, the prospect of yet more bad press was just too much for the Board.

It's interesting that the only Board member who came to Steve's defense was Court, who took him aside after the vote and said he didn't give a rat's ass what Steve did in his private life, and that if the company had learned anything from its experience with Ira it's that all shareholders and analysts and investors care about is profits. Court shared with him that Ira also thought letting him go was a bad idea, but didn't want to intercede on his behalf, given all the trouble he'd caused the company, which Steve understood. In the end all that matters is that when he walked out of PACBOND, he felt happy to be leaving that world behind.

He slows and eyes the "For Lease" sign in the window of the still vacant commercial property on a busy corner on Newport Boulevard in Costa Mesa. It's a perfect location and the only reason it's still available is the lousy economy. He parks and walks back and peers through the large plate glass window at the dark empty space. It's not much to look at now, but he sees the potential for a successful business. It'll be his legacy to his son. After all, Joey's the reason he's become passionate about this new venture. When his son was born, he found himself less interested in his work at PACBOND and more so in doing something he would truly love to do and devote himself to. What could be more enjoyable than satisfying people's sweet tooth? His settlement was generous, an amount most people would consider obscene and the Board's way of easing its collective conscience for firing him for such a relatively minor indiscretion. Unknowingly having sex with a seventeen-year-old is hardly drug trafficking. So, he has the money and, most important, Cyn's support.

He'll model it after the ice cream parlor in the Bronx he remembers so fondly, with white marble floors and table tops and black wrought iron stands for the tables and chairs with padded seat cushions and seat backs. Maybe he'll do a '50s theme and have the wait staff wear pegged black pants and skirts and white shirts. They'll serve ice cream in enough flavors to satisfy everyone and make it right on the premises so customers can see it being made. They'll offer Italian ices and pastry. It'll be a little piece of the Bronx right here in Orange County. The specialty of the house, of course, will be chocolate egg cream made with Fox's U-bet Chocolate Flavor Syrup, the real deal and delicious.

He smiles, remembering Cyn's expression as he described the drink to her. She looked every bit the girl from small town Indiana who'd never heard of a chocolate egg cream let alone tasted one. "So," she said with that cute perplexed expression, "let me get this straight. There's no egg?" It made him laugh.

He walks to the curb and stands looking up at the discolored rectangle on the building façade above the entrance where the previous business's sign had been. He can see it: "Aquilina's," definitely in script of some kind. "New York Ice Cream Parlor" or just "Ice Cream Parlor?" He'll think about it. No question about the logo, though: a cartoon eaglet, winking and smiling and holding a triple scoop ice cream cone. People love cute logos, especially kids, and kids are the sweet spot of the business. If kids want to come, their parents will bring them and once they do the entire family will be hooked. He takes out his phone, calls Cyn and puts it to his ear. "Hey," he hears her say. "Hey," he says.

"Whaddya think?" she asks.

"We should do it."

"Let's."

"Breastfeeding?"

"Yeah. Wish you were here."

He hears the smile in her voice. She wasn't kidding when she said nothing would come between them. The few times he'd seen women breastfeeding their babies it always struck him as a mother-baby thing, so when she brought Joey to the couch and sat at her end and put him to her breast, he naturally kept his distance and was surprised when she nodded him over. He thought she just wanted a family moment, the two of them sitting close together while she breastfed the baby and he watched, but she let him know with a look what she wanted, and he fed at her other breast while he pleasured her between her legs. What a woman. He's the luckiest man on earth. "I'll be home soon."

"Can't wait, baby."

He smiles and calls the realtor.

CHAPTER 25

Ensenada

Time's a tricky thing to Dee Dee. She always has the same feeling when she's looking forward to something. The time leading up to it is filled with anticipation and expectation. It's like a rubber band being pulled back in her mind for the longest time and then it snaps forward, and the moment suddenly arrives. As usual, this one seemed to take forever but here she finally is in the back seat of Matt's jeep, cram-packed with surfboards and camping equipment and duffel bags full of clothes and food, listening to Matt and her mom chatting and laughing up front as they head south on the 5 on a sunny spring morning toward Trestles for a day of surfing, and then on to the campground in Ensenada.

She watches the flock of concrete cliff swallows, decorating the wall by the side of the freeway in San Juan Capistrano, fly past. She's read about the swallows. They migrate from Argentina each spring and used to nest here, probably because for the longest time the mission was the tallest structure around, but since 2009 they've been building their nests in Chino Hills, considerably north of San Juan Capistrano. The city still has an annual Swallows Day Parade, though, and there'll always be that song "When the Swallows Come Back to Capistrano." It's hard for people to let go sometimes. She thinks she knows how it must feel to be a swallow, swooping the way they do. She feels that way when she's riding across the face of a wave. It's the greatest feeling in the world.

The woman on NPR is talking about the growing trend among women in India to have an abortion when they learn their baby is going to be a girl. It's against the law, but they do it anyway. It seems that boys are the preferred sex. How stupid! What will happen to India if there aren't any girls? Who's going to have babies? It doesn't make sense. It reminds her of the story she heard about girls in Afghanistan not being allowed to go to school when the Taliban were in power.

What do people have against girls? She feels fortunate to be alive and living in a country where girls have the opportunity to do anything they set their minds to, where they can pursue their dreams. Look at Sally Ride, a hero of hers. She was a physicist who wanted to be an astronaut and worked hard and made it and was the first woman to go into space. It's sad to think she might just as easily have never been born.

Dee Dee's really looking forward to surfing the best break at Trestles. Matt said she's ready. He stopped by and watched her that day when she was surfing with Janey and Cassie and Becca. They were the only girls in the water, and it felt special, like they were surfing for girls everywhere.

She reads the exit sign up ahead as Matt slows, "Cristianitos Road." She's not sure what "Cristianitos" means or if it's someone's name, but she knows it comes from "Christian" and that's what she feels like, a Christian on a pilgrimage to a sacred place.

Matt parks and they take their boards from the Jeep. He locks it and the three of them begin walking along the blacktop path toward the railroad trestle and the beach. Dee Dee sees couples and groups of people up ahead, some in wetsuits carrying surfboards and others in tee shirts and shorts and flip-flops, all headed in the same direction in a leisurely procession. They pass spray-painted graffiti on the path. Someone has written, "You're going the wrong way," and another, "F--k Hawaiians." She looks up at Matt. "What's that all about?"

"It's a turf thing."

"It's stupid."

"Yeah, well, some people are."

They walk up and over a rise in the path and there it is! The trestle! The wood is dark brown, almost black, and it looks old and rickety. Dee Dee hears the clang of the warning signal and the Surfliner suddenly appears and speeds past heading north, and the trestle doesn't budge. Matt told her that the bridge had been damaged by fires set by beachgoers and that the creosote protecting the wood had been eroded by the salt air, and that it had to be reinforced in places by concrete, but that it's still the same old bridge, the way Old North Bridge in Concord, Massachusetts, is and it means as much to surfers. It means everything to her to finally be here and she feels privileged to be looking at it.

They follow the path down to the trestle and now she can see the beach and the waves beyond. Walking through the crossbeams with the railroad track overhead, she's reminded of entering the church for Consuela's Thanks Action Mass, and as they emerge onto the beach, she feels like she's stepped into a cathedral as big as the ocean and sky. She sees where most of the surfers are and they head in that direction and stand at the shore and study the scene.

"Lowers," Matt says. "Looks like six to seven."

She stares at the advancing wave a surfer is gliding along and can see that it's higher than any she's surfed. She narrows her eyes and clenches her teeth.

"Gonna be crowded so be extra careful."

"I will," she says and kneels and fastens the Velcro strap around her ankle and eyes the waves. She's determined to do it, here, today, cutback on the face of the wave toward the white water and then cutback again and outrun it the way Bethany Hamilton does in the documentary. It's such a cool move! She almost did it on that last ride in when she was surfing with Janey and Cassie and Becca. Almost. "Have fun!" she hears her mom say and turns and sees her waving over her shoulder and jogging off down the beach. Dee Dee looks back at the highest advancing wave, narrows her eyes and clenches her teeth again. "All set?" she hears Matt ask. She nods and wades into the water.

With each ride she feels her confidence increasing. She's lost her balance and fallen off her board a lot but doesn't feel at all embarrassed. Each time she has it's been while trying to execute part of the move and when she resurfaces and gets on her board and looks around, she sees that some of the other surfers are watching her and following her progress. They know what she's trying to accomplish and how difficult it is to do.

They give her an encouraging thumbs up and she smiles and waves at them in thanks.

She and Matt paddle out again and she catches her wave and is able to cutback toward the white water and almost cutback again, but feels unsure of her footing, bails and just heads straight toward the beach. She manages to stay on her board and outrun the curl and settles into the waist-deep water. Almost. She's so close.

She turns and looks back out at her spot and one surfer in particular near it, a young guy with a mane of thick, curly black hair and a single, thick black eyebrow. This is the most crowded surfing she's experienced and she's been really careful about following the rules and not cutting anyone off or taking a wave if someone else is already up on it, but some of the other surfers don't seem to care all that much about the rules and this guy's the worst. He hasn't cut her off, but she's seen him do it to other surfers.

She lies on her board and paddles out and eyes him. He's sitting on his board with his back to her, talking with his two friends. They don't seem to be waiting for a wave and she reaches her spot and turns her board around and waits for hers, looking back over her shoulder. There it is, three back and rising up. She waits the first two out and times the third and catches it, and just as she's up on her board and steadying herself someone cuts her off and she falls off her board. She surfaces and grabs her board and sees it was the single-brow surfer. She climbs on her board and sits straddling it, watching him ride toward the beach on her wave. "What's up?" she hears Matt ask. "He cut me off. I was up first."

Matt follows her gaze toward the beach and sees the guy settling into the water. He doesn't want a confrontation to spoil an otherwise great day of surfing. "Just steer clear of him."

"I've been trying to. He should know the rules." She watches him paddle out to his buddies and get up on his board and sit straddling it with his back to her. "Hey!" she shouts. He looks over his shoulder at her and scowls. "That was my wave! You cut me off!" "Way to go, asshole!" she hears a surfer shout. "Dude, you suck!" she hears another shout. She sees him turn back toward his buddies.

She settles into the water on her last ride and stands and pumps her fists in the air and shouts, "Woohoo!" as loud as she can. She did it, maybe not as well as Bethany, but she did it! "Gnarly!" she hears a surfer shout and another, "You rule, girl!" She sees her mom standing on the beach, smiling at her and clapping and feels Matt's arm around her shoulder and looks up at him and sees he's as proud of her as she is of herself.

"Way to go, surfer girl! Wish Dibs were here to see it."

"Me too!"

"You can surprise him with the move."

Kate looks through the viewfinder at Matt and Dee Dee, standing together and holding their surfboards with the waves and surfers behind them, Matt with his arm around Dee Dee's shoulders and Dee Dee with hers around Matt's waist, both with big smiles on their faces and Dee Dee looking triumphant. There'll always be the photo, but this is how Kate wants to remember the moment and lingers before taking it. "Great!" she says and sees three young men carrying surfboards approaching, the one in the middle, she notices, with a single, thick black eyebrow. They stop behind Dee Dee and Matt.

"Hey," Dee Dee hears and turns and sees the single-brow surfer standing there with his buddies beside him, scowling at her.

He holds out his fist. "My bad," he says.

She bumps his with hers. "No problem." She sees him nod and watches him and his buddies walk off toward the trestle. Maybe he wasn't scowling at her. Maybe it's just that eyebrow that makes him look like he's scowling all the time.

* * *

The single-brow surfer has her thinking about appearances and how tricky to read they can be. We think we see things in people but maybe it's just our imagination sometimes. Take her mom and Matt here, sitting next to each other across the fire pit, their faces aglow. She's been looking at them and thinks they resemble each other in a way she didn't notice before, around the eyes and mouth, but maybe it's just that they feel the same way about each other and are expressing their feelings in the same way. It's tricky.

She lies in her sleeping bag in her tent, listening to the murmur of her mom's and Matt's voices coming from their tent and the sound of the waves breaking on the shore and the call of a bird in the distance. She wonders what type of bird it is. It isn't a gull, that's for sure. It's probably calling to its mate or trying to attract one. Its call sounds so sad and lonely, but it probably sounds pretty inviting to the female of the species. She assumes it's a male. Girls don't do that sort of thing, call in the night to attract boys, so why should female birds? Then again, maybe it is a female bird. There's that thought again, that things aren't always what you think.

She hears her mom giggle. There's no mistaking the happiness in the sound of it. She knew her mom and Matt would react the way they did when she said she thought they should get married, like they haven't been thinking about it themselves. She might be thirteen but come on! She knows when her mom says things like it's nice that she and Matt are surfing buddies and have such a great relationship that her mom's feeling her out about the idea. They should get married! They might as well be! She yawns, rolls on her side and tucks her knees up, lays her head on her camp pillow and tucks the sleeping bag under her chin. What a great day it's been, unforgettable, and the trip's just begun.

* * *

Dee Dee savors another spoonful of French onion soup and eyes the tourists from the cruise ship, streaming past their sidewalk table at Restaurant El Rey Sol, her favorite, on Adolfo López Mateos in downtown Ensenada. They saw the ship arrive earlier when they were hanging at the Malecon boardwalk, eating ice cream and feeding the brown pelicans. After a week here Dee Dee's begun to feel like a local and views the tourists as outsiders, which she knows is silly since she's one too. That's the way it goes. The longer you're in a place the more it feels like home. She's reminded that there was a time when the people who live here now didn't, that other people lived here before them and probably other people before them. Who were they? What did they call the place? What happened to them? There's so much she wants to know.

She dips her spoon into the bowl and brings another spoonful of soup and a chunk of Gruyère cheese with it to her mouth and savors it as she looks at her mom and Matt, sitting back in their chairs, smiling at each other and holding hands and chatting. What a pair of lovebirds those two have become on this trip! They're goofy and fun to watch. Well, she's done everything she can. It's up to them now.

It occurs to her that maybe this resemblance she thinks she sees between them is the result of their spending so much time together now. They say people come to look alike the longer they're together. Her grandparents do in a way, but maybe that's just because old people all look the same way, old. Her mom is older than Matt, but neither of them is old and they haven't been together that long.

She finishes up the last of her soup, puts the spoon in the bowl and sits back and looks again at the hands of the clock on the tower in the distance. They'll be heading home soon. It's been such a great trip and she knew it had to end, and now time feels completely different than it did at the beginning of the trip. It seems to be speeding up and she wishes it would stop or at least slow down.

She muses about what to share with Anneliese about the trip. Definitely surfing Trestles and nailing the cutback and her experience with the single-brow surfer.

Definitely the size of the Mexican flag in the Civic Plaza filled with sculptures of Mexican heroes here in Ensenada. It's humungous! If the size of the flag is any indication the people here are really proud to be Mexican.

Definitely eating octopus, a first! Matt ordered it when they had a late lunch at one of the stall restaurants the day they arrived. She watched the man behind the counter reach down and put a whole octopus on the counter, whack off one of its tentacles with a cleaver, chop it up into little pieces and put them in a large glass with lime juice and cilantro. Her mom said it was the grossest thing she'd ever seen and Dee Dee had to admit it did look pretty gross, but Matt grinned at her and said, "Try it," and she tasted a mouthful and it was delicious, chewy but delicious.

Definitely La Bufadora, the marine geyser south of the city, the world's largest blowhole. That was spectacular! Every minute or so there'd be a thunderous crashing sound and water would explode out of the hole in the rocks far below and shoot up high in the air, sometimes over their heads.

Definitely surfing San Miguel just north of the city! Matt said it could be gnarly, that the paddle-out could be slippery at times and that you had to time the sets to avoid being rolled down the point on the rocks, that it happens to people all the time. He was right and she was a few times, but overall, she was happy with her performance and he said she did great, considering it was her first time surfing the spot.

All day surfing at San Miguel she had her eyes on Todos Santos Island — two islands close together, as it turned out — about twelve miles off the coast where big wave competitions are held. Matt said surfers call the biggest and best break there Killers and she couldn't wait to get there and see the wave, whose face is sometimes sixty feet or higher, like the ones "Jet Ski" surfs. They rented a boat in Ensenada harbor and rode out to the island and Matt paid the boatman half the fare and told him he'd pay him the other half on the return trip, and when they were walking to Killers she asked Matt why he only paid the boatman half the fare and he said, "So we'll be sure to get back." She asked him if he really thought the boatman would leave them there and he said, "It happens," which seemed pretty sad, just as his saying about San Miguel that you can't leave your surfboard under your car if you're camping overnight because it might get stolen seemed sad and the graffiti on the path to Trestles did too. She realized that her image of surfers as being bonded together by their love of surfing and treating one another respectfully was naïve, that surfers are people like everyone else and don't undergo some magical transformation when they wade into the water with their boards.

She'll never forget standing by the lighthouse and watching the surfers ride Killers. The wave face was only about thirty feet that day, but she saw how difficult it is to surf a wave even that big, much less one 50 or 60 feet. All the surfers had big wave boards and full wet suits with hoods and booties because the water is so cold in that spot. Matt said it's because it comes up from a deep canyon. The more she studied the surfers' technique, though, the more she thought she could do it. If they can do it, she can. Killers is on her must-do list.

"Hey, surfer girl," she hears Matt say, "wanna get ice cream at the boardwalk before we head back?" She looks at him and then at her mom and sees they're both looking at her with amused expressions. She realizes she's been lost in thought, staring at the clock face without really seeing it. How long have they been looking at her like this? It's like they've been taking candids of her. "Sure."

Monday, June 18, 2012

Dear Anneliese,

There's so much great stuff I want to share with you about the trip, but it'll have to wait. I'm not really in the mood to tell you about it now. I wonder why things happen the way they do sometimes. Everything's great and then something bad has to happen.

Matt was hit by a car in Ensenada. We were on our way to get ice cream and I was crossing the street ahead of my mom and Matt and and heard my mom scream and tires screech and a thump and turned and there was Matt lying in the street. I saw his face was covered with blood and I bent over and threw up right there! I couldn't help it! It was awful!

They took him in an ambulance to the hospital and my mom and I got the Jeep and went there and waited for him in the waiting room for the longest time. Finally, the doctor came to tell us how Matt was. She said he was pretty banged up but was going to be okay. She said it was a good thing he was conscious and able to tell her he has hemophilia A. You should have seen the look on my mom's face when she heard that! It was like she'd seen a ghost! I'm sure she was just surprised to hear that he has the same disease she does. It's rare.

The doctor said it was pretty silly of Matt not to wear a medical alert bracelet or a neck tag but to only carry a card in his wallet. I'm pretty sure what she meant to say was "foolish" or "stupid" and was just being polite. My mom doesn't wear a bracelet or neck tag, either, so I know she wasn't too happy about what the doctor said.

Anyway, Matt finally came into the waiting room, and he had a bandage on the side of his face and his arm in a sling and said his ribs were taped up but that he was okay.

My mom did the driving on the way home. She was awfully quiet. They both were. It felt weird, the two of them sitting up there, usually so chatty but not saying anything to each other, or not much. I guess they were both in shock. I was. I kept asking myself why it had to happen. I know it was a silly question to ask because there isn't an answer. Bad things just do, and I have no idea why and don't like the fact that I don't.

So, now I'm thinking that maybe that's what religion is for, to calm you down when you get angry about not knowing why bad things happen, like Matt being hit by a car and my dad being shot in the head and dying. Good night.

Yours, Dee Dee

P.S.: Okay…a few deep breaths later. I won't forget to tell you about all the good things that happened. I promise.

CHAPTER 26

What If?

Kate sits at the kitchen table, puts the mail in front of her and stares it: a handful of envelopes and a 20% off postcard from Bed, Bath & Beyond. Like most everyone else these days she pays almost all her monthly bills online, and views what arrives in her mailbox as a nuisance she must dispose of and doesn't look forward to receiving, although she's felt differently about the mail for the last few days.

It's around the time the company said the test results would arrive and each day she's done the same thing, collect the mail from the mailbox without going through it and sit at the kitchen table, place it on the table in front of her and stare at, wondering if the envelope she's been waiting for is there, and if it is, if she'll open it. Of course, she knows she will. She must.

She puts the Bed, Bath & Beyond postcard aside and picks up the first envelope. She sees it's more 0% balance transfer offers from her bank and puts it on the postcard without opening it.

She feels guilty and a little ashamed that she's less worried about the news that her dad has been diagnosed with a very treatable form of prostate cancer than she is that the test results will come back a match, and it isn't really whether she'll open the envelope that she's been wondering about, it's what she'll do when she does and sees the results are what she's expecting. She's been preoccupied thinking about the possible scenarios. They go round and round in her head.

She puts the postcard appeal for clothes from the Veteran's organization on the discard pile. All the clothes she doesn't need have been donated to Good Will.

If she and Matt aren't a match, she'll feel relieved and they can get on with their lives. She might not even tell him about her suspicion and that she swabbed the inside of his mouth while he was sleeping and sent it off with her swab to be tested. That's why she's toyed with the idea of not opening the envelope, as if she could somehow spend the rest of her life not wondering and worrying if she didn't. She has to open it.

She puts the unopened envelope from her representative in Congress on the pile. It's good that he's trying to keep in touch with his constituents, but she suspects that if she read the letter, she'd find that its sole purpose is to cite all the reasons he should be re-elected, which is what being a politician is all about. She hates to be cynical. Maybe it's just her mood.

If she and Matt are a match, well, then that's that. It will be sad, and she'll probably spend the rest of her life regretting her decision to open the envelope. They couldn't stay together, could they? They're not like the whackos on those daytime TV shows. That's what has her really worried.

When the doctor in Ensenada told her the news and the thought immediately crossed her mind that he might be her son, her reaction was that they couldn't possibly remain together, but as time went by, she realized she didn't really feel that way, that she felt she'd been programmed to feel that way. The very idea of their remaining together should have seemed icky, but it didn't and doesn't. Her feelings for Matt are unchanged, and when she looks at him she doesn't see a man who might be her son, she sees the man she met and fell in love with and wants to spend the rest of her life with.

She stares at DNA Testing Labs' logo in the upper left corner of the envelope. So, here it is. She picks it up, opens it, removes the letter and unfolds and scans it: "Dear Ms. Beyer" — "results of mitochondrial DNA testing" — "with 99.9% certainty." She's reminded that it's the highest degree of certainty possible, that 100% certainty would be possible only if she and Matt weren't related biologically. She puts the letter on the table in front of her and stares down at it.

Well, she's satisfied her curiosity. What did she expect would happen, the world to stop turning and the sky to begin falling and her feelings to change? Everything's the same and it now seems to have been a pointless exercise, although she knows it wasn't. She had a responsibility to them both to find out and especially to Matt. He needs to know.

She read about incest — she hates the hissing sound of the word — when they returned from the trip. Relationships between mothers and sons and fathers and daughters are nothing new. They've always existed. Everything imaginable has happened between people in the course of time. She was vaguely familiar with the story, but reading it concluded that Oedipus got a bad wrap from the psychiatric community when it named the desire of a young boy to possess his mother and kill his father an "Oedipus complex." According to what she read, he didn't know he was killing his father or sleeping with his mother and did everything he could to avoid doing both. When his wife Jocasta learned he was her son, she hanged herself and Oedipus was so distraught he took the long golden needles that held her dress together and plunged them into his eyes. Oedipus and Jocasta were just like her and Matt, victims of circumstance. She doesn't know how Matt will react to the news, but she's certain he'll want to end the relationship. Maybe they can remain friends. Could they? Could she? She's getting ahead of herself.

* * *

Matt seemed to take forever to read the letter, although it couldn't have been more than thirty seconds. Kate watched his eyes and waited for his reaction. She remembers looking out the restaurant window at the boats in Newport Harbor, the lights in the windows of the houses on Balboa Island, the nighttime sky and thinking how tranquil the scene looked and how tumultuous she felt. Finally, he finished reading, carefully refolded the letter, put it back in the envelope and the envelope on the table and looked at her without expressing anything, at least nothing that she could see. They stared at each other and then she saw him slowly raise his eyebrows. It was maddening.

She wanted so much to hear what he had to say, but he didn't seem to have anything to say or wasn't ready to share it with her. She couldn't just sit there in silence any longer and told him the story, that she'd gotten pregnant when she was a high school senior and she and her boyfriend Bobby were planning to get married after graduation, but that late in her pregnancy he was killed in a car accident on the 405, returning with friends from a Lakers game, and she became deeply depressed and didn't want the baby and gave it up for closed adoption. She didn't want to know anything about him and didn't want him to know anything about her, because she didn't want him showing up unannounced in her life one day. She apologized for taking the DNA sample without his knowledge but said she had to know. She thought she'd feel relieved when he finally spoke, but she wasn't. "What difference does it make?" he asked, and she began blathering.

She cited every reason she could think of — legal, moral, social, ethical, genetic — why they should end the relationship, and he listened patiently and when she ran out of words, no, breath he said simply, "I mean about how you feel." She felt like a fool and realized the source of her turmoil was that she'd been hoping he would be the one to decide to end the relationship, and also that he wouldn't. In fact, knowing hadn't changed her feelings in the least, but she was too afraid to tell him, afraid of what would happen if she did. She was sure he could see the fear and confusion and worry in her eyes, and he studied them a long time and finally lowered his eyebrows and she knew she wasn't going to see those bright eyes and that easy smile of his.

He began speaking and sounded and looked like a different Matt, not the laid-back Matt she'd come to know, but a serious determined Matt. He said the test results, while surprising, didn't change his feelings for her, that when he looks at her, he doesn't see his biological mother but the woman he loves. He said that like Jenn, he'd been raised to know right from wrong and his love for her feels right, which is all that matters. As far as other people are concerned, it's nobody's business but their own, and as for having children, they can always adopt. He leaned forward and looked her in the eyes and said he wanted to spend the rest of his life with her and asked what she wanted to do. Did she want to end the relationship? If she did, he'd understand but hoped she didn't and held out his hand to her.

She stared at it and asked herself one last time how she would feel if he were out of her life and the answer was the same: empty and lost. She reached out her hand and took his and felt the years between them dissolve. She'd been so concerned about their age difference, but holding his hand she felt happy and secure, the way she used to when she was a kid and held her dad's hand.

They made love later that evening and Matt seemed unchanged by the knowledge. No, not entirely. If anything, he was more assertive in his lovemaking and whether it was to show her that he wasn't thinking of her as his biological mother wasn't important. It felt good, as did his tickling her afterward, which he's taken to doing after they've made love ever since she told him she hates being tickled. He doesn't do it the way the older girls at summer camp did, to torture her, but the way her dad used to, just enough in her sides to make her giggle and squirm delightedly. When Matt tickles her she's a kid again.

* * *

She pulls into her parents' driveway. She knows her dad well and knows he and her mom know. He stopped by the house after the trip to Ensenada and Dee Dee was telling him about it and got to the accident. She told him how she was so scared when Matt was hit by the car that she threw up in the street and how surprised she was when the doctor told them Matt has hemophilia A too. Kate will never forget the look on her dad's face and could see that piece of information got him thinking. She could hear the fact that he knew in his voice when he called a week later and said something had come up and could she please stop by. She didn't need to ask why.

She looks at herself in the rearview mirror and checks the calm and determined expression she'll show them. Strictly speaking, Matt was right when he said it's nobody's business but their own, but that's not entirely true. Their families are affected by their relationship. Her parents are understanding people, like his, but everyone has their limits.

She finds them sitting at the patio table, gives them each a hug and kiss and sits across from them. She puts her keys on the table and studies their faces. She sees concern and worry in their expressions, and they stare at her uncomfortably, her mom rubbing her index finger nervously against her thumb and her dad tapping his fingers on the table. It's obvious that they're reluctant to begin the conversation. What will they think when they learn she already knows and that it doesn't matter to her? That they failed as parents? That she's failed them as a daughter? Probably both. She looks at her dad. "Still have that 'panic attack pack?'" He nods. "Why don't you get it? I could use one." He goes to the kitchen and she and her mom sit searching each other's eyes uncertainly until he returns and hands Kate a cigarette and a lighter, then sits and takes a cigarette from the pack and puts the pack on the table. Kate lights hers, hands him the lighter and sits back and draws on her cigarette, inhaling the smoke deeply and blowing it out slowly. "I never thought I'd smoke a cigarette again," she says.

Gordon lights his and glances at Mary. "Neither did I."

Mary sighs. "Your dad's been smoking a lot lately."

"I bet," Kate says and sighs. "So, you know." They're shocked, of course, and stare at her wide-eyed.

"You mean *you* do?" Gordon asks. "How'd you find out?"

"I had our DNA tested. We're a ninety-nine percent match. Contact the agency?"

He nods.

"You weren't supposed to, Dad. That was the deal, remember?"

"I had to. I'm your father. I was concerned about you. What do you plan to do?"

Kate keeps her eyes on his as she draws on her cigarette and slowly blows out the smoke. "Nothing," she says and sees her mom put a hand to her mouth and her dad trying to contain himself. "I don't know what to say, other than that when I found out my feelings didn't change. I thought they would, but they didn't. I even tried to make myself feel differently but I couldn't."

"Does Matt know?" Gordon asks.

Kate nods. "It didn't change his feelings, either." Her mom takes her hand from her mouth and puts it back in her lap.

"Do his parents know?" Mary asks.

Kate nods again.

"How do they feel about it?"

"The same way you do I suppose, the way I would if I were you." Her dad draws on his cigarette and raises his eyebrows.

"Were you going to tell us?" Gordon asks.

"Honestly, I wasn't sure until Matt decided to tell his folks. I guess I was. You just beat me to it."

"It isn't right," Gordon says.

Kate sighs again. "I don't want to argue the laws of God and nature and man with you, Dad. I've argued long enough with myself. In the end, all that matters is that Matt and I love each other, and Dee Dee loves Matt. We're happy together. Not every family can say that. We don't plan on having children, so there isn't that to worry about." Her parents glance at each other. "I'm sorry if you think I've failed you as a daughter." Her mom's expression softens.

"We don't think anything of the kind, honey," Mary says. "We're just concerned about you and Dee Dee. She doesn't know, does she?"

"No."

"What if she finds out?"

Kate looks from her mom to her dad and narrows her eyes. "She's not going to. Not if I can help it. I'm not asking you to agree with me. All I'm asking is that you let us live our lives and continue being the loving grandparents you are to Dee Dee. How you feel about me and what you think of me is your business."

Gordon stubs out his cigarette in the ashtray. "Don't talk nonsense. Of course, we love you." He reaches for the pack but Mary stops him with a hand on his forearm and he sits back and crosses his arms and stares at Kate. "It's just a lot to digest."

"I know," Kate says. "I'm sorry for burdening you with this. I know what I'm doing goes against everything you believe is right. It isn't something I wanted to happen. It just happened and when it did, I found that what I thought I believed didn't matter. All that matters is our love for each other. It would be great to have your support, but I understand if you can't give it." She isn't expecting them to answer and they don't, but she knows they're weighing what she's said carefully and, being the loving parents they've always been, are trying to understand. Most people wouldn't and it occurs to her that she's not like most people, so why should she expect her parents to be? "Well, I have to get to work." She stubs out her cigarette in the ashtray, picks up her keys, stands and looks down at them. "Tell me honestly. What would you do if you found out you were brother and sister?"

Mary's quick to answer. "But we're not!"

"If you were, what would you do? Would you love each other less? Leave each other?" Kate isn't expecting them to answer now, either, and gives them each a hug and kiss.

Gordon and Mary watch Kate walk away, both struggling with the same thing, how to reconcile the fact that their daughter, whom they love and respect and know to be an intelligent, responsible and moral person, could have made the decision she has and believe it to be right. It seems beyond them, at the moment, anyway. When she's gone, they look at each other. Mary knows if she waits for Gordon to speak, she'll be waiting a long time. "What would you do?" she asks.

"I don't know."

"Neither do I. I can't imagine not being together."

He reaches for the pack and knows she won't stop him this time. It's the damnedest thing, but he should probably feel a lot worse about the situation than he does.

* * *

Saturday, August 11, 2012

Dear Anneliese,

YIPPEE!!! My mom and Matt are married! I'm so happy for them! My mom looked FAN-TAS-TIC!!! She wore a white strapless gown and Matt looked really handsome in his navy blue suit. I wore my emerald chiffon dress and my "grown up" makeup and hairstyle and looked like my usual gorgeous self. Just kidding!

So, now Matt's officially my stepfather, the way Mira's my half-sister. Who comes up with these names? I don't really think of him as my dad. He's more like a big brother to me. He's not that much older than Pauly!

I really enjoyed talking with the minister at the reception. Her name is Karen Whelan and she's a really nice person. She told me about what it's like to be a minister and where she's been in the world on missions. She's been everywhere!

I felt a little uncomfortable at first talking with her because my mom and I don't go to church, and I felt kind of guilty about it, but she didn't seem to mind at all. She said it would be nice to see more of me, that she thought I had a lot to offer the congregation and the rest of the people in the world and that got me thinking. That's what she does, helps people, and she travels all over the world to do it. What a neat job!

I told her that I didn't really know what I believed about God, and she just smiled and said that I shouldn't worry too much about finding God, that God would find me and that I should just concentrate on developing the gifts I've been given and putting them to good use.

It turns out she was a semi-pro basketball player when she decided to become a minister. I couldn't believe it! I mean she's tall, but I've seen women basketball players on TV and they're pretty rough and tough and I couldn't picture her mixing it up like that. She told me she meets with a group of women at a women's prison in San Bernardino and that they play basketball after the meeting. She invited me to go with her sometime. I think I will.

The only prison I've ever seen is San Quentin, the outside of it anyway, on a trip we took to San Francisco. It's a scary looking place. I can't imagine what it must be like having to live cooped up in a place like that. Karen (she asked me to call her that, not Minister) said the women's prison in San Bernardino isn't like

San Quentin. Still, a prison's a prison. It will be interesting to see what one's like on the inside and what the people are like.

My mom and Matt are going to Hawaii on their honeymoon and I'm going with them! Matt was there when he did that job for WestWave and my mom was there once when she was a kid, but I've never been and I'm really looking forward to it. Matt said we'd surf Pipeline. I've watched YouTube videos of people surfing it and it looks gnarly, but not as gnarly as Todos Santos. I think I can handle it. I'll give it my best shot.

So, here's some interesting news. I went to the movies with Rosa and Petey and Pauly. I was sitting between Rosa and Pauly and my arm was on the armrest (DUH!) and my hand was dangling over the edge and all of a sudden Pauly took my hand in his and I looked at him and he looked at me and smiled, and so did I and we both looked back at the screen and sat like that, holding hands and watching the movie. It felt nice. I have no idea what's going to happen between us, but I sure can't wait to find out! I'll keep you posted.

Yours, Dee Dee

P. S.: Rosa's parents took us to Aquilina's Ice Cream Parlor after the movie. I've wanted to go there ever since it opened. I love that place! The owner's name is Steve and he's really nice. He came over to our table to say "hi." He greets all the customers like that and, boy, there sure were a lot of them! There was a line of people outside waiting to get in! I had rum cake and a chocolate egg cream. I can't imagine life without chocolate egg cream now. I don't know how I lived without it! It's DEE-LISH-US!!! By the way, there's no egg! Go figure!

CHAPTER 27

Karen

Dee Dee feels off on a great adventure as she and Karen head toward the California Institution for Women in Chino. She listens as Karen tells her about some of the prison's well-known inmates.

"Cathy Smith did time there in the Eighties. She's the woman who killed John Belushi by injecting him with heroin and cocaine."

Dee Dee knows about John Belushi. She's watched old *SNL* episodes online and *The Blues Brothers* movie at Rosa's. He was funny and kind of whacky.

"Patricia Krenwinkel and Leslie Van Houten are still there. They were members of the Manson Family. Susan Atkins, another Family member, was there but died in 2009. They went on a killing spree back in 1969. They killed Sharon Tate, the pregnant wife of Roman Polanski, in their Benedict Canyon home in L.A., and three other people who were living there. Polanski was in London at the time. The next night they killed Leno and Rosemary Labianca in their home in Los Feliz. Charlie Manson, the leader of the Family, is serving a life sentence at Corcoran State Prison."

Dee Dee knows about Charlie Manson and Roman Polanski. "Why would anyone kill a pregnant woman?" she asks. "That's awful!"

"People do all sorts of crazy things, especially when they come under the influence of someone as charismatic as Manson supposedly was and are on drugs. He seems just plain crazy to me, but the Family members saw him as a kind of God. That's the way it is with cults."

Dee Dee agrees with Karen about Manson, but finds Polanski more disturbing because he isn't crazy and the girl he had sex with was the same age she is. He must have known she was underage. Dee Dee thinks of the way she looked at the wedding. Sure, she looked older, but clearly still like a kid. Anyone could see that. Why would a man Polanski's age want to have sex with a thirteen-year-old? It's creepy. "Isn't a cult kind of like a religion?" Dee Dee asks.

Karen glances at her. "Well, only in that the people who belong to them share a belief in something. Religion gives life meaning. All cults seem interested in doing is separating people from their money."

"But *you* ask people for money during the service, don't you?"

Karen glances at her again and laughs. "Yeah, but people don't have to give and the ones who do decide how much. Brenda Ann Spencer is there. She was sixteen when one Monday morning she began shooting at the school across the street from her house in San Diego. She killed the principal and another man and injured eight kids who were waiting for the principal to open the gate. When she was asked why she did it she said, 'I don't like Mondays. This livens up the day.' Bob Geldorf wrote a song about it, 'I Don't Like Mondays.' Heard it?"

"Yeah," Dee Dee muses. "I didn't know it was about that, though."

"Betty Broderick is there. She was a socialite in San Diego and married to a successful lawyer. She worked hard to help support them when he was studying medicine and then the law. He finally became wealthy, and she didn't have to work anymore, but he had an affair with his secretary, a younger woman, and divorced Betty and married his secretary. Betty shot them in their bed early one morning. She claimed she was suffering from "Battered Wife Syndrome," but the jury didn't buy it. There's no denying these people committed heinous crimes, but they're still people and the things they did don't make them any less human than the rest of us and they still need help, just like the rest of us. Ministering to the spiritual needs of prisoners has been part of the Methodist mission from the beginning."

"Why are Methodists called that?" Dee Dee asks. "I've always wondered."

"Well, Methodism was founded by John Wesley back in the eighteenth century. He was a member of the Church of England and he and his brother Charles started a Holy Club when they were students at Oxford University. The other students made fun of the way they went about living a religious life, systematically, using 'rule' and 'method' and called them 'Methodists,' so that's what they called themselves. Kind of turned the tables on them. Wesley believed the Church should serve all people, and especially the poor and the sick, and that's why the Methodist Church is known for its missionary work and its establishment of hospitals and universities and orphanages and soup kitchens and schools to follow Jesus's command to spread the good news and serve all people."

Karen's mention of Jesus reminds Dee Dee of the trip to the Getty and the religious paintings and their stories. "Do you believe Jesus was the Son of God?" She watches Karen and can see she's thinking carefully about her answer.

"Yeah, I do," Karen finally says. "We're all children of God."

It feels great talking so freely and openly with Karen about religion, but Dee Dee hesitates before asking the next question. "Do you believe Mary was really a virgin?"

Karen tilts her head, frowns slightly and purses her lips. Dee Dee's a sharp kid with an inquisitive mind and her questions are the same ones she asks herself and still struggles with. It would be so easy to prevaricate, but Karen feels she owes it to Dee Dee to be honest, to let her see she's not alone in her questioning. "I think that part of the story is symbolic, to reinforce the idea that Jesus was the Son of God."

"That's what my mom thinks."

Karen nods and shrugs. "Anyway, Jesus was also the Son of Man, so it wasn't like he was putting himself above people. He was one of us. He was born with original sin just like everybody else and had John baptize him to wash it away."

"I've heard of original sin," Dee Dee says, "but I'm not really sure what it is."

"You know the story of Adam and Eve?"

"Yeah. The snake tricked Eve into eating the apple from the tree God told them not to eat from, and God banished them from the Garden of Eden."

Karen nods. That's good enough. She's always wondered about this story. She's studied the interpretations of its meaning and symbolism, but why God didn't want Adam and Eve to know the difference between good and evil is beyond her. The God of the Old Testament has always struck her as a bit puzzling. "Christians believe that because of Adam's sin, everyone is born in a sinful state and unless they're baptized they'll go to hell."

"Do you believe that?" Dee Dee asks and watches Karen consider her answer.

"Let's just say that life can be hellish when you live in a sinful state."

"Do you believe there's a heaven?"

Karen glances at her and looks back at the road and nods. "Yeah, you're looking at it."

Dee Dee's perplexed and looks at the cars ahead of them and the stores passing by on the side of the highway. "I don't get it."

"Well, Jesus said his father's kingdom is spread out on the earth and people just don't see it. It's all in how you look at things I guess." Karen glances at her again. "I believe heaven and hell are ideas that serve as constant reminders of the importance of living a good life and the consequence of not doing so. Do you believe in Santa Claus?"

"Not anymore. I did when I was little."

"What happened?"

"I got older."

Karen nods. "Right. Our understanding of things changes in time. Some beliefs we outgrow, others we don't. We just view them differently. They take on new meaning."

Dee Dee thinks of her dad and her conversation with Pauly by the creek at Phantom Ranch. She feels she knows Karen well enough now to ask the most important question. "Do you believe in life after death?"

"I do."

"I don't," Dee Dee says. "I think people made that up because they're afraid of death, you know, afraid there isn't anything after they die."

Karen looks at her and raises her eyebrows and smiles. "You do, huh?"
Dee Dee nods.

"Well," Karen says, looking back at the road, "the idea of eternal life is a lot to get your head around. So, if people made it up, where did the idea come from?"

The answer seems obvious to Dee Dee and she's a little surprised Karen even asked the question. "People."

"You believe in a Creator, right?"

"Yeah. It all had to come from somewhere."

"So, if it all comes from the Creator, then the idea does too, right?"

"Yeah, I guess so," Dee Dee says a little uncertainly. "I hadn't thought of that."

"I think of death as being like fire," Karen says. "It transforms us from one state to another. I don't pretend to know what that other state is, but I believe we're with God, just as we are now, only in another form."

Dee Dee remembers gazing at the campfire in Ensenada and watching the wood slowly being transformed into falling ash and rising gas. She imagines being vaporized by a nuclear bomb in a flash of blinding light. It would be kind of the same thing only it would happen in an instant. Maybe Karen's right. Maybe death isn't the end, but just the beginning of something else. Dee Dee mulls it over as she gazes at a giant ferocious-looking gorilla with its arms outstretched floating above a passing car dealership. Why they think that will make people want to buy cars there is beyond her, just as so much about religion is. "The women we're going to see, why are they in prison?"

"Different reasons: robbery, drugs, prostitution. What these women did was wrong, but here's the thing to keep in mind when you meet them. They're all basically good people who come from poor families and none of them finished high school. When you put those two things together, poverty and lack of education, life is very hard, and you're forced to do whatever you have to just to survive."

Dee Dee tries to keep her eyes on Roxana's, but they keep returning to the word "L-O-V-E" tattooed on the backs of the fingers of her left hand and "H-A-T-E" on those of her right, and at the purplish gang tattoo — she's pretty sure that's what it is — that encircles her neck. She recognizes the tiny sentences to be in Spanish punctuated by crosses and what look to be teardrops.

Dee Dee studies Roxana's face. She's pretty in a rough sort of way. She must have had bad acne when she was a kid because her cheeks are pockmarked, and she must have used needles because the inside of her left forearm is lined with scars. Dee Dee listens to Roxana talk about how worried she is about being released from prison because she knows how bad the economy is and doesn't have any real job skills. She doesn't know how she'll support herself and will probably go back to prostitution and dealing drugs and doesn't want to, but how else will she manage to get by? She says she knows she'll probably end up in prison again, where at least she'll have a roof over her head and three meals a day. "Prison's okay," she says, "I've gotten used to it and it feels like home to me."

Karen nods and says she understands and encourages Roxana not to give up hope and sell herself short. She asks her to remember the lowest point in her life, not to share it with the group, just to remember it and think about where she is now, clean and sober with a good prison record, and about how far she's come and how much she has invested in herself, and about not giving up all that hard work, but putting it to good use instead. Roxana seems encouraged by Karen's words and says she'll try. Karen says she'll be there for her when she's released and will do everything in her power to help her find a job and keep her on track. Roxana says she knows Karen will and thanks her and says she needs all the help she can get. Karen looks at the faces of the women in the circle and says, "We all do," and everyone nods.

Karen asks Lashawna, the heavyset black woman next to Roxana, how she's doing and Lashawna says she's worried sick about her ten-year-old daughter Kiesha because her mother was supposed to be taking care of her, but her mother's drunk all the time and her boyfriend took Kiesha to live with him and she's afraid he's abusing her because that's what he did to his last girlfriend's two daughters. Karen asks if she means sexually and Lashawna says, yeah, that and beating her up if she puts up a fight. Karen asks if she's told Child Protective Services about her concern and Lashawna says she hasn't because she's afraid to, afraid of what her boyfriend will do to her daughter if she does and he finds out. Karen tells Lashawna she has to protect her daughter because she's her mother and the most important person in Kiesha's life, but Lashawna scratches her cheek and says, "Yeah, but look what kind of mother my baby's got, who can't even look out for herself." Karen says she knows Lashawna's afraid, that it's only natural to be afraid, but if she's afraid, think how Kiesha must feel and if Lashawna doesn't help her, who will? "Let's talk with CPS," Karen says, and Lashawna stops scratching her cheek, jabs her hands between her thighs, hunches her shoulders and looks around sheepishly at the other women.

"Do it, girl!" TJ says, frowning at Lashawna.

TJ is the only woman in the group Dee Dee finds intimidating. She's a buff, tough-looking young Latina with cornrows and the only woman sitting slouched back in her chair with her arms and long legs crossed. When it's TJ's turn, she and Karen talk about her plan to get a job as a personal trainer in a gym when she gets out, and Dee Dee hopes she does and bets she'll be a good one.

TJ looks at Lashawna, whom she can see is still troubled by her conversation with Karen. "She's your baby!" TJ says.

Lashawna shrugs, looks meekly at Karen and nods.

"Good," Karen says.

Dee Dee stands with the others when Karen does and takes Karen's hand and Ginger's, the only white woman in the group and here for bank fraud. Ginger's eyes and smile and the way she looks at her remind Dee Dee of Missus Harris, her third-grade teacher, who was always so nice to her and is her favorite teacher so far. Dee Dee bows her head with the others.

"Lord," Karen prays, "look upon my sisters and help them to see the goodness within themselves, for they are your children. Help them in their time of trial to overcome the temptations and wickedness of the world so that they may make a better life for themselves and their loved ones. Fill them with grace as you did Mary, for they are her sisters and as worthy. Give them the courage and strength they need to overcome the obstacles before them. I ask these things of you humbly. Amen."

"Amen," Dee Dee says with the others. The word feels and sounds different this time. Not being a churchgoer, she hasn't said it that many times in her life and realizes that when she has, it's been without thinking. She's thinking about it now, though, as she looks around at the faces of the women. She's spent an hour with them, but listening to them, she's gotten to know them and feels connected to them and wishes for them just what Karen prayed for, that they get out of here and somehow manage never to come back. She knows, as Karen said, that the odds are against them and they'll probably end up back here, but that's what she wants for them and if there were something she could do to make it happen, she gladly would and whatever "amen" means that's what she meant when she said it.

It occurs to her that she's been given so much in life, unlike these women, who've been give nothing and have nothing other than themselves and their troubles and Karen to counsel and encourage them. She can see in the women's faces how much they appreciate Karen being in their lives and that her being there for them makes a difference. Of all the things she'd like to do in life, helping people the way Karen does seems like the most important and worthwhile thing, and thinking about dedicating her life to the service of others fills her with a sense of purpose and makes her feel good about herself in a way she never has before. She feels Karen and Ginger squeezing her hands and glances up at them and sees them both looking down at her and smiling.

Karen looks around the circle. "Okay, ladies, who's playing?"

* * *

Dee Dee stands on the sideline and watches the women take practice layups and foul shots at opposite ends of the court. Karen and TJ are clearly the two best players and the leaders of their teams and Dee Dee can see that Karen is the better ball handler and shooter. TJ seems to work harder than Karen and the way Karen moves on the court is amazing to Dee Dee. She's only known Karen to be this laid-back person, walking the way she does in no particular hurry, but here on the court she moves like a cheetah, going from standing still to blazingly fast in a single step. The two teams practice a while longer and then TJ calls, "Let's go!" to Karen and bounce passes her ball to one of her teammates, who inbounds it to another teammate and TJ heads up court with Karen guarding her.

Dee Dee watches TJ's team pass the ball around the outside. TJ gets it, sees an opening and drives to the basket. Suddenly, Karen's moving even faster than when she was warming up and jumps in front of TJ as she shoots and blocks the shot toward one of her own teammates and TJ looks furious.

Karen breaks toward TJ's basket with TJ and one of her teammates right behind her. Karen's teammate passes the ball to her high over everyone's head and Karen catches it over her shoulder on the run and takes a step and jumps toward the basket with TJ and her teammate now hanging on her arms. Karen dunks the ball and throws her arms open wide, sending the two women flying backward. TJ lies sprawled on her back on the court, cursing in Spanish, and Dee Dee watches Karen walk away, slowly shaking her head.

* * *

"Well, there's good and then there's really good," Karen says as they head home.

Dee Dee knows it's impolite to stare, but she can't take her eyes off Karen's long arms and fingers and legs. She views Karen differently now, as two different people, the laid-back one here and the one she saw in action on the court.

"I was pretty good," Karen says, "not great, but good. A team probably would've picked me up, but I would've spent most of my time sitting on the bench and I thought there were better things I could do with my life than that. Helping people seemed like a worthwhile thing to do. So, what do you think?"

"Of the women?"

Karen nods.

"They're nice. I feel sorry for them, that they have to be inside a place like that."

"They did the crime, so they have to do the time. It's a waste, though. There used to be programs to educate prisoners and teach them a trade, so they at least had a chance of getting a job and bettering themselves when they got out, but this state's broke and all those programs have been cut, so most go right back to doing what got them arrested. They need all the help they can get. If we don't who will?"

The word "we" stands out in Dee Dee's mind and makes her feel even closer to Karen now, like they're sisters. She's been meaning to ask Karen why the only time she mentioned God was when she said the prayer and she never even mentioned Jesus. There are a lot of things Dee Dee's wanted to ask Karen, but hasn't had the confidence to until now. "Why did you become a minister? You don't have to be one to help people."

Karen glances at her. "That's a really good question. I asked myself the same thing when I was trying to decide what to do with my life."

Dee Dee listens as Karen tells her about growing up in Seattle. She isn't surprised to hear that's where Karen's from. She's heard people talk about Seattle, that it rains a lot there and that the place is filled with "tree huggers" and loonies, not that she thinks Karen's either of those. There's probably some truth in what she's heard, though, and she asks Karen about it.

Yeah, Karen says, there are a lot of environmental activists and people into alternative lifestyles in Washington and Seattle is a very Liberal city in a very Liberal state. Her folks were hippies in the Sixties and are vegans, which means they don't eat meat or dairy products. They're also animists who believe that animals and plants and rocks have souls. She remembers attending gatherings in the woods outside Seattle with her folks and their friends when she was a kid. They were like a big party with people carrying colorful streamers they'd tie to the limbs of trees. They'd stand in a circle holding hands and recite prayers they'd written and sing songs. She had the feeling even then that believing animals and plants and rocks have souls and thinking they can influence our lives is crazy but then, the whole hippie thing was kind of crazy.

Dee Dee understands pretty well what Karen means. She knows more about hippies and the Sixties than most kids because some of the old surfers she knows were hippies and still are in a way. She's heard their stories about the great times they had back then, getting high and surfing. Most of them smoke medical marijuana now, although everyone knows the "medical" part is a joke. She loves the old VW buses some of them drive because of the goofy way they look, and whenever she and Matt come across a new one in the parking lot when they go surfing, she always has him take her picture standing next to it holding up the peace sign. She has quite a collection now. Most of their owners live out of them and she likes the idea of their being able to pick up and go whenever and wherever they please and always have a roof over their heads. "Do your parents have a VW Bus?"

Karen smiles and nods. "Turquoise and white, held together with duct tape."

Dee Dee isn't surprised.

Karen tells her that she attended church service with her best friend Spring's family. They were Baptists and so she learned about Jesus and the bible, but she wasn't quite sure about the God of the Old Testament. He seemed like a crabby old guy and not the type of person she'd want to have as a father, and she was sure that whatever that ultimate higher power is, it doesn't look like an old white guy with long white flowing hair and a long white flowing beard.

"I don't think so, either." Dee Dee says. "That's like believing in Santa Claus."

Karen nods. Other than that, the idea of God seemed right. She could put her faith in God. God was above it all and when she realized that she was never going to excel as a professional athlete and decided that her true vocation was helping people, she thought the best way to do it would be within the structure of a religious organization dedicated to service and decided to become an ordained Methodist minister. She could have just joined the Peace Corps or some such organization but felt that if she were going to dedicate her life to something, it had to be something she really believed in and she had to put her faith in something greater than people. Karen glances at Dee Dee. "Don't get me wrong. I love people, but we're all human, imperfect beings. All the misery and suffering in the world is people's doing, not God's. I look at myself and see how imperfect I am. I think of the mistakes I've made in my life and how I've disappointed and hurt people. Why would I want to put my faith in the hands of someone like that? God is perfection. I know it exists because I can picture it in my mind. We can never achieve it, but trying brings us closer to God. It's like a magnet. Make sense?"

Dee Dee nods. "Yeah. Why didn't you talk about the Bible? You never even mentioned Jesus. Isn't that what ministers are supposed to do?"

Karen glances at her. "Yeah, well, there's a time and place for everything. Spending the time talking with the women about their lives is more important than spending it talking about the bible and Jesus, don't you think?"

Dee Dee narrows her eyes slightly and thinks about it a moment. "Yeah. You're right."

Karen smiles at her. "So, tell me about surfing."

Saturday, September 15, 2012

Dear Anneliese,

I went with Karen to visit the women's prison today. What an amazing experience! The women turned out to be people, just like the rest of us, but who've made mistakes in their lives. We all make mistakes, but some will land you in prison and that's the type of mistakes these women made.

Karen talked about them on the way there. She said a big part of the reason they did what they did is because they're poor and uneducated. It made me realize how lucky I am to have the family I do and that I do well in school and love to read and, really, it's all by accident. I mean I could just as easily have been born into a poor family and quit school because I had to go to work to make money to get by, and maybe I would have broken the law and gotten arrested and sent to prison. And the thing is, I probably wouldn't have known any better. So, if you don't know any better can you really be blamed for doing something bad? I guess you can, but it doesn't seem right somehow. It's like hitting a puppy for peeing on the carpet. The puppy doesn't know any better, either, so it's wrong to punish it. I dunno. I feel really confused about it.

Karen said when the women are released, most of them will probably go back to doing what they did that got them arrested and end up back in prison because there aren't any programs anymore to teach them a trade. What a waste! At least they have Karen. She's trying her best to help them, but it seems a lot for one person to do and she can only do so much.

I saw the way the women looked at her and listened to her whenever she had something to say, and I could see in their faces how much they respect her and appreciate the fact that she comes to visit them and listens to them and tries her best to help them. She makes a big difference in their lives. She's someone they know they can count on. She gives them strength and hope. It got me thinking about whether I'd like to be a minister and help people the way she does. It would be nice to do something with my life that makes a difference in other people's lives.

Karen visited a woman in another part of the prison before we left. I couldn't go with her and waited for her in the visitor waiting area. Karen said the woman is in prison because she killed her three children. Her husband left her and didn't give her any money to help with the kids and she wasn't earning enough to get by and she just lost it and set fire to the house one night when the kids were asleep. Karen said when the fire department got there, the woman was standing in the front yard in her bathrobe and slippers watching the house burn. She said the firefighters could hear the kids screaming inside the house but couldn't save them. What must she have been thinking and feeling as she stood there listening to her kids scream? I can't imagine, but Karen said the woman said she did it because she thought she was doing them a favor. She pleaded not guilty because of insanity but, as Karen says, the jury didn't buy it. I asked Karen what the woman is like and she said a nice person who wasn't thinking straight and made a bad decision that she'll pay for the rest of her life. She said that given the right set of circumstances, or the wrong ones I guess, it could happen to anyone. It's scary to think I could do something crazy like that. I don't think I could, but maybe she's right.

Karen played basketball with the women after the meeting. She is UN-BEE-LEEV-ABLE!!! She feels about basketball the way I do about surfing, which she asked me about on the ride home. Boy, was that a mistake! I couldn't shut up! I talked so much my jaws hurt, but she seemed to really enjoy listening to me. I'm happy to have her in my life the way I'm happy to have you in my life. You're both very special and important people to me.

Karen asked me if I'd be interested in attending a Methodist camp near San Juan Capistrano next summer. I told her I'd think about it. The camp part sounds like fun. I like camping a lot. I checked out their website and it looks like a pretty cool place. I'm not so sure about the Methodist part, though. I'm still trying to figure out how I feel about religion. I believe there's a higher power. Everything didn't just come from nothing. It couldn't have. Something must have created it all. What exactly it is I don't know, but I know it's definitely bigger than we are. The problem is that whenever I think about what it might be, I end up imagining a person and that doesn't feel right. Maybe because we're people that's all we can imagine God to be.

It was great talking with Karen about religion and to tell you the truth I was relieved to see she struggles with it as much as I do. And she's a minister!

Yours, Dee Dee

P.S.: When I told Karen that visiting the women and seeing how much she helped them and how much they appreciated it made me think that maybe that's what I should do with my life, she said the Greeks have a word for what I experienced: "epiphany." She said the Greeks have a word for just about every experience in life. I have the feeling that if I really want to understand what's happening to me, I'd better learn Greek!

Oh, yeah, I finally learned what "amen" means: "So be it." It felt like I said it for the first time today, when we prayed for the women to get out and lead a good life. A good life is what I wish for everyone, me included. Amen.

CHAPTER 28

Rosh Hashanah

Ira sips his morning coffee and peruses his emails, update and Bill about the company and his attorney about the upcoming trial. He was right when he assumed the government wouldn't be interested in a plea deal. The lead prosecutor indicated to his attorney they'd be seeking twenty-five years to life without the possibility of parole due to the aggravating factors that his criminal undertaking was for the benefit of organized crime and involved violence and the use of weapons. No surprise there. Ira's contributed generously through the years to the campaigns of powerful politicians in both political parties, but hasn't sought assistance from any of them and isn't going to. He knows no one would take his call. He's a pariah.

He closes his attorney's email reluctantly. It's the last of the new ones and now he has the rest of the day to look forward to with nothing much to do. He can only read for so long before his eyes begin bothering him. Adele's been suggesting he keep a journal or write his memoirs. He's been considering it. He's received several inquiries from book agents and one from a film producer interested in the rights to his life story. People would certainly be interested in it — *Schadenfreude* sells — but does he want to share it? Does he want to pull back the curtain the rest of the way on his life and invite people to scrutinize and judge it? It would have seemed unimaginable not so long ago but why not? What difference does it make now? There's not much left that remains concealed. Only his love of breath play and sex with young girls and he's confident no one involved will step forward and reveal that, well, as confident as he can be about anything anymore.

If he did write about his life, should it be a straightforward accounting of the facts or a cautionary tale? It would have to be the former. He has no stomach for moralizing. Perhaps he'll just begin writing and see what develops. He has to do something to keep his mind occupied. The trial is months away.

He hears a truck approaching, stands and walks to the window, pulls back the drape and peers out. Of course, it's Monday, the men from the groundskeeping service. He watches the truck with rakes and shovels and hoes sticking up from the posts on the sides in back pull up behind the security detail in the black sedan out front. The company was vetted and its employees are on a very short list of people who are permitted on the property. He recognizes the driver and watches him and another man get out of the truck and wave to the man in the sedan who returns the wave. A few men climb out of the back of the truck, carrying hedge clippers and rakes and leaf blowers. He watches the men, all Hispanic and wearing blue caps and shirts and trousers and black work boots, trudge up the driveway and disappear around the side of the house, He returns to his desk and soon hears a cacophony of leaf blowers.

So, back to the book. Where should the story begin, in his youth and work forward or in the present and work backward? There's a big difference between the two in terms of how the story would unfold. Perhaps it should begin with his time in Mossad and then at the London School and show how natural it was to apply what he'd learned in the clandestine service to business and how similar the two worlds are. If he goes that route, the book will almost certainly end up required reading at business schools everywhere. Perhaps it would do some good. He's not thinking about legacy. He's thinking about how he'll be judged and not by men but by God. After all, it's Rosh Hashanah.

He notices movement in the doorway of his study and sees one of the workers standing in it pointing a gun at him and motioning for him to follow. He does and is led to the dining room where he sees Adele, her eyes bulging, in a chair with black tape wrapped around her head and covering her mouth and her hands bound behind her back. He sits across from her and hears the tape being pulled and ripped off the roll. "Don't worry, my dear," he says and feels the tape being wrapped around his head and pressed against his mouth.

He and Adele have been sitting here alone, staring at each other for hours and it's getting dark outside. Ira's had plenty of time to appreciate just how vengeful a man Rios was, that he would reach out from the grave to exact his revenge. Finally, one of the men returns, gun in hand, and motions for Ira and Adele to follow. They get up with difficulty and follow him and are led to the back of the house. Ira sees the limp body of the man who was posted there slumped in a chair in the corner of the sunroom. He assumes the man in the car out front is also dead.

They're led into the backyard and Ira sees a black windowless van waiting at the bottom of the slope by the golf course. He was so concerned about attackers coming from that direction. He never considered them using it as an exit. They're led to the back of the van and helped in and sat down shoulder to shoulder on a mattress. Ira watches the door close, knowing full well what comes next, unlike the members of his family when they were herded into cattle cars and the door closed or when they were herded naked into the showers in the camp and the final door closed on them.

He estimates they've been riding about a half hour when the van slows and stops and then begins moving slowly forward and stops again. The door opens and he sees the wing strut of a light plane. They're helped out and led inside and he sees the fuselage is lined with seats running the length of each side and, when they sit, that the door opens inward. He knows what this type of plane is designed for: skydiving.

Four armed men sit across from them. One of them has a headset around his neck and Ira recognizes him. He remembers the well-trimmed Vandyke. You don't see them that often. The man puts on the headset and motions to one of the men standing by the open doorway, who pulls down the door, closes and locks it and the plane begins taxiing toward the head of the runway. The man with the headset gives instructions to the men seated on either side of him. One of them removes the tape from around Ira's and Adele's heads and cuts loose their bindings and the other retrieves a video camera from an overhead compartment and returns to his seat and points it at them.

Adele rubs her wrists and gasps for air. "Where are they taking us?" she asks, terrified.

Almost certainly over the ocean to throw them out, which is probably what she suspects. What good would confirming it do? Better to leave her uncertain than certain she's facing death. "I don't know, my dear." Her expression of terror changes to one of anger and Ira watches her give each of the men a long withering look. She rests her head on his shoulder and clings to his arm and he puts an arm around her and holds her close.

The engines gun and the plane lurches forward, picks up speed as it races down the runway and they're airborne. "I hate feeling afraid," Ira hears Adele say and feels her body trembling. He gives her a squeeze. He sees the red light on the camera and wonders, with Rios dead, for whose benefit they're being recorded. Pena? Is he carrying out Rios's plan to execute them out of loyalty to his lifelong friend and partner in crime?

Little is known about Pena, who was overshadowed by Rios. By all accounts he's a quiet clever man whose responsibility is to launder the cartel's money and invest it wisely, which he does in real estate throughout the Americas. Perhaps Pena felt compelled to exact revenge on Rios's behalf to put his rivals and his own people on notice that he's every bit as ruthless. Perhaps it isn't Pena at all. Perhaps it's a government, some agency. Perhaps it's God. Adele picks up her head and looks at Ira and he sees her cheeks are wet with tears.

"This is how they must have felt," she says and sniffs.

"I imagine so, my dear," their people, just before the Shoah, when it finally dawned on them that they were trapped and that what the Nazis had been saying they would do in their ridiculous and often incoherent speeches wasn't just empty political rhetoric after all. Ira gives her a squeeze. "We can't let them take our dignity," he says. "Whatever happens, we can't let them take that." She presses her face against his chest and clutches his shirt and he gives her another squeeze. He looks out the window and sees they're passing over Catalina now, heading toward the open ocean at an altitude of about fifteen hundred feet. Adele lifts her head and looks at him.

"I'm glad now we didn't have children," she says. "Imagine living with this for the rest of their lives." She presses her face back against his chest.

"I'm sorry I brought this on us," Ira says and hears her say, "I forgive you."

They sit quietly in the dimly lit cabin, Adele with her face against his chest and Ira staring at the men seated across from them. He doesn't look at the camera. He won't give whomever it is the satisfaction. He estimates they've flown about twenty miles west of Catalina when the man with the headset says something into the microphone and the plane's airspeed slows to what seems a crawl. One of the men stands and walks to the door, unlatches and opens it and the man with the headset motions for Ira and Adele to stand. "It's time, my dear," Ira says. "Be strong. Our journey's about to begin."

He helps Adele to her feet and they walk to the doorway, Adele keeping her face pressed against his chest. "Hold me tightly!" Ira shouts to be heard over the sound of the rushing wind and the loud drone of the engines. He feels Adele's grip tighten and her body shaking. He stares out the open doorway at the moon and down at its silvery light reflected on the surface of the Pacific far below.

How fitting that Rios would choose Rosh Hashanah, when God opens the books containing the deeds of all humanity for review. Will Ira be judged among the wicked? Will he be blotted out of the book of the living forever? It would seem so. Yet the same fate awaits Adele and she's certainly among the righteous. Now is not the time to second-guess the Almighty. Ira puts himself in God's hands and recalls the citation from Isaiah: "As birds hovering, so will the lord of hosts protect Jerusalem, He will deliver it as He protecteth it, He will rescue it as He passeth over." Ira looks back at the man with the headset, now standing behind them with the man with the camera beside him, recording. The man with the headset nods toward the doorway.

Ira hugs Adele tighter and she lifts her head and looks up at him. He sees what he always does when he looks at her, not her surgeon's handiwork, all, in the end, for her own benefit, not the imperfections of her flesh and the effects of age but the light in her eyes that's visible beyond the terror, her spirit, her soul, that perfect part of her that has remained unchanged in all the years he's known her and always inspires him. He smiles and kisses her. "You are the love of my life! Ready, my dear?" She nods and presses her face against his chest and he leans them toward the doorway and they fall together through the darkness.

CHAPTER 29

Absolution

Karen scans the draft letter on the screen, sits back and rubs her eyes. She wants this letter to argue as forcefully as possible for Evelyn's parole but already knows it's a futile effort, even though she's a model prisoner.

Evelyn killed her husband one evening when he was passed out drunk on the couch in front of the TV. According to her confession statement he had a long history of abusive behavior, both verbal and physical, but hadn't been that evening. In fact, they hadn't even been arguing. She was sitting at the kitchen table thinking about the hell her life had become and decided she'd had enough, got up and took a carving knife from the drawer, walked into the living room and stabbed him with it repeatedly in the chest. She called the police and they found her husband on the couch with the knife in his chest and Evelyn sitting at the kitchen table, staring at her folded bloody hands, waiting for them. She pleaded guilty and was sentenced to 25 years to life and has been denied parole twice and undoubtedly will be again.

Parole for prisoners serving life sentences is difficult enough, but Evelyn doesn't help matters. Each time she's appeared at her parole hearing she's been asked by one of the commissioners if she feels remorse and she's looked the person in the eyes and then in the eyes of the other commissioners and said very deliberately, "No."

Writing these letters on Evelyn's behalf is always mentally and physically exhausting. Karen's intimated that things might go better if

Evelyn weren't quite so honest, but Evelyn refuses to budge and while she's appreciative of Karen's efforts on her behalf, she pities her for her willingness to compromise herself morally. Is it ever right for a minister of God to blur the distinction between right and wrong, even if to try to secure parole for a decent woman who killed her abusive husband? Evelyn tests her.

Karen glances at the time in the corner of the screen. Almost noon. She has an uneasy feeling about this meeting with Kate. What's so important that couldn't have been discussed over the phone? It can't be Dee Dee. Karen knows her well and she's a great kid. She'd be very surprised if it's trouble in the marriage. She sees Kate and Matt often enough now, ever since Dee Dee expressed interest in attending service and they began accompanying her. They seem very happy together. No signs of strain that Karen can discern and she's pretty good at reading people.

She sees Kate pull into a parking space, get out of her car and walk toward the building. Karen can tell by Kate's expression she has a lot on her mind. "Nice to see you!" Karen says, welcoming her into the office.

"Thanks for seeing me," Kate says.

They sit facing each other and Karen can see Kate's troubled. "Something to drink? Bottle of water?"

"Thanks, I'm fine," Kate says, keeping her eyes on Karen's.

Clearly Kate isn't and Karen almost doesn't want to ask the next question. "So, how can I help you?"

"I came to ask for forgiveness."

Karen's surprised to hear this and raises her eyebrows. "Forgiveness? For what?" She listens wide-eyed to Kate's story and when she's finished stares at her as she tries to process what she's heard. There's a lot to process.

It's an extraordinary story and the most extraordinary thing about it is that their feelings for each other didn't change once they found out. Karen's surprised to hear their parents knew. She can't remember anything they said or did that day that seemed at all unusual. They seemed happy for their children. She's knows them to be decent people, yet they approved of the marriage and celebrated it. What's most interesting is that Kate isn't asking for God's forgiveness but her own for allowing her to marry them without her knowing. Kate said she knew if she'd told

Karen, she wouldn't have married them and she's right. Karen searches Kate's eyes. She doesn't seem in the least like a person who thinks she's offending God. Karen knows what Kate's answers to the questions she's about to ask will be but feels responsible to at least ask them. "You don't feel what you're doing is immoral and sinful?"

"No," Kate says emphatically.

"You feel God loves you and blesses your marriage?"

"Yes," Kate says even more emphatically.

Karen nods, slowly sits back and considers things, keeping her eyes on Kate's. As far as the state and its laws are concerned, Karen's under no obligation to notify anyone of anything and has no intention of doing so. Their conversation is confessional and confidential and she intends to keep it that way. In a situation like this most ministers would offer absolution and counsel Kate to end the relationship, but Kate's not asking for absolution and as for counseling her to end the relationship, it seems ridiculous. Karen leans forward and takes Kate's hands in hers. "Of course, I forgive you. Thank you for coming and sharing this with me." She sees relief in Kate's eyes and unburdening in the relaxation of her shoulders.

"Thank you," Kate says, "it means everything to me."

Karen stares out the window and watches Kate get in her car and drive away. She looks at the draft of the letter on the screen and pictures Evelyn looking at her with those pitying eyes of hers. She saves the document, shuts down her computer and goes where she always goes when she needs to be alone to think, or not think, to Joshua Tree National Park in the High Desert. It feels like a sacred place to her with its otherworldly landscape and the profound silence that engulfs it. It's where she feels closest to God.

* * *

She isn't surprised to see red on the fire threat level sign posted by the park entrance. She feels like she's about to experience God's wrath. She follows the road as it curves through the park, comes to the top of a rise and sees the sweeping valley before her. It looks to her like the

371

Almighty's upturned palm. She drives, zigzagging down to the valley floor, pulls off the road and parks and gets out. She locks the car and stands gazing at hills of weathered and crumbling rock in the distance, then begins walking toward them. With her car and the road and all trace of people out of sight, she sits on a rock, surrounded by cactuses with blood red blooms and tries to clear her mind of thoughts. Evelyn's letter is stubborn and the last to go.

Kate and Matt are members of her flock. Their souls are in her care. They might be unconcerned about their eternal destinies but as their minister she is. The teachings of the Church require that a sinner be repentant and accept Jesus's offer of forgiveness and new life in order to be saved, but does it have to be?

It happens sometimes that we forgive people without their ever knowing, people who have hurt and offended us and have no interest in being forgiven. She's done it herself. Why can't God?

She looks at the far end of the valley and then at the clouds, searching for a sign. She feels just as she did when she was in the twilight of literacy, staring at letters grouped on the page, struggling to sound out words and connect sounds and symbols to meaning. She could be staring at the answer now written in clouds.

Out of the corners of her eyes she notices movement and looks down in time to see a gecko, its tail shaped like a question mark, skitter under a bush in a spray of sand and disappear. She looks up and sees a coyote loping toward her, like Satan coming to test her. It sees her and stops and stares at her. She's sure she's imagining it, but its eyes look like Evelyn's. The coyote turns and lopes off in the direction it came from. She closes her eyes and listens to the silence, so profound it's more a feeling against her skin than the absence of sound.

Why is she so fearful? God sent Jesus into the world to forgive sins. Jesus gave his disciples the authority to do it and she's one of them. She wants to but feels that if she allows the words of the prayer of absolution even to enter her mind, God will strike her dead on the spot. In this vast space there is nowhere to hide. She feels small, tiny and imagines herself a grain of sand being held up by God for inspection. What is there to see but a minister who's always questioned her faith and who now presumes to know the mind of the Almighty.

She opens her eyes just enough to peer out and sees a raven nearby, standing on something it's holding pinned down in its claws. She opens her eyes wider and looks more closely at the wriggling thing and sees it's a small snake. The poor creature was probably sunning itself when the hungry raven spotted it. The raven pecks at the snake until it manages to sever it in two. It pecks off a piece of the tail section and gobbles it down. Does the same fate await her? She stands and the raven stares at her a moment, reluctant to give up its meal, but flies off a distance and lands. She looks down at the still wriggling snake and imagines suffering like that for all eternity. She walks off to find another spot so the raven can return and finish its meal and end the snake's suffering.

She notices a small bird on the ground by a bush up ahead. She stops and looks at it and recognizes it: a Killdeer. She slowly moves closer and sees it's sitting on its eggs in the nest it's made, just a shallow depression in the sand. When she gets too close the little bird raises its tail feathers and fans them out and spreads its wings close to the ground to protect its eggs. She stops and lowers herself to her knees, sits back on her heels and gazes at it. She wishes she had the little bird's courage. Faith requires it.

Reason tells her that belief in things that have no basis in fact and can't be proved is irrational. She's felt this way ever since she was a kid and accompanied her parents on those trips to the woods. Reason tells her that religion is part of the evolution of human psychology, that people conceived the idea to explain the inexplicable and comprehend the incomprehensible and that as time goes on and more is known, and human psychology continues to evolve, religion will ultimately cease to be. After all, it wasn't so long ago that Animism was pretty much the only belief system going and she can easily envision a time when Christianity is as obscure a religion as Zoroastrianism is today.

The little bird seems satisfied that its eggs are no longer in danger, settles back on them and tucks in its wings. It stares at her. She knows she's imagining it again but its eyes look like Evelyn's.

Christianity appealed to her. Ironically, it wasn't Jesus that did, although he fascinated her. He was this magical figure, fully human and divine. She knew her parents' feelings about religion in general and Christianity in particular, that belief in mystical figures like Jesus and their miraculous powers enslaves people intellectually and is the source of the Church's power over them. She wasn't sure about that, but it seemed to her that belief in Jesus's divinity was no more foolish then their belief that animals and plants and rocks have souls. It was unimportant to her whether Jesus was really the Son of God or just a prophet as the Jews and Muslims believe. She viewed him more as a literary figure.

What appealed to her was the good news Jesus brought to the world, of God's eternal victory over evil and the promise of eternal life and salvation for all people through divine grace. She often wonders where it came from and even though the logical explanation is that it sprang from the mind of an ascetic prodigy, who'd studied his people's history and was disgusted that they'd allowed themselves to be enslaved, and with how far they'd allowed themselves to stray from righteousness, it still seems to her to have come from outer space. Did Jesus have to be divine to come up with it? She didn't think so then and doesn't now. She's met people like him. They're a type: brilliant and persuasive, charismatic and maddening. Was being nailed to a cross part of a divine plan or just the result of his personality and penchant for bucking authority?

All these years she's skirted the issue of Jesus, as if it's possible to be "a little Christian" any more than it is "a little pregnant." His thinking was certainly divine. Doesn't that make him so? The simple truth is that there's no way to salvation but through Jesus and who is she to think otherwise? Even if everything she suspects is true is, and everything she thinks will come to pass does, what does it matter? Believing only in herself feels like Creation is mocking her.

As unworthy and unfit to be a minister as she feels she is, she bows her head and asks Christ to sow faith in her doubting mind and to accept Kate's and Matt's sins as his own and forgive them. The little bird blinks and cocks its head and stares at her, curiously it seems, as if wondering what she's waiting for.

She closes her eyes and recites the prayer of absolution, and the words seem sucked out of her mouth and absorbed by the silence. She's afraid to open her eyes, afraid she'll see the face of the Almighty in front of hers and not that of the benign quiescent God of the New Testament, but of that angry and vengeful God of the Old Testament, the God who commanded Abraham to sacrifice his son Isaac to test his obedience, who destroyed Sodom and Gomorrah because of the wickedness of its people and turned fleeing Lot's wife into a pillar of salt because she disobeyed God's command and looked back at the destroyed city, who visited ten plagues on Egypt for persecuting the children of Israel.

She opens her eyes and sees only the Killdeer, still staring at her curiously. She scoops up a handful of sand and sprinkles it on her head. It isn't ashes but it will do. She stands and the little bird raises its tail feathers and spreads its wings again and turns as she passes, keeping its eyes on her. They don't look like Evelyn's now but God's.

She sees her car in the distance parked on the side of the road behind a large bush, a tangle of brownish-gray bramble. The car is almost the same color as the bush and doesn't look so much like a car as the spirit of a car inhabiting the bush.

She takes one last long look around, letting what she sees sink in, wanting to remember always what this place looks like on the afternoon of this day, and when she closes her eyes and sees it vividly in her mind's eye, she opens them and gets in her car and drives back through the park toward the world where the souls of her flock and Evelyn's letter are waiting.

EPILOGUE

Dee Dee recognizes the house from Karen's pictures: ranch with blue shingle siding and white shutters and trim; flower beds flanking the brick front walk and under the windows; closed-in porch on the side; thick woods in back. The few times she's been to Seattle since Karen retired, they've gotten together in the city for lunch or dinner, but it's difficult for her old friend to get around now with her hips hurting her the way they do.

She steps out of the cab into the light misty rain, walks to the porch and let's herself in, as Karen asked her to. She finds Karen sitting at a small desk, peering at the screen on the wall with her glasses halfway down her nose and her fingers poised on the keycaps and her phone next to it. The technology's old but as Karen always says, she's an old-fashioned girl. Karen turns, removes her glasses and places them on the desk and looks at Dee Dee with that same kind welcoming expression she saw the first time they met. "Don't get up," Dee Dee says as Karen reaches for her walker. Dee Dee bends down and gives her a hug. She sits on the wicker couch across from Karen, takes her bag from her shoulder and puts it on the floor and folds her hands in her lap.

"It's so good to see you!" Karen says.

"It's good to see you too. It's been too long."

"How was the conference?"

Dee Dee shrugs. "Another conference. How's Frank?"

"Good, running errands. He'll be back soon. He's looking forward to seeing you."

"I might miss him. I have a flight to catch. The cab's waiting."

"Zach and the kids?" Karen asks.

"Fine, all doing fine."

"Can I get you anything? Something to drink?"

"I'm fine. How about you? Can I get you anything?"

"No, I'm fine."

Dee Dee glances at the walker. "You must be in a lot of pain." She anticipates Karen's shrug. "Miss the ministry?"

Karen tilts her head toward the screen. "It feels like I never left. I'm up to my eyeballs coordinating this summer's youth basketball camp."

"Yeah, well, you wouldn't know what to do with yourself if you weren't doing God's work."

Karen studies Dee Dee's eyes. "You look like you have a lot on your mind, Bishop."

A lot on her mind — her entire being feels like it's sagging, and Dee Dee's sure Karen can see it in her eyes. She has her mom's eyes, "eyes that can't lie," as her mom always used to point out whenever she tried. "We finally decided to go through their stuff in storage, get it down to something manageable we could store in the garage. It wasn't a lot of money each month, but it just seemed like a waste, you know?"

Karen nods.

Dee Dee reaches into her bag, takes out the envelope and hands it to her. "I found this."

Karen looks at it, reaches out slowly and takes it and glances at the front of the envelope and then at Dee Dee.

Dee Dee keeps her eyes on Karen's and studies them as she removes the letter, unfolds it, reads it, carefully refolds it and puts it back in the envelope and hands it back to her. She didn't think Karen knew but can see by her lack of surprise that she did.

Karen looks at Dee Dee compassionately. "Your mom came to me a few months after I married them to ask for forgiveness."

"Whose?" Dee Dee asks and sees Karen hesitate.

"Mine," Karen finally says. "She wasn't asking for God's forgiveness."

Dee Dee doesn't know what to say and searches Karen's eyes.

"Do you love them any less?" Karen asks.

"No."

"Do you think God does?"

Now Dee Dee's the one to hesitate. "No," she finally says. Karen looks weary now, like she's been carrying a heavy weight a long time.

"Neither do I. I nearly left the ministry because of it. It tested my faith and caused me to question whether I was fit to be a minister. In a way, that's when I became one. I have your mom to thank for that."

Dee Dee listens as Karen shares her mom's story with her and how she wanted to offer absolution, even though her mom wasn't asking for it, but couldn't bring herself to do it, that she felt she'd be overstepping her bounds and went to Joshua Tree to ask God to forgive them and believes God did. Dee Dee looks at the envelope in her hand, puts it back in her bag and stares at Karen. She feels limp, helpless. "I don't know what to say." There's that compassionate look again.

"Maybe there's nothing to say," Karen says.

Dee Dee searches Karen's eyes a moment longer and sighs. "Yeah. Maybe you're right." She stands, slings her bag over her shoulder, leans down and gives Karen a hug, then straightens up and looks down at her. She feels lost, like her moral compass is broken and she knows Karen knows just how she feels.

"It'll make you a better minister," Karen says. "You'll see."

It's hard to see how. She feels shaken to the core, like everything she thought she believed has been called into question and she knows that's Karen's point, that she's faced now with having to re-examine her faith, with breaking it down and picking up the pieces one by one and seeing if and where they all fit back together. It might be a blessing, an opportunity for her to reaffirm and strengthen her faith, if she chooses to view it that way. That's why Karen's the person she always turns to for spiritual guidance. "Give Frank my love. Tell him I'm sorry I missed him."

"I will," Karen says. "Love to Zach and the family."

Dee Dee stops at the door and looks back at her.

"Remember, Bishop," Karen says, "God's love is perfect and perfect love is all-forgiving."

"I will," Dee Dee says and nods. "Thanks."

It isn't until she's on her way to the airport that she realizes she didn't smile once during the visit, brief though it was, not once.

* * *

Sunday, May 21, 2050

Dear Anneliese,

I didn't think I'd ever be writing to you again and here I am, 35 years later. I'm making a mess of things with this pen, just as I did back then. It' a good thing you can't see all these smudges. It doesn't matter. I wasn't communicating with you through my written words, but rather through my thoughts, just as I am now. The diary is just a record of how I was thinking and feeling about things.

I owe you an apology for having stopped writing. I never stopped thinking of you, though. You've always been in my thoughts.

I came across my diary and pen when my husband Zach and I cleaned out the storage space where we kept some of Mom and Matt's belongings. They were in a box filled with my stuff.

You'd like Zach. He's a loving husband and father. We have two daughters, Katy and Rachel, both named for their grandmothers and both married with kids. Can you believe it? I'm a grandmother with three grandchildren! That's what happens when 35 years go by. We're far-flung, as most families are, and don't see each other very often, so it's special when we're all able to be together.

You won't be surprised to hear that I became a Methodist minister. It was Karen's doing. She planted the seed on our trip to the women's prison and nurtured it and my faith and interest in doing God's work grew. My ministry has taken me to many places in the world and it's been a rewarding and fulfilling experience.

I did visit the Secret Annex and it was an extremely moving experience. I'd spent so long imagining the place and what it would be like to actually be there. I thought I was prepared, but being there and thinking of you and everything that happened — Well, it was overwhelming.

I don't travel much anymore. I attend conferences and visit churches in my districts. Other than that, I spend most of my time behind a desk.

Speaking of experiences, I never did learn Greek, although I know quite a few Greek words. Karen was right. There's a Greek word for just about every emotion and experience in life and my favorite is still "epiphany."

I saw Karen recently in Seattle. She's retired now but still very active with youth groups, in particular a basketball camp she runs each summer. Her hips finally gave out and she's having them replaced soon. She continues to be my role model. She has shaped my life and enriched it in so many ways. I have immeasurable respect for her and am forever indebted to her for what she's given me. She's an inspiration, just as you've been to me.

I thought of you a lot when I lost Mom and Matt. They were killed in a plane crash in Libya, of all places. They were on their way from Tripoli to a location in the Sahara where Matt was going to do a photo shoot in a Bedouin setting for a Paris couture house. He became a very successful fashion photographer and was in high demand. Mom was his business manager and she was a good one.

They loved being together and traveled everywhere together and I try not to think about what the last few tragic moments of their otherwise happy life together must have been like. I try.

I was devastated by the loss and thinking of you comforted me. In a way you've always been the person closest to me. You know me so well, know things about me I haven't shared with anyone else. You're always there for me and I feel you've been waiting patiently all these years for my return. Now I feel even guiltier about not having written. Well, I know you understand and forgive me.

A week's gone by, but I thought I'd just continue the same entry. I took the opportunity to read everything I wrote to you back then. So many memories.

It was fun reading about my Quinceañera. I knew all along it would end up being a big party with me the center of attention in a beautiful dress. I smiled when I read the part about the Last Doll Rita had the dressmaker make for me and surprised me with, a blonde blue-eyed Barbie with the same white dress and gloves and heels as mine. It really was clever. It was in the box with my diary and pen. It's sitting here on my desk now, keeping me company. I don't know if I looked as pretty as this doll does, but I sure felt as pretty.

Mira and I became close friends and have remained so through the years. She was a teenager when she contacted me, saying she wanted to know more about our dad. Andrew's been a great dad, but she said there just seemed to be this empty space inside her that she felt knowing about her biological father would fill. I shared every memory of him I had with her and she ate them up. I've been her "big sister" ever since. We saw each other last at Rita's funeral. The years of drinking finally caught up with Rita. She died of liver cancer.

I visited Rita several times in the months before she died. I thought I knew her well but she shared things with me about her life I didn't know, and they were a revelation. Listening to her, I came to appreciate just what a courageous and strong person she truly was. Overcoming a disease like alcoholism isn't easy and finally coming to grips with the reasons you became an alcoholic in the first place is even harder. She managed to do both. To be sure, Andrew was a big help, but that woman was tough. She told me she lived with a death threat from a Mexican drug lord hanging over her head when she was pregnant with Mira. I can only imagine what that experience was like.

A few days later, same entry. I don't seem all that concerned about dating entries, which runs counter to the purpose of keeping a diary. Maybe I'm trying to decide if that's what I'm doing or maybe I just think of time differently now.

Anyway, I've been sitting here gazing at my Last Doll, remembering my Quinceañera and dancing with Pauly and taking that walk together in the parking lot. The moment when he took me in his arms and I put my arms around him and we kissed is vivid in my mind. That was the moment I stopped being a girl and became a young woman. It was magical.

I thought at the time that Pauly would be the person I'd make love with for the first time, but our relationship remained platonic. What we enjoyed most were our long conversations about books. I made love for the first time with Zach and he's been the only one. I guess I'm just an old-fashioned girl like Karen.

Pauly and I lost touch after he went off to college. Rosa's kept me posted about her brothers through the years. Pauly's a tenured Professor of History at the University of Wisconsin in Madison and Petey's a Foreign Service Officer in Mexico City. They're both married and grandparents.

Rosa's had a hard time of it. She married her college boyfriend and their daughter had cystic fibrosis. It proved too much for her husband and they divorced. Rosa doesn't do well without a man in her life, but she couldn't find one who was willing to enter into a long-term relationship with a woman with a sick kid, so she traded sex for temporary companionship. Her daughter died at 17 and by then Rosa had put on weight. Men are still interested in her for sex, though. I can't tell you the number of times I've been on the phone with her after she's been dumped. It's heartbreaking listening to her, but she's a dear friend and, after all, that's why I'm here. It's what I've dedicated my life to, helping people deal with their problems.

You remember Cryssie and Jenn's crazy romantic idea to have each other's baby and how amazing and confusing that seemed to me at the time? Well, they did, a boy and a girl, both married with kids.

Jenn joined Cryssie in Boston when she graduated from Stanford and they married. Same sex marriage has been the law of the land for decades now, so thankfully people no longer have to suffer the indignity and discrimination they and so many people like them once did.

Jenn became a psychiatrist, specializing in treating LGBT teens, and Cryssie got involved in politics. She was elected to the Massachusetts state legislature and served as a representative for many years. The issues of the poor in her district were her greatest concern and she was a fierce advocate for them. Jenn's still in practice but Cryssie's retired and has become a real "house husband", as she likes to call herself. They spend most of their time now at their Cape house in Truro near P-Town. I try to see them whenever I'm in New England. They're a great couple and two of my favorite people.

You remember Giselle, Phillipe's daughter, who came to my Quinceañera and how much she wanted to learn to surf? I lived with her and her mom in Paris during my senior year as an exchange student and Giselle and I took the train to Hossegor, a good surfing spot, and I taught her. She was a quick learner and became a really good surfer. We surfed Mavericks here in California on one of her visits, both of us for the first time. Matt and Dibs and Janey were surfing with us and Giselle got high marks from everyone, but especially from Dibs. She was over the moon.

I loved that year in Paris. I finally became conversant in French thanks to Giselle. She took me seriously when I said I really wanted to learn the language. Each time I tried to slip back into English she'd shake her finger at me and say, "No, no, en français, s'il vous plaît." She embarrassed me into learning. It was a humbling experience but a very effective technique. Giselle's a physician like her mom and dad and we've remained close friends through the years.

Amber took to the language easily. In fact, by the time I arrived for my stay, she'd transformed herself into a real "Parisienne." Giselle said her mom easily could have gotten her work as a model when she moved to Paris. Her mom had connections in the fashion industry. Amber wasn't interested. She taught finance at an American school and was perfectly happy. Amber is still BEE-U-TEE-FUL!!! Her beauty seems timeless.

Speaking of surfing, I did surf Killers. Mom and Matt and I made another trip to Ensenada the summer before I left for college. Mom seemed reluctant to make that trip and I thought at the time it was because of the accident, but I now know the real reason why. That's another story.

Anyway, talk about gnarly! The wave face was 35 feet that day! Not the 50 to 60 "Jet Ski" surfed but plenty big as far as I was concerned. The first time I got up on one of those waves my heart was in my mouth and it stayed there the entire ride. I didn't try anything fancy. I just concentrated on staying on my board and riding the wave and when I rode it out, I felt like I'd conquered the world! It was an unbelievable experience and feeling. Mom recorded me surfing and I have to say I looked pretty good, maybe not as good as Bethany Hamilton but pretty damn good.

I still visit Aquilina's now and then for rum cake and chocolate egg cream. That place was an important part of my girls' childhood. Steve's son Joey runs the business now and has for years. It's still a popular place.

Steve and his wife spend most of their time on their sailboat taking long trips. I got talking with him once when he happened to be at the store. He told me about how he started the business. What a fascinating story that was. I had no idea he once ran PACBOND. I was a kid when the scandal involving Ira Weiss happened and knew nothing about it at the time. Sad to say, people aren't always who they appear to be.

A few days later. I find myself reliving moments from my diary. It's funny. In a way I'm still the same person I was when I wrote to you back then, that kid sitting on a mule gazing out at the Grand Canyon, touching myself and being touched for the first time, coming face to face with that seal, riding a wave all the way in for the first time. I remember those moments and feel just as I did then. That part of me will never change. A part of me has changed, though, or I think it has.

You remember Pauly telling me that Orange County was called Valley of Saint Anne by the early Spanish settlers and how surprised I was that I'd never heard that and concerned that I might never have known had he not told me, and that there was so much more about life I might never know? I never thought I'd say this but lately I've been thinking there are some things in life you're better off not knowing, because knowing changes you profoundly and forever and perhaps in ways you'd prefer not to be changed. We'll see. I'll keep you posted.

Yours ever faithfully, Dee Dee

P.S.: I won't forget to tell you that story. I'm just not quite ready to yet but I will. I promise.

www.ingramcontent.com/pod-product-compliance
Lightning Source LLC
Chambersburg PA
CBHW050613110726
47899CB00001B/95